RELUCTANTLY ROYAL

ROYALS GONE ROGUE

ERIN NICHOLAS

ROYALS GONE ROGUE

The Series

Reluctantly Royal (Torin & Abigail)

Reluctantly Rogue (Jonah & Linnea)

Rags to Royals (Cian & Scarlett)

Recklessly Rogue (Henry & Ruby)

About the Book

A marriage proposal from a deliciously handsome and wickedly charming prince sounds like a fairytale.

But for a nerdy scientist with severe social anxiety, it's a horror story.

Prince Torin O'Grady, with his mischievous blue eyes and cocky grin, is always in the spotlight. And he needs to marry me to inherit the crown.

But we have nothing in common. He's a future king. And I'm perfectly happy slogging through mud in my work boots.

So why can't I stop thinking about him?

Maybe because he won't stop texting me. And sending me gifts. And making me feel like everything I find awkward and weird about myself is special and amazing.

And there's also that little detail of him offering me my dream job and telling me that together we can change the world.

Well, I could probably *work* for him.

And if I have to marry him *temporarily* to get what we both want, then fine. It's for the greater good.

It has nothing to do with the way he kisses me. Or that dirty mouth. Or the *royal treatment* he gives me in the bedroom.

Fine. Maybe it does. Still, it's only a year. Then I can turn in my tiara and come back to my normal, boring, behind-the-scenes life.

But Torin is determined to turn me from reluctantly royal to royally *his*.

A BRIEF HISTORY OF CARA & THE ROYAL FAMILY

In 1848 Tadhg O'Grady was an Irish sailor accompanying King Frederick VII of Denmark to the Faroe Islands. Their ship was attacked by pirates, and the ships were sunk. Fifty people perished, but Tadhg rescued three men, including King Frederick.

The King was so grateful that he gave Tadhg the southern-most island where they were pulled to shore.

Tadhg named the island Cara, the Irish word for friend.

The O'Gradys have ruled the small island in the North Atlantic ever since.

The Royal Family

Tadhg O'Grady (pronounced Tige (like Tiger without the closing 'r' sound))— first King of Cara.

King Diarmuid (pronounced Deer-mid)—King of Cara. Took the throne when he was 39 after his father died suddenly of a heart attack. He has ruled for 43 years. But he is now 82 years old and has had three heart attacks .

Queen Roisin (prounced pronounced Row-sheen)— 79 years old. Has ruled with her husband ever since he took the throne. Has equal power as long as he sits on the throne.

Prince Sean—only son of King Diarmuid and Queen Roisin, father of Torin. Killed in a car accident 21 years ago.

Princess Ábria (pronounced AH-bree-a)—Sean's wife, Torin's mother. Still holds the title of princess but has no formal power since her husband's death.

Declan—Sean and Ábria's first child, Diarmuid's eldest grandchild. Was in line for the throne until his abdication 14 years ago. Lives in the US where he has built up a multi-billion dollar company. Has not returned to Cara. Single.

Torin (pronounced Tore-in)—second son of Sean and Ábria. Now in line for the throne because of Declan's abdication. He also abdicated 12 years ago, but returned 2 years ago and rescinded his abdication.

Fiona— Sean and Ábria's third child and only daughter. Abdicated at the same time as Torin. Lives in the US with her husband and children.

Cian (pronounced Kee-an)—youngest child/ son. Abdicated at the same time as Torin. Lives in the US. Single.

Saoirse (pronounced Sear-sha)—Fiona's daughter. Now 12. Diarmuid's only great-grandchild. Is in line for the throne after Torin until/ unless he has children.

<u>Others:</u>
Jonah Greene— Torin's bodyguard and best friend
Colin Daly—Fiona and Saoirse's bodyguard and friend
Henry Dean—Cian's bodyguard and best friend
Lady Linnea Olsen (pronounced Li Nay uh)—woman arranged to marry Torin.
Astrid Olsen— Linnea's younger sister.
Alex Olsen— Linnea's younger brother.

THE DRUNKEN POKER
GAME THAT GOT OUT
OF HAND

Twenty-five years ago, Duke Alfred Olsen, King Diarmuid's best friend, and Diarmuid got very drunk one night while playing poker. As they often did. This night however, when only the two of them were left in the game, Diarmuid found himself out of money.

You might ask how a king runs out of money. And that is a fair question. That no one has been able to answer and that Diarmuid won't address even to this day.

But, as the story goes, because he had nothing left to bid, Diarmuid needed 'something of value' to stay in the game.

So he bet one of his grandsons.
Yes, a grandson.

Not even a specific one. He has three and any one of them would do. Of course, the one that would be King someday was most valuable.

And what did Alfred intend to do with this grandson if he was to win?

Marry him to off to one of Alfred's granddaughters, of course. He has two.

In the end, Alfred won.

And Alfred's oldest granddaughter, Linnea, was informed, at age four, that she would grow up to be a princess and then, someday, a queen!

Linnea embraced this news as any four-year-old would—as if it was gospel—and grew up to be a sophisticated, polished, intelligent, beautiful woman who was prepared to be queen.

But what she didn't know until she was seventeen and her would-be fiancé fled the country, was that the entire agree-ment—all fifteen words of it, including their signatures—is written out on the back of a playbill, and the words are smudged by spilled whiskey.

Still, the family lawyer has informed everyone who asks (and that is a great many people) that it's completely legal and enforceable since the men both signed it in front of witnesses.

Of course, that lawyer is also a very good friend of Alfred's and owes him money from another poker game. And is the son of a judge.

The most important fact in all of this, however, is that in

Cara, there's no need for lawyers and judges. King Diarmuid is the law. So the "contract" is enforceable in the stupid, archaic way that anything having to do with royal families is enforceable: with expectations heaped onto everyone from an early age, much manipulation, a lot of money, and a pretty good dose of guilt.

So now that Declan has left Cara, and Torin is set to be the next king, he and Linnea are "engaged". At least as far as both families are concerned.

Whether Torin and Linnea like it or not.

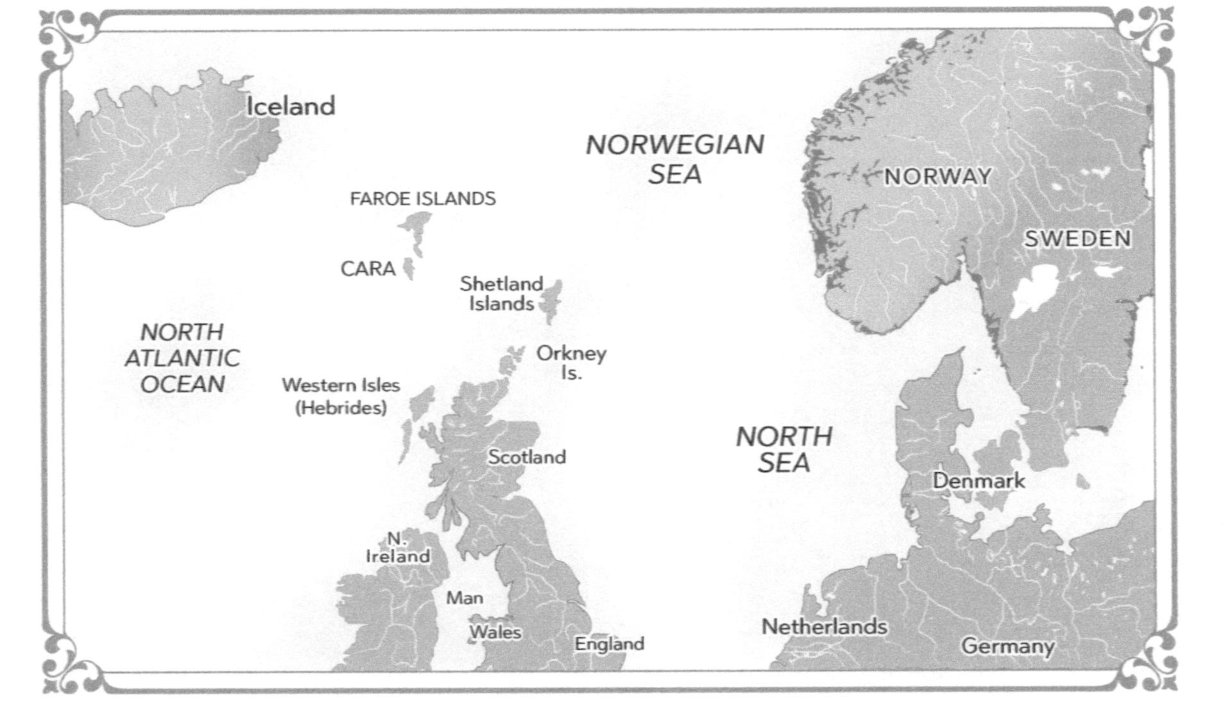

Iceland
NORWEGIAN SEA
NORWAY
SWEDEN
FAROE ISLANDS
CARA
Shetland Islands
NORTH ATLANTIC OCEAN
Western Isles (Hebrides)
Orkney Is.
NORTH SEA
Scotland
Denmark
N. Ireland
Man
Wales
England
Netherlands
Germany

"TRUST THE OVERTHINKER
WHO TELLS YOU THEY
LOVE YOU.

They have, most assuredly, thought of every reason not to."

– L.K. Pilgrim

CHAPTER I

TORIN

"We will announce the engagement in six months. Do what you need to in order to prepare."

I bite back the first four things I want to say and consciously work to make my tone calm, almost bored. "You mean, tell Samuel to get my best suit dry cleaned? Get a haircut? Hit the gym? That kind of thing?"

"I'm not in the mood for your jokes today."

The thing is, my grandfather is never in the mood for my jokes. He doesn't find me amusing in the slightest.

I assume he finds humor in *something*, but hell if I know what it is. The man hasn't smiled in my presence since I was about thirteen years old.

I'm now thirty-two.

"So, then I assume you mean that I should actually discuss this with a woman? You know, *propose* to someone so that there's an engagement to announce?" Now my tone is much less bored and calm. There's a definite edge to it.

He appreciates my sarcasm even less than he appreciates my humor.

He turns from the tall window behind his desk and clasps his hands behind his back.

The man standing in front of me is wearing a light blue button-down shirt and navy blue pants. He's not wearing a tie or a jacket. He's not wearing a crown. But I have no question that I am talking to King Diarmuid. Not my grandfather.

He's not scowling at me, however. He's giving me a look I hate even more. He looks at me with a condescending lift of one eyebrow as he says, "That's not really necessary. That was taken care of years ago. She'll be ready."

I grind my back teeth together.

She is Lady Linnea Olsen, the eldest granddaughter of the late Alfred Olsen. He was a billionaire, a duke, and my grandfather's best friend. And favorite man to sit across from at a poker table.

She's been my sort-of fiancée since I was five.

When my grandfather lost me in a poker game.

The agreement was written up on the back of a whiskey-stained playbill when my grandfather got too far in on a poker game and had to come up with something of 'value'.

Alfred won, and the fate of King Diarmuid's heir was sealed.

The "arranged marriage" has always been something of a family joke.

Until now.

Until I returned home to take my place as crown prince and my grandfather determined he didn't trust me and couldn't take me seriously, but that Linnea really would make a fabulous queen.

Oh, and Alfred died.

So there's no going back on the agreement. Linnea and I *will* be married.

That's what my grandfather has told me approximately a thousand times in the past two years.

We won't, though.

We definitely won't.

"I'm not marrying Linnea," I tell him, pushing up from the chair in front of the monstrous desk that has been in this office all of my life. Four generations of kings have sat behind that desk.

I've said exactly those four words to him repeatedly over the past two years I've been back in Cara.

"The day you marry her, the throne is yours."

I stop halfway to the door. I take a deep breath.

The entire reason I'm living in Cara, my home country, is because my grandfather is eighty-two years old, has had three heart attacks, my father is dead, my oldest brother is an asshole, and if I don't, my niece—my sister's oops-out-of-wedlock-adorable-spitfire-will-do-great-things-with-her-life-but-should-by-God-get-to-choose-her-own-destiny little girl—will have to take over the throne on her eighteenth birthday.

She's only twelve, but if he dies before her eighteenth birthday, she'll still have to take over. Of course, then my sister, mother, and grandmother will all have to be there every step of the way guiding and helping her. Which still won't be enough.

The country will be in turmoil.

As they should be if they had a twelve-year-old American who has only spent holidays in Cara sitting on the throne. Or a fifteen-year-old. Or even an eighteen-year-old.

So, I rescinded my abdication two years ago and came home.

And the old bastard has been giving me hell ever since.

I turn back. "It's been two years," I tell him. "I'm ready. I don't need Linnea."

Now he scowls. "The *country* needs her."

"I don't know what that means."

I do, of course.

Linnea is beloved in Cara. She's a celebrity of sorts. She put Cara on the world map.

She's the agent for two elite athletes from Cara who are now living in the US. One is an upcoming NHL star. A good-looking, charming, talented, all-around good guy. The other is a gymnast. Cara's first and only Olympian.

They are also Linnea's younger brother and sister. Their fame is because of Linnea's skills in PR. She also makes sure the fact that they are from the tiny island nation of Cara is mentioned in *every* story about them.

Now eighty percent of American sports fans can actually find Cara on a map. Probably eighty percent of those people could even tell you two or three facts about our country.

Three years ago, that would have been impossible.

National pride has soared, my grandfather installed a new satellite system so he and everyone else on the island can watch Alex's hockey games, and if Linnea wasn't his favorite grandchild before, blood or not, she is now.

Who am I kidding? She was totally his favorite grandchild before.

Now he wants to make her officially a part of the family.

"I can't keep waiting for you to take this seriously," my

grandfather finally says. "We need a plan. We need the people to know that there is a plan."

I feel my heart rate quicken. I need to keep my cool but...

"You're waiting for me to take this seriously?" I repeat. "I have been here for *two years*. I have attended every meeting, dinner, reception, and conference you have asked me to. I have listened to you, Emil, and Grandmother go on and on and on about our history and traditions and expectations. I have read every goddamned book, ledger, and piece of paper you have put in front of me!"

I am not successful at keeping my voice calm, but he's expecting this. All of our meetings end up with one, or both, of us shouting.

He waits, then takes a breath. "You've been back for two years. A miniscule amount of time. Linnea has lived in Cara her whole life. You, on the other hand, left Cara when you were still a boy, and hid out in the US for a decade."

I open my mouth to protest the 'boy' part. I'd been nineteen.

Also, the 'hid out' part. He'd assigned me and my two siblings each a bodyguard who kept tabs on every move we made. There was never a moment when he didn't know exactly where we were and what we were doing.

But he keeps going. "You marched into my office, lectured me about all of the ways a monarchy was an archaic, problematic institution, and gave me a dissertation on why we should change it."

I'd even had an impressive video presentation and colorful handouts. I'd worked on that presentation for months. At that point, my older brother, Declan, had already abdicated and left the country, so I was next in line. I knew I was the someday king. I'd always been interested in world politics and history, and I'd truly believed that

Cara should transition from a hereditary monarchy to a representative government. My presentation had outlined how that could happen over the course of ten years.

My grandfather had laughed.

But he's still not done. "Then, when I didn't immediately embrace the idea with enthusiasm and thanks, you abdicated your title and left the country in a colossal tantrum. With your siblings in tow."

It hadn't taken much encouragement to convince my sister, Fiona, and my brother, Cian, to abdicate as well. They'd been eighteen and seventeen at the time. *They'd* liked my presentation. They'd been fully on board.

Of course, I'd fully believed that once we left, the king would realize how serious we were, and he'd come after us —okay, he'd send people after us—bring us back to Cara, and have an actual conversation about my plan.

He hadn't.

He'd won that game of chicken, no doubt about it.

It wasn't as if we were in exile. We'd all lived happily in the US for ten years as undercover royals. We could have returned to Cara at any time. In fact, we did come back for holidays and such. But...we hadn't *officially* returned. Cian and Fiona are still very happy in the US.

But when I'm completely honest, I can admit that I was unhappy. I hadn't expected to be away from home for ten years. I hadn't expected my grandfather to be so fucking stubborn. I hadn't expected him to just go on without us.

"The entire country knows how you left, Torin," he says.

Of course, they do. Even if we weren't a very small country, news like the three grandchildren of the king—the only heirs—suddenly leaving the country would have spread.

"There's been underlying unrest ever since you left.

There have been questions about succession. More questions arose after Saoirse's birth was uncovered. Then my health concerns worried everyone even more. The country has been upset not knowing what's going to happen, and what the future holds."

Of course it has! I want to shout. He could have fixed all of that by reaching out, by *talking* to us, to *me*. I would have come home before this. But he would have had to meet me partway.

Diarmuid O'Grady doesn't do that. Apparently.

"I'm here now," I say, trying to stay calm so we can actually finish this conversation. "Tell them I'm ready, and crown me before you have another health scare." My mother and grandmother and his physician have told him this same thing, repeatedly. "You need to willingly, happily hand over the crown before you *have to* so the country knows that you have confidence in me, so they can as well."

I don't say the part about how if he dies and I take the crown because there's no choice, it will be harder for everyone to trust that I'm truly ready.

He knows this. Very well. He took the throne after *his* father's unexpected passing from a massive heart attack at the age of sixty-one.

That has, of course, also added to everyone's anxiety about *his* heart condition and the what-ifs.

He has to *give* me the crown.

And fuck, I want that.

I am an intelligent, well-traveled, highly educated man who loves his country and family enough to give up the life he knew, turn everything upside down, and come home to lead.

I love this country.

I loved it enough to advocate for a representative

government because I thought that would be best for the people, and then abdicate the throne to show how serious I was.

I loved it enough to swallow my pride and come back when it became clear the country, and my family, needed me.

"You returned only when you feared Saoirse might be called upon to come to Cara," my grandfather says, equally frustrated. "And now you jet off to America every time you get bored or don't get your way." He points a finger at me. "The people see everything, Torin. You have to remember that. If you're to be the leader, you have to accept that your actions, attitude, and words matter. All of them."

The media in Cara amounts to one newspaper and a radio station that has a broadcast that is also a podcast that posts on social media and blogs in addition to their three hours on air every day. The podcast is hosted by two women in their late twenties, Lindsey and Jen, who discuss everything from the weather to new recipes, women's health issues, relationship advice, politics, and celebrity gossip. The last two overlap often when it comes to the royal family of Cara, it seems.

The following for the podcast *Wait 'Til I Tell Ye* increased substantially after Astrid and Alex became known internationally. Now people from around the world, but particularly Americans, follow their podcast and social media posts.

Unfortunately, my grandfather is not wrong when he says they pay attention to me. The news that the crown prince of Cara had been in hiding in the US and had suddenly returned home to take the throne had been a huge story.

And the idea that I fly around on my private plane,

reportedly partying in Louisiana and shirking my duties in Cara, has been getting a lot of traction lately.

But I do go back to Louisiana regularly. It's where my siblings are. Where my closest friends are. My best friend, Jonah, finally came to Cara after staying behind for the first year. Thank God. That first year was rough. I haven't been back as often since he's been here but...

Fine. I do leave Cara a lot.

I feel so damned useless here.

He's also correct to point out that I rescinded my abdication for my niece.

Saoirse was the only O'Grady who had not officially abdicated. That had put her, technically, in the line of succession.

None of us had thought anything of that until my grandfather's third heart attack. They'd called my sister back to Cara to discuss with her the very real possibility that Saoirse could inadvertently become Cara's next ruler if our grandfather's heart finally gave out.

"I stepped up because Saoirse is a child," I say. "I did it to protect her, yes. If she was old enough to make the *decision*, and she'd *chosen* to come to Cara and take the throne, I would have let her. But as it is, I was the only one in a position to rescind my abdication."

My brother Declan should have. But he washed his hands of the throne long ago. He hasn't even returned to the island to visit. He's only in touch with us, his siblings, on occasion, and our mother. Most people also consider him the most successful of us. He's a self-made millionaire. Hell, he might even be a billionaire by now.

He owned and sold a professional football team. He owns a pro hockey team—incidentally, the one Linnea's brother plays on—a major tech company, a movie and TV production studio, and a few other things I don't remember off the top of my head.

He's obviously able to get things done and lead. But he has no interest in being an *actual* king.

He's got all the perks—money and power—without the pressure of affecting people's lives in a real, direct way. Why would he give that up to come to a windswept, remote island in the middle of the Atlantic Ocean?

My sister could have rescinded her abdication as well, but she has a life in the U.S. She's in love, living in a town where she has friends who are like family, and where she runs an animal sanctuary saving neglected, abused, and abandoned animals.

She's actually making a difference. Living a good life that makes the world a better place, and raising a daughter who will do the same.

Neither of them should be forced to give all of that up and come back to Cara.

And my younger brother, Cian, is...not ready to be a king.

He's still finding himself. And having a hell of a good time doing it. He doesn't want a crown, a throne, and a bunch of responsibilities.

So that leaves me.

I have no kids, no wife or even serious girlfriend, no tech or sports empire, no animal sanctuary. But I do have a head full of ideas and a desire to make a mark on the world, and...I have an opportunity to do so.

I am an O'Grady, a direct heir of Diarmuid, King of Cara.

Literally, five people walking the planet can say that.

I'd be stupid not to take this chance to make my life matter, to create a legacy, and to give my family and my country someone they can depend on.

"You came home to protect Saoirse. Not out of loyalty to me or Cara," my grandfather says.

He can believe what he needs to. I'm here now. I'm willing and able to take on this responsibility.

"While Linnea has been nothing but loyal, right?" I guess.

He doesn't even blink. "Yes. The people know she loves the country, and they will see her as steady, loyal, and serious. She is articulate, sophisticated, intelligent, kind, and beautiful."

Linnea Olsen is all of those things. She is definitely princess material. As Lindsey and Jen often remark.

He wants her to be my wife because she's adored by both Cara and Denmark, she will keep me in check, and it will give her the power to do amazing things for his country. And it will keep her close to him.

But there's a problem. Well, other than us not having even an ounce of chemistry.

And other than neither of us wanting to be forced to marry someone simply because our grandfathers were idiots when they played poker drunk.

Linnea is in love with someone else.

My best friend, to be exact.

But my grandfather doesn't know that. Because it's possible, *very* possible, that my grandfather will be so angry about it that he'll fire Jonah and banish him from Cara.

He might even banish Linnea.

And just to really piss everybody off, he'll live forever and never let me be king.

"And you honestly think I can't do this without her?" I ask.

"You haven't shown me that you can."

I scowl at him. "You haven't given me the chance. You haven't approved a single one of my plans or ideas."

"You talk and talk about your ideas and plans," he says, pacing behind his desk. "You go on and on about how we need new relationships, we need to be less dependent on Denmark—"

"Constantly having to travel to kiss ass and wine and dine men and women from another country with the hopes that they'll give a shit about us in the midst of their own issues and relationships with countries that can actually offer something in return is no way to deal with *our* people's security," I say.

He sighs tiredly. "Making and maintaining relationships will be important if you wear the crown. Whether it's with Denmark or another country."

I don't miss the 'if'.

"Of course. But being fully dependent on the goodwill and whims of a group of people that changes regularly and has their own responsibilities that have to come before ours is not a secure situation for *our* people," I reiterate. "We need to be more independent. We need to import less from Denmark. We need to expand our network or supply our own needs. We need to create jobs. We need to make our people feel secure, feel self-reliant, feel like *we* are our own country and not just an adopted child of Denmark."

Diarmuid moves around his chair and takes a seat. "You're a great talker, Torin," he says. "You're charming and confident. You create impressive presentations. You can write and give impassioned speeches on probably any topic. But I don't know that you can actually act on any of it or follow through on anything. Linnea gets things done."

I take a deep breath. I acknowledge that my grandfather actually included a few compliments in there. I try to see things from his point of view. I tell myself that he loves Cara. He's been the king for the past forty-three years. He has to be sure that his successor is up to the job.

"What do I have to do?" I finally ask.

"Show me that you're serious. Show me that Cara is your priority. I need to see commitment. That you will give your heart to Cara."

I open my mouth to declare that I've already done that, but I shut it again without a word.

Clearly, I haven't. Not to him.

Show him that I will give my heart to Cara.

Well, what the fuck does that look like?

"How long will it take to convince you of that?" I ask.

"Well, I suppose," he says, reaching for a folder on the side of his desk, a sure signal that our meeting is coming to an end. "If you don't want to marry Linnea, then you'd better hope that it takes less than six months."

CHAPTER 2

TORIN

I slam the door to my office behind me and stomp to my desk.

Of course I'm irritated by the idea of being forced to marry against my will. But this is not a new pressure. My arranged marriage has been a near weekly topic for months.

It's that every time, the conversation comes with the memory of bright blue eyes and long blond waves and a slightly lopsided smile where one side of her mouth tips up just a millisecond before the other.

And the scent of lavender.

Goddammit. It's been nearly two years and smelling lavender can still make me hard.

I lift the little glass vial that's been sitting on my desk for twenty-two months and remove the stopper, lifting it to my nose anyway.

. . .

June, two years ago

"What happened to your hair?" My niece, Saoirse, is studying me, now with her nose scrunched as if something smells bad.

I walked into this wedding reception only three minutes ago and she's the first to notice me. But she came running, clearly surprised, and happy to see me.

Despite her clear negative opinion about my new hair style.

I run my hand through the new very short style with the bleached tips. There's a lot of gel in it to get it to spike up just right too. "I cut it."

"Yourself?"

Okay, it does *not* look like I cut it myself. "Of course not."

"You paid someone for that?" She lifts the cupcake she swiped from the dessert table and takes a huge bite. Little candy sprinkles fall to the floor around her.

I sigh. My niece is only ten, but she definitely has opinions. And she's always willing to share them. She's also been hanging out with my sister, her mom, too much. She sounds just like Fiona.

"The color or the style?" I ask. Because it doesn't really matter if she likes it. The important thing is that it's *different.* I needed a fucking change.

I hate my job. I want to quit. But I can't.

I've only been doing it for two months, for one thing.

For another, it's not really the type of job you just quit.

So since I can't change my *life*, I changed my scenery— temporarily—and my hair.

Saoirse shrugs. "Both," she answers around a mouthful

of vanilla cake and pink frosting. "I also like you better with a beard."

I skim my palm over my newly shaven jaw. I do too. "It'll grow back."

"Good thing."

Okay, so the girl who is the reason my whole life is an upside down, bullshit, what-the-hell-did-I-do dumpster fire doesn't like my makeover.

But I don't regret my decision to upend my life for her. Exactly.

She's going to do amazing things with her life, and she deserves the chance to make the decisions about what those amazing things will be. It's not fair that her whole life was mapped out for her with a full list of expectations and responsibilities the moment she was born.

Still, my brother Declan would have made a hell of a king. He shares that I-don't-give-a-fuck-what-anyone-else-thinks that my grandfather has perfected.

Except Declan was smart enough to walk away, and not look back.

So now here I am. The middle brother. The one who's responsible and reasonable, and intelligent, who wants to do the right thing, be noble, and lead.

But I'm not leading a fucking thing. I'm not responsible for anything. I'm not *doing* anything.

"Uncle Torin?"

I focus on Saoirse, aware that I've been scowling at a spot on the floor just past her left shoulder. "Aye, *a stór*?" I ask, trying to soften my tone. I probably look mad, and I don't want her to think I'm angry with her.

She *is* the reason I did it, but it's not her fault.

"My mom says that Great-Grandpa is really mad at you."

I nod. "Probably."

"He's been calling her."

I sigh. I couldn't even have a weekend away? And why not? It's not like he's put me in charge of anything.

I'm just blowing off steam. *Enjoying* being a goddamned prince for a fucking change. Because I sure as hell don't enjoy it when I'm actually in the country I'm the prince of.

But my hair will grow out. My beard will grow back. And I can wear this fucking suit to the next godforsaken dinner my grandfather plans with my betrothed and her family.

I scrub a hand over my face and yes, it feels weird without my beard.

"Saoirse, your mom's looking for you." My best friend, Jonah Greene, is standing behind her, looking down from his six feet-four inches.

"Okay." She grins at me. "You better behave so Great-Grandpa doesn't get madder."

I nod. "I'll try."

Jonah chuckles as Saoirse runs off across the room and he drops into a chair at a nearby table. I join him. I'm not surprised that Jonah was the next person to notice me. But the rest of my family and friends will be over to chat soon enough.

"You're going to try not to make your grandfather mad? Since when?"

I roll my eyes. "No. I do intend to continue breathing and even that seems to annoy him."

I look around. I was pleased to get an invitation to this wedding. Charlotte Landry and Griffin Foster are great people and I know ninety percent of the people in this room. Spending the weekend in my favorite little American town with my favorite people is the perfect cure to my recent frustrations.

My gaze lands on a gorgeous woman across the room. Her light blond hair is twisted up on her head, and her pale arms and shoulders are bare in the peach-colored dress she's wearing. The puffy skirt covers her thighs fully, but it's clear that she's got one ankle propped on her opposite knee, rather than crossing her legs at the knees the way most women do when sitting in skirts and dresses. She's also sitting back in her chair, arms folded, looking incredibly annoyed.

I can't look away from her.

I don't know if it's because of the amusing image she presents or because I can relate to her demeanor.

Hmmm.

"Torin?"

"Yeah?" I ask Jonah distractedly.

She's sitting with the bride. Charlotte is delightful. She really is. She's bubbly and friendly and genuine. She can also be downright pushy, but her heart is always in the right place. I don't know anyone who doesn't like her. So the fact that this woman clearly is *not* enjoying the conversation is very interesting. Something about her makes me want to whisk her away from whatever is irritating her.

I don't need a psychology degree to understand what it is.

I have been forced to sit through so many conversations that have made me feel exactly what she's apparently feeling that I feel a moral obligation to help.

And when her eye roll is so big that I can see it from halfway across the room, I feel an instant connection to her. *Oh, sweetheart, I get you.*

"Your *Majesty*."

Jesus. I hate when he calls me that. I look at Jonah. "What?"

"What's with the haircut?" he asks, clearly for a second time.

I shake my head. "Don't do that. I know you heard about it on the podcast."

He chuckles. "It's about a fifty-fifty split between those who like it and those who don't."

"There's about a fifty-fifty split between those who like everything I do and those who don't."

"More than fifty percent don't like you always jetting off to the US."

"Jonah," I say, letting my fatigue and frustration show. "*Please* drop it."

"Fine. What do you need while you're here?" he asks.

I glance at the woman across the room. She reaches up, pulls on something in her hair, and suddenly it's tumbling down from the twist. The wavy blond tresses fall to her shoulders and down her back, past her shoulder blades. She puts both hands up, pushing her fingers into her hair, shaking it out, and I swear I can feel her sigh of relief from where I'm sitting.

Then she reaches into the front of her dress, and I watch as she seems to peel something off of her body, specifically her right breast, and pulls it out from the bodice of her dress. It's tan and round and when she tosses it on the table, the bride, Charlie, gives her a look that's partially surprised, partially amused, and partially exasperated.

Yeah, I've definitely seen *that* look from Fiona a few hundred times in my life.

The woman proceeds to do the same with a tan circle on her left breast, tossing it onto the table as well. Then she cups her breasts, takes a deep breath, and smiles.

Damn.

Come to think of it, it's been a while since I cupped any breasts.

That isn't helping my mood, I'm sure.

The blonde sitting on her other side—Amelia Landry, the bride's sister—says something, and the woman gets a wicked smile on her face. A smile I *really* like. Then she reaches out, grabs a shot glass from the table, and tips it back.

Wow. If that's Leo Landry's moonshine, she just drank it down without so much as a grimace.

I suddenly *must* talk to her. She definitely needs someone else to talk to other than the people making her roll her eyes. Maybe a dance and a little flirting will help. Because that's sure what I suddenly need. And there's something about her that makes me think I need it with *her*.

I rise.

"Where're you going?" Jonah asks.

"I think I need to dance."

Jonah follows my gaze. I guess it's clear who I'm looking at. His eyes widen. "Her?"

"Unless she's taken." In which case I need to know by who and how serious it is, because that's not an automatic reason to keep my hands to myself.

"No. She's not attached."

"Excellent." I take a step in her direction.

Jonah says, "Do you know who that is?"

I let out a breath. "I don't. But you know what? Tonight, I just want to be a guy who crosses the room and asks a beautiful woman to dance and lets *her* tell him who she is."

Now both of Jonah's eyebrows are up. "Okay." There's hesitation there, though.

"Don't worry," I tell him. "This is just a little fun. She only has to like me for tonight. We both know I can pull off twenty-four hours of good behavior."

"We do?"

"Okay, eighteen hours. If I stay away from the moonshine."

But Jonah laughs. "Good behavior is what you have in mind with her?"

I glance over at her again. No, not at all. "Sure," I tell him. "For the first twenty minutes or so." I grin and start in her direction.

Truth is, I can be charming as hell when I want to be. I haven't felt like I wanted to be in a while now, but watching this woman as she leans to one side and scratches at what might be her right hip, or might be her right butt cheek, I think maybe I feel a little charm coming on.

"Hey, Ami." I greet the beautiful blond sister of the bride, but I'm having trouble looking away from the woman next to her.

"Hi, Torin. It's nice to see you." Ami gives me a sweet smile. "Didn't know you'd be here."

"Sorry to crash the party."

Ami laughs. "You know you're welcome."

"It's fun to see everyone," I say with a nod. Then my gaze drifts to the woman with her again.

Ami quickly introduces us. "Torin, this is my sister, Abigail."

Her sister. That makes sense. *Abigail.* God, I love her name. "Hi, Abigail."

She looks at me for a long moment, seemingly cataloguing details about me. I just wait.

"Hi," she finally says.

"Torin is Fiona's brother," Ami tells her.

I am definitely dancing with this woman. I extend my hand. "May I?"

She lifts a brow. Then glances at her empty glass and hands it to me. "Yes, thanks."

I look from the glass to her, fighting a smile. She's messing with me. Right? "I was...asking you to dance."

Ami's hand flies up to cover her mouth as she gives a little snort.

Abigail frowns at her sister, then looks back up at me. "Oh. Well, no thank you."

She really thought I was asking to refill her drink.

I straighten. "Oh. You're kind of ruining my attempt to come to your rescue by sweeping you dramatically out onto the dance floor."

She looks confused. "Rescue me?"

"You don't look like you're having a good time over here," I say honestly, shooting a quick wink at Ami.

She doesn't look a bit offended. She's clearly amused.

"You've been watching me?" Abigail asks, looking up again.

"Yes," I tell her simply.

"Why?"

I decide to go for completely honest. "You're a beautiful woman, which is what first caught my eye." I smile. "You seem to be without a date, which kept my attention. You also seem to be..." I search for delicate words. "...in a bad mood. At a wedding. Even after taking..." I take in the glasses and plates on the table in front of her. "...at least a couple of shots and having cake. Which means it's serious. We might have some similar sorrows to drown."

She's definitely had more than a couple of shots. And maybe even more than a couple pieces of cake.

"The hot, rich guy is having a bad night?" she asks.

I almost laugh. I don't have to worry about wondering what she's thinking. "Do you like my suit or my haircut? They're both new."

She nods. "Both are good."

I tug on the lapels of my suit. "Thanks."

Her gaze roams over me from head to toe. And I enjoy every single second of it.

I hold my hand out again. "Now you have to dance with me. You're the only person I've talked to tonight who likes the hair."

She glances at her sister again. Ami looks…surprised.

But then Abigail starts to reach out. So I pull my hand back. "Do you need those before we go?" I point to the table where the tan circles she pulled from the bodice of her dress lie.

"Oh, no. I never want those things to touch me ever again," she tells me emphatically.

I fight another smile. "Are they what I think they are?"

"If you think they are stick-on bras, then yes," she says, getting to her feet. Without taking my hand, by the way.

I grin. Damn, I like this girl. She's fresh and surprising and there's just…something about her. "You don't need them?" I ask. All I really know about bras is that I like them *off* better than on. So those pads are fitting that criteria, I suppose.

She shakes her head. "I don't. I mean, unless we're going to jitterbug or something. Then things might get a little…bouncy."

I can't help chuckling. I take her hand and pull her toward the dance floor. "No jitterbug or other bouncy songs. Got it."

I turn to face her and immediately step in close, resting my hands on her hips. I can sense she's hesitant about this and I don't want to give her a chance to get away. It's a strange instinct, but I feel it strongly.

She takes a little breath that seems almost resigned and puts her hands on my shoulders.

"You know I'm feeling *very* cocky right now, don't you?" I ask her.

"Just right now?" she asks. "I get the impression that's kind of your usual state."

Yes, I really like her. There's no coyness here. She's not flirting. She's just telling me what she thinks. And I'm not so sure she's all that impressed by me. In spite of that being very unusual, I chuckle. Or maybe *because* that's very unusual.

"Fair enough. But I made the grumpiest girl...maybe the grumpiest person...in the room laugh and smile, so I'm feeling *especially* good about myself."

"Okay, but I also get the impression that you do *that* a lot too."

I'm surprised. That almost sounds like a compliment. "Thanks. You seemed like a tough case. And I'm not sure I've got my A-game tonight."

"No? Damn."

"So what was that about anyway? You really that down on romance and weddings?"

"What? No. I'm thrilled by the wedding."

She glances at the bride and groom and I realize that Charlie is also her sister.

"Other than the scratchy dress and stick-on bra and pinch-y shoes, I'm fine with the wedding."

I'm doing really well not looking at her breasts every time she mentions her bra, but I kind of need her to stop talking about it or I'm going to lose the battle. "So what was all the frowning about?" I ask.

"Oh that." She rolls her eyes.

"Yeah, that." I grin. "And you are an expert eye-roller."

"Thanks. Lots of practice." She sighs. "I just hate my job and was explaining that to my sisters. Nothing new or unique."

"Sorry," I say sincerely. "That sucks."

"It does. And I really want to quit but, to make matters worse, I have two fabulously amazing older sisters who are very successful and who would be very disappointed in me and a mother who would be very worried about me and... I'm weighing which would be more irritating—staying at a job I suck at or dealing with annoying family members."

Wow. Maybe that's what's drawn me to her. We have a lot in common it seems.

"What?" she asks after a few seconds.

I realize I was staring at her. "I just...know *exactly* what you mean."

"You do?"

"I'm in the same boat."

"You hate your job too?"

"Very much," I say. "And I, too, have incredibly successful siblings and a mother who will worry—and a grandfather who will be *pissed*—if I quit."

"Family business?"

That's one way to put it. "Something like that."

"Well, what makes mine even worse...I've only been at my job for two months." She grimaces. "I'm just not cut out for sales, I guess."

"Why's that?"

"I suppose it's mostly because I get easily pissed off when people don't listen to me talk about things I clearly know a lot about and when they need to be talked into doing things that are *obviously* a good idea."

I smile. Yeah, we have a lot in common. "That makes sense."

"I'm not really into...cajoling."

I laugh now. "I get it."

"You do?"

"I mean...I can understand that it could be frustrating. But I *am* actually very good at...cajoling," I tell her. I let my voice drop just a little on that last word, though.

I would really, really love to *cajole* this woman into a few things.

"But I've only been at my job for two months too," I add.

"What? Really?" She looks interested, as if she's realizing how similar our situations sound.

"Yep. I think I made a huge mistake telling my grandfather I'd take over the..." I hesitate. She clearly doesn't know who I am and I decide to keep it that way at the moment. "...business...from him."

"Wow. Sorry. Are you bad at the job too? Or do you just not like it? Is there not enough cajoling involved?"

I'm still smiling but I can feel it dim. "I guess the one person I can't cajole is my grandfather," I say. "Though I think I could be good at the job. My grandfather just doesn't want to listen to my ideas."

She nods. "That's frustrating." She pauses, then asks, "Is your job important? Are there things about it you like? Reasons you want to stick with it?"

I study her. Suddenly I want to know everything about her. What she does. Why she does it. How she feels about it. What she's good at. What she's not as good at. Where she wants to be in five years. In ten. Finally, I nod. "Yes. At least, it could be." God, there's *so much* I could do. That I want to do. "I have hopes it can be." I watch her as she takes in my answer. She looks pleased. "How about you?" I ask her. "Is your job important?"

She wets her lips and I don't even try to keep from watching that. Then she nods and my gaze locks on hers.

"Yeah. At least, it could be. I have hopes it can be," she says, echoing my words back to me.

That does something to me. I feel a hot kick in my gut and my fingers curl into her hips instinctively.

We have a connection. It feels like more than just having something in common.

"Okay, how about this," I say, after we stare at each other for a few seconds. "How about we both give our jobs another six months. Then we meet up here again, have a drink, and compare notes? See how it's going? Maybe knowing that we're in the same boat, that someone else is out there doing a job that's frustrating them but that has potential to be great will help a little."

"Six months from now will be Christmas," she points out.

"Perfect. We'll both be here to see family. We'll meet here at Ellie's and either toast to things being better or drown our sorrows together."

She nods and I feel a very strong sense of relief wash through me.

"Yeah. Okay," she says.

I give her a bright smile. "Great. I'll be looking forward to it."

I suddenly spin her out, then pull her back in, as the music shifts. Again. We've danced through two songs already.

Her smile is bigger now. "You're a good dancer."

"Thanks."

"You realize you are completely overqualified to be here, right?"

I chuckle and look around. I lived here in this tiny Louisiana town for a few months before going home to Cara and I always felt completely at home here. "I'm a bit overdressed, at least."

"Yes. And I, for one, greatly appreciate it."

I pull her closer. I can't help it. "So you *really* like my suit."

"It's not denim or flannel, so I'd probably like it no matter what," she says. "But...yes. I love it."

I knew this suit was perfect. "If you're not into denim, this is really the wrong place to be hanging out." Denim and cotton are the primary dress code in Autre, Louisiana.

"It's not that I'm against denim in general. It's just that all of the men I've been spending time with lately wear it exclusively. All the time. Work—which is fine—out social-izing, to church, to important meetings. And it doesn't matter if it's got mud, manure, or worse on it. They still wear it. Into public places. And then try to flirt with me."

I chuckle. And *damn,* I want to know everything about her, including where the hell she socializes that has mud and manure in such close vicinity, and what she orders when she's there.

I also want to know about these men who are flirting with her. Like names, addresses, and social security numbers. It will make it easier to send my people to get rid of them. "Men have been hitting on you with manure on their jeans?"

"Yes."

"But it hasn't worked?"

"It most certainly has *not* worked." She seems almost affronted that I would think for a moment that it *might* work. Then she leans in and takes a deep breath. "In addition to your very nice suit, you also smell very good. Something else I really appreciate."

There is no way for me to resist pulling her even closer after that. She can sniff me all she wants. She can do any damned thing she wants to do to me.

"Thank you," I tell her. "And ditto." *God*, I'm not sure I've ever wanted to bury my face against a woman's neck and just *smell* her more than I do in this moment.

But she laughs. "I realize that I set the bar low when I said that I don't like the smell of manure."

"You think I'm just returning the compliment?" I ask.

"Yes. I don't wear perfume."

Well, it might not be perfume, but this woman smells fucking amazing. And...fuck it. I lean in, put my nose against her neck, and take a deep breath.

A little shiver goes through her body, and I want to put my mouth against that skin I just sniffed, so damned bad.

Instead, somehow, I lift my head and meet her eyes. "Well, then I guess it's just the smell of *you* that I really like." Then I lift a hand and drag my thumb and forefinger down a strand of her hair. "It might be partly this."

I hold up my finger. There's cake frosting on it.

Her cheeks flush, but she grins. "Oops."

I laugh. She's real, and intriguing, and also cute as fuck. "Chocolate's my favorite."

Her eyes brighten. "Chocolate is superior to all the others."

"Well...it's definitely in my top three flavors."

Her brows rise. "You like *vanilla* frosting better?"

I decide to test this chemistry. I don't have to try to make my voice a little gruff though. "I wasn't talking about frosting."

The song ends, but it doesn't matter because we stopped moving about a minute ago.

She pulls back and puts a hand on her chest. Her eyes widen.

And I think I just fucked up.

"So, two dances is kind of my limit," she tells me.

"Are you okay?" Her cheeks are flushed, and she's breathing a little faster now, but not in a good way.

"Just need some air."

I nod. "Do you want some company?"

But she shakes her head quickly. "I don't. Just need…a minute."

Well, fuck. I don't want to let her go. Not only because I just really don't want to be without her, as strange as that sounds, but now I'm concerned about her. "Do you need water or anything?"

She takes a breath, shakes her head slowly, and even gives me a smile. "No, I'm okay."

I don't believe her. At all. But I step back. She doesn't want me to go with her so, okay, I'll give her some space. It's her sister's wedding. I'll see her again. "Well, I'll be here. Come find me when you come back in."

"Thanks for the dances." She glances over toward the table where her sister and a woman I assume is their mother, are sitting. "And thank you for the rescue."

"Those of us with opinionated sisters need to stick together." I give her a smile as our gazes meet again and I feel that *connection*.

Then she says, "Okay. Um, bye," before spinning and heading toward the kitchen.

Okay. Well, maybe she needs water but wants some space too. Or she needs another piece of cake but doesn't want anyone to comment on that. Or maybe her grandpa has some moonshine stashed in the kitchen.

I'll see her when she comes back in and will make sure she's okay.

I hold my breath until she stops in the kitchen doorway and glances over her shoulder.

Then I relax. Yeah, I'll see her again in a few minutes.

I already can't wait.

And I'm pretty sure I'm going to kiss Abigail Landry tonight.

Things are definitely looking up.

CHAPTER 3
TORIN

My office door opens, pulling me back to the present.

I spin, ready to tell Jonah, my best friend and body-guard, or Samuel, my butler and personal assistant, to fuck off and just give me a damned minute.

I get out, "Can you just fu—" before I realize it's not either of them.

Linnea Olsen closes the door quietly and then crosses the room to stand in front of my desk.

The sound of the two-inch heels on her black pumps against the stone floor is muffled by the sixty-year-old woven rug. It's one of the newer things in the room.

This was my father's office. Most of the first floor of a modest-sized home in Louisiana could fit inside this one room. The ceiling is thirty feet above me, and the grand chandelier hanging in the center is as old as the castle walls themselves.

The wall behind me is made up of floor-to-ceiling bookcases with more books on the balcony level above, accessible by the spiral staircase in the corner. Most of the books in here are older than I am. Many are older than the rug.

To my right is a huge stone fireplace, above which hangs a painting of my great-great-great-grandfather, Tadhg O'Grady, the Irish sailor who saved the life of Frederik the Seventh, then King of Denmark when pirates attacked their ship. That King of Denmark was the one who gave the island to Tadhg as a thank-you. Tadhg named it Cara, the Irish word for friend.

And thus began the O'Grady family's rule of the tiny island nation that almost no one even knows exists.

I spent a lot of time in this room growing up. I loved the history, the books, the maps, the sense of being a part of something important that could be traced back so far and so directly.

Now, I feel restless in here.

I'm doing nothing inside this room. I have ideas. I come up with concepts. I think about the future. But I'm not *doing* anything *now*. I'm not conducting meetings. I'm not getting reports. I'm not negotiating, or brainstorming solutions, or watching anything actually come to fruition.

"We have a timeline now?" Linnea asks, planting her hands on her hips. "Six months is no time at all! You *have* to get us out of it, Torin."

I'm not even going to ask how she already heard about the date of the engagement announcement. She knew about the meeting, and she and I both guessed our "arrangement" would come up, so she'd made sure she was here for tea with my mother and grandmother earlier.

"It's fine. I've got it under control," I tell her, sitting back in the high-backed leather chair behind my desk. This was my father's chair.

"How?" she asks. "What are you going to do?"

"I'm going to...convince him that I'm serious about the title. That Cara is my number one priority and that I'm committed and giving it my whole heart." I'm staring at the center of my desk.

How the hell am I going to do that? What would convince him of that?

"How are you going to do that?" she asks.

I look up at her. "It would really help if *you* could stop being amazing. Maybe you could piss him off. Make my grandfather a little less enamored with *you*."

She gives me a small smile. "Sorry."

I roll my eyes, but I smile at her. "It's really too bad we have no interest in one another."

She nods. "I know. It's annoying how much I *don't* want you."

"Not to mention how much I *do* want her."

Damn, Jonah's stealthy for a guy who's six-four and two hundred and thirty pounds of muscle.

Jonah Greene is the big, sarcastic American who was assigned as my bodyguard when I was only nineteen. He's been with me for twelve years. He knows me better than anyone.

And about once a week, I feel bad about making him come to Cara and leave everyone else he knows and loves for a tiny, remote, windswept island that is sadly lacking in a social scene, single women our age, American pizza, his favorite coffee, his favorite beer, bowling...okay, *lots* of things.

Well, I felt bad about it before he confessed that he'd

fallen in love with my fiancée.

I'm still glad he's here, of course, even if he's not here *just* for me anymore. And even if I don't really need his protection. Not only is there full-time security at the palace, but Cara is an *island* in the north Atlantic halfway between Iceland and Norway. Nobody is getting to me here. If there is anyone who even *wants* to get to me.

Still, when he'd decided to move to Cara with me after leaving me here alone for a year, I'd nearly wept for joy.

"How'd it go?" he asks.

"I have six months before my grandfather announces my engagement to Linnea," I say.

Jonah frowns. He looks from me to Linnea and back. "Excuse me?"

"We're working on a plan," Linnea says.

Jonah looks at me with an eyebrow up. "Work faster."

I chuckle. "It's been ten minutes."

"Yeah. Exactly. That's about nine and a half minutes longer than I'm comfortable with people contemplating how to announce that my girl is marrying another man."

He stops next to Linnea and rests his hand on the back of her neck in a very possessive gesture. He's still eight inches taller than her even with her heels on. She looks up at him with a grin.

"I'm not marrying anyone else." Her smile turns sly. "Probably."

He gives a low growl, and I see his hand tighten on her neck. He leans in and says something in her ear.

Her cheeks get red, she swallows hard, and then she says, "Um, yes, please."

"Good girl," he says, kissing the top of her head before straightening.

Okay, what is *that?*

I lean back in my chair. I've never seen Jonah in love. Not in all the years I've known him. This is...fascinating.

"Am I interrupting? Would you like me to leave you alone?" I ask dryly.

"Actually—" Jonah starts.

"Of course not," Linnea says over him.

Jonah chuckles and I get the impression they will be picking that conversation up later when they *are* alone.

"We were discussing how Torin is going to show the king that he's fully committed and going to give Cara his heart," Linnea says.

Jonah's thumb is stroking up and down the side of Linnea's neck.

I watch that, and the rest of his body language. He's standing close, his body angled toward her. He's all about her. When he first told me about his feelings for her, he'd said they'd fought it, him even more than her, but he finally just couldn't any longer. Being without her, seeing her with other people, not being there when she needed him, when she was upset or hurt or sick, was harder than anything that could happen if they were together. He was willing to do anything. Even risk upsetting our friendship. Or angering the king.

"What does that mean?" Jonah asks. "Fully committed and going to give Cara your heart? You're here. You're stepping up. What the hell else does he want?"

"He wants proof," I say, my thoughts spinning. "He wants to see *evidence* that I'm here to stay."

"Okay." Jonah looks down at Linnea.

She's watching me with a frown, but not saying anything.

But these two have given me an idea.

"Yes. But I think I know how to prove to him that I'm here to stay. That I'm putting my *heart* into Cara."

"Okay. How?" Jonah asks.

"I need a wife."

When I say it out loud, it seems like an even better idea.

There is a long pause. Neither of them say anything.

Then Jonah says, "No."

I frown up at him. "What?"

"No. You're not marrying Linnea even if it's fake."

I shake my head, frowning. "I'm not talking about Linnea."

He scowls at me. "Then who?"

"Someone special." My thoughts are spinning. Oh, yes, I like this. "Someone who will see Cara for the amazing place it is, with lots of potential for more. Someone who will commit themselves to our country in a way that will impress my grandfather the way Linnea has. Someone so incredible, that I can convince my grandfather, and the media, she is the reason I've been going back to the States so often for the past two years. Someone who I can seem so in love with that the king will believe I've brought my *heart* here and that I'm ready to settle down, put down roots, and truly stay."

I pick up the bottle of lavender oil and take a long inhale.

Jonah and Linnea are both watching me with wide eyes.

"But..." Linnea starts. "You *are* ready to settle down here and put down roots...right?"

"I am. But the king isn't seeing it. Me saying it is obviously not enough. So I need to give him something more apparent to prove it."

Yes, this is a good plan.

Linnea looks up at Jonah, then back to me. "So you want to find someone to fake marry you?" she asks.

"No. *Real* marry me. It has to be real." My grandfather could easily verify something like that if he suspected I was doing it only to get the throne.

"So you need to find a girlfriend and get her to fall in love with you and agree to marry you in the next six months," Jonah says.

Okay, yes. Love would be great. And to him and Linnea, that doesn't sound crazy because it's essentially what happened to them. He was supposed to help find her another guy to fall in love with so my grandfather would drop the idea that she and *I* would get married.

I didn't mean for *him* to fall in love with her. Or vice versa. Because...well, I didn't see that coming.

And because it's made things complicated. Jonah doesn't have the...pedigree...that my grandfather will accept for a husband for Linnea. And if he finds out that Jonah is wrecking all the plans he has for me and Linnea, he will be so pissed.

"Sure," I finally say. "Let's try that." I finally look up at my friends. They're both watching me with wide eyes. But neither is saying this is a bad idea. "You think this is a good idea?" I ask.

"I think you being king is a good idea," Linnea says. "Your grandfather needs to step down. He deserves to rest. He also deserves the peace of knowing that his beloved Cara is in good hands. He deserves to see *you* being a good king. You deserve the chance to show him that. I'd love to see the two of you mend your relationship." She meets my eyes, and I see her sincerity. "But I don't think that will happen until he steps aside, and you have the actual chance to lead. So yes, if you're ready to fall in love and get married then I think this plan is...not terrible."

I clap my hands together as I rise. "Wonderful. Then let's go get our princess."

"Wait," Jonah says. "You have someone in mind?"

I grin. Then I lean over and click on a file on my desktop. Then I step back and point at my monitor.

Jonah and Linnea both lean in.

Then Jonah looks at me. "Uh...that's Abigail Landry."

"Yes, it is."

"Abigail Landry doesn't like you."

"That's a bit of an overstatement," I say.

"Well...she didn't seem to really be into you," Jonah amends.

I tuck my hands into my pockets. "That will change when she finds out that I have something she wants."

Jonah straightens and faces me. "And what's that?"

"Her dream job."

Did her comment about hating her job when we danced intrigue me enough to look into her? Yes. Have I now learned everything about her in the past two years? Yes. Does that make me a stalker? No. Obsessed? Maybe.

"What's her dream job?" Linnea asks.

"Eliminating world hunger," I say. It's a *very* simple summary of the things that Abigail Landry studies, works on, writes about, and wants to do.

I go on when they just stare at me. "Specifically, she wants to build indoor farms in food deserts and supply fresh food to people, especially children, year-round regardless of climate and terrain."

They just blink at me.

"Cara is a food desert," I say. "We can't grow anything here! Our soil is too thin and rocky, and our weather is too cool and windy. We import everything. It's terrible for our economy and our ability to be independent and have strong national relations."

"So you think she'll want to come here because this is the perfect place to do her work and you, as the prince, can give her all the resources she could possibly need," Linnea says.

"Exactly," I give her a smug grin. I mean, I hope the chemistry between us is part of it too, but yeah, giving her a chance to do her life's work on an international stage won't hurt. The woman is passionate about what she does, and she did tell me she hated her job two years ago. She's with the same company. I can only hope it still sucks.

That sounds bad. I don't want her to be miserable.

Unless it means she'll marry me.

Surely being my princess is a step up from miserable.

"If it will keep the king and the country from looking at Linnea as the next queen, then I'm on board," he says. "The sooner *you* are on the throne, the sooner Linny and I can come out and be a couple in public without worrying about how the king will react."

He's got a point. King Diarmuid might still be pissed when he finds out, but he won't be able to fire Jonah or banish either of them if I'm king.

"Then we're all in agreement," I say.

"We are," Jonah says. "And if we leave in the next two hours, we can get there just in time."

"Where are we going?" I ask.

"Louisiana. For a wedding." Jonah grins. He rounds the desk and takes Linnea's hand, starting for the door.

"Torin's wedding?" Linnea asks.

Jonah looks back at me. "Maybe. But first...Amelia Landry is getting married this weekend."

Amelia. Ami. Abigail's other sister.

Obviously, that means Abigail will be in Autre this weekend.

She rarely is. In all of the times I've been back to Louisiana, we've never run into each other again.

Which is fine. She's not interested, so that's that.

But, if I *had* ever run into her, I would have asked her *why* she isn't interested.

That just doesn't really happen to me. Women like me. Hell, most *people* like me.

My grandfather, and Abigail Landry, are truly the only exceptions to that rule I can really think of.

I look down at Abigail's photo on my computer screen. God, she's so fucking beautiful. And brilliant. And amazing.

And I'm still thinking about her two years later.

So yes, I'm going to Louisiana for a wedding.

And to get myself a princess.

CHAPTER 4

ABIGAIL

I'm going to be sick.

Literally.

At my sister's wedding. In front of my entire family.

I *told* Ami this was a bad idea.

Actually, it would serve her right if I passed out or puked in the middle of my maid-of-honor speech. She should know better than to make me do any public speaking. Even if the "public" we're talking about here is mostly my own family.

I was *just* here, two years ago, in another bridesmaid dress in this bar at another sister's wedding reception.

Thank God I only have two sisters.

I suck in a deep breath of the humid night air behind my grandmother's bar. I press a hand against my stomach, willing it to calm down.

For fuck's sake. Just lift your glass and say congratulations. That's it. It doesn't have to be elaborate.

My self-talk never works. I don't know why I still try it. Habit, I guess. All of those pep talks from friends and family and teachers and counselors trying to help me over my "stage fright".

But this isn't just stage fright. And this *does* have to be elaborate. This is my *sister*. It's her wedding. I'm her maid of honor. And she wants me to say something meaningful. And I'm going to speak after Charlie, her matron of honor, does. Articulate, charming Charlie, who always says the perfect thing.

Perfect, wonderful Charlie, who did *not* make me do a toast at her wedding.

Maybe I can go first. I can just do the obligatory *I love you, congratulations* and then Charlie can take over and no one will remember what I said. Or didn't say.

I wrote a speech. It's pretty great. *Writing* things isn't my problem.

But I can *not* make a speech in front of a roomful of people. Period.

I grip the metal railing that runs down the side of the three cement steps and breathe deep.

What am I going to do?

"Abigail."

I freeze.

What?

No. It can't be.

Oh, *no*.

No, no, *no*.

But I know that voice. That deep, smooth voice, with just a touch of an Irish accent that gets thicker when he's being flirtatious.

Not out here of all places.

I'd carefully scanned the church pews for him earlier. I'd

seen his name on the guest list lying on my mother's kitchen table about a month ago. I'd been shocked by the way my heart had tripped just reading his name on a piece of paper. I'd felt butterflies in the last few days thinking about seeing him again.

And then...I hadn't. Torin O'Grady had *not* been at the wedding.

I'd been disappointed. And a bit relieved.

But now...he's here.

Out *here*. During the worst time for me to be around *anyone*.

"Abigail?"

I feel him move closer.

"Are you okay?"

So, very not okay.

"I'm...uh...."

I haven't turned around. I've got a death grip on the railing and my eyes closed and I'm working hard on not bolting down these steps, across the street, up to the bedroom on the second floor of my grandmother's house, and under the covers on the bed.

I feel his hand on my upper arm, and I suck in a breath.

"Abigail?"

And, God, I want to look at him.

I haven't seen him in almost two years. It's not like I think about him every day. But I do think about him. Sometimes.

Like every time someone asks me to dance.

That doesn't happen very often. I don't go out, much at all, and especially to places where people dance. But there's a little bar in Sapphire Falls, the town where I'm currently living and working, and every once in a while the girls will talk me into coming out with them and sometimes a guy will ask me to dance.

And I always think of Torin.

And I always say no.

I tell myself it's because I'm not very social and don't really like dancing. Both of those things are true.

But if I was *really* honest, it would be because I know I won't enjoy any dance as much as I did the one I had with Torin.

And now he's here. *Right* here. Touching me.

The air around me heats, at least it feels like it does, with him right behind me and I have to finally let out the breath I've been holding.

I don't want to turn around.

I'll act like an idiot. I'll blush. I'll probably start sweating. I might even throw up on him. I *might* cry. That doesn't happen as often, but if I puke on him, I'll definitely cry.

He's tall and just seems to take up space with attitude, or confidence, or just *presence*.

He's one of *those* people.

Like Charlie. My driven, can-do-anything-she-sets-her-mind-to sister.

Not like me.

"Abigail," he says again, softer, gruffer, while touching me.

And now I have to turn around.

When I do, I'm struck with *oh, that was a really bad idea.*

I stare at him. The last time I saw him he had short, spiked up, blond-tipped hair and a big grin, and gorgeous blue eyes that freaking twinkled.

He looks different now. And *amazing*.

He's hotter, bigger somehow, darker. More of...everything I remember.

He'd been wearing a light gray suit last time. I'd really liked that suit. He'd been polished, and clean-cut, and charming. The suit had been a light color. His hair had been a light color. His smile had been bright and easy.

Now he's wearing dark jeans and a dark button-down shirt, rolled up on his forearms, and untucked. His hair is a deep brown, and it's much longer now. I want to run my fingers through it. He also has a beard now. Yeah, my palms are itching to glide over that as well.

Until ten seconds ago I would have said I'm not a beard girl. I like clean-shaven, and short, well-styled hair.

I would have been lying, apparently.

At least when it comes to Torin. This longer dark hair and beard really work.

He's also not grinning at me like he did the first time we met. He's watching me with an intensity that I swear I feel from my scalp to the bottoms of my feet. My body suddenly feels like it's humming. Like it's a tuning fork that's been struck against something hard.

Hard.

Yes, he looks harder than the last time I saw him. Physically—either that suit was covering up some serious muscle, or the guy has been putting in some manual labor since June two years ago. And emotionally. There's something in his eyes that seems less carefree and fun.

He made me laugh when we danced. He'd seemed very determined to do so and very pleased when it happened.

Tonight, he looks determined. But not in a mood to laugh necessarily.

Still, the look in his eyes makes my stomach flip.

"Hi," he says simply.

"Hi."

"You're not leaving, I hope," he says.

I want to leave so badly the soles of my feet tingle at the thought of walking away.

But other parts of me are tingling for other reasons standing this close to Torin. Alone.

"No. I have to…" I swallow and the reason I'm out here comes rushing back. "Give a speech in a minute."

"Oh. Good."

Actually, it is the complete opposite of good. Speeches and me are…so very not good. With the reminder, my palms get damp, and I feel my breathing pick up.

"Then we'll dance again after that."

He doesn't phrase it as a question. I get the impression Torin rarely *asks* people for things. I'm sure he's used to just telling people what to do.

"I, um…don't know." That might have been my answer even if I wasn't distracted by my racing heart rate and the sudden queasiness in my stomach. But I am, so my attention is not fully focused on him.

I'm sure he'd be appalled to know that.

"We will," he says confidently. And almost…soothingly?

I don't know why he seems to be reassuring me about that. Dancing with him is the second of the three problems I have right now.

My social anxiety.

Him.

Getting the fuck out of here.

Those are my problems. In that order.

"I can't really think about that at the moment," I tell him. I need to get rid of him before I puke. "Can you…go back inside?"

Of course, if he's inside when I give the fucking speech,

he'll know very well that there's no way I rehearsed what's sure to be a jumble of words and nervous laughter, fidgeting that makes everyone in the audience uncomfortable as well, and the reddest face he's ever seen.

He moves to lean against the railing next to me, definitely not leaving. "You can practice on me."

Oh. Fuck. No.

"That's a terrible idea." Those words aren't self-deprecating. They're a warning.

"I give a lot of speeches. I can give you pointers."

I hadn't known who he was when we first met, but I do now.

He's a prince. The leader of a country. He gives speeches to presidents, prime ministers, parliaments, and other world leaders. And I bet he's never once puked because of it.

Those thoughts are *not* comforting.

"No, thanks," I tell him, gritting my teeth. Because the sick feeling is definitely growing. "I really just want to be alone right now."

"I know what you're thinking...he's naturally charming and clearly intelligent and passionate," he says. "But I do practice my speeches before I give them. Every speech is important in its own way. Your audience wants to hear what you have to say about what matters to *them*."

My stomach tightens. "That's really not helping."

"Obviously, when it comes to making a speech at your sister's *wedding* you want to do a good job—"

"Oh God. I'm going to throw up." I spin and lean over the railing.

I'm shocked to feel his hands in my hair. He grabs my hair in both hands, holding it back just as I retch over the side of my grandmother's steps.

I've thrown up so much that I'm able to appreciate his lightning-fast reflexes and that what I said registered in time for him to react.

Not to mention how helpful it is having him hold my hair back.

I stay bent over, breathing for a few seconds. I've also done it enough to know when I'm finished.

I push myself upright and reach for my bag. He lets go of my hair as I rummage in the depths of the big purse. But he doesn't move back.

I pull out the package of tissues and a bottle of water. I clean up, swish water in my mouth, spit it out—it's not ladylike, but it's very hard to spit water out over the edge of a porch gracefully...especially after throwing up over that same porch—check the front of my dress and give thanks that I missed everything but the grass at the base of my grandma's steps.

Then I take a deep breath and look up at him as I unwrap a piece of gum. I start to chew as I wait for his response. Which I assume will be some mumbled excuse about why he needs to be back inside and away from me.

"Did you know that was going to happen?" he asks. He seems to already know the answer.

"Yes."

"Then you probably shouldn't have taken your hair down."

I blink at him. I think about his words. And I realize... he's right.

"Good point. I get a little impatient when it comes to being uncomfortable and that twist was killing me." Then I frown as I realize what his comment means. "You saw me before this?"

"You took it down after you took two shots, ate a cupcake, and..." His gaze drops to the front of my dress, then returns to my face with a faint smile. "...you took off what I assume are adhesive bra pads."

I stare at him. All of that happened. And honestly, only about twenty minutes ago. And in fairness, I was *very* into trying to get comfortable and *all* of that played into that, so I wasn't really looking around the room. I'd already looked for him and not found him. I didn't know he was here.

"And you really don't like shoes," he says, looking down at my feet.

Yes, I'm barefoot. Again. When we'd danced at Charlie's wedding, I'd been barefoot too.

"Unless you've worn adhesive bra pads and had your hair up in a twist, you don't get to judge," I finally say.

"No judgment at all," he says, a full smile finally forming.

"Well, I'm glad you have such good reflexes."

He nods. "You're welcome. You can pay me back with dance number four."

My eyes widen. He wants to dance with me? After watching me throw up? "We only danced once before."

"Twice. We paused for about a minute in between two songs, so that counts as two dances. Even though the first dance was actually two songs."

"But dance number *four* will be for holding my hair just now?"

"Yes."

"So what's dance number three for?"

"I asked for dance number three before you came outside. Two years ago." He gives me a little frown. As if I displeased him back then. And for some reason that makes me want to make it up to him.

That's stupid. What are you thinking?

"You didn't *ask*," I point out. "You *told me* to come back and find you."

"But you didn't."

"No."

"Why not?" He leans in a little.

Somehow, that makes my stomach flip again. I pretend it doesn't, though.

"I didn't want to." That's the truth.

He overwhelmed me. I don't like being overwhelmed.

And now...he's even more overwhelming.

He's a prince—a real honest-to-god-you-have-to-be-kidding-me prince. My sisters had told me about the royal family living in Autre after I'd met Torin at Charlie's wedding. I'd met Torin's sister, Fiona, his brother, Cian, and his niece, Saoirse. They'd told me about Cara, and because I'd thought they were kidding, I'd looked it all up and...it's all real.

He lifts a brow. "If I'd *asked*, would you have come back?"

I find that amusing for some reason. This guy definitely doesn't ask a lot of questions. I just know it. So, I take it as something of a compliment that he's even contemplating asking me something. And I give him the courtesy of actually considering the question. "Probably not. I'm not really into dancing. Or parties. Or staying up late," I tell him honestly.

He watches me as he ponders that. "So I should be grateful for the dances I got."

"Yeah, something like that."

"Okay," he agrees. "Then I'll be *extremely* grateful for getting *four* tonight."

My mouth drops open, and I shake my head as I fight a

smile. God, he's pushy. "How do you say incorrigible in Irish, or whatever you are?"

He frowns as if confused. "I'm not familiar with that word," he says.

I can tell he's kidding. I'm sure he knows the word well. Though I'm also sure he's unapologetic about being the very definition of the word.

He leans closer. "But you know *exactly* what I am, don't you, Abigail?"

"I don't know what you mean."

"You looked me up after we met, didn't you?"

That's pretty arrogant of him. But it's also true. "Oh, you mean the prince thing?" I ask.

"Yes, the prince thing." He looks mildly amused.

"Yes. I know about that."

"And what do you think?"

"That a prince is a strange, and awful, cross between a politician and a celebrity."

He considers that for a moment. "True."

"And I would never, ever, date either a politician or a celebrity. So I *definitely* wouldn't date a prince."

He lifts an eyebrow. "Good thing no one said anything about *dating* then."

I blush. Okay, that was presumptuous of me. But the guy is looking at me like he wants to eat me up.

There. I said it. That's exactly how he's looking at me.

And no, I suppose we wouldn't have to *date* for that to happen...

He finally smiles. One of those smiles from the first night we met. And my heart does a stupid little trippy beat.

"Abigail—"

The back door of the bar bangs open just then. "There you are!" Charlie exclaims. "Are you read— Oh! Torin! Hi."

"Charlie."

I swear Torin gives her a little bow. It's actually imperceptible, but it's like it's implied or something.

"I saw you come in, but I didn't know you were out here...with Abi." Charlie's eyes dart back and forth between us. And they sparkle.

That's not okay. Charlie doesn't need to be sparkling about me and Torin being out here together.

I'm out here puking. And he just followed me.

And is demanding dancing. Which I don't want to do. Much.

You're such a liar.

"Yes. I'm ready." I step around Torin. I'm not, of course, but staying out here with Torin is a bad idea.

His hand settles on my upper arm, stopping me. "Actually, she's not quite. We were just fixing her hair."

What the hell is he doing? I start to respond, but, as if she's hypnotized, Charlie nods.

"Oh, okay, sure. Great. I'll stall a little longer." She smiles brightly. "See you inside." Then she turns and the door bumps shut behind her, leaving me with Torin again. Alone.

I spin to face him. "What was that?"

"You're not one hundred percent *not* going to puke again, are you?" He digs into my bag. Without *asking* by the way.

"Well...no." I can't guarantee there will be no more puking.

He pulls out a hair tie, then settles his big hands on my shoulders and turns me to face away from him.

"I—"

But I don't remember what I was going to say because he starts pulling his fingers through my hair, combing it out, and gathering it at the back of my head and I can't think enough to form any thoughts other than, *um, wow.*

It feels so damned good. And now...he's braiding my hair. Wait, what? How does he know how to do that? And why?

"Why are you so nervous about this speech?" he asks.

His voice is low, and he's really taking his time running his hands through my hair. I could have had it put up in a ponytail in twenty seconds. But his fingers are gliding over my scalp and down the entire length of what seems like every strand of hair and...I don't hate it.

My eyes slide closed and my head tips back a little, and I hear the breath escape my lips. It sounds like a sigh.

"Um..." What did he ask me? Oh, the nerves and the speech. "I'm just not good at public speaking."

"It's your family."

"Not all of them. And even my family is prone to teasing."

His fingers pause their stroking at my shoulder blades. It's just a moment's hesitation, but I feel it. Dammit, I shouldn't have said that.

"Who?" he asks. His voice is a little harder now.

"Who what?" Honestly, he needs to move his hands again.

"Who teases you? And what the hell could they possibly tease you about?" His fingers start stroking through my hair again.

That's probably why I actually answer. *God,* that feels good. "Oh, just my cousins. Zeke and Owen and those guys."

I hear what sounds like a low rumble that seems to come from his chest. But it's definitely not an amused sound.

"What do they tease you about?"

The backs of his hands coast down my neck and upper shoulders and I just keep talking. It's like I can't help it. "It was worse when I was a kid. Just about being too smart for the rest of them. How I always wanted to be inside. How I didn't want to hang out with them because I had to dumb down everything I said for them."

"Is that true?"

I feel him wrap the hair tie around the end of the braid. His hands feel huge against my head and neck and it's really hard to keep my train of thought moving forward.

"Of course not. But..." I only debate for a second about saying the rest. "Okay, sometimes maybe."

"Why?"

"I wanted to spend time reading and in the garden instead of swimming and boating with them."

"Did you sometimes use big words or talk about things that would bore them so they would leave you alone?"

I pause. How the hell did he know that?

"Abigail?" he asks when I don't answer.

His voice is low, almost husky, and one of his hands settles on the back of my neck.

Holy crap, his hand is hot. And big. That feels so good.

I nod, then remember he's holding onto my hair. That little tug on my braid sends a shiver of heat through me.

I clear my throat. "Um...okay, maybe. Just once in awhile."

He makes a noise that sounds amused and *I-thought-so*.

"But that wasn't the only reason they got annoyed with me. When I played hide and seek with them..."

He's stopped playing with my hair and I suddenly hear what I'm saying.

Torin's hands both settle on my shoulders, and he turns

me to face him. "What happened when you played hide and seek with them?"

I swallow. "It doesn't matter."

"Tell me."

See? He doesn't make requests.

I sigh. "They got in trouble a lot because they'd lose me."

His eyebrows rise. I see every tiny motion in his face because we are standing really close now.

"They'd *lose* you? On purpose?" He seems angry.

"No. Not on purpose," I say quickly. "I'd get lost. Accidentally. I'd wander off because I'd get distracted by a bird or I'd start to collect bugs and frogs and turtles. But they'd get blamed because they were older."

"They'd get in trouble because they couldn't find you?"

I nod. "Or because I got stung by a bee. Or bitten by a snake."

His eyes widen. "Yeah. I can understand that."

"But it wasn't their fault." I sigh. "But they got to the point they would stop inviting me to go play. They were *fine* with me staying behind to read in the house, or mess around in Cora's greenhouse because then they wouldn't get into trouble."

My grandmother's best friend grew everything from vegetables to flowers to herbs. She made a lot of her own lotions and salves and treated everyone in town with her natural remedies. Cora's greenhouse had been like a treasure trove to me.

"And now they make you nervous when you have to get up in front of them?"

"I get nervous up in front of any crowd," I tell him honestly. "It's just not something I'm good at. And when I know people in the crowd are thinking about how different I am from them, it makes it worse."

He watches me for a long moment, and I wonder why I told him all of that. Dammit. He saw me throw up and then ran his hands through my hair and now I'm telling him all my secrets? What's wrong with me?

It probably has something to do with the fact that his hands are still on my shoulders and the heat from his skin against mine is scrambling my brain.

"I'm very different from most of the people I speak to," he finally says.

That isn't hard to believe. Even without the prince thing, I sincerely doubt many people have Torin O'Grady's combination of good looks, charm, and confidence. "But you don't think about that?" I ask.

"I do, actually."

"It doesn't make you nervous though?"

"No."

"Why do you think that is?"

"Because I know that what I'm saying is important. Either to them or to me. So the other stuff doesn't really matter."

Cognitively, I know he's right. If what I'm saying is important, it shouldn't matter what the people listening think of me.

It doesn't help to know that.

"But there *are* people in the audience judging if you *should be* saying whatever you're saying, if you're good enough, if you deserve it," I say.

Of course, that all isn't about the speech I'm about to give at my sister's wedding reception. I'm her sister. Of course, I'm supposed to give this toast.

But the other times I've been asked to speak, and the

times in the past I've had to give speeches and have been sick about it, paralyzed in front of my audience, embarrassed down to the toenail on my pinky toe, have been about being judged by my audience.

He gives me a slow smile.

"What?" I ask.

"Nothing."

"What?" I insist. That smile is full of...something.

"I just..." He shrugs. "I always think I deserve to be the one speaking." His smile grows.

But it's self-deprecating and I'm not sure I've ever seen anything sexier.

I can't help the little laugh that escapes me. "That must be nice."

"You need to start feeling that way."

"I think it might just be something in your blood. Or maybe something they put in your bottle when you were a baby or something."

"I'll have to ask my mother about that."

"If it *is* something they can bottle, let me know. I'd like a little bit of that."

"Would it be worth a fifth dance?" he asks.

Now *his* eyes are sparkling.

I've been around my sister's sparkling eyes long enough to know that's trouble. It always means I've-got-an-idea-you'll-maybe-hate-but-I'm-going-to-convince-you-to-go-along-with-it.

"You keep jumping over that third dance," I say. "You don't even have that one promised."

"Don't I?" He's leaning in again and now his gaze drops to my lips.

Dammit.

If this confidence *is* something he could sprinkle in my iced tea, I would *really* like some.

"Come on, Abigail. You're going to give me that third dance tonight just for asking, aren't you?" His voice is low, and I feel goosebumps rippling over my skin. "I've waited for *two years*."

Finally, I say, "You are going to *ask* for a third dance?"

He smiles. "I don't have to ask people for things very often. Most people *like* to give me things."

"Oh, I'm sure." I roll my eyes. I'll bet women people in particular like to give this guy things. Like their panties.

"But I have a feeling you could be the exception to a few of my rules."

Yeah, well, I think he could probably get my panties from me pretty easily. I don't think I'm an exception to *that*. But I like the idea that I might be different for him in a few ways.

I should *not* like that.

I lift my hand to the back of my head and feel the braid he did. "How did you..."

Finally, his hands drop away from my shoulders, but it almost feels as if he's reluctant to stop touching me.

"My sister was a single mom until a couple of years ago. She needed all the extra hands she could get. I've known how to do hair since Saoirse was about three."

I shake my head. "Well, maybe I'll give you a third dance for this braid."

He smiles a slow, sexy half-smile. "Nah. I want the third dance just because you want to dance with me." He steps to the door and holds out his hand. "But let's go inside and see if I can do something to earn dance five."

I take a breath as he pulls the door open.

"By the way," he says as I step past him. "If you're

thinking about using big words and trying to bore me in an attempt to get me to leave you alone..."

I look up at him.

"It's not going to work."

I nearly trip over the threshold of my grandma's side door.

But Torin's hand is there on my elbow to catch me.

CHAPTER 5

TORIN

As Abigail steps past me into the bar, she stumbles slightly on the threshold. My hand on her elbow keeps her from falling, and I get a whiff of the scent of lavender.

And it has the usual effect.

I'm *so* fucked here.

This night *is* going to end differently than the last time we were together.

Because last time I was attracted to her. *Very* attracted, but it was all based on her sweet curves, and that intoxicating scent, and the way she looked at me with those big blue eyes that seemed both wary and interested at the same time. She'd been a little awkward but had made me feel protective, made my skin tingle, and had made me smile.

Now? Well, now I know that the woman who shot me down two years ago, who I've thought about every time I've set foot in this bar since then, is a gorgeous genius who wants to change the world. And actually has a plan for it.

And I want to help her do it.

I watch her sweet ass as she crosses the kitchen and pushes through the door that leads into the main portion of the bar. I study the way the braid I created touches her upper back as she joins her sisters at the head table. Her hair is so silky. I can still feel it against my skin. Did braiding her hair take several minutes longer than it needed to because I just wanted to run my fingers through it? Definitely. I lift a hand and sniff. Yes, I can smell lavender on my hands.

This beautiful woman, who is so nervous about giving this toast that she literally got sick, is a literal genius. She graduated *summa cum laude*. Three times. She has master's degrees in biology and conservation ecology, and a doctorate in agricultural engineering. She's only twenty-three, which means she got through college, possibly high school, *far* ahead of schedule. She's clearly brilliant.

She now works for IAS, a Nebraska-based company that is internationally renowned for pioneering agricultural solutions to food crises around the globe.

And now I'm with her again, and I'm even more attracted to her now than I was before, and I need a princess.

I won't let her walk away from me again.

In fact, I'm ninety-nine percent sure I'm going to propose to her tonight.

"Owen!" I greet Abigail's cousin with a big smile and a handshake as she makes her way to the head table.

"Hey, Torin." The other man gives me a friendly grin.

Owen Landry is a great guy. Fun-loving and a well-known troublemaker, for sure, but kind-hearted, family-oriented, hard-working, and loyal. He and his wife Maddie own part of the swamp boat tour company in town and they've adopted three boys who were in their home as foster kids first.

But he makes Abigail uncomfortable when she has to give a speech in front of everyone, so he has to go. Temporarily, of course.

"Hey, I wasn't sure who to tell," I say, "but I was just outside, and I heard some kids, teenagers, talking about heading down to the docks and checking out the airboats. Maybe they're just taking a look, but I thought I'd let you know."

Owen frowns. "Dammit." He looks around, probably searching for one of his cousins who owns the company with him. "Thanks. I'll sneak out and check on things."

"It's probably nothing, but I thought I'd let someone know," I tell him.

"Yeah, thanks. Better to just check it out."

I watch him get up and say something to his cousin, Zander, who's one of the local cops. Zander gets up and follows Owen out.

Damn. I'd hoped Owen would take Zeke, the other cousin Abigail specifically named as someone who makes her nervous.

I see Charlie pick up the microphone, clearly preparing for her toast, so I head toward Zeke. I exchange pleasantries with the big man, then get him out of the building with a made-up story about overhearing some teenagers talking about sneaking around the barn at the petting zoo. It's not unique from the teenagers-and-boat story, but I didn't have much time to prep. And it will work. His wife, Jill, is one of the vets at the animal park and is very protective of the animals, so I know Zeke will want to go handle any potential trouble without her finding out.

By the time Owen, Zander, and Zeke realize there are no teenagers causing trouble, hopefully Abigail will be finished with her speech.

But when I glance at Abigail, she's noticed that not only have both Owen and Zeke left the room, but I can tell that she knows I had something to do with it. She gives me a questioning look. I just wink at her. Which causes both of her eyebrows to arch.

My first priority was getting anyone out of the room that made her uncomfortable, but if she knows I had something to do with it, and it makes her happy, all the better. Do I want to be on this woman's good side? No question about it.

Maybe that will help me get my fifth dance.

Or better yet, everything else I want from Abigail Landry.

The sound of silverware clinking against glassware calls everyone's attention to the head table. Charlie is beaming at the crowd.

The bride and groom, Ami and Michael, are sitting next to her with brilliant smiles on their faces. Amelia Landry is a beautiful woman, but after everything she's been through and with the glow of love on her wedding day, she's breathtaking.

Then there's Abigail. Who's no less beautiful, but right now, looks like she's about to throw up again.

Instinctively I move closer. I lean casually against the end of the bar, as close as I can get to where she is standing, without actually joining the people at the head table.

I clear my throat. She looks over at me. I give her what I hope is an encouraging smile.

She just frowns at me.

"Hi, everyone," Charlie starts. "I'm so happy that you're all with us today!"

I barely register what Charlie is saying. My attention is fully focused on Abigail.

She's pale, her hands are shaking slightly, and her eyes are unfocused. I would bet that she hasn't heard a word that Charlie has spoken.

These nerves are a little bit more serious than I thought. Obviously, throwing up at the thought of giving a speech is fairly significant, but this is clearly not something that passes easily.

Charlie goes on to talk about a few memories from childhood with Ami, about the first time the girls met Michael as kids, how Michael had been there for Ami as she recovered after a car accident, how Ami had bonded with Michael's son Andre, the proposal, and on and on. It's a heartfelt, beautiful speech. It's clear that Charlie and Ami are very close, and that Charlie is thrilled about this wedding.

All of that is lovely.

But all I can really focus on is the path I'll take to get to Abigail if she faints.

Finally, it's time for Charlie to hand the microphone to Abigail.

I tense up as she takes the mic.

I watch her swallow hard, then lift the microphone to her mouth. "Hi. I'm Abi. Ami's other sister."

Okay, her voice is a little shaky, but she's smiling. Kind of. It's definitely forced, but she's upright. And not puking.

So far.

"Congratulations to Ami and Griffin... I mean, Ami and *Michael*..." Her cheeks are now bright pink, and her smile is gone. "And…" She glances at her new brother-in-law, who is smiling at her, obviously not offended that Abi didn't get his name right on the first try. "I love you both," she says. "And…"

She glances at me. My heart thumps and I give her an encouraging smile.

"Good luck and…may the wind be always at your back, and the…"

She trails off, and I realize she's got no words left.

Light laughter trickles through the room and I can't keep my mouth shut. I simply have to save the day.

I'd like to think I would've done it for anyone, but that probably isn't true.

But hey, she started a line from an Irish wedding blessing. It's like she summoned me.

"Feck, sorry, I missed my cue," I call out as I make my way toward where she's standing. "Sorry, Abigail. You set me up perfectly." I flash the room a smile. "I told her outside that it's a custom in Ireland, that we've adopted in Cara, that *everyone* offers up a blessing and she thought that was lovely and asked if I'd be willing to start the toasts and blessings from the rest of the room." I don't stop until I'm standing between Ami and Abigail. I don't touch her, but I'm close enough now that if she starts to crumble, I can catch her.

And if she throws up, my shoes are toast.

"And you all know I'm always happy to say a word. Or two," I say. "Or a hundred or two."

The room fills with laughter again, but now it's directed at me.

I can *feel* Abigail's astonishment, but I know how this will go.

Perfectly. Thank you very much.

I know how to handle myself in front of a room of people, whether I know them or not, and I have zero trouble being the center of attention.

"So..." I lift my beer to the room, then look down at Ami and Michael. "May the sun shine warm upon your face, and the rain fall soft upon your fields. Until we meet again, my friends, may God hold you in the palm of his hand."

Jonah, my sister, and my brother Cian, all call out, "Sláinte" and I'm more grateful for them than I have been in a while.

The rest of the crowd follows suit and calls out, "Cheers!"

Everyone drinks and then Cian, my wonderful, impossible-to-embarrass baby brother—who definitely got a dose of the O'Grady confidence in his baby bottle too—gets to his feet and says loudly, "May your mornings bring joy and your evenings bring peace. May your troubles grow few as your blessings increase. May the saddest day of your future be no worse than the happiest day of your past. May your hands be forever clasped in friendship and your hearts forever joined in love!"

Again, everyone hoists their glasses and bottles high, with a chorus of, "Cheers!" before drinking.

"Okay, well, this is fun." This comes from Owen, who was already back. But now I'm happy to see him. Owen Landry is absolutely not shy of the spotlight either.

He makes a toast. Then others follow suit, including the bride's and groom's parents and grandparents.

But I don't register a thing anyone else says, because Abigail moves in close, rises on tiptoe and says, "Okay, fine, you can have dance three, and five, for that."

And that is all I need to hear.

I just stand next to her, grinning like an idiot, for the next fifteen minutes.

Then, as soon as the toasts and the first dances—the bride and groom, the bride and her father, and the groom and his mother—are over, I turn to Abigail and hold out my hand.

"May I?"

She lifts a brow. "Wow, you really are asking."

"Of course."

We both smile at that. It's probably good she knows I don't ask permission for much. I do have manners. I do understand how women think. I just...haven't had to worry about that in...far too long.

She takes my hand, and I head straight to the middle of the dance floor.

"No one else is out here right now," Abigail says, tugging on my hand as if to slow me down.

"That doesn't matter."

"But everyone will be watching us."

"I love being the center of attention," I tell her honestly.

"I *hate* being the center of attention."

"You won't even notice anyone else once we start," I tell her with a wink, stopping when we are exactly in the center of the 'dance floor', which is actually the middle of the entire room.

She sighs and starts to put her hands on my shoulders, but I ask, "Do you need those?" I point to the floor under the table where she was sitting earlier. Her shoes are lying there. Yes, she's been barefoot this entire time.

She looks up at me, a tiny twitch at the corner of her mouth. "Do I need to worry about my toes? You didn't step on them last time."

I'm actually an excellent dancer, but we'd safely swayed

together last time. Nothing fancy. I nod thoughtfully, though. "What if I twirl you? I don't want you to get a splinter."

The bar's floor is wood, but it's been smoothed by *years* of foot traffic.

Now there's a definite curl to one side of her mouth. "*Are* you going to twirl me?"

"I can't promise *not* to."

She glances at her shoes, then back at me. "I think I can survive twirling."

"What about flipping?"

Her eyebrows lift. "We're going to need to negotiate any flipping."

I grin. "I'm just making sure I understand the parameters I'm working within."

"I don't think I'm the flipping type. With or without shoes on," she says.

"Hmm." I pretend to contemplate that. "Okay. But you should know, dipping is a requirement."

"I'm not sure I've ever been dipped."

"Oh, we're going to fix that. For sure."

This playful teasing makes me feel light and *very* optimistic. Maybe she doesn't dislike me after all. She *almost* laughs. I can feel it *right there* almost bubbling out of her.

"Thanks for the warning."

"But let's just be sure your toes stay safe." I let go of her hand, bend over, and untie my shoes. I toe them off and toss them over toward the table where Jonah and Linnea are watching us. And judging my seduction techniques, I'm sure. I resist the urge to flip him off. I face Abigail again, arms outspread. "Okay, I'm ready."

She finally fully smiles at me. "That's really nice."

"Oh, I'm charming as hell."

"Isn't that kind of a requirement for the whole prince thing?"

"As a matter of fact, I've known a couple of princes who were real assholes." My grandfather had been a prince at one time, after all. And no one would describe my brother Declan as friendly or charming in the least. He's even been described in the media as a grump when they're being respectful and an asshole when they're not.

"Interesting."

"Do you know how to waltz?" I ask her. My arms are still outstretched, waiting for her to take that step that will bring her completely into my personal space.

She looks at me, wide-eyed. "Do *you*?"

I give her a *really?* look. "With the way I *ooze* charm and charisma? What a ridiculous question. I can even do it without my crown slipping."

Her lips almost curl again. "Even the twirling, flipping, and dipping?"

"I take twirling, flipping, and dipping very seriously. I wouldn't offer it if I couldn't deliver."

Now she laughs. She fucking *laughs*, and I feel stupidly triumphant over it.

"This song isn't a waltz," she says.

I tip my head, listening to the music. "It'll do." I curl my fingers in a *come on* motion.

She steps closer. "Why a waltz?"

"I want to impress you."

She looks completely surprised. "Why?"

"I haven't been able to impress anyone lately, no matter what I do," I tell her honestly. "It'd be nice to remember what that feels like."

Her gaze softens. But she warns me, "I'm hard to impress."

Oh, I hope so.

I'm surprised that's the first thought to roll through my mind. But then I realize it's true. I don't want a woman who will agree to the crazy proposition I'm about to make this one because of the money, or the celebrity that will go with it. I don't want someone who wants to live in a palace and be waited on hand and foot. Who is easily impressed by things like private jets and jewels. I want someone who will understand what we can *do* with the money, power, and influence. The good that can come of it all.

I think Abigail is that woman.

And I'm glad she's not easy to impress. That means when I do, it will be even sweeter.

"Challenge accepted," I tell her.

Finally, she takes that last step that brings her close enough to dance.

Our hands meet, her other rests on my shoulder, and mine settles on her hip.

And the song switches.

"Come Away With Me", by Norah Jones floats over the dance floor.

It's a romantic song for a wedding reception, for sure. It's also got a three-fourth time signature.

Like a waltz.

I give Abigail a wink. And she laughs.

We dance without speaking for the first two songs.

Then she asks, "Is that two dances?"

I shake my head. "One."

"But it was two songs."

"But one long dance."

The corner of her mouth tips up. "So we have to have a break where we're apart for a period of time and then come back to the dance floor together?"

My fingers curl into her hips, and I bring her closer. "Technically."

She swallows. "I don't want to dance with anyone else."

"I wasn't going to let you dance with anyone else."

Her eyes round slightly, but she doesn't tell me that's ridiculous or call me on the possessive tone in my voice.

She seems to move in closer. "I don't really want to take a break either."

My body heats, and if she gets any closer, she's going to feel *real* evidence of how I'm reacting to her. I'm getting hard just from dancing with her, smelling the scent of lavender floating up from her skin, and her saying things like that.

"If you dance with me the rest of the night, and I get to see you tomorrow, I'll consider it all even," I tell her.

She smiles, but she's shaking her head.

Goddamn it, I want *yeses* from this woman. She needs to start practicing that word with me.

"Yes, Abigail," I say, lifting my hand to run my thumb over her jaw. "I want more than just dancing."

Her pupils dilate, and her breath catches. Her gaze drops to my mouth. But she says, "I'm leaving really early tomorrow. I have to get back to work."

"On a Sunday?"

"Yes."

"I can get you out of it." I've already been in contact with her bosses at IAS. I called them from the plane. They like me—and my bank account and title—*very* much.

"I'm in the middle of a big project," she says with a soft smile. "I actually *want* to get back."

"You haven't heard what your other options are," I tell her, pulling her even closer. "You don't know what you could be doing instead."

Her cheeks get pink, and her gaze drops to my lips.

Yes, sweetheart. Exactly. All of that and more.

The song ends just then, and she wets her lips. "I, um... need to go to the ladies' room."

I let her slip out of my hands, and as I do I feel a niggle that tells me not to. "When you come back, it will be dance number four."

She nods. "The one for holding my hair back."

"Right."

"I'm keeping track," she tells me.

Then she turns and winds her way across the room, disappearing down the hallway that leads to the restrooms.

And the back door of the building.

Which I don't realize until it's too late.

CHAPTER 6
TORIN

"Are you just going to sit staring at the door for the rest of the night?"

I shoot Jonah a glare. "No. She's got about three more minutes before I go after her."

"This seems familiar," he says, lifting his beer.

Yeah, yeah, she left like this at Charlie's wedding too.

"Just go after her," he says. "Abi always stays at Ellie's when she's in town. She is about thirty yards away."

I turn toward him. "You call her Abi?"

"Everyone here calls her Abi."

"She introduced herself as Abigail last time, and I called her Abigail tonight. She didn't correct me."

Jonah smirks. "I guess her *friends* call her Abi."

I give a little growl. For some reason, I don't like the idea of Jonah and Abigail being close enough that he calls her by the shortened form of her name.

"What is going on?" Fiona asks.

My sister and her husband, Knox, joined us as soon as we got here. I love seeing them, of course. I love that my niece has been over to say hello and keeps stopping by in between dancing with her friends and nabbing treats from the dessert table. My brother and his best friend, Henry, also sat for a while to catch up, but there are lots of pretty, single girls here, and they can't be expected to sit with family for too long.

"I thought you filled her in," I say to Jonah.

Obviously, everyone in our inner circle would notice that Jonah and Linnea are here together. And they will also completely understand why that has to be kept from the king. Or really anyone else in Cara.

"We told her about us," Jonah says. His arm is over the back of Linnea's chair. Now he moves to rest his hand on the back of her neck in that gesture that's already becoming familiar. "But didn't want to get ahead of ourselves on your...situation."

"Situation?" Fiona pivots on her chair to face me, her eyes wide. "You have a situation?"

I shake my head. "No."

"Not yet," Jonah supplies.

I shoot him a frown. That's not going to help quash Fiona's nosiness.

"What situation are you *going to* have?"

"I'll tell you when I have it," I say. I frown at the door where Abigail disappeared again.

"He's here to find a wife," Jonah says. His smirk says that he's been very much looking forward to this particular conversation.

And I understand why when I realize that my brother and Henry have just returned to the table.

Like Jonah was to me, Henry was assigned as a body-guard to Cian immediately after we left Cara. Cian was seventeen, and Henry posed as his best friend, college roommate, and general sidekick. He played the part well. Very well. Sometimes I think Henry forgot it was just a part.

"A wife?" Henry asks, dropping into a vacant chair at the table. "Do tell." Henry is British, and everything he says sounds pompous, I swear, just because of his accent.

"I'm looking for..." Fuck. I'm not looking for anyone. I've found her. She's the gorgeous blond who just bolted out the back door after dancing with me. Again.

"A princess," Jonah says. "Or at least someone willing to play the part until your grandfather forgives him for all his past sins."

Fiona is staring at me with her mouth open.

"So is this a want-ad situation? Or a dating app profile thing?" Henry asks. "Wanted: fair maid to assist belea-guered prince in his quest for a happily ever after."

"Does she need to have a wicked stepmother, or is that just a bonus?" Cian asks.

"Yeah, we can start looking around for carriages made out of pumpkins, but pretty sure the animal park would have been notified if anyone had run across any talking mice or birds," Knox adds.

Everyone laughs.

I sigh.

Even Knox is into this. My grumpy, everything-about-the-royal-family-thing-is-kind-of-ridiculous brother-in-law.

"You're one to talk," Jonah says to Cian. "Who's been looking for the girl he had a one-night stand with for over a year now? And you don't have her shoe, but you do have her keychain or some damned thing, right?"

Cian pats his pocket. "Bracelet." Then he points to his left bicep. There's a new tattoo. It's an elephant holding something in its trunk.

"What is that?" Jonah asks, leaning in.

"It's the design on the bracelet," Henry says with an eye roll. "An elephant holding a jewel of some kind. Probably a birthstone. Of course, he has no idea whose birthstone or what it means. It could be this woman's husband's birthstone, but he still put it on his body permanently."

"So after I find her and return the bracelet, I'll still have it with me," Cian says.

Henry gives us all a wide-eyed look that I know means he thinks Cian is a little nuts.

Cian is a little...exuberant...about the things he loves, that's for sure. And this woman has had him knotted up. He's been searching for her for months. After spending one night with her.

But...

I look toward the back door of Ellie's again.

Goddammit. I'm starting to understand my little brother's obsession. I haven't even slept with Abigail Landry but I know that I'm not going to be able to just leave her alone.

"I'll see you later," I tell them all as I shove out of my seat.

My best friend grins at me knowingly. "Where you going?"

Abigail's been "getting some air" for nearly twenty minutes. If she was going to come back, she would have.

That means I'm going after her.

"For a walk."

"A walk about thirty yards long?" he asks.

"Yeah, something like that."

I start for the back door in case she really is still out

there on the back patio. But just as my hand hits the handle, I stop, turn back, and stomp over to the table where Abigail had been sitting with her sisters.

I hook my finger under the straps of her shoes, then carry them with me as I head out into the night.

I stalk across the dirt parking lot, the dirt road that runs between the parking lot and Ellie Landry's side yard, and over her grass to the front walk. I intend to charge up the porch steps and bang on the front door.

But I realize someone is sitting on the top step.

I stop at the base of the steps and look at Abigail. "Got enough air yet?"

She's changed out of her dress. She's now in what look like pajamas. It's a T-shirt and shorts set with a matching pattern of either polka dots or flowers. In the dim light cast by the moon and the tall street lights in the parking lot of Ellie's I can't make out details.

Her hair is still up in the braid I did for her though.

She's also barefoot again. Or still.

"Just waiting for the window AC unit to cool the room off. Then I'm on my way to bed."

It's June in Louisiana. It's hot and humid. It's hard *not* to sweat in Louisiana in June, no matter what you're doing. But I want to scoop her up, carry her upstairs, and show her a level of sweaty she's never imagined.

I hold her shoes up, letting them dangle by the strap from my fingers. "You left your shoes behind."

"Those shoes aren't really my style," she says. "I'm okay without them."

"As a prince I'm kind of obligated to return shoes to beautiful, intriguing women when they leave them behind after we dance," I tell her.

That makes her smile. "Right. I wouldn't want you to lose your Prince Charming card."

I lean over and set the shoes on the bottom step. "Really? Because I'm thinking if I didn't have that, you might have stuck around for the rest of our dances."

She doesn't respond right away. Then she asks, "You're really that disappointed about not getting all those dances?"

"I am. But I want more than the dances, Abigail."

She presses her lips together, takes a breath, then asks, "What else do you want?"

I decide to be honest. "I want to whisk you away on my private plane to an actual palace and give you everything and anything you could ever want or need."

Her eyes widen. "You don't even know me."

I tuck my hands into my back pockets. To try to look casual. But also to keep from reaching for her.

"I've read all about your work," I tell her. "I started by just wanting to know about that job you said you hated so much. But then I kept reading. I know all about your degrees, what you want to do for the future of farming, how you see farming changing, and how indoor farms can combat a lot of the current challenges to food production and can fill in the gaps where people are hungry and where those gaps are only going to increase in the future."

She's staring at me. She's sitting up straighter now and even in the pale light, I can see her shock.

"You...read about me?"

"Not just *about* you. I read all of *your* papers. Your work in college. Your dissertation. The articles you've published. I even stumbled upon some social media posts."

"I...Oh..." She shakes her head. "I thought you wanted to sleep with me."

I chuckle softly. "Oh, Abigail, I most definitely want to sleep with you."

She swallows hard.

"I wanted that before I knew you are a damned *genius* who could come to my country and revolutionize agriculture, give us food security and independence, and completely overhaul our economy."

I can see that she's breathing faster now.

"So you want to hire me?" she asks. "Which means we *can't* sleep together because you'll be my boss."

I step up on the first step.

"I don't want to hire you. But I do want to bring you to Cara to do your work."

She stands. "But you won't pay me?"

I grin. "Well...you'll have plenty of money."

"I don't understand."

I step up onto the next step, but she doesn't back up. There's only a step between us now. "I want you to marry me."

Her eyes widen. But she says nothing.

"Be my princess," I go on. "You'll have influence, and resources. You can do anything and everything you've ever wanted to do. And my country will have indoor farms that will revolutionize our agricultural programs and our economy."

She's staring at me. Then when she realizes I'm done talking, she laughs.

"Marry you? Is that how things work for you? You just smile that smile, waltz a couple of waltzes, and women just say yes to anything? Even *marriage*?"

Well...

"I've never asked anyone to marry me before so I don't really know," I answer.

She's still smiling. "Thank you for the offer. But I'm not going to marry you."

"As princess of Cara you could build as many farms as you want to. You can see your plans in action. Right now, they're all just on paper. You're not actually *doing* any of it. Don't you want to see it come to life?"

Now she's not smiling. She's just watching me. She takes a deep breath. "Of course I do."

"This is the perfect way. There's no red tape. Nothing between your amazing brain and making it all happen for real."

"What's the catch?"

"No catch. My country needs a prince and princess in place before my grandfather steps aside as king and I ascend to the throne. The country deserves to know who will be there to step up and take care of them. My grandfather needs a successor in place before his heart gives out."

"He has a bad heart?" she asks.

"He does. He's already had three heart attacks. I really need to get married to give him and the country peace of mind."

"So you're serious about finding a wife?"

"I am." My heart starts pounding.

She steps down a step.

"Abigail."

"Yes?"

"If you step down one more step, I'm going to kiss you."

She wets her lips.

"So if you want to just keep talking, you need to keep your sweet ass right there on that step."

She looks down at the step that would start the kissing.

"And if you don't want to keep talking...or anything else... you need to go back inside."

She meets my gaze. But doesn't move.

"*And*," I say, feeling like I need to lay it all out. "If I start kissing you, the only way to stop me from that, and more, is to say the word elephant."

She meets my eyes. Then nods. "So that's our safe word?"

I almost groan. "Yes."

Her eyes widen at how serious I sound.

"I might need a safe word?" She says it almost on a whisper. But she doesn't seem concerned.

"Typically, I would say no. Not the first time I ever kiss you. But judging by the way I have felt unusual things for you since the very beginning, I just want to cover all the bases right up front."

She's staring at me. But she seems more fascinated than anything. "Okay." Then she tips her head. "Why elephant?"

The word will definitely make me think of my brother's new tattoo and my brother himself, which will definitely cool any sexual thoughts I've got going on.

"It's just a really good anti-sex word for me."

She gives me a half smile. "Okay. I understand."

"Good."

Two heartbeats pass.

Then she steps down onto the step right above mine.

I groan and cup her face, bringing her mouth in against mine.

She tastes sweet and minty, like she just brushed her teeth and I want to run my tongue over every inch of her mouth. Every inch of her body.

She opens when I lick over her bottom lip, and her body presses against mine as she wraps her arms around my neck.

My hands drop to her ass. She fits perfectly in my

hands. I squeeze and she moans into my mouth. My fingertips brush the smooth bare skin just under the curve of her ass and I realize she's not wearing panties. My cock hardens and I press into her.

She gasps, then arches closer.

I run my fingers back and forth along the soft, smooth skin and feel the way she shivers in my arms.

I drag my mouth along her jaw to her ear. "You feel and taste amazing."

"Ditto," she says breathlessly.

I move my hands, sliding them up and down her back, then dipping under the hem of her shirt so that I can feel bare skin. There's no bra either. I run my fingertips over the bumps of her spine.

"I want to touch you all over," I say, my voice rough.

"I want that too." She laughs lightly. "We could go inside."

I lift my head and pin her with my gaze. "If we go inside, I'm getting my hands all over you."

She nods. "Good."

I step up onto the step she's on, and she steps up to the step above. I do it again. She does too. I walk her backward to the door. I press her against it, my hands moving around to her sides and running my palms up and down over her ribs, just brushing my thumbs against the underside of her breasts.

"Be sure," I tell her.

"I'm sure."

Then I'm cupping her breasts, her nipples pressing into my palms. They're the perfect size. I want them against my chest, against my tongue.

Her head thunks back against the door and she takes a deep breath. "That feels good," she tells me softly.

"It sure as fuck does," I agree.

I can't get over the fact that this gorgeous thing in my arms is also probably the smartest person I've ever met. That she's letting me close like this, letting me touch her, is amazing.

I dip my knees and take her nipple in my mouth through the soft material of her shirt. I suck, then bite down gently.

"Oh my God!" Her hand slides to the back of my head, holding me close.

I roll her other nipple between my finger and thumb.

She's panting. "More," she tells me, her gaze locked on mine.

I move her shirt up, exposing one breast.

She's gorgeous. I can't see everything with the lack of light, but I don't need to. She's the most beautiful woman I've ever seen. I lean in and take her nipple in my mouth, sucking hard. Then swirling my tongue around the tip. Her fingers dig into my scalp.

"Inside," she says, the word barely audible.

I reach past her hip, twist the door knob, and push.

We stagger over the threshold, and I immediately scoop my hands under her ass, lifting her. Her legs go around my waist, and I turn, slamming the door and pressing her against the wall next to it.

We're in the foyer. There are shoes along the wall to our right underneath hooks overflowing with jackets and hats. But there is one section of wall that's empty. I press her into it, my mouth hungry on hers. I cradle her hips in my hands, holding her against my cock as I grind into her.

She whimpers into my mouth. "That's so good."

I trail my lips down her neck, sucking lightly but not

hard enough to make a mark. Not this time. Though the idea of marking her as mine has my cock pulsing.

I slide one hand under the loose edge of her shorts, palming her bare ass and sliding forward.

"What's your safe word, pretty girl?"

"Elephant," she says. Then she pulls back, "But I'm not saying it. That's just what it is."

I grin. "Good girl." Then I cup her. I love how baggy these shorts are. My whole hand covers her pussy. She's hot, and so wet.

"This all for me?" I ask.

"Yes."

The fact that I can make her needy like this makes my entire body hot and hard. I groan and lean in to kiss her neck as my middle finger strokes over her slickness, then slips inside her. "Christ, you're so tight. So wet."

She wiggles against my hand. "I need more."

It hits me that I can't fuck her. Not like this. Not tonight. She's staying with her grandparents upstairs. I'm staying in the house where I used to live with Henry, Cian, and Jonah. It's a really nice house. Big. I'd have my own room. It's definitely a few steps above a frat house. But... when we're all there, it does kind of have that feel.

I could whisk her off to New Orleans to the Waldorf Astoria.

But...I want her just barely satisfied. I want her to think about this. I want her to want more.

I slide another finger into her, deep, curling against her G spot.

She gasps my name.

"Fuck, I love hearing my name on your lips." I kiss her again.

"Do that again. I'll say anything you want," she says against my mouth.

I growl. "I like the sound of that. The idea of making you do whatever I want."

She circles her hips, trying to rub harder against my hand.

"I've got you," I say softly. "I'm gonna give you what you need, sweet girl."

Well, most of what she needs. I'm going to give her an orgasm, but she doesn't get my cock yet.

I thrust my fingers in and out, then press my thumb over her clit.

She's grasping my biceps and circling her hips. She doesn't have much leverage, but her thighs tighten around me, and she's grinding against my hand.

I want to spread her out, touch her, lick her, suck on her from head to toe.

Another time.

This is just a taste of what she can have with me.

It's going to kill me to give her this, and walk away, but it will be worth it in the end.

I move my fingers deep again. Damn, I don't think I can get a third finger in.

"Come on my fingers, Abigail. I want to taste you."

Her thighs tighten. She gasps.

"Play with those pretty nipples," I coach. "Help me make you come."

She reaches up under her shirt, cupping one breast, her thumb moving over her nipple. Then I see her pinch it lightly. I feel her pussy squeeze around my fingers in response.

My cock is angry, pressing against my zipper, protesting being left out of the fun.

I finger fuck her faster, my thumb swirling over her clit.

"Be a good girl and come on my fingers," I tell her. "Let me feel this pretty pussy soak my hand."

Suddenly she gasps, and I feel her pussy clench around my fingers. She comes then with the prettiest little moan.

I like that.

But next time, she will be crying out my name.

I slide my hand from her body, then lift it between us and let her watch as I suck each finger clean.

She watches, breathing fast, her cheeks flushed.

"You're amazing, Abigail."

I don't want to call her Abi. Everyone calls her Abi. I want to be someone unique in her life.

She looks up at me with a sweet smile. "Do you want to go upstairs?"

"I want to go upstairs more than I want to take my next breath," I tell her honestly. "But I can't do that tonight."

Her eyes widen. "Why not?"

Because I am either the stupidest man walking the planet, or the smartest.

"Because I want you to want another time."

"Oh." She doesn't know what else to say to that.

I grin and lean in to kiss her. I hope she can taste herself at least faintly on my tongue as I stroke along hers.

When I lift my head, I say, "Next time we'll have a lot more space and a lot more time and a lot fewer relatives around." I lower her feet to the floor and cup her face, giving her a last deep kiss. "I loved every fucking minute tonight with you."

She nods. "Me too."

I straighten. "I'll see you tomorrow."

I turn and let myself out before I give in to my new biggest weakness—Abigail Landry.

But there's plenty of time for me to be weak over this woman. When she's my princess, in my bed, in my palace, I'll be able to indulge in every single thing either of us would ever want.

Convincing my grandfather and the people of Cara that I'm crazy about this woman shouldn't be difficult at all.

The next morning, I text her the moment I wake up.

I want to see you.

She doesn't respond.

I assume she's still asleep. So I shower, dress, and head for Ellie's house. There's supposed to be a brunch with the family, and I know I'll be included.

But I stop by the house first.

As I walk up the front walk, I immediately see that Abigail's shoes are still sitting on the bottom porch step. Right where I put them last night.

Smiling, I pick them up.

I bound up the steps and lift my hand to knock. The door swings open before I connect with the wood though.

"Well, hey there," Leo Landry, Abigail's grandfather answers.

"Uh, hey, Leo. Good morning."

I try very hard not to feel guilty about what I did to this man's granddaughter against his foyer wall mere hours ago.

"You comin' over for breakfast?" he asks, stepping out onto the porch and pulling the door shut.

"Yeah, sure," I answer. "I was just..." I hold Abigail's

shoes up. "Found Abigail's shoes." That was true. "Thought I'd return them."

Leo chuckles. "Well, she's already gone. But I don't suppose she'll have a lot of use for those. Abi's not really the rhinestones and high heels type."

"Gone? She's over at Ellie's?" I ask.

"Nope. Back to Nebraska. She had an early flight."

Leo starts down the porch steps. I glance at the front door of the house, then at his retreating back.

She's *gone*? She told me last night she had to get back to work but...

Fuck.

She's gone.

She had to catch a flight. Sure, I get that. But...we're engaged.

Aren't we?

Okay, she didn't say 'yes, I'll marry you', but she didn't say no either.

Well, she said no, but then I talked her into it.

Didn't I?

But no matter the status of our engagement, she left without a goodbye. She knew I was expecting to see her again. Just like both times she left Ellie's "to get some air".

I'm getting very tired of being left behind by Abigail Landry.

"You comin'?" Leo asks from the bottom of the porch steps.

"Uh, yeah." I follow him across the road but my mind is *not* on grits and pancakes and bacon.

And there is something about me that Abigail needs to learn right now.

My "prince card" doesn't just come with an obligation

to be charming. It also makes me a very entitled asshole when I need to be.

CHAPTER 7

WAIT 'TIL I TELL YE

EPISODE 741 TRANSCRIPT

Lindsey: So our illustrious prince has once again jetted off to the US for the weekend. Ugh!

Jen: For a friend's wedding! That's sweet.

Lindsey: Yes, we wouldn't want his duties as prince to get in the way of a good party.

Jen: What duties? He's not really doing that much. <laughs lightly> And did you hear? Linnea Olsen went with him.

Lindsey: Wait, what? I love Linnea.

Jen: Everyone does. I mean people have always talked about how perfect they would be together. Okay, at least since Torin first came back two years ago. Their families have been friends for a long time. They've known each other since they were kids.

Lindsey: No question. Linnea is one of us. And she's definitely princess material.

Jen: For sure. So maybe their get-away is more than just a weekend of partying in Louisiana. Oh! Maybe he's introducing her to his friends there! And his brother and sister are there! They know her too, but it's been a while. It's a good thing for them to all spend time together if Torin and Linnea are dating!

Lindsey: Okay, I'm not so mad about this trip now. But, Torin, if you're listening, we're going to need to hear something concrete soon! Spill the tea, Your Highness!

CHAPTER 8
TORIN

I waited twelve hours to text her. Mostly because I was waffling between texting, calling, and just getting on my plane and flying to her.

But it seems Abigail thinks she doesn't want to spend more time with me, so I've decided to take things a little slower.

My phone dings two minutes later with a text from her.

I honestly wasn't sure she'd respond at all.

I open it immediately.

It's just a photo.

Of her legs. Propped on the wooden railing of what looks like a porch. And she's wearing cut off denim shorts and ugly green rubber boots that go up to her knees.

And my dick gets hard.

She has great thighs. They're smooth and tan and trim and I vividly remember how they felt wrapped around my hips as I finger fucked her.

It was only last night that I felt that sweet, hot pussy but I feel like I've been starving.

But fuck me...it's also the boots. Or, more specifically, that she's wearing boots like that.

Those are not heels. Those are not pretty sandals. Those are...work boots. Waterproof, stomp-through-mud-and-shit boots. Getting dirty boots.

I fucking love those boots. I love getting dirty. In every way I can mean that.

> Where are you?

> Just got home from work. Having a beer on my back porch.

My dick twitches again.

> Those are your work boots?

She's a farmer. I know this. I've read all of her papers and all about the company—Innovative Agricultural Systems—and what she wants to do with her research and development. But I hadn't pictured her in green rubber boots.

Now I have a new turn-on.

> Yep. What I wear every day. I told you those sandals aren't my style.

I also love that. Oh, I love heels. Don't get me wrong. But those boots would be perfect on my ranch.

Cowboy boots would be better, maybe, but honestly, a pair of good rubber boots, when things are muddy and sloppy, are even better.

I'm guessing they're not your style either, so you can toss them.

I focus on her next text. I frown. I'm not tossing these shoes. They're a little piece of last night. I want her to want them back.

Okay, I want a reason to take them to her.

Dammit. Courting a woman from thousands of miles away—there are three thousand, eight hundred and ninety-one miles between my palace and Sapphire Falls to be exact—is not easy. Or practical.

Which is why I'm still in the US.

I respond to her, trying to keep it light.

Damn, they don't fit.

Good thing I showed you how fun it is to dance barefoot.

Indeed. It was an absolute pleasure.

As were the other things we did while you were barefoot

Several seconds tick by before she replies.

She finally sends a blushing-faced emoji.

Okay, that's cute. My gorgeous genius is also cute as fuck.

Marrying her is going to be the easiest thing I've ever done.

As soon as she fucking says yes.

I'm thinking July eighteenth

For what?

Our wedding.

Fine. I'm taking it *a little* slow. I'm not pushing this in person, at least. And that's a month from today. I want the wedding next week, but I realize that's probably overreacting.

Her reply is simply three laughing-crying emojis.

I frown.

You'd rather do it sooner?

I'm not marrying you, Torin. Though I do think you should still consider indoor farms for Cara. They would be perfect for you.

I focus on the first five words at first, feeling frustrated and almost panicked. I need her. For so many reasons.

But then I read the entire message again. And again.

You looked up my country, didn't you? And our agricultural status. And our environment. And our economy.

It's nearly three minutes before she replies and I've almost given up when a text finally lights up my screen.

Yes.

I grin. She was curious. That's good. That's very good.

Come to Cara, Abigail. Be my princess.

> That's such an overreaction! I can just come and build farms for you.

Yes, she could. Of course. But I need a princess and I want her. Those two things should go together.

> I need to get married. And if it's not you, I don't think whoever ends up as princess will appreciate how I feel about the gorgeous scientist who is revolutionizing agriculture in my country and making me hard every time I see her in green work boots.

Again, it's several minutes before she replies.

> Thanks for checking in about the shoes.

Changing the subject won't work. Not forever. I don't actually give a fuck about the shoes. Especially if she doesn't want them back, and I can't use them as a completely valid reason to fly two hours to see her.

I start to type, but then another message from her comes in.

> I'm going to get in the shower.

> You could take the phone with you. But, of course, we should probably switch to a video call.

Again there are several seconds before she replies.
And then it's with another blushing emoji. And a,

> goodnight, Torin.

She's now metaphorically walking out the back door. Dammit.

Talk to you soon, Abigail.

That's a promise.

CHAPTER 9
ABIGAIL

I don't *hate* going out.

I *hate* presenting in front of professional colleagues. I *hate* going on sales calls. I *hate* parsnips. I *hate* when men other than my grandpa Leo call me "sweetheart" and "darlin'".

But I don't *hate* going out.

I don't really like it either, though.

This is why I've only been at the bar for about an hour before I excuse myself from the table I've been sitting at and go up to pay my tab.

Sapphire Falls is a nice town. The Come Again is a nice bar. It's clean and not too loud—for a bar—and the general atmosphere is very come-as-you-are and laid-back. The guys who have flirted or outright asked me out, take 'no thanks' in stride. The people I work with are great, and the locals are friendly, so saying 'sure' to an invitation to show up for a drink or two isn't terrible once in a while.

For some reason, tonight, though, I'm less enthusiastic about socializing than usual. And that's saying something.

I'm thinking about Torin.

That's not new, but it's been happening a lot more than it used to.

In the three days since I got back from my sister's wedding, I've thought of him seemingly constantly.

I've replayed his crazy proposal. Both of them.

I guess it was one proposal, but he brought it up twice. Once on my grandmother's porch steps and once in text.

I've replayed what he said about reading all of my papers. And that he's not only actually interested in my work, but that he wants to make my ideas reality.

I've definitely replayed the make-out session against the wall of my *grandmother's house* every single night. And I haven't felt nearly as weird or guilty about it as I probably should.

I maybe shouldn't have let that go as far as it did after he'd essentially proposed. But I said no. He knew where I stood.

It was just that...I *really* wanted to kiss him. And then he affirmed that he was really serious about finding a wife, and I realized that was probably my only chance to kiss him. It's not like we run into each other often. And if he *needs* to find a wife, then the next time I see him he could be engaged. Or married.

Or I might never actually see him again.

So I took the opportunity to kiss him. And when it went further than that, I just enjoyed every damned minute.

I've also re-read the texts he sent over and over and over.

After I sent him the photo of my green work boots and turned down his proposal *again*—and then ignoring how the idea of him marrying someone else makes my stomach feel—he'd sent me a photo with the caption *my work shoes*. They were shiny black dress shoes and they'd been propped up on what was clearly the leather seat of an airplane. A *private* airplane.

Lord, we have nothing in common.

But the next morning, I'd sent him a photo of my bare feet in the dirt beside my strawberry plants. I'd added, *No shoes required.*

He'd sent me a photo of his bare feet propped up on a chaise lounge chair by a bright blue swimming pool. *Same.*

I'd laughed.

We are definitely *not* the same.

So what the hell is the point of being interested in him?

He's a *prince*. He's *in charge of a country*. He's up in front of people, in the public eye, constantly being watched. He's the absolute opposite of my type as a guy could possibly get.

Still, tonight I'm thinking about him again, and I've had a couple of drinks, and I want to call him.

I'm not going to, of course. I have way more self-control than that. Not to mention self-respect.

But texting is different. If there's a good reason for the text.

I look down at my feet and think about the fact that he texted me first. About my shoes. And ignore that he also mentioned setting a wedding date.

So...fuck it. I'm texting him tonight.

I snap a photo of the low-heeled leather ankle boots I'm wearing tonight. They're not sexy or especially cute. They pull on and scrunch a little at the top, but they're plain black without any adornment. They're definitely cuter than the green rubber boots, though. I'm wearing these with a sundress that hits me just above the knee, so I make sure to get some leg in the photo.

Why?

I don't know.

To me, flirting is a little like sales: you're trying to convince the other person they're interested in what you've got by putting all the *good* things up front and hiding the bad.

And I *suck* at sales.

Because I think people make better decisions when they know all the *facts*. There's not really "good" and "bad" in most things. What one person thinks is a pro, can be someone else's con. In my opinion, that goes for pancakes, cars, innovative agricultural systems, shoes, and even other people. I think it should all be spelled out from the beginning.

I open my texts, find the ones from him, ignore the way my heart does a little flip in my chest, and start a new message.

> Thought you'd like to know I do have other boots.

I attach the photo and hit send.

Even having this text open, this tiny connection to him, makes me feel excited.

I set my phone down and pick up my drink.

My phone pings with a text less than a minute later. I'm surprised. It's only about ten p.m., and I'm thinking about heading home, but that's me. I don't do late nights out. I'll stay up until one reading, but I'm never out much later than this. I still didn't expect to hear from him immediately.

Or maybe at all.

Actually, that's a lie. I knew he'd text back. And that makes my stomach flip.

But I really didn't expect how hard my heart thumps in my chest as I pick up my phone and open the text.

> You look so fucking good in both. And out of both. And I'll bet out of everything.

My breath catches. God, I love his intensity. I should *not* love that. I don't like intense things. I like quiet, calm, and even-keeled.

You also thought you didn't like beards and you ended up with this guy's hands in your pants in your grandma's foyer, I remind myself.

Yeah, okay, fair enough.

> It's late to be working, isn't it?

> Not work boots. Down at the bar.

I look around the bar. I'm not having a bad time. Everyone here is so nice. But two messages from Torin, and I want to text with him for the next hour instead of sit in a bar and drink and dance.

Yeah, that's totally normal. I sigh.

> Since you're not barefoot, I'm going to assume you're not dancing.

I read his text twice. I'm sure if anyone is looking at me, my smile is big and goofy.

> No dancing

> Good.

Something about that single word from him makes my

heart thump again and a hot ribbon of heat slides languidly through me. I squeeze my thighs together.

> They two-step here. No waltzing. Though there is some dipping

> You can't get good dipping just anywhere

I actually laugh softly at that. And he's not wrong.

> Not to mention twirling.

> Remember that.

I have no idea why my stomach flips at that. That response sounds almost...possessive. But that's ridiculous.

> Do you like the two-step

I'm not much for dancing period.

> I've never done it. But seems like it could be fun.

> You just tell me what you want to try, Abigail. Anything at all. I'll make it fun.

Whoa. I feel my eyes go round. My brain takes his word choice and pretends he's offering to do *anything* I want to do. And maybe even teach me a few things.

I take a deep breath.

Then read the text again.

The use of my name, even in a text, makes the heat in my lower belly and between my legs intensify. I shift on the bar stool.

How many drinks have I had? I study the bottle of hard

cider on the bar in front of me. Two. I'm almost certain. That is *not* enough for me to blame this reaction on the liquor.

I swallow hard. I have to text him back. And *not* throw myself at him.

But he did just promise to make whatever I want to try fun…

I pull my lower lip between my teeth and pray I don't sound like an idiot.

I guess as long as I can do whatever it is barefoot.

His reply is almost immediate.

You can wear, or not wear, whatever you want.

I quickly set my phone on the bar and pick up my bottle to take a drink. Yeah, this bottle isn't even half empty. I haven't even had two full hard ciders. But my imagination is running away with that.

"Hey, Abi, you're still here. You want to come back and sit with us?" Riley Wright and Peyton Hansen, two Sapphire Falls natives, are suddenly leaning onto the bar beside me. I didn't even see them approach.

Riley's husband, Derek, is the bartender so she's up here often, flirting and teasing with him. They're adorable. I really like them both.

Peyton has returned some empty glasses and is apparently waiting for refills. She grins at me.

I look over at the table where we were all sitting together a few minutes ago. Peyton's husband, Scott, is there with her sister and brother-in-law, Hope and TJ. My boss Lauren introduced me to Riley and Peyton because they're closer to my age than she is. But I think Lauren is starting to figure out that I have more in common with her nerdy, introverted, bluntly-says-whatever-is-on-his-mind best friend and business partner, Mason, than I do with the fun, vivacious Peyton and Riley.

I'd told the group I was getting ready to leave and had come up to the bar to settle my tab. Then I'd decided to finish my cider, and I'd started texting Torin. "Oh, no, sorry. I was on my way out and...got a text."

Riley grins at me. "I didn't know you had a boyfriend."

I shake my head quickly. "I don't."

"Well, a *potential* one then."

"No."

She lifts a brow. "You're smiling and blushing over texts, girl. Do you have a *girlfriend*?"

I look down at my phone. "Oh. I mean, it's a guy. But it's not...well, it is, but..."

"Is he hot?" Peyton asks, interrupting my stammering.

He is. Very. I nod. "Yes."

"Are you related?"

"No."

"Is he married?"

I swallow hard. *Not yet. But he's going to be soon. To someone.* I hate how that makes me feel. It's almost like I'm... jealous. Which is stupid. There's not even a fiancée to be jealous of, and *I'm* not marrying him—I've literally said no to marrying him—so it's absolutely ridiculous for me to be jealous. "No."

"Have you ever masturbated while thinking of him?"

I choke.

Yes.

"Jesus, Peyton," Derek says, sliding the refilled drinks across the bar to her.

"What?" Peyton asks. "That would be a pretty good sign that she's into him."

Peyton is also very blunt and says whatever is on her mind. But in a very different way from the kind-of-grumpy-socially-awkward genius scientist, Mason. Peyton is more live-out-loud-and-don't-give-a-fuck.

And now I'm definitely blushing. Hotly.

Riley and Peyton both notice. And give me knowing grins.

"We'll let you get back to the sexting," Peyton says, picking up the tray of glasses and bottles. "But if you want to really do it right, you need to go home and get naked. Or at least go into the store room. Derek will unlock it for you."

"Peyton," Derek says, his tone full of warning, but it's clear he's fighting a smile. "Go away."

"Yeah, *we* might need the storeroom in a little bit," Riley says, winking at her husband. "You should go home to sext him," she says to me.

My cheeks are hot.

So are my panties.

"Um...thanks for the tip," I finally say. Because I want to be the type of girl who's fine talking about sex and hot guys and flirting and all of that with two really nice and fun women who should be my peers.

They both grin and head back to their table. But as they go, I'm hit by the realization that they're not really my peers. They're easily six to eight years older than me, but we still should have *similar* interests, watch the same videos on line, listen to similar music, read the same books, be into the same things. But we don't. I know that without even asking.

They're the types of girls I tried to fit in with for years.

In grade school, I tried to fit in with the girls in my

classes at school, but they were three years older than me. It was impossible. I tried to hang out socially with girls my age, but we never saw each other at school since I was in classes three grades ahead of them, so we didn't have the same experiences and didn't know the same people.

Plus, sleepovers, dances, and pool parties have never been my thing, so I was fine staying home on the weekends.

College was a little easier. No one there knew that I'd skipped three grades, so I could fake "normal" there. Or so I'd thought. I know exactly why I'd slept with Matthew Latham, the one and only guy I've ever had sex with. The *entire* reason. Because normal eighteen-year-old girls in college are supposed to meet cute boys and have sex with them once in a while.

Just like normal college girls are supposed to go to football games and have fun. And out to bars, where they do shots and dance to the current top forty. And stay up with other girls in the dorms, eating pizza and talking about their hopes and dreams until three a.m.

I did all of that. Even though at eighteen, I was actually a senior according to my hours and in classes with people who were at least three years older than me. And kicking their asses on exams and papers.

I'd faked it and lied about the classes I was taking to the girls in the dorms—the freshmen who were my age but way behind me academically. Yes, I'd lived in the dorms, where I'd hoped to have a "normal" experience.

Turns out that lying about what you do, want, like, and are interested in doesn't actually produce a normal experience at all.

It was exhausting. I wasn't interested in watching reality TV every Thursday night, or parties at the frat houses, or getting a tattoo that meant nothing, or group study sessions for Sociology 101. I'd taken, and aced, Soc 101 as a freshman in *high school*.

They all thought I was stuck-up and weird. I thought they were silly and immature.

I'd moved home after that one year in the dorms and worked on my advanced degrees from my childhood bedroom.

I look down at my phone and re-read Torin's text.

> You can wear, or not wear, whatever you want.

Well, hell, that makes me hot all over. But I have no idea how to sext. Maybe I should tell Torin *that's* what I want to try. I bet he'd make that fun. He can make me horny just by texting about dancing and shoes.

That's probably weird.

I pick up my bottle and finish off my cider, then take a deep breath.

> Are you wearing dancing shoes right now by chance?

I frown at the words. That sounds like a version of "what are you wearing?". Maybe cheesy. But he'd texted me that same thing essentially a few days ago. And I want to know. It's crazy, but I'd love to see a photo of Torin's shoes.

Okay, that's definitely weird.

I push send and then rub my fingers over the center of my forehead. What am I doing? He's a prince.

I cannot date a prince.

I can't sleep with a prince.

I definitely can *not* marry a prince.

So I shouldn't be texting and flirting with a prince.

Besides, he could also be a raging alcoholic.

Or he could hate cats.

Or love NASCAR, like my cousins do.

Or he could be into absolutely nothing I have any interest in.

Or he could just be an asshole.

My phone pings and my heart jumps. I take a breath as I pick it up.

> No dancing for me tonight either.

And then there's the photo.

And...

Oh. My. God.

The shot is down his body. From mid-thigh to his feet.

It's mostly white. Because he's covered by a pristine white bedsheet. One foot and the bottom portion of his left leg are showing, the sheet tangled around his muscular calf. The rest of the sheet clearly molds to his thigh and his other leg.

He's in bed.

I suck in a breath.

He's. In. Bed.

And holy crap, I wish he'd taken that shot from a little higher. I'd love to see the rest of what that sheet is clinging to.

That's all I can think of.

My face feels hot again. The rest of me gets melty. Yeah...that was a good text.

I don't know what to send back. Except...

> Good.

I don't like the idea of him dancing with anyone else, either.

Which is, admittedly, problematic.

If I don't want him *dancing* with anyone else, how am I going to feel when he's engaged to someone else? Marries someone else? That will probably hit the news here. I'll probably have to see photos of that.

My stomach churns a little.

Yeah, I won't like that.

I shouldn't be flirt-texting with this guy.

> You've ruined me for dipping anyone else.

I stare at the words, as warmth spreads through me. And yes, it's heat from the innuendo but it's also a softer feeling in my chest that feels more like just...happiness.

Well...crap.

I don't want him dancing with other women and I really like the idea that I'm on his mind and that he doesn't *want* to dance with—or "dip"—anyone else.

I consider my response. And then I decide to keep it simple. And honest.

And blame it on the hard cider.

> Good.

Okay, that might have been a mistake. I don't want him to think...

> It's all been so very good, Abigail.

I read that over. Four times. Well, damn. I never should have texted him tonight.

But as I tuck the phone into my purse, pay my tab, and head out into the June night, I can feel that I'm still smiling.

CHAPTER 10

WAIT 'TIL I TELL YE

EPISODE 749 TRANSCRIPT

Lindsey: He's *still* in the US? What the hell is going on? It's been over a week since the wedding.

Jen: Yep. He's still there. But so is Linnea. It seems that the prince has been taking the duchess out to dinner and enjoying the local culture in Shreveport.

Lindsey: *Shreveport.* What's in Shreveport? When he lived in Louisiana, it was down around New Orleans, right? And I always forget Linnea is a duchess.

Jen: Right. Her grandfather, besties with King Diarmuid, was given the title and all that land way back. She looks amazing in that green dress in those photos from their night out.

Lindsey: She does. But *why* Shreveport? Anyone know? If you have a theory, call in or comment on one of our social media posts. They've been seen entering and exiting the Magnolia Hotel, which is *very* posh. They're in the penthouse. Jonah Greene, the prince's longtime friend and bodyguard, is there with them so this must be palace-approved, right?

Jen: Oh, it is! Didn't you see the statement from the palace?

Lindsey: Wait, there's an official statement?

Jen: Yes! And I quote, "The Prince and Duchess have known each other since they were children. That they have a close friendship should be no surprise and their families are delighted that they enjoy spending time together."

Lindsey: Okay, that sounds like the royal family is on board with this trip...and all it entails.

Jen: It really does. Oh! What if he *proposes* to her while they're in the US?

Lindsey: Instead of doing it *here*? He should propose in Cara, don't you think?

Jen: I know *I'll* be disappointed if it happens somewhere else. Even if the US is meaningful to the prince, *this* is their home.

Lindsey: I agree. Okay, listeners, let us know what you think.

CHAPTER 11

ABIGAIL

I don't *hate* my job.

I even *want* to love it.

I'm just not very good at it.

I like the company. What they do is amazing and I'm proud to be a part of it.

And my bosses are amazing. Objectively *and* in my opinion.

Mason Riley and Lauren Davis-Bennett have been best friends since college and business partners since Innovative Agriculture Solutions, better known as IAS, was first conceived.

IAS is an incredible company, on the cutting edge of innovations in agriculture at almost every level. Mason and Lauren started out bringing agricultural systems to areas of the world that most needed increased access to crops, literally feeding hundreds of thousands. They've now expanded to research and development in making farming more resilient to climate change and more efficient for feeding the continuously growing population of the planet.

Mason and Lauren have met with leaders around the world. They've presented to Congress and the United Nations. They have a direct line to the White House. They've been published and featured in every scientific journal that has anything to do with agriculture or humanitarian efforts.

So when they recruited me as a junior in college based on a paper I wrote about using indoor farming technologies to solve the problem of food deserts in the United States, I was flattered and excited. I signed up immediately.

I didn't ask any questions. I didn't worry about a thing.

One of the most respected companies in the field of agricultural engineering and conservation wanted me. Of course, I wanted to work for them.

I didn't realize that they would want me to go out and try to convince farmers and ranchers to use our technologies. To *explain* to people why they should convert to our systems. To *talk to people* about what we could do for them and why partnering with us would help them and their communities.

Lauren and Mason thought that the people actually developing the systems were the best to educate people about why they were beneficial.

They're probably right on some level.

But I'm not the right girl.

I think that people should respect that *experts* know best and should just use technologies and systems that we tell them they should use.

Of course, I also don't like talking to people, so there's that too.

I'm meeting with *two* men today. Just two. Outside on

their ranch. It's not a big roomful of people. It's not a wedding toast for one of my two sisters.

I still threw up right after I got out of my car.

I parked near a ditch specifically because I knew that was going to happen.

"Hi, Abigail, I'm Dean Simons."

I shake the man's hand. "Nice to meet you."

We're fifteen miles outside of Bayard, a little town in the panhandle of Nebraska. I'm here to try to convince Dean to put one of IAS's feeding systems on his ranch.

I can get excited about these systems. At least in theory. The idea is very much like the indoor farms I'd like to build across the country. Those farms would supply a variety of fruits and vegetables to an entire community, while the system I'm showing Dean specifically grows the feed the rancher needs for his livestock. But the idea is the same— an indoor space that protects the plants from extreme weather, seasonal changes, pests, and disease, making terrain and climate a moot point.

"You too." Dean turns to the young man beside him. "And this is my son, Tyler."

"Hi, Tyler."

Tyler takes my hand with a grin. "I was an agricultural engineering major in college. All of this is right up my alley."

"Oh, great."

He just gives me a wink as he shakes my hand.

I really hope that's great. He could be an asset in this meeting if he's into new, innovative ways of growing food.

Dean is probably in his mid-fifties. He is in a faded Nebraska Huskers T-shirt, blue jeans, and cowboy boots that are scuffed and obviously worn a lot.

Tyler, on the other hand, is wearing jeans, a button-down shirt, and cowboy boots that are very clean and look almost new. He can't be much older than me. He is also very good-looking.

"I figured Tyler should be here to help me explain all of this to everyone else," Dean says. "The guys all think I'm nuts to even be talking with you."

"Why's that?" I try *really* hard not to frown.

"Well, it's expensive as hell," he says with a chuckle. "And we've been getting by all this time. The guys think we're getting a little excited about things."

We're standing along the fence line looking out over one of Dean's pastures where I can see several cows off in the distance. It's beautiful here. I can see for miles over the gently waving grasses.

"Things?" I ask. "Like climate change? The fact that your grain prices are going up every single year? The fact that corporate farms are coming in and buying up family farms left and right?"

Dean shrugs. "They think you all are just a bunch of corporate bigwigs trying to scare us into spending our money. You know how it goes."

I definitely know how it goes. I know how big corporate *farms* try to keep small family farms from expanding and thriving. I know how big corporate farms don't worry about things like weather and disease wiping out feed crops because that simply drives up their beef and pork prices, and all they need to do is go to the government for bailouts.

Scare you? I want to ask. *By telling you that extreme temperatures and weather events are going to keep getting worse? Because that's just true. By telling you that the world's population is going to keep growing and will still need to be fed, but the land available for planting is shrinking every year? Because that's also true. Is it scary? Sure. But we're not saying that to make money. We're saying it because we need to find solutions, and the people out here already growing the food should be the ones who care the most.*

I rein in those thoughts and smile at Dean. "Okay, let's back up a little. What our systems do is actually really simple. It's the same crops you grow now. But everything is grown indoors so the plants are protected and the environment is controlled. Your cattle will have fresh feed *all year*. You won't have to worry about the weather. You won't have to worry about having another company supplementing you. You won't have to worry about storage and transportation. It will all be right in your backyard."

He nods. "I get that. But we're doing okay. The guys—"

As Dean goes on about what the other ranchers are telling him, Torin's words from the night on my grandmother's porch play through my mind.

You could build as many farms as you want to. You can see your plans in action. Right now, they're all just on paper. You're not actually doing any of it. Don't you want to see it come to life? There's no red tape. Nothing between your amazing brain and making it all happen for real.

Dean stops talking and I force a smile and go back to attempting to convince him that his rancher friends don't know what the hell they're talking about. Nicely, of course.

Okay, kind of nicely.

I think I need a new job.

I'm back at my hotel an hour later, with a cheese pizza that I am going to eat *alone*. I'm dreading calling my boss and letting her know that I didn't make this sale either.

I stare at my phone, chewing on my bottom lip for nearly five minutes before I finally pick it up and dial.

But it's not Lauren's number I punch in.

"Abigail?"

God, I love his voice. Why have I only been texting this man?

Oh yeah, because I should just be leaving him alone entirely. He needs to find a wife. And I don't want a husband who's a prince.

"Hi," I say softly.

"Are you all right?" Torin's tone is sharp. "Where are you?"

"Yes," I say quickly, even as my stomach flips over how concerned he sounds. "I'm fine. I'm just...bummed. Had a bad day at work."

"Where are you?" he asks again. His tone is gentler but still firm.

"Bayard, Nebraska," I say with a little laugh. "Tiny little town out west. I'm in a Travelodge."

"What can I do?" he asks. Then he swears. "I hate how far away you are."

Okay, now it's not just my stomach flipping. That almost feels like my heart flipped a little.

"Tell me why you think what you read about me and my work is so amazing," I say before I can swallow it. "I guess I need an ego boost after talking to a couple of ranchers today who think that our indoor growing system is too expensive and we're overreacting about climate change and I'm too pretty to know about ranching, anyway."

I hear a little growl on his end of the line. "Did someone tell you you're too pretty to know about ranching?"

"He called me a pretty little thing."

"I'm going to need his name and address," Torin says tightly.

I laugh. His protectiveness feels good. I don't care what

that says about me. "He wasn't hitting on me." I pause. "But his son did ask me to dinner after our meeting."

The next growl is a lot louder. "Bayard, Nebraska, you said?" he asks.

I laugh again, feeling lighter now. "I said no to dinner. And to giving him my number."

"You better have said no."

I lie back on the pillows on my bed. I feel a little...sassy, actually. "Oh? Why's that?"

"Because you had *my* fingers in your sweet pussy nine days ago, and you came all over *my* hand. You're spoken for, Abigail."

My eyes go wide and my breath lodges in my chest. Holy crap. I did *not* expect him to go there. "Oh." That's all I manage to say.

"As to why you're amazing," he says, as if he didn't just say something incredibly filthy to me and practically set my panties on fire. "You want to put an end to childhood hunger by building indoor farms for every school, incorporating the farm into the curriculum from kindergarten through high school, including science classes, cooking classes, business classes, and even history and social science classes. You want the farm to supply fresh food to the school, but also provide a place for families to acquire fresh food for use in their homes. You believe that when people know how to grow their own food, right in their own kitchens or backyards, they feel more secure, and are more empowered. You are looking for people to help you not only build and maintain the farms, but you want to include social scientists, psychologists, physicians, and economists to study the long-term effects because you believe these farms can significantly impact the physical, mental, and social well-being of communities, villages, and neighborhoods."

I'm staring at the ceiling. But I only see Torin's face.

I'm *more* amazed by what he just said than I was by his dirty words about his hand in my... I can't even think the word he so easily said.

I sit up. "You...I..." I take a deep breath. "You really did read all my stuff."

"All of it." He pauses. "I'm fascinated to know where it all comes from though," he says. "Why are you a farmer, Abigail?"

I only hesitate for a moment. I don't remember the last time someone asked me about this.

"When I was ten, I decided I wanted to be a vegetarian. But I was picky about textures and strong flavors. And there were times when I wanted something we didn't have, and I didn't drive or have my own money to go get what I needed. It was frustrating, and I felt...helpless. I never went *hungry*, but I wanted to eat a certain way, a way I felt strongly about for ethical reasons, but I couldn't because of various limitations. So I decided to grow my own food. That way I always had food I liked available."

He's quiet, and I wish I'd thought to video call him so I could see his face.

"So you understand what it's like to have your food options limited," he says.

Yes, he gets it.

"I was *really* privileged. It's not the same as people who have limited access to food because of true financial or mobility or access issues," I say. "They're limited in accessing *all* types of food. I was just picky. But I remember how it felt, and I can easily understand how awful it would feel to be unable to provide good food to your whole family, your *children*, on a consistent basis."

I run a finger over the design on the hotel room duvet, thinking about what all to tell Torin.

"Anyway, I started growing vegetables in a garden, but of course not everything can grow all the time. So I moved a bunch of plants to pots inside. My parents got sick of having pots all over the house, and I wanted things that took up more space. Strawberries, melons, bushes for berries. So...I built a greenhouse."

"You *built* a greenhouse by yourself?" he asks.

I smile. "I designed it and was planning to, but my dad did jump in along with a few of his friends. And I've built two since then."

"And then you grew...everything?"

"I slowly added onto it. As I learned about different plants and what they needed to grow. And as I wanted to try different foods. And the feeling of security that came from being able to provide for myself that way really stuck with me."

I frown. "Then I started my college classes, and learned about food insecurity and was appalled to learn that Louisiana is one of the hungriest states in the US. *My* hometown, where I was growing my own food in my backyard, has so many families who don't always have enough. That shook me. I can't believe that in the *United States*, one of the wealthiest countries on the planet, we have *children* going hungry on a *daily* basis."

I feel the familiar rage and frustration tightening my chest. "I know what it feels like to be empowered by being able to provide for myself in that very basic way, and I decided to help find a way to give that to everyone. Especially kids. They are, obviously, dependent in so many ways.

But if they can access *food*, understand how food grows, and that it can happen anywhere they are if they are just a little creative, that will make them feel secure in a way that can influence so many other things. And doing that through their schools just makes sense. It combines education with simple *access*. Kids have to go to school. So helping provide their most basic needs there seems like a no-brainer."

He's quiet for several seconds, and I worry that I scared him off. Or put him to sleep.

I'm amazed by how many words I actually said. I'm not one to go off on rants or give eloquent monologues. Or any monologues. But with Torin, the words just...come out.

"That's incredible, Abigail," he finally says. His voice sounds gruff.

"It has the *potential* to be incredible," I say. "We're not to the incredible stage yet."

"The passion behind it is incredible," he says, firmly. "All you need to do is convince people who have the resources to give them to you. Like me."

I shake my head even though he can't see me. "It's basic human decency. Things that keep people alive and healthy shouldn't be for profit."

"Agreed," he says.

"I shouldn't have to appeal to corporations or billion-aires or even nonprofit foundations. I believe governments should pay for these farms." I wait to see what he says to that. He *is* the government in Cara, essentially.

"Why?" he asks after a moment.

He knows the answer to this. He's read all my papers. But if he wants to hear me say it, I definitely can. It's not every day I have the chance to personally appeal to someone in a position to actually *do* the things I believe in. I'm not going to pass this chance up.

"That's what government, at its most basic level, is about—gathering the resources and distributing them to the people. It's what taxes do. It's what public education does...and could do better. It's what emergency services are. Food should absolutely be the same."

"You believe a government should feed its people."

I absolutely do. "In the US, the federal government pays out *billions* in farm subsidies every single year," I say, feeling myself about to get on another roll. "A huge portion of that goes to big ag corporations rather than to small family farms. And nearly two-thirds of it goes toward meat production with less than two percent going to fruits and vegetables despite everything we know about healthy diets. Because of big lobbies. We need to divert the money in politics out of influencing votes to make people bigger profits and into making sure people are taken care of. If even a *portion* of the farm subsidies was invested into indoor farming, threats to crops like weather, climate, and disease would be a moot point. Food would actually be produced, and people would actually be fed."

I take a breath and then say, "Being in a position to *truly* do something about that...to make decisions that impact people's lives every day...*that* is incredible, Torin. *You* can make people's lives better and easier and happier and healthier with the swipe of your pen." I pause. "Right? I mean, Cara doesn't have a congress or parliament. It's just you."

"My grandfather," he corrects. His voice sounds gruff.

"For now. Someday it will be you. And that's amazing."

He clears his throat. "You've studied Cara's government?"

I feel my cheeks heat. I'd started out wanting to know more about agriculture in the country, but I'd kept going. "I was…curious." I'd read everything I could find. Which wasn't enough. I want to know more.

"I'm glad," he says. "Makes me feel a little less like a stalker with everything I've looked up about you."

I feel myself smile. "Maybe we're both stalkers."

"Just one more thing we have in common," he says. "A passion for making people's lives better, hot as fuck chemistry, and stalker tendencies."

This man, no doubt, has women throwing themselves at him all the time. To hear him say our chemistry is hot is… amazing. I mean, *I* think it's great, but I have very little to compare it to.

"If you tell me you believe peanut butter Oreos are far superior to regular Oreos, we're practically the same person," I tease.

"Alas, I prefer the mint Oreos to all others."

I giggle. And I honestly don't remember the last time that happened. "Well, I still like you anyway."

"I like you too, Abigail." His voice is husky again.

That is *so* not dirty, especially compared to what he said just a little bit ago, but a swirl of heat twirls through my belly and between my thighs.

"You don't think a monarchy is an outdated model of government that should be abolished and replaced by a representative government of some kind?" he asks, a moment later.

I think about his question. "Not necessarily."

"No? Nineteen-year-old Torin is on the verge of launching into his lecture," he says with a soft laugh. "But I'd love to hear your thoughts on why not."

"I'd like to hear nineteen-year-old Torin's lecture," I say, meaning it.

He clears his throat, then says, "In a nut shell, I think

people should have a say in the policies and programs that govern their lives. One person shouldn't decide that for everyone. Especially someone who sits on money and power and has no idea what the average, and below average, citizens' lives are like."

I'm sure his 'lecture' is more in depth than that, but I like his summary. I agree with it. But... "Okay," I say. "I was more of a science geek than a history or poli-sci girl, but..." I decide to say the first thing that occurred to me when he asked the question. "I think it depends entirely upon the monarch. A benevolent one, who truly cares about his or her people, and listens to them, can be even more effective in a lot of ways. If he or she takes the time to understand what needs to be done and then takes action, it saves a lot of time and red tape and *time* in making things happen."

He chuckles, and the sound rolls through me like a swallow of cocoa...sweet, and warm, and very satisfying.

"I'm going to assume you've run into a lot of red tape and people who have policies about the policies applying policies to things?" he asks.

"Oh my God," I groan. "You have no idea. In the US, getting things changed and moving forward in agriculture and food production is a nightmare. Throw the public school system in, and there are even more hoops to jump through and people who think they need to be involved. There is *so* much time wasted. And money. And there are all these people involved in decisions who don't really know what they're talking about." I slump back against the pillows again. "Why can't they just trust the experts to know that what we're saying is the right thing?"

He's quiet for a long moment.

"You still there?" I ask.

Damn, maybe I finally scared him off.

I've never been able to talk to a guy I also wanted to kiss about all of this. I probably went overboard. That's what happens when you bottle everything up and don't really talk to anyone about anything you really care about for, oh about a decade.

He clears his throat. "I am. I just...I think you're one of the most amazing people I've ever met. You're definitely the most amazing person I've ever kissed."

I don't know what to say to that.

"I can't stop thinking about you," he says, his voice gentler.

I know it's dangerous to admit I can't stop thinking about him either.

He's the epitome of 'give him an inch and he'll take a mile'.

But I don't think there's a single other person on the planet who could have said all of those things about my work without prompting. Not my family, not my peers in school, not my professors, not even my bosses.

My professors and bosses, even some of my peers, would certainly understand all of it if they read it.

But no one has ever delved into my work like Torin has. Not on their own, without *having* to read it for grading purposes, or to offer me a job. And even then they only read pieces and parts.

Torin read it because...he's interested. In me.

And because he's the leader of a small country that he said could use my ideas to revolutionize agriculture, give them food security and independence, and completely overhaul their economy. Yes, I remember all of those words from the steps of my grandmother's house a few days ago.

"Me too," I finally admit out loud. "But...I can't date a prince, Torin."

"Why not? You and I could do amazing things, Abigail."

My heart flips. He's right. With his influence and resources and the way he seems to understand what I do, I could actually make my dream farms a reality.

"Maybe I should explain why your prince thing is a problem for me."

There's a beat of silence. Then he says, "Okay, I'm listening."

"When I was growing up, I was three years behind everyone in school."

"I know you skipped grades." His tone of voice sounds almost affectionate.

I swallow. I don't know how he knows that, but it wouldn't be hard to find out. "At first it was just one grade, but then they realized that wasn't enough and they bumped me up two more grades the next year. That put me in class with kids who were twelve when I was only nine." I take a breath. "You can imagine that I was...behind, socially. We didn't have the same interests. I was behind them developmentally even though, academically, I could keep up."

"That's a big difference at that age," he says.

"It was. So the kids in my classes had one of two reactions to me. They thought I was weird and immature and wanted nothing to do with me. Or they were intimidated. I was competition to some of them. The ones that were the best students, who liked being at the top of the class, the straight A students. So, I ended up either ignored and left out or..." I pause, then shrug. "Made fun of. Bullied."

"Bullied?" His tone is sharp now.

It reminds me of how he reacted at the wedding when he found out that my cousins sometimes left me out of games. It feels protective and possessive. I like it, I have to admit.

"I was a threat to a few of them. So they took every opportunity to make sure I didn't get too full of myself or ever forget that they were older and more important than I was. They couldn't do much to me when I just stayed to myself, but if I ever tried to talk to them, or God forbid we had group projects—" I shudder thinking about those even now. "—or, worst of all, presenting up in front of the class, they made fun of me and made sure I knew they were judging every single thing from what I was wearing, to each word I chose, to my actual conclusions and results."

Torin sounds angry when he asks, "How could they dare? You're brilliant."

I shake my head. "Academically, book-wise, sure. But I was a *kid* in a high school environment. I was socially awkward and naïve and immature."

"That wasn't your fault."

"No. But most people who get bullied aren't at fault."

He takes a long, deep breath in. "Would you give me their names if I asked?"

I actually smile at that. "Would you track them down? Now? This many years later?"

"I would."

"And do what?"

"Show them how fucking amazing, and accomplished, and generous, and gorgeous you are," he says without even thinking. He pauses. "And then punch them in their arrogant, smug faces."

My heart squeezes. "You think I'm *generous*?" I ask softly.

"Abigail," he says, his voice scratchy. "With your brain you could have done *anything*. You could be a multimillionaire by now. But you've used your brilliance and spent your time and energy on agriculture and conservation. Your passion is finding ways to feed more people." He pauses, then says his voice gentler, "Yes, I think you're generous. Among many other things."

My throat feels tight. I've learned over the years that I don't need to be admired by everyone. Just certain people. People who are working to make things better for others, like Mason and Lauren. And now Torin. He understands what I do and his admiration matters. "You don't need to track them down for me."

"I still want to."

"I appreciate that. But they don't matter."

"Don't they?" he asks. "What they did to you has made it so that you won't get up in front of groups and talk about the amazing things you want to do, the amazing things you *are* doing."

He's right.

The trauma from those years, the desire to shrink into myself and not call attention to my words, my work, *myself*, has made it hard to talk about my work. "But I'm still *doing* the work," I say. "What I learned from all of that is that the best way to shut up those judging me is to *show* them what I can do. They can't argue with results."

"You never held back." It's a statement, not a question.

"Never. I avoided presentations and group work when I could. My teachers understood my anxiety, and my being so much younger did make them pay a little more attention to that. They'd sometimes let me test out or do projects alone instead of in a group. But if I *had to* present, I'd go throw up and then I'd do the presentation. It didn't matter if the other kids thought I dressed like a little kid or didn't understand their jokes and innuendos and references. At the end of the day, I *was* their competition. And I won. Every time. My projects, my papers, my experiments, my essays, my tests were always the best."

"You always gave it your best, even knowing they'd make fun of you?"

"They were going to make fun of me anyway. I started going for *really* pissing them off. The meaner they got, the more confident I got."

"Why?"

"Because it meant I was doing something right. They wouldn't have cared otherwise. It meant I really was a threat." I still feel the weird mix of thrill and terror thinking about it now. Every time I turned in a project or took a test, I felt that nauseating mix of adrenaline. Even in college. I knew I was going to poke the bears who wanted to tear me down, but I did it anyway. "They used words to try to hurt me, to *say* I was a wannabe, to say I cheated, to say I was a loser, and that no one liked me and that everyone thought I was weird. But I used actual *actions*, and produced actual results that *proved* I was no wannabe, I didn't cheat, and *I* was the winner. Over and over and over."

I realize I'm clenching my fists and I'm scowling.

"Were you valedictorian of your class?" he asks. His voice is a little gruffer now.

"Of course."

"Even being three years younger than everyone else."

I nod. "Yes. And the salutatorian from my class doesn't have even one master's degree." I can't help but frown when I add, "He's on the city council in Shreveport and is in engineering, though."

"Why does that matter?" Torin asks.

"Because I want to build indoor farms in Shreveport and I'll probably have to talk to him to get that done," I say.

Then I shake my head. "But that's not important right now."

He clears his throat again. "Everything about you is important, Abigail."

God, how am I supposed to resist him when he says things like that?

I *really* need to resist him. I can't be in the public eye. I would be a terrible princess.

But still, stupidly, I say, "I still owe you two dances."

"You do," he says, something in his voice making goose-bumps break out over my arms.

"Does this mean I'm going to see you again?" I ask. "So we can...dance."

I shouldn't. It's not like I can *keep* seeing him. But when he was in Autre, it didn't feel like he was famous or anything. There was no one around taking his picture or making a big deal about him. It felt normal. Safe. I could probably do that again for a weekend.

"Yes, Abigail." His voice gruff, but firm. "You are going to see me again."

I shiver. And take a deep breath. And let the meaning of that sink in. He knows why him being a prince is a problem for me, but he wants to see me again anyway.

Okay, we could have a weekend together.

Before he finds a wife.

My stomach tries to drop at that, but I ignore it.

I smile. "Good."

"It will be very good," he promises.

I mean, I have no idea what exactly I'll do with him once we're together again...

But I have a feeling that the leader of a country, even a small one, will be happy to take charge and I think I'm okay with that. For one weekend.

CHAPTER 12
TORIN

I do not have a foot fetish.

I have an Abigail Landry fetish.

But I can understand how someone picking up either of our phones might think we are both a little too into feet. Most of my texts to and from Abigail have consisted of a lot of photos of our shoes. And feet.

And hell, I won't deny that I can't wait to prop her pretty heels up on my shoulders.

I drag in a deep breath and study the photo she just sent.

Her feet are bare, resting on the edge of a bathtub. Her ankles are crossed and bubbles cling to her feet and calves.

And I swear I can smell the lavender. That has to be what her bathwater is scented with, right?

Fuck that's hot. The photo, and the fact that she sent it. The photo is hardly dirty. Certainly not as dirty as I would like. But damn, this subtly flirtatious, sweet-but-tempting photo will haunt me.

Honestly, though, I love the one of her toes in the dirt just as much.

I've sent my own feet and shoe photos. And none of the captions have read, *I want you. Marry me. I'll do anything.*

So far.

This is actually my second photo from her today. And that makes my heart beat a little harder.

The photo from this morning was her in work boots again, her foot on the pedal of a four-wheeler, a sprawling cornfield all around her.

I'd teased her with my photo today without her even realizing it. It's been two weeks since the wedding and Monday through Friday both weeks I've been in meetings. I needed to get outside. I found a horse ranch an hour outside of Shreveport and gave them a sizeable donation to go riding. The photo I sent Abigail was of my foot in the stirrup.

No!! You're a cowboy?!

I have cowboy boots. And horses. And a ranch.

I'd waited for a moment and then added,

Are these bad things?

She'd responded after a couple of minutes.

I'm just so not into cowboys.

I chuckled. I wasn't worried.

> You'll feel differently when the right cowboy is into you.

Was that on the nose? Yep.

Did it make her blush? I hope so.

But did it remind her of the minutes against the wall in her grandmother's foyer and make her want more? I'm betting on it.

I got that cute blushing, sweating emoji in return and felt stupidly triumphant about it.

And then I promptly got online and placed an order for a special gift to be delivered to her in Sapphire Falls. Well, after I'd texted Jonah to get her mailing address in Sapphire Falls.

She's staying in touch.

She likes me.

This texting is strangely fun. We're giving each other peeks at our days, letting the other know we've been thinking of them. I can't explain why it feels intimate in a way, but I'm enjoying the hell out of it.

And being stuck in Shreveport putting together the perfect proposal for a genius scientist I want to marry so she can help me with...so many fucking things—take care of my people, and make my country stable and independent, and enable my best friend to be publicly, obviously in love, and get my grandfather to happily take off his crown and rest his heart—isn't so bad when she's flirting with me.

But I *really* want to be with her. I need to get this project in Shreveport to the point where I can present it to Abigail. Along with a crown of her own.

Does this mean I'm going to see you again? So we can...dance.

I cannot stop thinking about her asking me that.

Fuck yes, she's going to see me again. And we are most definitely going to 'dance' again.

That night when I went to bed, I sent her another photo of my feet in bed, the sheet draped over my lap.

Her return text woke me right up.

> You're such a tease sending bed photos only knees down.

Oh, really?

> If I show you mine, you have to show me yours.

I would pay this woman a million dollars cash for a nude photo.

My phone lit up with a text two minutes later.

> I've never done this before. Like this?

It was her in bed, hips down, no sheet covering her. But she wasn't naked. She was wearing those shorts from the night at her grandmother's. And pink, yellow, and green striped socks that started at mid-thigh and covered her legs and feet completely.

Those fucking socks still made me hard.

So, I'd responded with a sweating, hot-faced emoji of my own.

She'd sent back a laughing face emoji.

This is the silliest thing I'd ever done with a woman. And I haven't had this much fun in a very, very long time.

But now I'm firmly, fully obsessed with Abigail Landry.

I text her a photo of my bare feet propped on the railing of my hotel balcony. It's risky, actually. She could recognize the section of Shreveport in the background. I want to surprise her with the project in her hometown.

Did I know that she wanted to build indoor farms in Shreveport? Yes. I'd read it in one of her essays. Shreveport is a classic example of food deserts inside a metropolis. It's the type of place that surprises people by having a lack of accessibility to fresh food in sections of the city.

But after hearing her talk about her school experience here in this city, in the school where I'm building this farm, has me all the more certain that Abigail and I are destined to be in one another's lives. I'd started the project before I knew just how meaningful it would be to her. Now I'm even more eager for her to see it.

I hit send on the photo from my balcony despite the risk. Then I follow it with another text.

> Wish I was there with you instead.

It's less than a minute before I get her answer back.

> My bathtub isn't big enough for both of us.

My cock is immediately hard.

> Don't worry, Abigail, we'll fit.

I get the impression that she isn't as experienced as most of the women I've been with. I know she's not as experienced as I am. But I hope she understands *all* of that innuendo.

> You wouldn't mind smelling like lavender?

I smile even as heat slides through me. Running my hands through her hair at Ami's wedding made my palms smell like lavender. Our bodies rubbing against one another all night long will ensure that I smell lavender on my own skin.

Oh, I'm quite looking forward to it.

She doesn't respond to that, but I still grin down at the text conversation on my phone.

Abigail Landry *is* into me.

I'm ninety percent sure.

Okay, maybe seventy percent.

And yes, going from text-flirting to *I do* is a pretty big leap, but I'm more optimistic by the message.

And I *am a* prince.

Getting my way comes with the territory.

CHAPTER 13

WAIT 'TIL I TELL YE

EPISODE 757 TRANSCRIPT

Lindsey: Okay, you all had *a lot* of opinions about Prince Torin proposing to Linnea in the US rather than here. I'm not surprised. I feel the same way as eighty-two percent of our listeners. That would be crappy.

Jen: I get it. I do. They're from here. They're two of Cara's most beloved public figures. But what if there's some special spot in Louisiana that's really meaningful to him? That could be really romantic. The US was part of his life for ten years!

Lindsey: He did not live in Louisiana the whole time. And *Cara* is his country. And he's not just some guy. He's our prince! No. The engagement needs to happen *here*.

Jen: I guess we'll see. They've been over there for a long time. You don't think...never mind. I don't even want to put that out there.

Lindsey: Well, now you have to. What are you thinking?

Jen: You don't think they're considering *staying* there, right? Or buying a house or land there?

Lindsey: Why would you say that? He's our *prince*. How could he stay there?

Jen: I don't know. I just saw a report that he was on a ranch outside of Shreveport two days ago. Maybe that was just...for fun? But he has a ranch here that he loves and I was just wondering if he's staying there this long to look for property? Maybe just someplace to stay when he's there?

Lindsey: I don't even know what to say. Why would he need a place to stay? Especially in Shreveport rather than near New Orleans where his family and friends are? And he needs to be *here!* Oh my God, Torin, Linnea, one of you has to be listening to us! You need to come home! Tell us what is going on!

Jen: This is why I didn't want to bring it up. But on the bright side...at least we'll have a royal wedding to look forward to, right?

Lindsey: Well, we'd better!

Jen: The palace has released another statement! Quote, "the royal family already considers Her Grace a part of the family and are enjoying seeing the reports and photos of the prince and duchess together as much as everyone else is."

Lindsey: I swear to God, I'm more invested in this than I am my own dating life.

Jen: Oh, hold on, *you* have a dating life? Now you need to start talking!

Lindsey: And that's a wrap for us today! Tune in tomorrow! Just wait 'til we tell ye!

CHAPTER 14

ABIGAIL

"Abigail! You in here?"

I'm crouched in front of the lower-level shelves, checking on the new seedlings we started last week in the smallest of our greenhouses.

It's small enough that it really only takes one of us to keep up on the plants inside and since I'm the one who loves and knows the most about tropical plants—this is where my beloved cacao and coffee trees are—I've kind of adopted this greenhouse as mine.

I stand and wipe my hair away from my cheek with my forearm, trying to keep my dirty gloves off my face.

"Yeah!" I call back to Austin, one of my fellow ag engineers.

"Delivery for you." He comes around the end of the aisle with a huge box.

My mouth falls open. He's not carrying a brown cardboard delivery box. It's a box wrapped in cream paper with gold swirls and a gold ribbon crisscrossed over it with a huge gold bow on top.

"What is this?" I ask. "I didn't order anything."

Austin has a very serious girlfriend named Veronica. This is not a gift from him.

I hope.

"Someone sent it to you," he says with a grin. He props the box on one hip as he swipes a gloved hand over the wooden table next to us, dusting potting soil to the floor. The space on the table is hardly *clean* when he sets the box down, but at least there's not a quarter inch of dirt underneath the box.

"Apparently, there were very explicit instructions about how to deliver this," he tells me. "It had to arrive today. Had to be unwrapped in the office so that *this* is all that showed up for you. And then it had to be brought directly to you no matter where you were."

I stare at him. "Really?"

"Yep. And I won the contest to get to be the one who brought it down here."

"There was a contest?" I ask, now staring at the box. My heart is racing. I never get surprise gifts.

"Well, it was rock-paper-scissors." He grins. "But there were several rounds, and I was the champ."

I laugh. "Thanks. I had no idea you were all so bored that me getting a package would be so exciting."

"But it's a really fancy package with super specific instructions," he says. "And it's *you.*"

"What's that supposed to mean?"

He leans a hip against the tall table. "You're not really the secret admirer type," he says. But then he narrows his eyes. "Or maybe you're *really* the secret admirer type."

I frown. "And what does *that* mean?"

"You're a little mysterious."

"I am not." I roll my eyes.

"You are. You're quiet. Super smart. You don't really socialize. But you're gorgeous and brilliant. It's like you're secretly a super hero or something."

I laugh out loud at that. "No. I'm not a super hero. I'm a nerdy farmer. Just like I appear."

"Hmmm…" He doesn't seem convinced. "Well, open the damned box. You know I've been ordered to report back."

I study the box, then look at him. Opening a surprise package in front of someone I don't know all that well seems a little vulnerable. But that's ridiculous. Someone is sending me a *gift*. That's a nice thing. And it's something that someone put a lot of thought into. From the wrapping to the method of delivery…

And it hits me.

I know exactly who this is from.

It's no one in my family. They send me stuff sometimes, of course. My grandmother will send me treats, but those come in cardboard boxes delivered to my house by the post office. My sisters send me gifts sometimes—little things they see when they're out together like notebooks or socks, like the ones I wore in the photo I sent to Torin, or pajamas like the ones I wore the night Torin came over to my grandmother's house. Those also come to the house in boxes addressed by one of them. There's no fancy paper or bows.

This is from Torin.

Butterflies kick up in my stomach.

This is exactly something he would do. From the elaborate bow to the special delivery instructions, he would go above and beyond to send me a gift.

I press a hand against my stomach and look up at Austin.

I want to open it in front of him. And I want him to go back and tell everyone that Torin O'Grady went out of his way to send me something.

Okay, I probably won't tell them his name. They *might* know who he is and I'm not ready to tell people I'm getting gifts from a *prince*.

But I'm also not feeling shy or weird about this attention suddenly.

I usually would. Definitely. I hate being the center of attention. But because this is from Torin…I don't.

I just feel special.

I give Austin a smile and then reach for the bow. I pull it loose and tear back the paper. Inside is a beautifully decorated cardboard box. It's immediately obvious what's inside the box.

Austin chuckles. "Cowboy boots?"

I'm grinning. I realize I should have been expecting this.

I lift the lid and then laugh out loud. These are not just cowboy boots. These are so unlike anything I would ever buy for myself that I stare at them in wonder.

You'll feel differently when the right cowboy is into you.

His message comes back to me immediately. As does the heat and dampness in my panties.

Would I wear these cowboy boots for Torin O'Grady?

Yee fucking haw.

"Who sent *you* cowboy boots?" Austin lifts one of the boots out of the box and holds it up. "*Pink* cowboy boots?"

I laugh, and I can feel I'm blushing. The boots aren't just pink. They are *hot* pink. With white trim.

"A guy I'm…talking to."

"A cowboy I'm guessing?" Austin asks. "He knows

you're more in farm country here than rodeo country, right?"

I laugh. "I'm not sure he cares. He kind of does what he wants."

I'm actually delighted by this gift. I'm shocked by that, but definitely delighted. I'm sure Torin doesn't care if Sapphire Falls is farmer or cowboy country. *He* has a ranch. *He* likes cowboy boots.

"Wow," Austin says, leaning in, watching my face. "You really like this guy."

I do. He's charming, and sexy, and funny.

And he makes *me* feel charming and sexy and funny.

That's huge.

"Yeah. I do."

"Well, you might have to wear those out later," Austin says, putting the boot down. "Not sure anyone will believe me that you have pink cowboy boots."

I laugh. "We'll see. Right now, *these* are more practical for what I have planned today." I tap the heels of my green rubber boots together.

Austin nods and pushes off the table. "Same. I'll see you later."

He leaves and I tell myself to get back to work. But I can't stop looking at the boots.

It only takes me one minute to decide to call my sisters.

"Good morning," Charlie greets.

I hear goats bleating in the background. "Are you at the animal park?"

She laughs. "Yep. The petting zoo, actually. We have a kids' event coming up this weekend." Charlie is in charge of all the marketing and PR for the animal park where Griffin is one of the veterinarians.

"I don't supposed Ami is around too?" I ask, running my finger over the white trim on the boots.

"Uh, I haven't seen her yet this morning," Charlie says. "Why?"

"I…"

Charlie and Ami are both madly in love, but we've never really talked about guys before. Mostly because I wasn't interested. In high school, the boys were way too immature for me. In college, the guys I was in class with, who I could talk to about interesting topics, were older and a lot of them saw me as a kid. And even if they didn't, I wanted to *talk* to them. Not kiss them.

The one guy I slept with was my attempt to do something normal. To do what the girls around me were doing. I was hoping I'd understand the hype once I'd done it.

I didn't really.

Now I do have a guy I want to talk about, though, and these are the only two women I can be that open with. I have some female cousins and *lots* of female cousins-in-law, and I like them all. But I can't talk to them about this.

However, I have two sisters. Two nosy, outgoing, in-love sisters who would not only be ecstatic that I have a crush, but thrilled they can actually give me advice.

"I met someone," I say. "A guy." I don't know why I feel the need to clarify that, but I want her to understand that I'm calling for boy talk.

Charlie is quiet for a second. Then she yells, "I'll be back later!"

I wince. She's clearly yelling to someone there with her in Autre, but she didn't cover the phone.

Then she's in my ear babbling. "Oh, my God, Abi! That's amazing! Someone there in Sapphire Falls? Who is he? Are you dating or do you just like him? Have you gone out? Do you work with him? What's he like? What's his name?"

When she pauses for a breath, I say, "You know Ami will kill you if you get info before she does. Where is she?"

"I'm on my way to her right now," Charlie says. "She might still be in bed. Do you realize it's only eight a.m.?"

"She's up before now usually, isn't she?" I'm a morning person. For sure. Eight seems late to me.

"Yes, when school's in, but Andre's off for the summer so they sleep in," Charlie says of Ami's twelve-year-old stepson. "Of course, Rosie might have them up."

Rosie is my baby niece. Rosie is only a little over a month old. Ami and Michael had gotten married at the courthouse in New Orleans shortly after Ami found out she was pregnant. Then Rosie had been born in March and they'd had their big wedding ceremony and reception this past weekend. The order of things didn't really matter. No one who had ever seen Ami and Michael together doubted that they were going to be together forever.

"Well, call me back after you're with Ami and you guys are able to talk." I pause and give my sister something that will make her entire day...maybe her whole week. "I need some advice about this guy."

Charlie squeals. Actually *squeals* in my ear. I hang up laughing.

Then try to get some work done.

But I'm so distracted.

I want to text Torin.

But I want to talk to my sisters first. This is all happening really fast with him. We *just* met.

Sure, we met two years ago at Charlie's wedding technically, but I didn't really know him then. I'd totally written him off, in fact.

You should still be writing him off, the voice in my head tells me. *He's still a prince.*

Yeah. He is. All of the reasons I can't be involved with him are still there.

But it doesn't *feel* the same now. Now that I know him better. Now that he knows me better.

Charlie and Ami call me back only ten minutes later. And it's a video call.

I take my gloves off to answer and prop the phone against the boot box. "Hey," I answer.

"You met someone?" Ami squeals. "Oh my God, Abi! That's amazing!"

I laugh and shake my head. "Why do you both act like I just won a Pulitzer? He's a guy. There are literally hundreds walking around here. Meeting them isn't hard at all."

Charlie laughs. She's got a cup of coffee in both hands, and I can tell she's sitting on the floor in front of Ami's couch. Ami is on the cushion behind her so they both fit in the frame. There's a baby blanket draped over the back of the couch, and a swing in the background. Ami clearly just woke up, and she looks a little sleepy, but happy.

"You winning a Pulitzer is way more believable than you meeting a guy you want to call and talk to us about," Charlie says.

I shake my head again. They say stuff like this a lot. And it's supportive and really nice in many ways. But my family actually has no idea what I do.

Abi's just always in her own world.

Oh, Abi is just so smart, we can't even keep up with her.

She's going to do amazing things, and we just need to stay out of her way.

I have no doubt they're proud. But they figure that whatever I'm doing must be so advanced and amazing that they'll never be able to understand it anyway, so they don't really ask much about it.

"Well, surprise," I say. "He's real. And I need advice."

"Oh my God, I'm so excited," Ami says. Then she yawns.

I laugh. "I can call later."

"She'll be yawning later too," Charlie says, patting Ami's knee. "Talk. Now."

I reach for one of the boots and hold it up. "He sent me these. Today. Special delivery."

Charlie's eyes go wide. "Um..."

I take a breath. "He doesn't live here. We've been texting a lot. And he sent me a photo of him wearing cowboy boots, and I admitted that I'm not crazy about cowboys."

"Which is ridiculous," Charlie says. "Cowboys are hot. Everyone knows that."

She hasn't met the cowboys I've met.

Ami leans in. "Looks like he's trying to change your mind."

"And I think maybe he could," I say softly.

Charlie squeals again. "Oh my gosh, tell us everything. How did you meet him?"

"We met at your wedding, actually, Charlie."

Both of my sisters stare at me. "Oh, really?" Charlie asks.

I nod. "And then we met again at *your* wedding," I tell Ami.

They exchange a look. Then Charlie asks, "It's Torin, right?"

Hearing his name makes my stomach flip. I nod. "How did you guess that?"

"There were definite sparks between you," Charlie says.

"And I caught you on the back step with him." She looks at Ami. "That's why we..."

Ami's nodding. "Yeah."

I frown. "Why you what?"

"We thought maybe you were interested, which is super weird because of the whole..." Ami trails off.

"Prince thing?" I ask.

They both nod. "Yeah, that," Charlie says. "We figured no way would you be interested. But we saw how he was looking at you."

My stomach flips again. "How was he looking at me?"

"The way Michael looks at Ami," Charlie says with a grin.

Ami laughs. "And the way Griffin looks at Charlie."

I feel my cheeks heat. Even *I've* noticed the way my brothers-in-law look at my sisters. And yes, it's hot and possessive, but it's also full of love and affection and an emotion I can't name. It's just...I-can't-believe-you're-mine. That's the best way to describe it.

"He did not look at me like that," I say softly.

"Kind of," Ami says nodding. "He seemed *very* into you. So..." She sighs. "We checked on him. Kind of for fun at first. Like what the palace looks like and what the interior of the private plane looks like and if we could find any photos of him in his crown."

I can't help myself. "Did you?"

She nods. "And he looks *very* good in it."

Well, now I'm going to have to see that.

"But..." Charlie says. She doesn't look happy.

"What?" I ask suspiciously.

"We found out some other stuff. Well, one other important thing."

Obviously, it's not something good. And I don't think

it's about his crown. "I thought you knew him," I say. Torin had lived in Autre for a few months. And my sisters know his sister really well.

"Sure. Kind of," Charlie says. "I mean, I know he's a great guy. Funny. Intelligent. There for his family. Cocky, but in a charming way."

"That seems like how he is to me too," I say. Not to mention sexy as hell and a dirty talker and very good with his hands, but I don't need to tell them those details. At least, not yet. They're really making me hesitate to go into this any further. "What did you find out?" I ask, feeling my stomach twisting.

"Well..." Ami starts. Then she says, "Fuck," softly. "I'm sorry, honey."

"Sorry about what?" I lean forward. "What did you find out?"

What could it possibly be? He's not a criminal or a... well, dammit...maybe he is a criminal. Maybe he's embezzled money from his country. But can a prince do that? Do the people of Cara pay taxes? And how do monarchies really work? I'm not sure. I need to read more about that. Presumably, the royal family can spend the money how they want. So it wouldn't *technically* be embezzlement. But it would be a pretty shitty thing to do. Which would definitely make me not like him. Or...maybe he's passed some law I'd hate. Something like allowing some rich chemical company to poison the water. Or making people pay exorbitant amounts for prescription drugs. Or...

"Did he put someone to death?" I ask.

Charlie and Ami both swing around to face the camera. "*What?*" Charlie demands.

"You're acting like you found out something terrible about him," I say, my heart pounding. "Do they execute people in Cara? Did he sentence someone to death? Or did he take away women's rights? They don't vote for leaders there, but do they vote for other things?" I'd briefly looked up the hierarchy of government but hadn't dived into voting procedures or their constitution. "Do they only allow men to vote? Or did he burn down a rainforest or something? Tell me!"

"Holy crap," Ami says, her hand on her chest. "No. It's nothing like that." She frowns. "It's..." She looks at Charlie. "Better than that?"

"I'd think it's better than killing people, yes," Charlie says dryly.

"What about the voting thing? Will she think it's better than taking women's rights away?" Ami asks.

Charlie has to think about that. "Yes," she decides after a second. "I think she would think rescinding voting rights would be worse. But what *do* they vote for in Cara?"

I pick up my phone and bang it on the table. "*Hello*! Sister having a meltdown here!" I hold the phone up in front of my face. "What. Is. It?"

"He's not killing anyone or burning anything down," Ami says quickly. "He's just...engaged."

I let out a breath. "Oh." Then her words sink in. *Really* actually sink in. I stare into the phone. "He's *what*?"

Ami winces and Charlie shakes her head. "He's *not* engaged." Now she grimaces too. "Yet."

"What is going on?" My voice is shaky and my heart is pounding so hard I can hear my blood rushing in my head.

I know he's supposed to get married. Before his grandfather has another heart attack. He's very serious about that.

But he just proposed to *me*.

And he's been flirt-texting with me ever since.

He can't be engaged to someone else already.

Can he?

He proposed to you the second time you ever saw him. He could totally be engaged to someone else by now.

"He's apparently involved with a woman named Linnea Olsen," Charlie says. "She's kind of famous in Cara. Her brother is Alex Olsen, a hockey player here in the US. And her sister is Astrid Olsen."

I frown. "Astrid Olsen, the gymnast?"

"Yes. Do you know who she is?"

"Everyone knows who Astrid is," I say. "She's like Tom Brady or Michael Phelps or Simone Biles. She's so big and popular that everyone knows who she is, even if they're not a fan of the sport."

I don't follow sports. I'm vaguely aware of team names simply because my family is full of football, hockey, baseball, and basketball fans. But Astrid Olsen really is that big. She was a favorite for the Olympic Gold, but she fell during the qualifying round and was badly injured. The fall happened on live television and was replayed over and over and over. Everyone in the US has seen that clip. Her rehabilitation was covered extensively, and she is now an advocate for athletes with disabilities and is a national speaker and book author.

"So that's Linnea's sister. Linnea is Alex and Astrid's agent," Charlie says.

"Oh."

"Torin and Linnea's families are really close," Ami says. "Their grandfathers were best friends. She and Torin are..." She swallows. "...together right now. Here in the States. On some little vacation."

I reach behind me, finding the shelves of seedlings, and slowly sink to the ground, my phone still in front of me. My stomach feels like I swallowed a rock. My heart actually hurts. Because…I believe this.

He needs to get married.

He and Linnea have been friends for a long time.

He asked me and I said no.

Clearly, he asked a woman he knows well and likes. And she said yes. Because she's obviously a very smart woman. Who wouldn't want to marry Torin?

You. You said no. Remember?

"How do you know about this?" I ask.

"There's this podcast out of Cara called *Wait 'Til I Tell Ye*. They talk about all kinds of things, but they cover politics and celebrity gossip and that includes Linnea's brother and sister and…the royal family. According to them, everyone always hoped Torin and Linnea would get together, and they're thrilled. The palace has made two official statements. The first one just said that they've been friends since they were kids, and the palace is happy they're spending time together. But there was another one yesterday. It basically said that the royal family already considers Linnea a part of the family."

My whole body suddenly hurts.

What the *hell*? He's been texting with *me*. He's been on the phone with me. He told me *I* was 'spoken for'. And all this time he's been *here*, in the U.S. with another woman? A woman he's going to marry? That feels really icky.

"Then I was concerned because I knew he'd flirted with you," Charlie goes on. "And Leo said Torin had been looking for you the morning after the wedding."

My heart beat stutters. Torin had told our grandfather he'd been looking for me? My face gets hot thinking *again* about what happened in the foyer of Leo and Ellie's house.

"What did you do?" I ask Charlie, knowing my big sister's concern would lead to some kind of action.

"I asked Fiona what the deal was."

I take a deep breath. Torin's sister would know. "And?"

"Torin doesn't want to marry Linnea. But the king expects it to happen and he's not turning over the crown until it does."

"Torin would be a really good king I think," I say quietly. I do think that. He wants programs like my farms. That shows very good judgment in my opinion.

Charlie frowns. "So what the hell is Torin doing sending *you* boots?"

I take a deep breath. "That is a really good fucking question."

"Oh, Abi," Ami says, her voice gentle. "You look really sad."

"I *feel* really sad," I admit. Which is stupid. I knew we couldn't flirt, or even have a fling, forever.

"You really like him?"

I nod. "But I'm also...really..." I frown. "What is he doing? He's cheating on his fiancée with me? Even if he doesn't want to get married to her, *that* is not okay."

"Well, the engagement isn't official," Charlie offers. "It's an arranged marriage between their grandfathers."

This is what annoys me about words and talking and debates and explanations. What's the difference between an arranged marriage and an engagement, really? They're both going to end up with Torin and Linnea married. She'll be his princess, then queen. So who cares what it's called? The *action*, the outcome, is the same no matter what words surround it.

"It doesn't matter," I say, suddenly shoving to my feet.

"Wait a second, *cheating* with you?" Ami asks. "Did

something happen between you? Something more than dancing?"

"Yes," I say, adrenaline pumping hard now. "Kissing and an orgasm! And a bunch of texts. And a really great phone call. And now... cowboy boots!" I pick up one of the boots and throw it. It thunks against the trunk of a cacao tree.

"An *orgasm*? I want to know more about—"

I cut Charlie off. "No. It doesn't matter."

Ami just grins at me. "You aren't going to start an international incident, are you?"

I sigh. "I'm not *at all* the international incident type." Not even a little. "This is actually great," I tell my sisters.

"It is?" Charlie asks.

I take a deep breath and even manage a small smile. "Yes. Before this goes any further, I already know the most important thing I need to know."

Charlie winces. "What's that?"

"That nothing romantic can ever happen between me and Torin O'Grady."

CHAPTER 15

TORIN

I'm not into cowboys.

I've thought about that text from her too fucking much.

Wrong. She's wrong. And I want to prove how wrong she is so much I think about it all the time. And the thoughts are very fucking dirty.

Now I know that she has the cowboy boots I sent her—the delivery service sent me confirmation—but I don't have a text from her yet.

I want a photo of her in those boots.

I blow out a breath and stare at my dark phone screen. It's been twelve hours since she got the boots.

I haven't heard from her all day.

Is she all right?

I know she's physically all right because I called IAS and asked if she was at work today. She is. The woman I spoke to personally saw her with her own eyes. Or so she told me when I insisted on speaking to someone who had.

But is she feeling okay? Why hasn't she responded to the text of my running shoes with the puppies? I'd been in the park this morning, and the two adorable Dachshund puppies on a walk with their new owner decided I looked like the kind of guy who would stop in the middle of his run to give tummy rubs and...they were right.

But Abigail didn't respond to the photo. Is she not a dog person? Is her phone working? It rang through when I *called* and left a voice message.

Abigail, call me. I figured that was pretty straightforward.

Regina, the same woman I'd called to ask if Abigail was at work today, assured me that the cell phone towers in Sapphire Falls were working and told me that she was ninety percent sure she used the same carrier Abigail did and that there were no system problems as far as she knew, when I called a second time.

I would have preferred that she be one hundred percent sure, but she only said that she'd ask Abigail who her phone plan was with when she saw her next.

Regina did not offer to go find her, or to call me back with any further information, however.

The annoying thing about being the Crown Prince of Cara hanging out in the US? I'm not actually the boss of any Americans. Sure, some are impressed by my title, my connections, and my money. I can get things from *those* people.

Regina doesn't seem to be one of them, however.

"This is Torin O'Grady," I'd told her.

"Yes, you said that when you called before, Mr. O'Grady," she'd said.

"*Prince* Torin. I've been working with Mr. Riley and Ms. Davis-Bennett."

"Okay." She'd sounded bored.

"There's *nothing* else you can do?" I ask.

"I can put you through to Mr. Riley or Ms. Davis-Bennett."

"I don't need to talk to either of them."

"I can take a message."

"I've already given you the message."

"Then no, there's nothing else I can do."

I'd gritted my teeth.

"Have you considered," Regina had asked, with a tone that made me think she and my grandfather would get along well. "That if the phones are fine and Abigail is fine, there *is* still a third potential reason you're not hearing from her?"

Yes, Regina, I have definitely considered that. But hey, thanks for the punch-to-the-gut confirmation that it's me.

Abigail doesn't want to talk, or text, with me.

I pick up the glass of whiskey sitting on the desk in the hotel suite next to the final plans I wanted to review. I haven't been able to concentrate on them. I down the rest of the liquor, glaring at my phone.

Fuck it. I'm going to text her.

But rather than all the words I want to say, I pull back my frustration and need and kick off my shoes, prop my feet on the desk in the hotel suite, and take a photo of my stocking feet.

My socks are pink, yellow, and green striped. They're not the neon colors of hers, but they're...bright. Nothing like what I typically wear. They also don't go up to my thighs, but I definitely thought of her when I saw them and had to have them.

I send the text with a simple

> thought of you all day.

Then I wait.
And wait.
I finally text her again.

> You should know…I am into cowgirls.

She replies within two minutes this time.

> I'm not a cowgirl. I just happen to have some boots now.

I frown at the message. That doesn't sound flirtatious. Or like a thanks. And she didn't comment on the socks I'm wearing.

> You could definitely be a cowgirl, Abigail.

With me. *For* me. On my ranch.
She's wearing those damned boots the first time I fuck her. Whether she knows it or not.
Another text comes in, but it's not from Abigail.
It's my sister.

> Fiona: Um…Abigail knows about Linnea.

I scowl at the screen.

> There's nothing to know.

> Fiona: Right. Well…

Then she attaches a link to the podcast *Wait 'Til I Tell Ye.*

I click it despite wanting nothing to do with this. If Fiona thinks there's something here I need to see, then I'll look.

The last few episodes have titles like, "Not Just Another Getaway", "Penthouse to Palace", "Perfect Proposal Tip #1: Don't Do It In Shreveport", and the latest, "Are Those Wedding Bells? They Better Fucking Be".

My fist tightens around my phone.

Fiona also sent a link to the recent statement from the palace. Part of it reads *the royal family already considers Linnea a part of the family.*

Just fucking great.

If Abigail thinks I'm with Linnea...

Fuck.

I call Regina back.

"Sir, really—"

"I need to speak with Lauren. Right now."

"Of course."

I think Regina is relieved to have something to do that will allow her to turn me over to someone else immediately.

"Your Highness," Lauren Davis-Bennett greets.

I've told her to call me Torin, but I don't have time for that right now. "I need Abigail in Shreveport, at the farm site, today."

"All right," Lauren says smoothly. She's used to dealing with politicians and full-of-themselves American business-men. One demanding prince is nothing. "What should I tell her?"

I've told her I don't want Abigail to know about IAS building this farm with me until I give the word.

"That you're sending her for business. That no one else can go and that she'll understand everything when she gets there."

"She won't like that," Lauren says.

"She'll like it better than the truth at the moment."

There's a pause on Lauren's end. "I have to ask, Torin, will she eventually like the truth?"

I appreciate that Lauren feels protective of Abigail. She was also incredibly impressed with the farm plans I presented her and not surprised to find out that Abigail was the mastermind behind it all. Lauren knows Abigail is special and I like her very much for that alone.

"Lauren, I'm betting *everything* on Abigail liking the truth eventually."

CHAPTER 16
ABIGAIL

I'm not mad.

I'm not even hurt. Not exactly.

I guess I could be. He shouldn't have been flirting with me, and kissing me, and *more* if there was actually another woman. I knew there was *going to be* another woman. That there was the possibility of another woman. But if there was one who was actually planning a wedding, then he should have stopped it all with me.

But I'm...disappointed.

Really fucking disappointed.

I knew I wanted to kiss Torin again, but until I realized that I'd lost the chance for good, I don't think I realized how *much* I wanted to kiss him.

A lot.

I'd say more than I've ever wanted to kiss anyone, but that's not really saying much. I've never been that into kissing.

Until Torin O'Grady.

I study the photo I just took. It's my feet in the hot pink boots he sent me this morning, the heels hooked on the bottom rung of the barstool I'm sitting on. I make sure that it's clear it's a barstool.

Why?

Because I'm considering sending this photo to him.

Because I want him thinking about me. Thinking about the fact that I'm out where there might be other men. Other men who might like how these boots look on my feet.

There I said it. Okay, I *thought* it. Still, I admitted it.

Do I want to make Torin jealous?

Yes.

Dammit.

It's an airport bar, but he doesn't need to know that. There are other men here.

I'm on my way to a work site. In Shreveport. I don't know much about it, but some guy has already bought an IAS system and wants someone there to "go over a few things".

Lauren didn't ask me to go so much as she told me she was sending me to handle the last-minute request.

She probably thinks I'm willing to go since it's home and I could visit my parents. But they made the trip to my dad's hometown for Ami's wedding into a mini-vacation and they're still in Autre.

It's fine though. Being in Sapphire Falls reminds me of Torin, stupidly. The texts I've sent have been from my back porch and bathtub and the bar and it all makes me sad now.

So I'm in the Chicago airport waiting for my connecting flight to Shreveport.

And thinking of him anyway.

I blame it partly on the three hard ciders I've had. And I'm sure this time that I've drunk three full bottles.

Still, I realize this is childish. And such a waste of time. What if he *is* jealous? What does that accomplish? Then we're both upset with emotions that don't matter and that we can't, ultimately, do anything about? I will *not* be some 'other woman' or mistress to a prince. I won't be some secret affair he has while he's publicly marrying another woman.

Then I frown.

A secret affair should be exactly what I want. Especially the secret part. I don't want to be in any kind of spotlight. I don't want anyone knowing anything about my personal life.

Hell, I have a hard time talking about my *professional* life. That's why my bosses don't know how passionate I am about building community-based indoor farms and that I have a plan that IAS could implement tomorrow to start making those happen around the country.

One of these days I'll get the nerve to sit down with Lauren and Mason about my ideas. But fuck, how does someone go to two literal geniuses who have years of hands-on experience, who have traveled the globe and seen agricultural issues up close, gotten their hands dirty in fields ravaged by natural disasters and plagued with famine and drought, met with presidents and Nobel prize winners, and say, "Oh, hey guys, I've got this amazing plan that I think you should implement"?

Who am I? I need to prove myself. I need to earn the right to sit at the table with them and share ideas and plans.

So, yeah, if I don't have the experience or confidence to talk to my bosses about ideas in my professional field of study, how can I possibly face a personal life that involves *dating* a *prince?* I've slept with one guy. Kissed two. And I only *liked* kissing one of them.

I was thinking *maybe* Torin and I could have a hot weekend together in Autre where everyone would keep our secret.

I definitely don't want to go public with anything with Torin.

When it comes to a man who could have any woman he wants, there would constantly be questions. Fair questions. *Why her? What could she possibly have that a million other women don't? Did you see what she said at that state dinner? She's so weird. She can't possibly be that good in bed.*

And they'd be right.

I can't possibly be that good in bed.

"Hi. Can I buy you a drink?"

I focus on the man who has just taken the seat beside me at the bar.

He's handsome. He's wearing a suit and a big smile. And I'm not interested. At all.

"No, thank you."

"Sorry, I didn't see a ring," he says, looking at my left hand. "Not that you need to have a ring to say no," he says quickly. "Just took a chance."

I nod. "It's okay. No ring."

"You're not taken then?"

Torin said I am. That's the first thing to go through my mind. But *he's* the one who's taken.

"No, I'm not," I tell the good-looking stranger who I should at least have a drink with.

Instead, I hit send on the photo of my boots on the rung of the bar stool.

Torin's reply comes in only three seconds later.

Where are you?

That's all his text says. It doesn't say anything about the boots. There's not even one emoji.

I frown. I could ignore him. Keep him on read. Maybe make him sweat.

But my fingers are already moving. The jealous, petty, childish side of me types the words

at a bar.

You better not be dancing with anyone else wearing those boots, Abigail.

What is it about him using my name, even in a text, that causes a little shiver to dance down my back?

I'm the only one you dance with in those boots

I actually laugh at that. He sounds jealous. Good. He can act as possessive and bossy as he wants. Yes, that's a little hot, but there's nothing he can do.

Tell me you're not dancing in those boots tonight, Abigail.

I frown. I want to dance with him. In these boots. In any other shoes. In my bare feet again. I've been turning down other guys for dancing because of a guy who is a fucking *prince*, who I can never be with.

I'm irrationally annoyed at him. None of that is actually his fault. Though I can definitely blame him for my attraction to him and how flirtatious and funny and charming he is.

I text back, feeling sassy.

> What if I am?

I never feel sassy.

> Then I would have to remind you that you're mine.

> Though I would very much enjoy that.

I actually laugh at that. He doesn't know that I know about Linnea. Fine. He wants to just keeping digging this hole he's in deeper and deeper?

> Sure. From thousands of miles away?

> You don't think I can make it very clear to you and any other man who even looks at you that you are spoken for?

My heart pounds. See? This is what I'm talking about. *This* kind of stuff, this possessive, flirty, I-want-to-be-your-boyfriend bullshit and how it makes me feel *is* totally his fault.

He's engaged. He's engaged-ish at least. And he's not here.

> I think you're texting the wrong number. This is Abigail. Not Linnea.

There is more of a pause before he responds. Oh, did I surprise the cocky prince? Good.

> Linnea and I are not engaged, Abigail.

I simply send him the link to the podcast that Charlie sent me.

Linnea and I are friends. We are not getting married. Also, she's in love with someone else.

I study the words. I want to believe them. So much.

Why does this podcast and 'the palace' think you're engaged?

Because my grandfather is a terrible listener and he loves Linnea. He's also king and that seems to make him think he can make whatever he wants to happen, happen.

That is pretty much what that means right?

Unfortunately.

So you have to marry her?

Unless I marry someone else who is just as good, or better, for the country. Who my grandfather will also love and trust.

Why I'm continuing this conversation I have no idea. This is all crazy. Still, I read the 'unless I marry someone else' over and over.

He *is* engaged to Linnea. Kind of.

But he says he doesn't want to be.

And there is a way to get him out of it.

Still, I have to ask a question.

Once you're king, you could just get divorced, right?

Yes. But I'm not marrying Linnea.

You should. Temporarily.

My best friend would never forgive me. And
I won't do that to him.

I frown, reading that over again. Then it clicks.

Jonah is in love with Linnea?

Yes. And you're now in on a huge secret,
Abigail. He would be fired and likely
banished if my grandfather found out.

So Torin *can't* marry Linnea.

But he still needs a wife.

If it's not Linnea, it will be someone else.

Torin will marry *someone*.

I stare at my screen, my thoughts swirling. I know if I
don't respond, he's going to text me again. And I don't
know what to say. So I simply text,

I have to get on the plane now.

And then I shut my phone off.

CHAPTER 17

ABIGAIL

There's a black town car waiting for me when I land.

I'm not sure exactly where this IAS project is, but I'm confused as we head into the city rather than to a site outside the city limits.

"I'm sorry," I say to the driver. "I'm here to check out a farming site. Are you sure you have the right address?" Am I about to get murdered?

"Yes, Ms. Landry. Here's the address of the project site." He hands back a piece of paper.

I read it. Then stare at it.

This is in my old neighborhood. This address would put the site right across the street from my old high school, two blocks from my elementary school, and five blocks from my parents' house.

I text Lauren.

> What kind of system are we installing in a
> residential neighborhood?

But I don't hear back from her even five minutes later.

So I call Regina, Lauren and Mason's executive assistant.

"Innovative Agricultural Solutions, this is Regina."

"Hi, Regina, it's Abi. Can I talk with Lauren?"

"Hi, Abi. Lauren is in a do-not-disturb meeting."

"I understand, but I just landed in Shreveport for this site visit, and I think I need to know more about it before I get there."

"Oh, yes, she said you might call about that and to tell you that it will be fine, and it will all make sense when you get there."

I don't know what to say to that. "Uh. O-kay."

"Have a great day, Abi!" Regina says brightly. Then she hangs up.

What is going on?

I look down at my boots. The pink boots from Torin. The prince who is *not* currently engaged to anyone. The prince who loves my ideas for *my* farming systems.

That gives me a little surge of confidence. Torin is...or will be...in charge of an entire country and he thinks that my ideas could benefit *all* of his people.

I can definitely check out this one site and answer whatever questions these local people, my people, have about this one system. I don't love selling people on systems they're skeptical of, but these people have already bought this one. They just need some expert input. I can do that. I don't need to prepare ahead of time. I know IAS systems inside and out.

But, for just a second, I think about how much I'd enjoy

touring a site where one of *my* farms had been built in Cara for Torin's people.

And then I shut that down.

Because I can't possibly go to Cara, where Torin *will* be marrying some other woman. Even if he's not currently engaged. I can ignore all of that news and those photos and stories here in the US, probably, but no way will I be able to avoid it if I'm *in* Cara.

However, I could teach someone else at IAS about my systems so *they* can go to Cara. Because my systems really would be wonderful for Torin. I mean, for Cara.

The car finally pulls up at our destination.

And I gasp.

We are at the curb beside the building that was an apartment building the entire time I was in school at Clover Park Elementary and in high school right across the street. About six years ago, the building was sold and turned into offices. But three years ago, the company defaulted on the loan and it's been sitting empty ever since.

"Here we are," my driver says. "I'll wait for you."

"Okay, thanks," I say absently. I get out of the car slowly, staring at the building.

Because it's not empty anymore.

And it doesn't look like an apartment building or an office building.

It looks like...an indoor farm. One that I've described a number of times. On paper.

This one is in real life. Huge and shiny and...gorgeous.

My gaze finds the sign sitting in the dirt next to the brand-new front doors.

Clover Park Indoor Farm.

What.

The.

Hell?

"Abigail! Welcome!"

My gaze is jerked away from the building to the man approaching me with a wide smile and his hand outstretched.

Holy. Shit.

The Mayor of Shreveport is coming toward me. And he knows my name.

"Um. Hi." I run my hand over the skirt of the dress I'm wearing. It's blue with little pink flowers that match my boots. It's sleeveless, the skirt is loose and flowy with the hem hitting just above the top of the boots, and it ties loosely at my waist. It was comfortable for the plane but looks dressier than blue jeans. Which is basically every-thing that's in my closet. "Mayor Aiden." I extend my hand. "It's nice to meet you."

"Johnny, please," Johnny Aiden—a hometown boy who played football for LSU and won in a landslide, because what better qualifies someone to govern a city than being a star running back?—says, clasping my hand in a warm handshake.

I notice that there are a number of people standing around on the sidewalk.

It's mostly men in suits and ties, though there are a few contractors in jeans and tool belts, and a couple of women in business wear.

The man next to the mayor reaches out as well. "Abi. It's great to see you again. Thank you for everything you've done here."

And I'm suddenly facing Brady Schuster.

My number one bully. The guy who made me feel like a silly, stupid little girl who didn't belong in the same rooms with him. Ever.

He is now the city council member from this district. He's in his mid-twenties. He's an engineer. He's married with a little girl. We're both adults.

But the little girl who is still inside of *me* doesn't care. My stomach still knots, and I feel a wave of nausea.

I've more than proven that I *did* belong in those rooms with him. Hell, I belong in even better rooms. But I'm standing just across the street from the school where Brady would whisper and laugh when I stood in front of the class to present, and while he's taller and broader than he was back then, his eyes are the same.

I definitely feel sick.

I swallow. "Brady," I say, tightly.

His smile wavers. Clearly, I'm not feeling very friendly.

"This is all so amazing," he says, and his tone is sincere. "Thank you so much for choosing to put the farm here."

"Well, I—"

"You have to see how much we've gotten done," Johnny says, ushering me toward the front doors. "We're very proud of the progress and the prince insisted a tour be the first thing on the agenda."

My feet suddenly feel stuck to the sidewalk. I stop and stare at the mayor. "The *prince?*"

He laughs. "Yes. He was adamant. He's been pushing hard to get things done, kind of riding our asses, just between you and me." He grins and gives me a wink. "But we have to admit that it's all impressive and the neighborhood—hell, the whole *city*—is so excited to see it come to fruition. His passion and"—Johnny grins and lowers his voice—"his money and influence with some pretty impressive people, have made this project really come together and we couldn't be more thrilled."

"But he's been singing your praises since the first

minute," Brady adds, stepping past my other side to pull the door open. "I was initially surprised to hear a name I know from the past, but when I thought about it for even thirty seconds, I realized I shouldn't be surprised the smartest girl to ever come out of Shreveport is the one giving back to us like this."

I look at him, my brow lifting. "Smartest? I don't remember you ever using that word to describe me."

I can't believe I said that out loud.

Brady can't either. He stares at me for a few seconds, then has the grace to get a little red in the face. "I'd like to think that *I've* gotten a little smarter over the years. That I've learned how to treat people a little better."

I lift my chin.

"I'm sorry, Abigail," he says, and he sounds sincere. "I was terrible to you in school, and you didn't deserve that. The fact that you've come back to do all of this for our old neighborhood in spite of the fact that there are probably some not very good memories here for you, says a lot about how much better a person you are."

I swallow hard. I didn't expect to get an apology from Brady. Ever. Certainly not when I woke up this morning, or even when I got on the plane to Shreveport. But...it does help.

"Thank you for saying that," I tell him.

"Of course. And I should have done it before now. I hope you don't think it's only because of the farming program you convinced the prince to facilitate here."

"No, I believe you," I say, trying to be gracious. Then because when Torin is on my mind, I can't concentrate well on *anything* else, not even a long-time-coming apology from my childhood nemesis, I look at the mayor. "Torin told you this was my idea?"

"Of course. He had us all read about your plan to bring farms like this to neighborhoods like ours. To involve the schools, various neighborhood groups, including medical clinics." He motions to two women standing next to the building. "This is Dr. Felicity Wilson, she's the superintendent of schools. And this is Dr. Amanda Connor. She's the physician at the local clinic. They're both very excited about the program and look forward to being involved. We've also got scout leaders, church groups, child advocates, food pantries, and others asking how they can help."

I feel tears well up suddenly and I have to blink rapidly.

Torin did all of this.

I haven't even stepped inside the building yet and I'm already overwhelmed.

I smile at the women and then let them all escort me into the building.

For the next hour, they lead me around, showing me the farm, explaining the discussions the school board, faculty and parents, and even the city council have had. The farm isn't complete, but they have a clear vision for the areas that aren't finished and...it's amazing.

I choke up several times and have to swallow down emotions.

Torin asked me if I wanted to see my ideas come to life.

I did. So much.

And he's made it happen.

I don't really understand why. At least, why *here*? But it's real.

This farm was drawn up according to sketches given to an interior architect who turned it into a to-scale model and then builders and scientists and farmers, some from IAS in Sapphire Falls, turned that model into reality.

Johnny tells me Torin did those initial sketches himself,

but it's obvious he did it based on my papers. It's exactly as I described it.

"We built everything exactly as Prince Torin drew up, right down to which crops were planted," the mayor says.

"It's all...incredible," I tell them. "I'm so impressed with how quickly you've done it and I'm so excited about the enthusiasm around it."

"Would you like to say a few words to everyone?" Brady asks.

I freeze. No. I absolutely would *not* like to say *any* words.

"Yes, please," Johnny adds. "Torin has spoken with the group a few times and they love hearing that they're doing good work and making the vision come to life. He's so passionate about the project that it really rubs off on every-one." Johnny chuckles. "Between your brains and his charisma, I dare anyone to say no to the two of you about anything."

I actually am able to give a small smile at that. He has a point. Torin and I could do some pretty amazing things.

But then I realize he's leading me toward a small stage with a freaking podium. I actually dig in my heels. "No, I really don't need to say anything. I'm the behind-the-scenes girl. Torin is the speaker."

"Sure," Johnny says. "But everyone knows that this project is your idea. Torin never lets us forget that." He gives me another wink. "Just say something about how this is the first of its kind—they love that—and that when you first thought it all up you didn't know how great it would be in real life, and maybe throw in something about how great it is to be doing this in your hometown."

He's a *mayor*. Of course he thinks this is no big deal. Just stand up and talk to a crowd of people off the cuff.

If only the 'off the cuff' part was the whole problem. I

would still be sweating and nauseated even if I'd prepared a speech.

And here I am, only a few yards away from my high school, the place where I first learned that I'm weird and it doesn't matter what you *say*, it matters what you *do*.

People can say that you're strange and a "mutant", that no one likes you, and that you're nothing special. And it doesn't matter if you *tell* them they're wrong.

But when you ace the test, solve the problem, get the award, earn the scholarship, and the degree, and the prestigious position, what they said doesn't matter. If you give your detractors irrefutable proof that you are actually special and bright and worthy, then you can show them that all of their words were wrong.

But here I am about to *speak* about the real-life embodiment of my greatest idea and dream with Brady Fucking Schuster in the audience. Apology or not, I don't want to speak in front of him about something that matters this much to me.

I just want to show him. Them. Everyone. I want them to just implement the programs, feed the kids, and then they'll see for themselves how great it is.

But no, we have to *talk* about it first.

I swallow hard.

I guess if I puke in front of these people, it won't be any worse than...no, it will be the worst of the times I've puked in public. But I guess they won't ask me back to speak again, so there's that.

I try to make my feet move, but I can't. It's like my boots have been nailed to the floor.

"I...um...I need a second...to...um...think of something to say," I mumble quickly and start to turn away.

And suddenly there's a big arm around my waist, practically lifting me, hurrying me away and around the corner and shoving a plastic bucket in front of me.

I throw up.

And I feel a big hand grasping my hair, holding it back.

And after my stomach empties and I suck in a deep breath, it hits me that Torin is here.

I lift my head and blink.

"Hey," he says with a grin.

"Oh my God!" Immediately I cover my mouth with my hand.

He hands me a bottle of water.

I look around but am horrified when he takes the bucket from my hands. He sets it down by a large bin and a coiled water hose. I take in more details. We're around the corner from the front section of the farm where there are placards explaining the farm and displaying a map of where various crops are planted. Then the farm starts about fifty feet behind that with common plants like tomatoes, peppers, and leaf lettuces.

Where we're standing now seems to be a storage area where fertilizers, implements, and hoses are kept. Along with buckets. Lots of different sizes of buckets.

I twist off the top of the water bottle, take a mouthful and swish it around, then swallow. I take two more long drinks.

Then Torin hands me some gum.

I take it from him wordlessly, before moving to clean the bucket I got sick in. I dump it out in a big trash bin full of weeds and mud, then use a hose to wash it out. I place it by the others of the same size.

Finally, I face him.

"You're here?"

"Are you *really* surprised?"

I start to say that yes, of course I am. By *all* of this. But now that I know he's behind this farm being built, no. Of course he's here. I prop a hand on my hip. "You've been hiding? I haven't seen you until now."

"I wanted you to enjoy it without me taking up the spotlight."

That should sound arrogant, but it doesn't. It's a fact. Torin *basks* in the spotlight. He naturally drifts to the center of any room or group. And here, he's the man funding the project. The one really leading it from the sounds of it. Of course, they would have been talking to him and including him.

But since the mayor and Brady and everyone else didn't know he was here, they gave *me* the VIP treatment.

"Thank you," I say. "It's…" I take a breath. "Incredible. Perfect."

His smile is so bright, and so genuine that it takes my breath away. "I'm so glad."

"And you *have* to build farms in Cara, Torin. You said it would enhance your agricultural systems and improve your economy, but from what I've read, you have almost no agriculture. Your climate and terrain make it impossible to grow almost *any* crop." I start gesturing with my hands, my stomach completely settled now. "You import *everything*. Your economy is kept alive by fishing, which is also being threatened by climate change, and your attrition rate of youth to larger, more stable countries in Europe and the United States is alarming. But these farms can help all of that. Especially if you're willing to start some programs where students can become a part of green energy engineering. Because powering these farms is the biggest hurdle, and we need to keep working on those alternatives. But yes, you definitely need these farms."

He's staring at me.

And my *God*, he looks good. He's in blue jeans, and a casual blue button-up that brings out the blue in his eyes. It's even a little rumpled. He looks like...a guy. Any other guy on the street. Except that he wears his confidence and power and passion like a cologne or something. Something that just floats up around him and fills the air. It's an aura. He just oozes charm and I-can-do-anything. And I'm so drawn to that. Because as much IQ as I have, I don't have *that*.

My sisters have it. My grandmother has that. But I don't. I know I'm good at things, but I'm happy to just do my thing, quietly, in my little bubble. I'm not the type to tell people that they *must* listen to me. I'm not the type to sell people on my ideas. I'm not the type to proclaim...anything.

I need someone like Torin to do that for me.

He swallows hard. "Abigail." Then he just reaches for me and cups my face between his hands. "You are—"

"No!" I shove him back. Oh my God! He can't kiss me right now!

He stares at me, his hands suspended between us.

"I just *threw up*," I remind him, my eyes wide. I slap my hand over my mouth. "I...want to kiss you so badly," I say from behind my hand. "I want you to kiss *me* so badly. And we should definitely do that before you actually get engaged to anyone. But not *now*."

The words sink in, and he starts grinning. "Well, I can think of *many* places I could kiss you that don't involve your mouth."

My aforementioned mouth falls open and I gasp softly. But then, without really thinking, I ask, "If I say I want to brush my teeth first anyway, will you still kiss me in those other places too?"

His gaze turns immediately hot. "Where is the closest toothbrush?" he practically growls, moving to stand nearly on top of me.

I keep my hand over my mouth, but answer, "In my purse, over there, but we should just go to my parents' house."

"Your parents' house?"

"That's where I'm staying."

"Yes," he agrees quickly. "Yes, we should."

"And…I think I still need to give a speech first."

His grin is quick. "Yes, you do."

This man built me a farm. In my hometown. I have so many questions for him.

"Okay. I'm ready."

"Make it quick," he says.

Yeah. I want that.

I take a deep breath and step around the corner and into the main area again. I plaster on a smile and walk toward the stage and that fucking podium. But just as my steps start to falter, I feel Torin's hand on my lower back.

He steps up onto the stage with me and I feel the butterflies in my stomach settle into little flutters instead of sickening swooping.

I move behind the podium and grasp the sides, facing the audience in front of me. And then, I just say what's on my mind.

"Hi, everyone. Thanks for being here. Not just today, but every day you've been here making this happen. I'm Abigail Landry and…this farm was my idea."

I smile as they applaud. Okay, that's not so bad.

Torin gives me a smile and I feel mine grow as I meet his eyes.

I turn back to the people in front of us. "Torin O'Grady

and I believe that everyone deserves access to fresh, healthy, affordable food year-round. And, because Shreveport is where I first found my love for growing things and the empowerment that comes from producing food, it makes sense to start my..." I look up at him again and find him watching me with an expression that seems to be a mix of admiration and affection. My chest warms. "*Our* farms here."

Everyone is smiling back at me, and I feel great. This is... so damned great. They are all interested and open. Like they really do think I have something interesting to say.

I open my mouth and...my mind goes blank. I have nothing else. I have no idea how to continue the speech or, worse, how to end it.

Torin slips an arm around my waist, and I lean into him.

He asks softly, "Want me to take over?"

I do so fucking much. I look out at the audience. "I learned a lot at that school across the street, but I'll be honest, public speaking was not, and is not, my gift."

People laugh lightly but I think it's in understanding rather than judgment.

I look up at Torin. "I think it's in the prince's handbook that you're obligated to save the damsel in distress. And I'm definitely in a little distress."

He gives me a smile that makes my knees wobble. "I've got you." And then he proves it. He turns to the audience and starts talking about the farm.

And ten minutes later, I'm staring at him with my mouth hanging open.

Holy. Shit.

He just told this roomful of people all about food deserts, and child hunger, and even used current statewide and national statistics. He emphasized the importance of access to fresh produce year-round. He highlighted what a gift an indoor farm could be to a community. He told them how he'd had *them* in mind when he'd designed the farm and chose every single crop for this farm, without putting a single person to sleep. And without using a single note card.

I didn't have to tell him any of this. I didn't have to explain or teach him a thing. He's done his homework.

This project really does matter to him.

He's up here selling it, *very* convincingly, as if he planted every single seed.

He keeps his arm around me as he steers me off the stage.

"There are some people we need to talk to," he says. "I'll talk, but I need you beside me, okay? We're the team. You're the brains and heart, and I'm the voice and the money."

I look up at him. "You are most definitely the heart too," I tell him sincerely. "Without your heart, you wouldn't have understood the project. You wouldn't have been able to draw it up like you did. You wouldn't have cared enough to do it."

The look in his eyes as he looks down at me is hot and sweet at the same time.

But before either of us can say a word, three men approach. One is the mayor, but the other two are strangers.

"Torin," one says, extending his hand.

"Hey, Steve. Bob," he says, shaking hands with another man.

"Good to see you, Torin," Bob says.

The mayor also shakes Torin's hand.

"This is impressive," Bob says.

"I agree," Steve tells him. "But we have concerns."

"Tell me what they are so I can tell you why they're not an issue," Torin says with a smile.

I watch, fascinated. I've seen my sister do this—wrap people around her finger in thirty seconds. It's smiles and tone of voice and eye contact and a bunch of stuff she's tried to teach me.

"Regulations," Steve says. "No matter how much we'd like to partner, I don't know what we can do and who we need to clear things with."

Torin nods. "I understand. I've got it covered. You don't need to worry."

Steve leans in. "That's it? Just you've got it covered and don't worry?"

"Of course not," Torin says with a laugh. "I'll get all the paperwork you need. I'll have the right people call you. I have a meeting with the Governor and the State Superintendent of Public Instruction and the Director of the Department of Agriculture next week," he says. "They're all very interested and excited about the farm. They think there is huge potential in Abigail's program ideas."

Steve, Johnny, and Bob all look at me now.

"Is that right?" Steve asks.

I just arch an eyebrow.

"I'd love if you wanted to join the meeting," Torin says smoothly. "This site will be a fully functioning farm for this area, but it's also going to be a trial site and when it's successful, they'll want local business people and school administrators presenting and adding your perspective when they talk to other communities around the state and, of course, when we go out of state."

Steve looks surprised, then straightens slightly, smoothing a hand down the front of his shirt, and nods. "I see. Of course, I'd be happy to join the meeting."

Well played, Torin. I don't know who Steve is or what he does, but it's clear that he's got an ego and thinks he's pretty smart. Of course, the man would want to be regarded around the state as an expert in something new and potentially so impactful. That will make him feel important and maybe add something to his resume or portfolio or whatever.

I just want him to do it because it's the right thing to do.

But I guess this will work.

"It would be great to have you in on the meeting as well," Torin says to Johnny. "As Mayor, we'll also want your perspective when we talk to other towns." Torin reaches out and claps Johnny on the shoulder. "This is going to be big, guys. It's great to have such a supportive and enthusiastic team here as our foundation."

The men all look at one another, sharing proud smiles.

"Abigail is going to do amazing things with her plans. It's incredible that this neighborhood is the starting point for some of it," Torin adds.

Steve nods, giving me a smile. "We are grateful, Ms. Landry. I hope you aren't offended by my concerns and questions. We're not just proud of this farm, but proud that the woman behind it is from right here."

I nod. I should be happy that they're now recognizing me and my contributions. It's what I wanted when I was in school here.

But now, it doesn't matter if *they're* pleased.

Torin O'Grady, Crown Prince of Cara, thinks I'm amazing and I'm realizing his opinion is worth more than every single person I went to school with put together.

Because *he's* amazing. And he really sees me.

"I'll be in touch," Torin says. "Right now, Ms. Landry

and I have somewhere else we need to be. In fact, we're running a little late."

With that, he turns me and starts for the front of the building, his hand resting hotly against my lower back. We have somewhere else we need to be? I just want to go to my mom and dad's. And my bedroom there. Like, right now.

I've missed him. I've wanted to see him again. And that was before I actually saw him again.

Now, I want to kiss him, and strip him naked, and... well, damn. I think I might have a proposal for him.

"Where do we need to be?" I ask, as he holds the door for me and ushers me out onto the sidewalk.

"Alone somewhere. As soon as possible," is his gruff, quiet answer.

I trip over the toe of my boot as I try to turn to look up at him. He keeps me from falling and keeps me moving forward.

Until we're standing in front of Jonah. Who is standing beside a large black SUV.

I look around. The car that brought me to the farm is gone. "Uh, where's my car? Where's my suitcase?"

"It's in the back of the SUV. I dismissed your car," Jonah says, opening the back door of the SUV.

A beautiful brunette is standing next to him. "Hi, I'm Linnea Olsen."

I whip around to look at her fully. "You're Linnea?" Oh, damn. She's gorgeous. And...yeah, she's got a regal air about her.

But she winces. "Yes." She says it almost apologetically.

I look up at Torin.

He just shakes his head. "I told you we're friends. And she's with Jonah."

I look to the other man. He steps closer to Linnea and puts a hand on the back of her neck. She leans into his touch, her expression relaxing into a smile. And I take a deep breath.

"Yes, you did. It's nice to meet you," I tell her.

"You too." She gives me a very genuine smile.

Torin helps me up into the back seat of the SUV while Jonah holds the front passenger door open for Linnea. Then the men round the vehicle and get in, Jonah behind the wheel and Torin in the back next to me.

"We have another stop?" I ask.

Torin shakes his head. "Even though your parents' house is closer—" He shoots me a grin. "We're heading back to the hotel. We booked you a room at the same place we've been staying."

My heart rate speeds up. Oh, that's...good. Probably better than my childhood bedroom that only has a twin bed. And that I'll have to stay in on future visits home. I'm not sure I want to think of Torin every time I'm in that room after today. Christmases could be a little sad. And possibly sexually frustrating. Which is not ideal.

But I would very much like to spend some time with Torin. Alone. In a room with a bed. Before he's completely off limits because he's engaged to someone else.

My stomach drops at the thought, and I realize that the crazy idea that drifted through my head earlier is maybe not so crazy.

Well...it's still crazy. But I can make it make sense.

To both of us.

And making it make sense to myself is a big deal.

"I can't believe you built that farm," I tell him, pivoting in my seat to face him. "That's just...I don't even have a good word for it." I laugh lightly. "Words aren't really my forte anyway, but that farm is just…" I feel my eyes filling with tears again.

He takes my hand, lacing our fingers together. "It was my pleasure, Abigail."

"You did it exactly according to my plans."

"Of course, I did. Why would I change anything?"

"Why didn't you tell me you were doing it?"

"I wanted to surprise you."

"You did." I laugh lightly. "I can't believe Brady was there. He was one of the guys who…you know."

Torin nods, his jaw tightening. "I'm aware."

"You are?"

"I did some digging. I already knew you wanted to start a farm in Shreveport from one of your essays. After you told me about your experience in school, and that one of your classmates was on the city council, I asked around. I very much wanted to be sure he was there to see you shine."

I swallow hard, studying his face. He means that. He wanted to give me a moment to show Brady what I'm capable of. "He apologized."

"Good."

"It didn't matter."

"No?" Torin watches me.

"No. I've realized that I don't care what he thinks. I don't care what very many people think. But—" I swallow again. "I care what you think. And I'm really glad you think my farms are a good idea."

His eyes are locked on mine, hot and intense. "I think they're a lot more than simply a good idea."

I nod. "And I'm glad you think I'm…" I trail off, not sure how to fill that in.

"Amazing. Special. Incredible. Fascinating. Addictive. Pick an adjective, Abigail." Torin's voice is low and rough.

I'm breathing faster. "Why did you build the farm? I mean, specifically. Why did you do it here? Now?"

"You're not really a dozen roses kind of girl," he says, a grin teasing his lips. "I knew I needed to give you more than that."

"Why did you need to give me anything at all?"

"Because I want you."

That makes the air in my lungs whoosh out. I don't know if he wants me for my farms, or for sex, or what, but...

"Okay, then—" I squeeze his hand. "I have a solution for how we can both get the things we want."

He leans closer. "I'm listening."

I take a deep breath. "I think you were right. We should get married."

CHAPTER 18

TORIN

Shock rocks through my body. I stare at her. Then I look toward the front of the SUV. Linnea has pivoted in her seat and Jonah is staring at us in the rearview mirror.

"Road," I say to him.

He jerks his attention back to the street in front of the SUV.

Then I look at Abigail again. She's just watching me.

Maybe I misheard her. Because what she just said is something that I want to hear and do so much that it's possible I made it up.

"What?" I finally ask simply.

"I've been thinking, and I realized that you and I getting married would solve a lot of problems."

Linnea and Jonah look at one another, then look at me, then look back at Abigail.

"You do?" I ask.

"Yes." She meets my eyes directly. "These farms *are* a good idea, Torin. They *will* be good for Cara."

I nod. "I know." My heart is beating so hard, I almost can't take a deep breath.

"And we're obviously an amazing team," she continues, "So, how long do you think it would take for your grandfather to feel like you're ready to take over the throne?"

"Um...a year?" I say it with a definite question mark at the end. I glance at Linnea and Jonah. Linnea nods and lifts a shoulder. Okay, yeah, a year.

"Great. If we ship in already established plants, then we can have a farm up and running in a few months and then get several programs going within a year," she says.

"We don't have to do it all in one year," I assure her.

She wets her lips. "I think it's a good idea if we have a timeline. And some established guidelines."

"Okay." I want her. I will probably agree to anything that gets my ring on her finger.

"You want the throne. I want a farm that can feed an entire village and proof that it can positively impact the physical and mental health of the people as well as the economic and societal well-being of the village. Cara is perfect because you don't have any programs already in place and, because you're the prince, we won't have to talk to a bunch of people and jump through a bunch of hoops. You can just make them all do what we want. It will be faster and easier to get things established and providing data."

It's true. I would like to think I'd use more tact than just ordering people around, but I know Abigail well enough by now to know the lack of administrative bullshit is very appealing.

"I mean, even here in Shreveport, with you fully

funding the farm, you still have to convince people to get on board and do paperwork and have inspections. In Cara, we can do whatever we want. Right?" she asks.

I nod. "More or less." Again, I'm tactful and like to get people on board with ideas and plans, but yes, I can get things done without forms and meetings and approvals.

"Great." She gives me a smile full of relief. "So that's the plan. We get married for one year. The goals are you on the throne and a fully functioning farm where we can measure outcomes for the village."

"What happens after a year?" Jonah asks.

I look up to find him frowning in the rearview mirror.

Abigail shrugs. "We divorce. Or annul it. Or Torin just cancels it or whatever. He'll be king then. He won't need a queen." She looks over at me with a sweet, genuine smile. "Just because his grandfather thinks he does, doesn't mean it's true. But we'll do what needs to be done to get him on that throne. Then he can blame our breakup on the crazy American who never quite assimilated." Her smile fades and she looks down at our hands as she says, "They'll probably think I'm weird and stuck up anyway. I won't be making public appearances or be out amongst the people, so they won't miss me when I'm gone. They might even be glad I leave."

I frown. This is her biggest vulnerability, this idea that being introverted and having social anxiety makes her strange or wrong. I will *not* put her into positions that will make her anxious or uncomfortable, but I also won't let people think she's anything but intelligent and passionate and amazing.

"Abigail." I squeeze her hand and she looks up at me. "*No one* is going to think you're weird. They're going to be enchanted and intrigued."

She gives me a little smile. "Well, *that's* not necessary."

"They might not be able to help it." I lift her hand to my lips and kiss her knuckles. "I know I couldn't."

She rolls her eyes, but I see her smile grow. "*Anyway*," she says. "This is a specific plan with a clear timeline and goals. No need to get worked up over anything else. We just need to focus on the throne and the farm."

I agree that there are some specific goals to be attained here, but I don't like the idea that it's *all* about business. I'm very into the idea of having Abigail as my wife. In every way.

And I really don't like the timeline. A year seems like nothing. I'm ready to make this a long-term thing. Very long-term. But she keeps mentioning a year. And hell, the fact that Abigail is considering this at all is awesome. If my gorgeous scientist needs specific parameters, I can go along with it. For now.

If that's the only way to have her, then of course I'll agree.

But surely, she'll fall in love with me in a *year*.

Right?

Or maybe, if not, then yeah, letting her go might be the right thing to do.

I'm frowning down at our entwined fingers when she says, "And we'll just elope before we leave the US."

My head comes up as Linnea turns in her seat again.

"You're not going to have the wedding in Cara?" Linnea asks, clearly not a fan of that idea.

Abigail shakes her head and looks at me. "I'm sure it won't shock you to know that the idea of standing up in front of a huge crowd of people all staring at me like that is the *last* thing that sounds good to me. But I also don't want to tell a bunch of lies."

I lift a brow. "Lies?"

"Yes. I don't think we should stand up in front of family and friends and your entire country, in a *church*, and say that we love each other and vow to stay together for the rest of our lives when we know it's only going to be a year," she says. She takes a breath and sits straighter. "So no talking about love or forever or hearts or anything like that. The ceremony can be at the courthouse, and we can stick with *do you take this man to be your husband?* That's a yes or no question. No need to involve emotions."

"But—"

"No." She pins me with a serious look. "Words can be misconstrued. Words mean different things to different people. They can be confusing, and they can...get complicated. Let's just stick with facts. And actions. We'll *do* the things we need to do to get you on the throne and to get crops growing in Cara. No need to add a bunch of emotional extras that could muddle things. Let's keep things pragmatic. This is a *practical* solution."

I watch her as I take all of that in.

She's...not wrong.

This *is* a practical solution.

Emotions *can be* confusing and complicated.

And I agree that actions can be quite effective in proving what's important.

The next second, her eyes widen. "Oh! And we don't have to lie about how we met or any of that. We can share our real story. That we met at my sister's wedding, then we reunited at another sister's wedding, and we got to know each other via texting and calls after that."

I'm just watching her process all of this in real time. It seems that all of this is just occurring to her now.

"Abigail—" I start.

"Oh! *And*," she says, reaching out to grip my forearm.

I'm falling more in love with her just watching her speak. She might struggle with presenting plans and concepts to certain groups of people, but when she gets going with *me*, her words and enthusiasm just tumble out. Back at the farm site, behind the wall from the main area, she forgot there was a crowd, she forgot she had to make a speech, she just launched into a whole monologue about Cara's fishing economy and attrition rates.

"You're the *prince*," she says. "You need to just start building the farms when we get there, okay? Don't ask the king's permission. Don't spend time talking about it. Just tell people to start doing it. They have to listen to you. *Then* we'll be able to *show* him our plans." She squeezes my arm. "He'll see that you're committed and ready to be in charge. Don't wait for the title. Just be the king you want to be right now."

I'm staring at her. She's so fucking gorgeous when she's wound up like this and right now, she's wound up over *me*.

I want her so much.

I think about what she told me about her past. The times when she gave her presentations and projects her best even when she knew the people out in the audience were judging her and wanting her to fail. I think about how she said that the best way to shut them up was to just *do* the thing and prove them wrong. I think about the fact that she's convinced the people of Cara are going to think she's weird, but she's willing to come and build these farms anyway.

I feel a surge of adrenaline. I need to just *do* the things my grandfather won't listen to me talk about. She's right. I don't need the title of king to do important things.

And do I want to *marry* this woman? Fuck yes.

"So, you're proposing to me then? Is that right, Abigail?" I finally manage, my voice rough.

She gives me a little grin, her hand still on my arm. "I guess I am."

I reach up and cup her face even as I shake my head. "Of course, you got there on your own."

There's a little wrinkle between her brows. "What do you mean?"

"It means that I was going to propose to *you* again. After you saw how the farm came together. I was going to do whatever it took to show you that you should be Cara's princess, but you, my gorgeous genius, got there on your own."

Her eyes widen on the word 'princess' and I grin. *She* proposed to *me*, but me using the word 'princess' surprises her?

"You...were?" she asks.

"I was." I meet her gaze directly.

"And that means I'll be the pri..." She presses her lips together and swallows. Then she swallows again.

"The princess thing is just now sinking in?" I ask, reading her.

She nods. "That's crazy, I know. I was thinking about you being the king and I'd told myself I won't be the *queen*..." She takes a breath. "But you calling me...that... suddenly made me realize that I will be...*that*. At least for a little while. Won't I?"

I press my thumb into the tip of her chin. "You were thinking about me. About helping me. And about making the farms happen." I lean in, putting my nose against hers. "And maybe about how you didn't want me to marry anyone else."

She nods. "Yeah," she admits quietly. "You shouldn't *have* to get married if you don't want to. This way it's only temporary."

I don't want it to be temporary. But I do love that she doesn't want me to marry anyone else.

"But you can't even say the word princess out loud?"

She shakes her head.

"Abigail, you're going to have to say the word."

She wets her lips. "I don't know."

"Yes." I nod. "You're going to have to."

"Is this a bad idea?" she asks softly.

"This is the best fucking idea either of us has ever had," I tell her. "And you're a genius, so that's saying something."

"I'm probably going to be bad at it."

God, I'm seriously in love with this woman. "No, you're not," I tell her firmly. "And when it comes to speeches and stuff...I've got you. Just like at Ami's wedding. Just like today."

"Okay," she finally says. Though she doesn't sound fully convinced.

"Okay," I agree with a nod.

"*Okay?*" Jonah asks from the front seat.

I meet his eyes and nod. "Yes. Okay. This is great. Abigail is right about all of it."

He rolls his eyes.

But just then he pulls the SUV into the circular drive in front of the Magnolia Hotel. The bellmen come forward and Jonah opens his door to get out to hand over Abigail's suitcase.

"Jonah," I say.

"Yes?"

"Have them take her things to my room."

He just lifts a brow.

I look back at Abigail. "It's only *practical* to have my fiancée staying in my room with me, isn't it?"

She sucks in a little breath. But then she nods. "Yes. That seems...rational."

"Oh, boy," Linnea mutters as she lets herself out of the car.

I'm grinning as I get out and go around to help Abigail out. When I open the door, she's just sitting there, staring at the back of the seat in front of her.

"You ready?"

"To go up to your room?"

"Up to *our* room," I say. "Unless you want your own room. I will let you have your space." I don't want her to have space, but I don't want to push too hard. At least, right now.

She looks at me for a long moment. Then shakes her head. "I don't want my own space."

I blow out a relieved breath. "Good. Let's go, princess." I hold out my hand.

She hesitates for just a second. "We're going to start using that nickname, huh?"

"Yes. We are." I grin.

"And if I come upstairs with you, you're going to make me say the P word too, aren't you?"

I give a surprised huff of laughter. "Yes, I am. A couple of them."

She sucks in a little breath, her eyes widening. Then she takes my hand. But doesn't say a word.

I grin. There will be time for words. Lots and lots of words.

I tug her out of the SUV and tuck her tightly against my side.

As the doormen swing the big glass doors open and I sweep her across the marble-floored lobby to the gold elevators and press the button for the penthouse, I definitely feel like a fucking king.

CHAPTER 19
ABIGAIL

So, we're engaged.

Torin isn't going to marry anyone else.

At least, not for a year.

He's going to become king.

I'm going to get my farm.

And this all feels really, really good.

And I'm wondering if being incredibly turned-on can make people make terrible decisions.

Like proposing to a prince.

The door to the penthouse shuts softly behind Torin. My suitcase sits just inside the door, having already been brought up. The view from here is beautiful. Hell, even the drapes around the windows showing off the view are beautiful.

But I can't focus on anything except the man who is stalking toward me.

"Did you just fly back from Cara today?" I ask as the thought occurs to me.

The penthouse looks lived in. It's neat and tidy, I assume because of the maid service, but there are folders and papers on the desk, two other pairs of shoes near the door, and up a step and through open French doors I can see a suit jacket lying on the bed.

"No. I've been here working on the farm," he says, stopping right in front of me.

"For how long?" It would be difficult to put this all together long-distance.

"Since the wedding."

My eyes widen. "You've been here for the past two weeks?"

"Sixteen days. That's how long it's been since I last saw you."

My breath catches. This man is…so much. He's over-the-top. Everything feels extreme with him. He doesn't just dance, he waltzes. In the center of the room. He doesn't just go for a walk when he's frustrated. He gets on a private jet and spends a week in another country. He doesn't just wake up each day and go to work. He wakes up in a *palace* and his job is *running a country*. Or, at least, it will be.

Clearly, he's willing to go to any length to make things happen his way.

That should be a red flag to someone like me. Someone who doesn't like a lot of attention. Who prefers quiet and alone-time and to be behind-the-scenes.

But I step closer to him.

"Thank you."

He puffs out a breath that's part laugh and part sigh.

"Abigail, you need to know that I had no intention of just letting you go." He shakes his head. "Of just taking your 'no' at face value. Not without a fight." He reaches up and cups my face. "I couldn't leave you alone that easily."

My heart rate kicks up even faster, but it's not out of fear. This guy is intense. And typically, I don't like that. If someone had told me he was this intense I would have said that he was absolutely not my type.

But...

I love that he's here.

I've never been pursued. I've never been *wanted* like this.

I've had people impressed with my work. Lauren and Mason came to recruit me, in person, when I was a junior in college. That felt pretty great.

And it was a tenth of what I'm feeling from Torin.

Guys don't ask me out more than once. They don't even ask me to dance more than once. I'm pretty good at saying no.

Except to this guy apparently.

I have this feeling he's never going to let my answer just be 'no'. He's going to make me truly think about it, explain it *face to face* rather than in a text, and really mean it.

I am happy in my little bubble in the middle of Nebraska. When I can just be in the fields or inside the greenhouses, I'm happy. It's easy. When I can just go home, and read, and not try to figure other people out, I'm happy. Because it's easy. When I can just socialize with people like Peyton and Riley and their husbands, which is honestly more of a spectator sport, it's easy.

Even my own flirting with Torin has been easy and comfortable because it's mostly been via text. And most of the texts haven't even required that many words.

But now there is a big, used-to-getting-his-way prince

staring down at me with an expression that is a mix of determination, and heat.

I have a feeling things are about to get less easy.

His thumb drags over my cheek. "*Fuck*, I've missed you."

That makes heat swirl through me. I've honestly never had anyone try this hard to get close to me. No one's ever cared this much. I swallow.

"I need you, Abigail." His expression is still full of what almost looks like respect and, if I'm not mistaken, wonder.

His words make my heart flip. "You...do?" Need is different from want. It seems deeper. More primal.

"Cara needs you," he says with a nod. "You are completely right when you say that your farms can change so many things for us. But I need so much more from you."

I stare at him for a few beats, his words sinking in slowly.

He takes a tiny step forward, fully moving into my personal space. He's looking at me with an unreadable expression, his thumb still moving over my face.

I wet my lips. God, his hand feels so good. It's big, hot, a little rough...real.

Just like that my mouth is dry, my heart is pounding, my palms are tingling, my thighs clench. And I look past him to the door.

His fingers grasp my chin and move my face until I'm looking up at him. "Oh, no. You're not walking out that door. You're not walking away from me. Not again."

My breath catches in my chest. A shiver goes through me. But it's not a bad shiver. That's a shiver of desire.

This man wants me.

And I'm intelligent enough to know that all of the things I'm feeling—the adrenaline pumping, the mind whirling, the electrical pulses along my nerve endings—are from wanting him too.

They just feel like all of the fight or flight reactions I've had to bad, uncomfortable situations over the years and my primal brain is telling me to run.

"You'll *make* me stay here?" I ask. My voice is breathless.

"I'll make you *want* to stay here," he promises.

God, that confidence.

I press my lips together. I know he won't force me. If I pull back and tell him I want to leave, he'll let me. I know he won't give up. But he'll give me space. He said so in the SUV.

But I don't want space.

I really don't.

"I need to brush my teeth first," I say.

He blinks. Then his brow wrinkles. Then he smiles. "I'll get your bag."

He pivots and strides toward my suitcase. He carries it into the bedroom and tosses it on the bed. Then he steps out into the living room area. "Hurry up," he says.

I grin, all of my nerves melting away. "I will."

I grab my toiletry bag out of my suitcase and duck into the en suite bathroom.

It's enormous. And gorgeous. It's all marble and gold accents and there's a deep tub that would be perfect for soaking with a good book.

But there's a hot prince outside the door—who I'm *engaged to*—and I am startled to realize that I'd rather be with him than in that tub with a book. Wow. Now *that* is something.

Don't worry, Abigail, we'll fit.

I shiver as I remember his text after I told him we

wouldn't both fit in my bathtub in Sapphire Falls. I would definitely be willing to try *this* tub out with him though.

I toss my gum into the trashcan, apply toothpaste to my brush, and scrub my teeth quickly but thoroughly as I imagine Torin and me in that tub.

Then I glance out at the bed. The huge, king-sized bed with the thick white duvet.

Then I think about the sofa out in the living room area. And the desk. And the dining table.

There are lots of places that I'd be willing to try out with Torin.

I rinse my mouth and my brush, then set my brush next to the blue one that is clearly Torin's. Huh. Our toothbrushes are already next to each other.

I like that. A lot.

"Okay, how are you going to make me want to stay here?" I ask as I step down into the living room. I have some ideas about how I hope he does it, but I'd really like to see what he's got in mind.

His smile grows as he approaches. He stops when he's nearly standing on the toes of my boots. He reaches up, grips my ponytail in his hand, and tips my head back. "I'm so glad you asked that." Then he kisses me.

Finally.

His lips touch mine softly. Just for a second. Like he's giving me a chance to adjust. Not pull back, not say stop, not run. Just adjust. Prepare.

And then he *kisses* me.

His hand tightens around my ponytail. His other drops to my hip, his fingers curling into the side of my ass.

I grip his shirt on both sides, going on tiptoe to get closer, reveling in the heat that courses through me.

I do the opposite of what I usually do with intense emotions. Instead of pulling back and balling up inside of myself, I feel like I'm opening up, expanding, and wallowing. I want more of this. I want to draw him closer. I want to give him more area to touch and be against.

He's still a prince. He'll be a *king* someday. I've only got him for a year.

But right now, right here, in this moment, he's just Torin. Just the guy I have a huge crush on. The guy I've been flirting with via text. The guy who can heat me up with just a few words.

I want as much of him as I can have for as long as I have him.

He drags his mouth over my jaw and tips my head back so he can kiss down my neck and to the front of my throat. His beard rubs over my skin and I feel the friction between my legs. He sucks softly at the base of my throat, then pulls in a deep breath. "Your scent is imprinted in my brain. Anything lavender makes me hard. But I still seek it out."

I suck in a quick breath.

He lifts his head. His eyes are dark. "I've needed to taste you for two *years*, Abigail."

The roughness and need in his voice make my pussy clench.

"Yes," I say quietly. "Please."

He growls softly as he takes my mouth again. As he kisses me, he turns me and walks me back, until my butt hits the desk. His hands go to my waist, and he lifts me up, setting me on top.

I pull back, breathing hard. "Will this hold me?"

He leans in, his lips brushing mine. "If it doesn't, I'll buy them a new one." He kisses me deeply, then says, "But I want to make you come all over these plans and sketches for that farm right here in the spot where I've been sitting for two weeks, thinking and dreaming about you."

I actually wiggle as desire hits me. Why is that so dirty and delicious? That farm is good and noble, but I want this man to do wicked things to me on top of the plans? But looking up into his heated stare, looking at the mouth that has already made me needy and wet, and thinking about the things he's already made me feel...yes, I do want that. It's all already melded together in one I-can't-believe-this-is-real fantasy come true. Why not add some filthy sex with the only man who has ever made me actually understand lust?

I moan, and I kiss him this time, his face in my hands. My tongue strokes over his lips, and his hand goes to my hip and squeezes as he groans, opening for me.

When he lifts his head, he stares down at me. "I can't believe I've only ever kissed you once before. This feels like..."

I frown. "Like what?"

He shakes his head as if he can't believe what he's about to say. "It feels like I've only ever kissed you. I don't remember kissing anyone else ever."

My heart does a little stutter-beat, but I laugh softly, running my hands down the sides of his neck to his shoulders. "You don't have to say stuff like that. I'm not leaving this time."

He frowns and suddenly grips my chin, making me look into his eyes as he says, "You *are* going to get used to someone telling you what he's thinking and feeling about you, because he's fucking fascinated and in awe and can't get enough of you. I know people have used words to belittle you, and make you doubt yourself, but the only time *my* words will be used to put you in your place is when

I say *get on your hands and knees* or *spread your legs wider* or *kneel*."

My breathing is ragged, and my whole body feels like it's melting, but because of his words I feel a sudden jolt of boldness, and I ask, "Will I kneel for you while you're still the prince or does that wait until you're the king?"

CHAPTER 20

TORIN

She's sassing me.

Quiet, bottled-up, genius scientist Abigail Landry is *sassing* me. About kneeling.

And that makes me so fucking hot.

I put my mouth against hers. "There's no way we're waiting until I'm king for you to be on your knees taking my cock in this pretty mouth, Abigail."

She sucks in a breath and says quietly, "Good."

Too quietly.

I tip her head back by tugging on her ponytail. She looks up at me. "Tell me what you're thinking."

"I—" She shakes her head and swallows hard.

At this moment I love that words are difficult for her, because hearing them will be so much sweeter.

"I'm obsessed with you, Abigail, and I'm going to need

words back. My huge...ego...wants to know everything you're thinking and feeling and needing from me."

"I'm an *action* girl, not a words girl," she says. She tries to lean in to kiss me.

But my hand on her hair won't let her.

"Abigail." I make my tone low and firm, tipping her head back even further and leaning in. "If you don't tell me how much you want my tongue and fingers and cock, I can't give them to you. I need to hear you."

"Oh God," she breathes out. "I, um...Torin, will you please..." Then her brow furrows. "I don't know how to say it."

"Say, 'Torin, will you please eat my pussy the way you dreamed of last night'." I brush my lips over hers. "That will do it."

She takes a shaky breath.

I lift my head to look into her eyes as a thought occurs to me. "Have you ever said the word 'pussy' out loud to another human?"

She shakes her head, though it can't move much with the way I'm holding her hair.

Need like I've never felt knifes me in the gut. Fuck. This is going to be so damned good.

I know even what she's shared with me about her past and her passions is more than she shares with most, and that's got my heart in a chokehold.

But right now, I need words she's never given anyone else.

"This mouth, that has said incredible, innovative, passionate things about work that I'm fucking fascinated by is now going to say dirty, hot as fuck things to *me*, and only me," I tell her.

She looks at me like she still doesn't know what to do.

My mouth ticks up at one corner. "I will give a thousand dollars to the charity of your choice to hear this sweet mouth say *please lick my pussy, Torin.*"

Finally, she gives a soft snort of laughter. "Oh my God."

"You can say that too, *while* I've got my tongue inside you. Right now, say the first words I need, Abigail."

She takes a deep breath and starts to drop her eyes.

"Oh, no, princess, you look at me when you ask for orgasms."

Her cheeks are flushed and she's breathing hard, but finally she says, "Please put your mouth on me, Torin."

I grin. Okay, we'll play. We'll work up to this. I've got all the time in the world.

I actually don't. I've got one year, apparently. But that doesn't start until she says, 'I do'. And I'll take all the time I need to get Abigail Landry talking dirty to me.

I lean in and kiss her again. I make it deep and hot, but it's slow and my hands don't move from her hair or her back.

God, she tastes amazing.

Finally, I let her go. "There. My mouth on you."

"More," she says, breathlessly.

"Where?"

"All over."

I lean in, putting my nose against the base of her throat. I breathe in her scent again, then drag my mouth up her neck to her ear. "Abigail, I'm not going to make you come until you say what I want to hear."

Do I love words? Do I love to know exactly where I stand with people? Do I love to know when I'm making people happy and especially when I'm doing something no one else has done? Yes, yes, I do.

But this? With this woman? Right now?

Oh, fuck yes. More than I've ever needed those things before.

She's going to talk to me. And she's going to love it.

I let go of her. She makes a soft sound of protest that I love, but I keep my eyes on hers as I unbutton my shirt, shrug out of it, and toss it to the side.

Her eyes on me make my skin tingle and burn and my cock ache. She takes in every detail, and I want *her* hands and mouth on me so fucking bad I'll gladly beg. I know *all* the words.

"You have tattoos," she says, her gaze on the ink that starts on my left pec and continues over my shoulder, upper bicep and upper back as well as the tattoo on my right rib cage.

"I do." I move in closer.

Her hands run over the images. Holy fuck I love her hands on my bare skin.

I press her left hand against my right ribs. "This one symbolizes the way Cara was founded." It's a trident speared through a shamrock and a daisy, binding them together. "The shamrock for Ireland and the daisy is the national flower of Denmark," I tell her.

I drag her right hand up to the tattoo that's over my heart. "This is a Celtic knot. Specifically, a Dara knot. A traditional Irish symbol that means anchoring or strength. The knot symbolizes the magnificent root system that holds up majestic, heavy oak trees."

She's listening raptly and I would bet good money that she'll be looking all of this up later. The idea of Abigail learning more about Irish tradition, and maybe even researching more about Cara's history, is almost as hot as the idea of her saying words like *pussy* and *fuck me* and I know I'm at risk of getting in very far over my head with this woman.

"This—" I move her hand over the ink that wraps around my upper arm. "—is another traditional Celtic knot, called the sailor's knot, in memory of how my great-great-great grand-father went from sailor to king in one act of selflessness."

She squeezes my bicep and runs her hand over my skin, up to my shoulder. "Turn."

I shift slightly between her knees so she can see the ink on my back. It comes down from my shoulder, across my shoulder blade, to the top of my ribs.

Abigail strokes her hand over it. "This is the shape of Cara."

I look at her quickly. "How do you know that?"

She smiles up at me. "I Googled you."

The outline is, indeed, of the island. But the full picture is made of a shamrock, a daisy, and wings.

"Wings?" she asks, tracing her fingertip over them.

"I got it after I left Cara and came to the US."

"Ah. Your wings," she says. "Flying away from home but taking your history with you." She looks up at me. "Escaping?"

I nod. "At the time."

"What about now?"

"I don't have wings anymore. But at least I have a private plane."

She smiles a small smile as she nods. She knows I'm trying to make light of it, but she senses the seriousness of it all.

Her gaze drops to the tattoo again. "I like that your tattoos all mean something. Mine is just a stupid attempt to fit in. I knew even at the time that it wouldn't work."

"You have a tattoo?" I turn back to her. I have to admit I wasn't expecting that.

"I do."

"What is it?"

"A honeybee."

I study her eyes. "And that doesn't mean anything?"

She lifts a shoulder. "It's tiny. And I was with these girls...they were getting butterflies and flowers and one got the word *believe* on her wrist." She rolls her eyes. "I was sitting in the tattoo parlor, knowing it was so stupid for *any* of us to be there. The tattoos meant nothing really and we were all putting something permanent on our bodies. But I was..." She stops and takes a breath. "I was trying to fit in. I was usually fine with *not* fitting, but every once in a while I'd have a weak moment and do something that I thought would make me more like them, more normal. Like the time I had sex."

I feel my eyes widen, but I don't say anything.

"So I drank two wine coolers and said yes to the tattoo," she goes on. "But when we got there, I just couldn't do any random flower or butterfly and if I was going to do words, I would have done a quote or something meaningful, you know? So I just picked a honeybee."

I want her even more in that moment. "God, I hope you are well over wanting to be normal," I tell her. "Because you're just not, Abigail. I've met hundreds of normal people in my life, and I don't remember a single one of them. But you? I danced with you *once* and couldn't forget you. You will never be normal. And that's such a great thing. For me. For my country. For the world."

She is staring at me and for a moment I think she might cry.

So I say, "We need bees for plants and flowers to

survive. It makes sense to me that *you* would pick a bee even subconsciously. Maybe some people don't think they're as pretty as butterflies, but they are vital."

"Honeybees pollinate around eighty percent of all flowering plants, including one hundred and thirty types of fruits and vegetables," she says.

Of course, she knows that.

I lean in with a grin. "So you did get a meaningful tattoo."

She nods. "I did."

"Where is the tattoo?" My gaze sweeps over her legs. I've seen her arms and wrists and hands. I've seen her bare legs and ankles and feet in photos that I've studied like I'm going to be tested on the composition of the entire picture. No honeybee tattoo.

When I meet her eyes again, she gives me a sly little smile that shoots straight to my cock.

"I guess you'll have to try to find it."

Oh. Fuck. Yes.

"You're right," I say, my voice low and gruff. I reach behind her and pull the tie on her dress loose. "There's not going to be an inch of you I won't know *very* soon."

Her breath catches as I take hold of the fabric on either side of her waist, tugging. She leans onto one buttock, letting me pull the skirt up, then shifts to the other side, allowing me to hike the rest of the skirt up. I meet her eyes, give her a grin, then sweep the dress over her head.

Then she's sitting on the desk in only a tiny white bra, simple white silk panties, and the pink boots I sent her.

And I can barely breathe.

"You're fucking gorgeous, princess," I rasp.

"Should I take the boots off?" she asks.

"Absolutely not."

She moans as I run my hand down her side, over the swell of her breast, the dip in her waist, the curve of her hip, and down the outside of her thigh.

I wrap my hand around that thigh and pull, widening the space between her legs and stepping closer. "You okay?" I ask.

She nods.

"Abigail."

She licks her lips, clearly understanding what I want.

"Yes. I'm…great," she says.

"Good girl," I tell her. "Love your words. And I want to be *sure*."

I press against the center of her chest, laying her back on the papers behind her on the desktop. I run my hand up her inner thigh. "Because I want to talk about your sweet pussy. And how I've thought about you while I've had my fist around my cock *every* night since Ami's wedding. I want to tell you how much I want to see this gorgeous, grumpy farmer spread out and dripping wet and wild and begging me to fuck her until she screams my name."

"Oh." It's kind of a whisper, kind of a moan, kind of a gasp.

I nod. "I get kind of graphic." Then I lean over and say, "You've been warned," just before I press a kiss to the strip of bare skin on her stomach just above her panties.

Her nipples are hard against the front of her bra, and I can see the exact size and shape of her sweet tits.

I run my hand over her bare stomach. "You like results, right?"

She nods.

"I promise you amazing results if you talk to me this whole time."

"Okay."

"Okay. Let's start with this." I run my hand up and down from the waistband of her panties up between her breasts. I just stroke the silky soft skin and absorb her heat. "How many guys have you been with?"

"Why?" she asks.

Because she said *the time I had sex* earlier when talking about getting the one tattoo she had and that's been niggling at me. And because I want to know. "Because I need to know what you can handle. I don't know if you're ready for how much I want you. It's been a long time for me." And because the things I want to do to this woman are not gentle and sweet.

She frowns. "You've been with other women, right?"

"Well, yes. In the past. But not since I've been...back to Cara."

Her eyes get huge. I chuckle.

"The prince thing has taken up some time." A lot of fucking, frustrating time that hasn't left me in the mood to *entertain*. Plus fucking around on the island with my people just didn't feel right. I could have found women in Louisiana on my visits, and I think I assumed I would, but I just haven't. Not since I met her. I ask again, "How many men have there been?"

I want to kill them all. With my bare hands. Slowly.

She seems still preoccupied by what I shared about my own sex life. "None," she says. "I mean, one. Once. A while ago. Two years. No, wait, three."

My hand stops moving on her stomach. "One?" I repeat. "Only one, ever?"

She presses her lips together and nods.

"Were you...in love with him? High school sweetheart?" If there was someone Abigail had given her heart to, I still wanted to kill him, but that seems more in character. She definitely doesn't seem the type to have a string of flings.

"No. I didn't date in high school. It was just some guy in college. One night. I met him at a party I didn't want to be at, had a couple of shots I didn't want to drink, told him I was a freshman with an undeclared major, and I was so happy to get out from under my controlling parents' thumbs and have some fun."

I just watch her gorgeous face. "You weren't a freshman?"

"I was a freshman in college when I was fifteen. Sex with a nineteen-year-old college guy would have been gross. And illegal," she says. "The guy was a freshman, and I'd just started grad school. We were both nineteen though."

I take a breath. She is *so* not normal, in so many ways, and I love every single one of them. "Was this another night out with the girls like the tattoo?"

She nods. "Trying to be a regular college girl."

"And you were a virgin."

"Yep."

"And it was just that one time with that one guy?"

She lifts a shoulder. "People don't really try to get close to me," she says simply. "Especially this close."

I stare at her. I imagine the look on my face is the same expression scientists wear when they first look at a previously undiscovered galaxy through one of those incredible new high-powered telescopes—the beauty has always been there, but no one has ever *really* seen it before. And they get to be the first. And *they* truly understand how amazing and special it is.

"Idiots," I say simply, because there's no real way to express how stupid I find every other man who's ever met

Abigail. And how fucking glad I am that they're all imbeciles.

She smiles. Then it grows into a grin that even lights her eyes. Then she says, "You know what? Sometimes words are good."

And...fuck. I'm done.

"Words are really good, *princess*," I say. That word, in particular, is very, very good. And then I move my hand up and down her body again, this time brushing over one breast, the hard nipple imprinting into my palm. "And I'll agree that *actions* can be really fucking good too."

"Torin?" she asks, my name husky.

"Yeah?"

"Can you say something completely filthy to me?" she asks. Then adds, "Please?"

My entire body hardens. "I absolutely fucking can." I lean in and kiss her belly again. "And then I can *do* some completely filthy things to you."

"Oh, *yes*," she says.

And yeah, words are really damned good.

I stand and hook my fingers in the top of her panties. "Bra off," I tell her.

She reaches back and unhooks her bra, tossing it to the floor as I pull her panties down her long, smooth legs, loving that I have to work them over the boots.

I look up and I freeze for a second.

Her breasts are perfect. I like breasts in general, to be honest, but these are the ones I've been waiting my whole life for. "Fuck, Abigail."

Her panties are wet, and I lift them to my nose, my eyes on hers as I take a deep breath. Fuck, even her pussy smells like lavender. And Abigail. It's intoxicating.

Her legs are bent, and she squeezes her thighs together.

"Spread your legs," I tell her. I want to hear her words, but I also want to see how she responds to *my* words.

She swallows and does it, straightening one leg and letting the other knee fall to the side.

"So fucking beautiful."

Her skin is golden from the sun, and faint lines show where the straps of her tank tops and the edge of her shorts fall.

I run my hand up the inside of one thigh. My mouth is watering for a taste of her.

She wants filthy? I can so do that.

"Did the idiot college boy make you come?" I ask as I lean over her, kissing her, then dragging my mouth and beard down her throat to one breast.

She shakes her head. I cover her nipple and lick, then suck lightly. "What? I can't hear you."

"No. He didn't."

"Do you make yourself come?" I run my hand down her body, over her belly to her mound where I cup her. "Do you give this sweet pussy that relief at least?"

She nods, but remembers to also say, "Yes."

"Good," I tell her, sucking on her nipple harder.

She arches closer, her hand going to the back of my head. I press the heel of my hand against her clit.

"Do you use your fingers? Or a vibrator?"

I rock my hand over her clit and suck on her nipple again.

"Oh God," she pants. "Um...both. Vibrator mostly. It's faster."

I smile against her breast. "You like it fast?"

"I just...do it for relief."

"How often?"

She pauses, and I lift my head. I run my finger along her

pussy, feeling how hot and wet she is. But I just glide the pad of my fingers over her bare, sensitive flesh. "How often, Abigail? How greedy is this pretty pussy?"

"Um...a lot since I met you."

Her cheeks are flushed as she says it and she's looking at my chin, not my eyes.

I dip my finger into her, just barely. God, she's wet. And then lift my finger to her lips. I paint her bottom lip, then slip my finger into my mouth, sucking. "Fuck, you taste good. I love that I do this to you."

Her tongue darts out, licking over her lip. Maybe instinct, maybe curiosity, maybe she knew I was going to make her do it. Either way, she tastes herself. I wish I'd changed into more comfortable pants before I started this. My cock is almost painful against my zipper right now.

"Don't ever be shy or embarrassed about telling me what you feel and like and need," I tell her. "If I make you hot and wet and needy, and you get yourself off every fucking day thinking about me, all that's going to make me think is how can I make you need that vibrator *twice* a day."

She lets out a long shaky breath. "Torin."

She's not asking me for anything. She's not protesting. She just needed to say my name and I fucking love it.

"And the next time you use it, you can imagine it's my fingers and tongue, just like this." I run my finger down along her soft, wet lips again, then slide inside. "You're so fucking tight. Do you know how much I love that you haven't been with anyone else in so long? That the first cock to stretch you in *years* will be mine?" I ask as I pump my finger in and out. Her pussy grabs onto me, and the heat and slickness make my cock throb.

"Torin!" She grabs onto my wrist, but she's holding me in place.

As if I'd be *able* to pull away.

"Did the dumbass dare to put his mouth down here?" I ask her.

She shakes her head. "God, no. It was missionary, in the dark, didn't even last ten minutes."

I'd figured. But that was all excellent to hear.

"I'm really glad he didn't take a taste of *my* pussy," I tell her. I slide a second finger into her, slower, stretching her as I go. "No one else deserves to know how sweet it is, how wet you get, how you smell and taste and feel."

She just gasps and her fingers tighten around my wrist.

"Come for me, Abigail," I tell her. I pump in and out, pressing and circling her clit with my thumb. I want her to come so badly, *I'm* aching with it.

"Torin, God, that feels so good. I...it never feels like this."

Fuck, I love her words. "No one will ever take care of you like I will," I tell her, meaning that with everything I've got. "Give me your first orgasm like this. Then I need you to come on my tongue."

She lifts her hips closer to my hand. "I'm so close."

"What do you need?" I suck on a nipple, thrusting my fingers deep, curling them against her G-spot.

"You...just you...don't stop."

"No way I'm stopping, princess."

"Keep talking to me," she says, practically panting.

"Now you like the talking?" I ask, grinning against her breast.

"So much."

"Is your vibrator just a clit stimulator or does it stretch you out?" I move my fingers faster.

"Just...Oh! Um..." She arches her neck and I lean over,

and kiss then suck at the base. "It's just a stimulator. Small."

"Tell me where you put it."

"On my..."

I brace for hearing the word clit from her because it's going to make my cock ache.

"Tell me, Abigail," I say nipping at her nipple.

"On my clit."

Fuuuck.

"I'm buying you a vibrator. A long, thick one that you're going to fuck yourself with when I'm not with you. I'm going to pick it out myself so I know exactly how it looks and can picture it sliding in and out of this gorgeous pussy," I tell her, sucking on her nipple again, then continuing down her stomach. "And maybe we'll start texting something other than our shoes and feet."

She gasps. "I can't send you those kinds of photos!"

I curl my fingers just right and thrust hard. "Yes, you can."

"Torin!" she cries.

And then I feel her tighten around me and come.

It is the most beautiful thing I've ever seen. Her body bows, her chest, throat, and cheeks flush, and my hand is coated in sweet stickiness.

I immediately move to the end of the table, spreading her thighs, and lean in to lick.

"Torin!" Her cry is much louder this time, and she tries to squeeze her legs shut.

I grasp both thighs and press them toward her chest. I give her ass a little slap and look at her. "*Mine,*" I tell her. "You're going to come again. On my tongue this time, Abigail."

She sucks in a breath and then her cheeks get even

pinker, but she says, "Aren't I supposed to say something before you do that?"

I freeze.

And I think I fall a little bit more in love with her.

I nod slowly. "Yes. Yes, you are."

She wets her lips, takes a deep breath, and opens her mouth, but her eyes shift to my chin.

I pinch her thigh. "Eyes on me."

Her big blue eyes latch onto mine and she says, "Torin, will you please eat my pussy the way you dreamed of last night?"

Yep. Totally. In. Love.

I growl.

I might be a someday king, but this woman can definitely bring me to my knees.

CHAPTER 21
TORIN

I kneel and start licking, sucking, nipping, and fucking her with my tongue until she's writhing in my hands, gasping and crying out a combination of, "Oh God!" and "Torin!" and "Yes!" and "More!"

It only takes a few minutes for her to come again and *God* I've never needed a woman like this before.

I swiftly stand and lean over to press my lips to hers. She grasps my face with her hands and kisses me back eagerly, her tongue stroking along mine. It's dirty and amazing and I still need more.

"More," she says against my lips.

I grin. "You're getting good with the words."

"Turns out I really like the results," she says.

I coast my hand down her side. "Told you."

She laughs lightly. Then says, "More. Please."

I reach between us and undo my jeans, pushing them out of the way.

She pushes me back so she can prop up. "I want to see you."

My cock pulses in my hand. I give it a squeeze and a stroke, trying to tamp down some of the urgency to rush to pound into her.

But I'm still between her spread legs and she's wet, pink, and glistening. She's ready.

She reaches out. "Can I touch you?"

"It might kill me, but fuck yes," I tell her, as I move my hand.

Her smaller one wraps around my shaft. I groan as she squeezes, then strokes the way I did, but with light pressure. Too light. I wrap my hand around hers and show her how hard to grip and stroke.

"This is even better," I tell her. I move her hand to her pussy and run her fingers through her arousal. Then I move it back to my cock, painting the wetness along my length. "Now stroke."

She does and my eyes nearly roll back in my head.

I let her move for as long as I can take it, but finally I say, "I can't hang on."

She actually scoots her ass closer to the end of the table. "Okay."

I shake my head. "So greedy."

"Yes." She meets my eyes. "Please. Fuck me, Torin."

Fuck. I scoop under her ass and bring her the rest of the way to the edge. I notch my head at her entrance.

Then freeze.

No.

No.

I squeeze my eyes shut and breathe.

"What?" she asks. "Do you want something else? Just tell me what to say."

Christ. The talking…

I open my eyes. "Condom," I say shortly. I don't have one. I haven't needed them in a long time, and getting her here was such a last-minute thing, I didn't think about getting condoms too. I just needed *her* here, at the farm site. *Fucking dammit to hell.* And there's no way she has one.

Her eyes widen. "Oh. I don't…have any."

"I haven't been with anyone in over two years and I get regular physicals from the palace physician," I say.

There's a little wrinkle between her eyebrows. "Okay."

"I'm saying, I don't have any…issues…" Dammit, this isn't hot or romantic. "If you're on birth control, we can do this without a condom. If you want to."

"I'm not on birth control," she says. "Why would I need to be?"

Right. She doesn't do this.

I blow out a breath. And step back and pull my pants up. And try very hard not to look at her naked body spread out like a feast.

I fail at that last one. I brace my hands on the desk on either side of her hips and curse. "I'm sorry. I didn't plan for this. Exactly." I've been thinking about it almost non-stop, but not really *planning* for it.

She's quiet for a moment. Then she sits up. "I want you to feel good too."

I give her a genuine smile. "I feel fucking fantastic, Abigail."

She blushes but grins. Then says, "I mean…there." Her gaze drops to my dick. That is still very prominent against the front of my jeans.

I lean in and put my mouth against hers. It will be

torture, but I want more words from her. "You mean my cock? That's throbbing for you? Harder than it's ever been because of *you*?"

She nods.

"Say the word *cock* for me, Abigail."

"Cock." She didn't even hesitate. She didn't whisper it. She's already getting more confident.

And yep, I'm aching. But it was worth it. I capture her lips in a kiss. "This mouth..." I say. "I fucking love everything about it."

"I want to help you with your hard, aching cock, Torin," she says against my lips.

My knees actually wobble a little.

I pull back. "Do you now?"

She nods.

"I can't fuck you. Not right now. But I *will* get condoms and then, I probably won't let you out of bed for days."

She grins. "Good."

God, this woman. "So what do you think you're going to do to help me right now?" I ask. I have about twenty ideas.

"Are you going to take care of it yourself?" she asks.

"Am I going to jerk off thinking about you and your sweet tits, and your tight pussy that tastes and feels like heaven? And the way you sound, and look, and taste when you come? And imagine that it's your pussy squeezing me instead of my fist?" I ask.

She takes a breath, but nods.

"Yes, I am."

"Can you do it here so I can watch?" She waits a beat and then says, "Or can I help?"

I don't even think about it for three seconds. "Anything you want, Abigail."

She reaches for my fly and pulls my cock out again. I'm

so hard it's nearly painful. She wraps her hands around me and strokes me, then she reaches between her legs, gathers some of her arousal on her fingers, and then coats my shaft the way I showed her.

I brace my hands on the desk, not sure I'll be able to stay standing for this. I let her play for a few minutes. "Talk to me, princess."

"You're just so big," she tells me, watching her hand on my cock.

I know she's not saying that just to talk. She's telling me what she's thinking. Exactly what I want.

I reach up and push her hair back from her face. "Your pussy is going to grip me so tight."

She nods. "That's going to feel so good." She moves her hand faster. "Can we do that *soon*?"

"So fucking soon." My voice is tight as I struggle to hang on.

Then she leans in and puts her mouth against my neck, stroking me faster, and says, "I want you to come for me, Torin."

Fuck.

I nudge her back. "Show me your pussy. Play with your clit," I tell her.

She spreads her legs, her fingers going to her clit, where she starts circling. I step in closer, jerking my hand over my cock, my eyes on the wet, sweet pinkness I want to bury myself in over and over, for days.

"God, Abigail, I'm never going to recover from this."

And then, of all the dirty things she's already said, that made me hot and hard, and stupidly proud, she says one word that sends me over the edge.

"Good."

I look up and she's watching me with...satisfaction and

heat and, is that possessiveness? As if *she* wants to claim me as well?

I lean in, jerk my cock three more times, and then I come, spilling over her, painting white ribbons on her stomach, mound, and inner thigh, marking her.

"*Fuck*," I groan. "My God, Abigail."

She takes a long, deep breath. Then she props herself on her elbow and looks up at me. "Wow. Talk about the royal treatment."

I just stare at her for a few seconds. Then I feel myself grinning. Then laughing. I clasp my hand around the back of her neck and bring her up off the table and against my lips. I kiss her deeply. "I like you so fucking much," I tell her.

I want to tell her that I'm falling in love with her, but words are a big deal with this woman, a big deal between us, and I don't want to freak her out. She said not to bring emotion into this. She specifically said she did *not* want to use words like love and forever. So...I won't. Right now.

"Same," she says, smiling brightly.

I tuck myself back into my pants and take in the picture she presents. She looks perfect perched there, wearing those boots, covered in my cum on top of a polished wood desk covered in plans I've drawn up to make her dream a reality. But fuck I love that her cheeks are glowing, and her eyes are bright and that she's got whisker burns from me adding to that picture of happiness and contentment.

I pick her up in my arms and head for the bathroom. I clean us both up, then carry her into the bedroom. I set her on the bed.

"I'm staying in here, with you, right?"

"Yes."

"And we could do...some more."

I lift a brow. Already? I love that she wants more.

And I fucking hate that I don't have any condoms. I could get some from Jonah. Or send someone out for some. Or run out myself.

Or I could rein all of this in, take a deep breath, and just get them when we go out for dinner.

I step close enough that our knees bump.

She looks up at me.

I reach out and brush a strand of hair back from her eyes. "There is going to be time for more. So much more. I promise you."

She runs her hand up the outside of my thigh, and I quickly move to stop it, smiling and shaking my head.

"Don't be naughty."

"You make me want to be," she says.

This woman does things to me. "You know," I tell her, walking back into the living room for my shirt. "I think this is your punishment."

Her eyebrows lift. "Punishment?"

"For the times *I* wanted more, but you walked away." Yeah, that sounds good. God, I want to give her so fucking much more right now. She looks soft and happy and open.

A smile teases her lips. "That really bothered you."

"It really did," I agree.

"Okay," she agrees. "But, after this we're even."

God, I really do like her.

"We'll get married tomorrow. At the courthouse. Before we fly to Cara," I say, to test her reaction.

She nods. "Okay."

That's it. No surprise, no argument, no negotiation.

"Okay. I'll get it set up."

She gives me a little smirk. "You can do that? Just set it up? Last minute?"

I turn to face her fully, buttoning my last button. "I can."

She looks pleased by that. And maybe a little turned on. My girl likes that I have the influence to get things done. That will be very good for us going forward.

"Great," she says.

"Do you need to go back to Sapphire Falls? Wrap anything up? Grab anything?"

She shakes her head. "I'm assuming Lauren and Mason won't be surprised I'm coming to work for you in Cara?"

I grin. "I don't think so, no. They might be surprised we're getting married."

She sits up a little straighter. "Oh, well, they don't need to know that part. That's really just... kind of a business arrangement. And it's just a year. To get things moving and done. They can just think I'm taking a job with you."

My smile drops. I take a breath. She has a point, I suppose. "The people of Cara *will* know about our marriage, Abigail," I say anyway. "It will be a real marriage in every way. No matter what other stipulations you put on it."

She meets my eyes. And nods. "I know." She swallows. "But Lauren and Mason aren't the types to keep track of the social life of a prince in another country," she says. "They won't know about the marriage part."

I feel my jaw tighten and work to relax it. "What about your family?"

"My parents aren't the celebrity gossip or podcast types. My sisters will know, but they'll know the truth behind it too. And they can run interference with anyone else."

"The truth being that you're doing it for the farm program and only for a year." There's an edge in my tone I can't hide.

"And for *you*," she says.

Right. She's doing it to help me get the throne and to keep me from walking down the aisle with someone I don't want to marry.

I should be glad about this.

I *am* fucking glad about this. I get Abigail. Even if it's for only a year, I get *her*.

And I'm going to do whatever I can to make sure it's for more than a year.

"Okay." I give her a smile. "You can move to Cara without going back to Sapphire Falls?"

"I rent the house I live in. Peyton and Riley will be happy to pack up my stuff and ship it—though I doubt many of my clothes or shoes are princess-worthy. And if I'm going to be married to the prince, I trust I don't need a passport or immigration papers or anything?"

I outright grin now. She just kind-of said the word 'princess' and she didn't even stutter. "I can get your dual citizenship taken care of. And we'll definitely get you new clothes. Though you'll want your regular stuff too. You are, after all, still going to be farming."

Her smile is bright. "That's true."

I pick up her dress from where it got tossed to the floor. "Let me take you out to dinner tonight."

I think she might say no, because someone might see us out and snap a photo and send it back to Cara for the gossips to talk about.

But she smiles. "Okay."

She must not know that there are eyes and ears even here. Fine. *I* certainly don't care who sees us together and starts talking. Maybe it will make our imminent wedding announcement less of a shock.

She scoots off the bed and heads into the bathroom.

"Just let me shower quick," she says, tossing a sly smile over her shoulder.

Right. Because she's probably still sticky from my cum.

Heat arrows through me at the thought.

And the thought of the very long night ahead of us.

Because I've decided that I'm not fucking Abigail again until she is my *wife*, wearing my ring in the palace.

Is that an overreaction to how adamant she is that this is all more of a business arrangement than an actual marriage? Maybe. But there are two things Abigail wants: that farm, and, now I'm very pleased to know, my cock.

And she doesn't get either one until she is announced as the Crown Princess of Cara.

Maybe *then* we'll be even for my two years of being obsessed over her.

Four hours later we're back from dinner with Jonah and Linnea, who helped fill her in on what to expect when we get to Cara. They warn her that people, especially the King, will be displeased the wedding happened in the US instead of in Cara. That doesn't seem to faze Abigail and I know it's because she thinks that being a princess who isn't all that well-liked will actually help in the end.

Which makes me irrationally cranky. She's right in that assumption. It *will* make ending the marriage easier.

I suppose if I wanted the marriage to end, I'd be more on board.

Linnea tells us she's going to handle our social media and spin the story so people believe the relationship has been happening over two years—true, for me—that I've been in the US working on my proposal—also technically true—and that we simply couldn't wait any longer and just *had* to elope—also true.

But, despite all the official talk, dinner is very pleasant. Abigail seems comfortable around Jonah and Linnea and it feels more like a double date with my best friend and our girlfriends than four people setting up a marriage of convenience to further a political, business, and personal agenda.

We get back to the hotel and Jonah leaves the SUV with the valet. We all head inside.

"Hey, Torin, can we talk for a second?" Jonah asks. "Alone?"

I nod. "Of course." It wouldn't surprise me if he's gotten an earful from staff in Cara, passed down from my grandfather. I've been gone for longer than I expected and I'm sure my grandfather is beyond annoyed.

"I'll meet you upstairs," Abigail says as the elevator doors swish open.

"I'll be right up."

She and Linnea step onto the elevator and the doors shut on them. Linnea will be sure Abigail is settled upstairs.

I turn to my best friend. "Is there something from Cara?"

"No. Well, yes, but that's not what I want to talk to you about right now."

"Are you going to congratulate me?"

He isn't. I can tell.

Jonah stuffs his hands into the pockets of his pants. He regards me with a serious expression. "Should I congratulate you?"

"The woman of my dreams proposed to me. She's going to be the princess. I'll have the throne within the next year. Her farm will make a number of positive changes for our country. Isn't that all cause for congratulations?"

"Yes. I heard her lay out all of the practical reasons why the two of you getting married was a good idea."

I sigh and lean back against the wall. "What's the problem, Jonah?"

"I just want to be sure that you still think this is the right idea."

I frown. "Of course. This was the plan when we got on the plane in Cara. I'm crazy about her. You know that."

Jonah moves closer. He pulls his hands from his pockets and crosses his thick arms. "I do know *you're* crazy about *her*. That's what concerns me."

"You're *concerned* that I'm crazy about the woman I'm going to marry?" But I feel a niggle behind my breastbone. I know exactly what he's worried about. And once he says it out loud, I'm going to have to acknowledge it. To him. And to myself, officially.

"You're in love with her."

The words hit me directly in the chest. But I don't even have to think about them. I nod. "Yes."

"And does she love you?"

I open my mouth to answer with a flippant *what's not to love*, but I stop. This is my best friend. He knows me better than anyone. And he just hit on something I've been trying to ignore.

Of course, he did.

I take a deep breath, then ask, "What are you asking me exactly?"

"Abigail has laid out all of the good reasons why you should get married. No one can really argue with any of them. It is, in fact, a very good, *practical* idea. But was one of those reasons, at any point, in private between the two of you, because she's in love with you, too?"

It wasn't. She has never said that.

"No," I admit to Jonah. "But I haven't said it to her either."

"Why not?"

"Because she's not the whirlwind romance, head-over-heels, follow her heart kind of girl," I say honestly. "It's been fast. And it's all a little crazy."

"Exactly," Jonah agrees.

"And that concerns you. You think she's marrying me for my money? Or to get what she needs professionally from me?"

"I think the reasons she's marrying you are not...the same reasons you're marrying her. But," he adds. "I think she *thinks* she's marrying you for the same reasons. So I can't really fault her."

I sigh. "I'm marrying her for the same reasons she's marrying me, *too*," I say. "The farms, Cara, Linnea, my grandfather."

"But you're making a mess of this."

"Because I haven't told her I'm in love with her?"

Finally, he drops his arms and takes a big breath. "I'm talking to you as your best friend now. Not your bodyguard. Not a member of the royal staff. Not even just a guy. But as someone who considers you a brother."

I prepare myself. "All right."

"I don't want you to get your heart broken. And I think there is only one thing, and two people, in the world who can do that. Your country. Your grandfather—who has repeatedly done it, especially over the past year. And now Abigail Landry. Who is going to come to Cara with you, and potentially break your heart over and over again every day."

Well...damn.

I swallow. "She and I are an amazing team. We can do really amazing things."

Jonah nods. "I think that's absolutely true. I think Abigail should come to Cara."

I nod. "Good."

"But I don't know if you should *marry* her."

I feel my gut tighten. I *am* marrying Abigail and I really want my best friend on board. "It's the best way."

He gives a single nod. "In a lot of ways, I think that's true." He pauses. "But, if you do it, you need to remember it's a *solution to a problem*. You're going to be king, Torin. You're going to be faced with difficult decisions every damned day. And you're going to sometimes have to make choices that really suck, that are going to break your heart. I don't want your personal life making you feel shitty too. You deserve to be happy. And if you're happy, you'll be better for Cara."

I take a deep breath. "Abigail *is* the right choice for Cara. I thought you understood this was the plan all along."

"Making a *deal* with her to be princess. Sure. I actually thought the plan was exactly what Abigail seems to think it is," Jonah says. "And seducing her? Sure. I saw how you looked at her clear back at Charlie's wedding."

I shift, and clear my throat, but nod.

"But falling in love with her? Especially without anything reciprocal from her? That's...dangerous."

"I think she really likes me," I say, trying for a light tone.

He doesn't smile. "Everyone likes you, Torin." He says it like it's just a fact. "Even your grandfather *likes* you. He still makes you fucking miserable because he doesn't give you anything more than that," Jonah says bluntly. He's frowning again. "I like Abi. She's brilliant. And yes, I'm sure she *likes* you. But she proposed and specifically said she doesn't want it to involve any emotions. And she said she wants it to only be for a year."

"So you're trying to protect me."

"Well, it's kind of a habit now after eleven-plus years," he grumbles.

"It's because *you* love me."

He looks at me for a long beat. It's not as if we've never said this, but a lot of times, there's liquor involved. Or we just had a narrow miss with something dangerous, or potentially illegal.

"I do love you," he says. "And you deserve to be loved and appreciated a fuck ton more than you are."

A little choked up—the bastard—I lean over and clap him on the shoulder. "Thank you. And, just so you know, I think I can make her fall in love with me."

"Should you maybe wait for that to happen before you marry her?"

I give him a grin, actually feeling okay about this. "Maybe."

"Really?"

"How long do you think it will take?" I ask.

"A month. Maybe two," he says, with a shrug.

I actually chuckle at that. "Thanks, man. I was going to say six months."

He rolls his eyes. "If it's going to happen, it's going to happen."

I guess he would know. He and Linnea fell hard and fast. He even tried to fight it.

"A month," I muse. "That's nothing. So no, I'm not going to wait for that to happen before I marry her."

Jonah groans. "I just want her to be as into you as you are her. That's not so much to ask."

"I'm going to make her a princess. Give her a crown. Jewels, a palace, a private jet."

Jonah lifts a brow. "Yeah. Too bad none of that really matters to this particular woman."

I actually smile at that. "I guess I'll have to throw in some fruit trees and green rubber boots."

Jonah shakes his head. Then he reaches over and stabs the elevator button for the penthouse. "Well, if you're going to make her fall for you, I guess you better go up and get started."

I laugh and we both get on the elevator.

Yeah, I have some work to do, it seems.

When I get to my room, I find my fiancée—I really fucking like that term—already under the covers of the bed we're going to share.

"Did you get condoms?" she asks.

I give her a grin as I undress down to my boxers. Her gaze is on me the entire time.

"I did not."

She frowns. "Why not?"

"Because we're going to wait."

"Wait? For what?"

Until she's officially *mine*.

"Until our wedding night, of course." Which is, after all, tomorrow night.

She seems stunned. She watches me as I go into the bathroom to brush my teeth.

"You should know, I'm not wearing pajamas," she calls.

Ah, she's going to tease me.

Bring it on, my little introvert. I love the idea that she's feeling sassy and sexy and wants to try to tempt me. "Sleeping naked is really comfortable," I call back agreeably.

"And I like to cuddle."

I almost snort. She sleeps alone. She likes to do most

things alone. She is *not* a cuddler. I already know this about her without anyone needing to tell me.

"Can't wait. I love how you feel and smell," I tell her. I rinse my mouth and lay my toothbrush next to hers. The sight of the green and blue plastic handles next to each other on the counter seems right. As silly as that sounds.

I step into the room, switching off the bathroom light. The only light in the room now is the lamp on the table on my side of the bed.

Seeing Abigail in my bed, her gorgeous hair spread out on my pillow, the sheet pulled up under her arms, knowing she's naked underneath has me battling my conviction that I need to wait.

You didn't get a condom, so you're out of luck, buddy, I remind myself.

There's plenty of other stuff you could do to her, I also remind myself.

I round to the other side of the bed, pulling the covers back.

"I can't believe we're not going to have sex," she pouts.

I fight my grin. Making her *want* it is a good move. I intend to fulfill every need, want, or wish this woman will ever have.

Once she's officially mine.

And on *my* terms.

She's calling the shots on all of the stipulations surrounding our marriage, so I'll call the shots in the bedroom.

Before I slip between the sheets, I open the bedside table and withdraw the item inside that I want to give her.

Turning on my side to face her, I reach out and tuck her hair behind her ear, needing to touch her somehow. "I'm so glad you're greedy for more, Abigail," I tell her gruffly. "But

I realized that when I finally sink into your tight, hot pussy, and call you my good, sweet, dirty, fucking princess, I want you to actually *be* my princess."

I see her suck in a sharp breath and her gorgeous blue eyes widen.

I grin. "Yeah. That will be hotter when it's *really* true, right?"

She swallows hard. "That will be...yes."

I have to be sure she's going to walk down that aisle. Or into the judge's chambers as the case may be.

Jonah's concerns have only served to heighten the unease that's been nagging me since Abigail insisted we not talk about any feelings and put an end date on us.

She's not in love with me.

But she *is* in love with these farms.

And maybe she's in love with the things I can do to her body. That's not bad for a guy's ego.

Surely all of that will get her to 'I do'.

But I'll do whatever I can to *ensure* it.

She's studying me with a look I can't quite decipher. I just let her. I could simply look at her for hours.

"I can't believe that you shared my farm plans with Lauren and Mason," she finally says.

"I can't believe that *you've* never shared the plans with them," I say. I can't tell if she's happy or not.

"Coming up with ideas and plans is never the problem," she says softly. "Convincing other people to get on board is."

"You mean, putting your ideas out there to be judged is," I say, one brow arched. "Because it took no convincing at all for them to get on board. But they'd never even heard the idea."

She slowly nods, her cheek rubbing against the pillowcase. "Yeah. I need a spokesperson. Someone who can understand what I want to do and why and can communicate that to other people with passion and charm and patience."

I feel a swirl of *fuck yes* go through me. We are going to be an unstoppable team. "It seems you do. But I know a guy."

She smiles. "I texted Mason and Lauren before dinner to tell them I'm taking a job with you. Lauren just texted me back while you were still downstairs with Jonah. She's thrilled for me. And she said she thinks the farm plan is amazing."

"It *is* amazing."

Abigail shakes her head. "It's only amazing if it gets *done*. Otherwise, it's just an idea. Maybe a good one, but still just a thought. *You* sold them on it. And paid for it. You made it real."

I take her hand, linking our fingers on top of the duvet. "All I did was say the idea out loud. I used *your* words. Your explanations, descriptions, and statistics." I give her a little grin. "It wasn't hard. I've literally been talking since I was one."

She laughs softly. "Torin, I appreciate your attempt at humility, but I've known you long enough now to know that when *you* talk it's different than when other people do."

I feel warmth spread through my chest. I stroke my thumb across the back of her knuckles. "Well, it's very easy to be enthusiastic about you and your work."

Her expression is soft as she smiles at me. "I still can't believe you did this."

"It was supposed to be a grand gesture," I say. "It had to *really* matter."

"It does." She wets her lips. "But why did you need a grand gesture?"

"I was hoping the farm would help you say yes to my *third* proposal."

"Third?"

"Your grandma's porch was one. I asked you again in a text."

She nods, then blows out a breath. "It would have made me say yes."

I lean in further. "You know, it occurs to me, that you didn't actually say *those* words to me."

Her eyes widen. Then her voice drops even though we're very much alone. "I *did* say...both P words."

Heat jabs me low and hard. "Yes, you sure fucking did," I say gruffly. I'm semi-hard again remembering. "And I'm going to hear them again." That isn't a question.

Her eyes widen slightly. And she wets her lips.

"But I'm talking about the other four words."

"Which ones?"

"You said you were proposing to me, but you never said, 'will you marry me?'"

Her pupils dilate and her lips part. She clears her throat. "No. I guess I didn't, did I?"

"So..." I pull my other hand out from under the pillow and hold my palm out.

Her eyes widen and her gaze flies from the object I'm holding to my eyes.

The ring I'm holding looks exactly like the one my mother wears.

"This is the Princess Ring," I tell her. "It matches the tiara you'll wear. And the crown I wear."

Her eyes are on mine, not on the stunning ring that is probably worth hundreds of thousands of dollars. I don't actually know. It's always been in my family and has never been appraised as far as I know.

"The center stone is a diamond, surrounded by purple stones. Purple is the color of the king and the crown prince. My siblings wear crowns with different stones. The crown for the second in line—now Declan, though it was mine growing up—has maroon stones. Fiona's, third in line, has green, and Cian's, fourth in line, has blue." Then I shake my head. "Though I guess Saoirse gets the maroon ring and crown now." I hold the ring up. "Anyway, when you become queen, you'll wear the Queen's Ring that my grandmother wears now. It's a purple stone, surrounded by diamonds instead. The King and Queen's crowns are the same, with the purple stones at the center." I reach for her left hand. My chest feels tight suddenly and I have to clear my throat. I look into her eyes. "Abigail, will you marry me?"

She looks from my face to the ring, then back to me. "It's a very...practical decision," she says. "For both of us."

I smile even though her words make my stomach clench. Of course, the scientist in her needs this to make sense. She can't just meet a guy at a wedding reception, have intense chemistry with him, text him for a few days, and then marry him on a whim. It's too fast. It's too sponta-neous. And that's even without all the royalty stuff.

I nod. "It's a very smart thing to do."

It is. It's more than that, but if she can't say that yet, that's fine.

She will. She has to. Because I know I'm in love with her.

She takes a breath and nods. "Yes. I'll marry you."

Relief and triumph and possessiveness all surge through me as I slide the ring onto her finger. "Some of my favorite words of yours so far, princess," I tell her.

She's staring at her hand now. "They're not your very favorite?" she asks.

I lean in, my mouth against her ear. "It's going to be *very* hard to top hearing you say, 'please eat my pussy'."

She gasps and jerks back, staring at me with her mouth open.

I grin. "But I'm *very much* looking forward to hearing 'I do' from that pretty mouth."

Her gaze drops to my mouth and she murmurs, almost as if to herself, "It's a very practical decision."

It is.

And it's so fucking much more.

I have no more words for her. At least, none that I can say. My ring is on her finger, I can't—or won't—fuck her tonight, and I can't tell her I'm in love with her. So I reach over and switch off the light.

But soon she'll be *mine*. Officially. And everyone will know. And I will be able to say and do whatever I want to.

I turn back to my side and reach for her, knowing that having her up against me all night is going to make me hard and hot and a little miserable, but unable to not hold her.

She wasn't lying about being naked under the sheet. I groan as my hand splays over her bare belly, hauling her against me.

But as her ass fits against my hips, her back against my chest and her head under my chin, and she makes a happy, contented sound, I realize something deep in my very soul —she's already mine.

CHAPTER 22

ABIGAIL

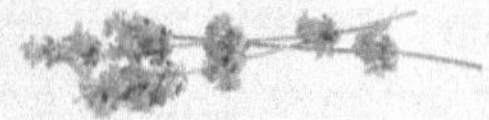

I sleep later than usual the next morning and I wake up to a note telling me that Torin has gone out for a run, and he'll see me in a little bit.

So I basically wake up to butterflies in my stomach and tingles all over and a huge smile on my face and the awareness that my crush has turned into a little more than a crush.

We slept together last night. *Slept* together. Just that. Well, sure there was more before that, and I wanted *more*, but sleeping up against him, his arm around me, his big hand splayed possessively over my stomach and his face tucked against the back of my neck is...more. It really is.

I text my sisters. *Get somewhere together, I need to talk.*

Then I shower quickly, get dressed, and pull my hair up.

My phone rings just as I finish brushing my teeth and blushing just from looking at Torin's toothbrush.

But that toothbrush has been in his mouth.

His very, very talented mouth that says very, very dirty things that I love so much more than I would have ever expected.

I fumble for my phone and answer the video call.

"Hi!" Okay, that was *way* too enthusiastic. They'll know something is up.

But then I grin. Something *is* up.

"Uh, hi," Charlie says. "We're calling for our sister Abigail? She looks a little like you. Is she there somewhere?"

"Ha, ha," I say, sinking down onto the bed.

My butt just touching that mattress makes me blush too.

"What's going on? You said you needed to talk and we had to be together," Ami says. Then she yawns.

I grin. "How's Rosie?"

"The light of my life." She yawns again. "And my nights. And my three a.m.s." She shakes her head. "We're not talking about my baby or how I may never sleep through the night again. We want to know about *you*."

"Okay, well, I just thought I should tell you..." I take a breath. "I'm getting married." I hold up my left hand to show off the ring.

The absolutely gorgeous ring that Torin slipped on my finger last night...while denying me sex. But I immediately focus on my sisters as they both gasp, then scream.

I wince. And give them a minute.

"Oh my God!"

"Abigail!"

"What?"

"Is it Torin?"

"What happened?"

"What is going on?"

"When?"

"Oh! My! God!"

When they both stop babbling, I fill them in. On all of it. How he and Linnea were never really engaged. Why he has to marry *someone*. What our goals are. When we're doing it. And then I re-emphasize that it's just a temporary arrangement to meet two very specific goals.

They both sit blinking at me.

"Did you get all of that?" I ask.

"What I got was that we don't get to come to your wedding," Ami says.

"Because it's not a *wedding* wedding. And if you come, everyone else will find out about it and that's unnecessarily complicated."

"But..." Charlie says, frowning. "You *like* him. And you're attracted to him. And he *built you a farm*. He's basically giving you your dream job! Why wouldn't you want to stay married? I mean, you could fall in love with him!"

I'm shaking my head by the time she finishes. I can *not* fall in love with Torin. That would be a really terrible thing to do. "I have to be a...pri...*princess* as it is," I say with an eyeroll. That word really is hard for me to say. But I'll be anti-social and probably not well-liked or popular and I'm used to that, and it will make it a lot easier on the people of Cara when I leave. "If we stay married, I'd have to be the *queen*." I give a humorless laugh. My chest feels tight as I think about it. "I would be so, so bad at that. You know that."

"Abi," Charlie says gently. "It won't be *easy*, probably, but you can do hard things."

I stare at the carpet.

Can I?

I actually haven't done that many hard things. The professional things I do come so easily to me. And the things I don't want to do, people don't really *make* me do. They either chalk it up to general weirdness or they want to protect me.

When I was a kid, I got out of fishing and swimming. When I was a teen, I got out of sleepovers and dances. When I was in college, I got out of parties and *most* tattoos. As an adult, no one pressures me to go out, or to spend time on things I don't care about. Even the guys asking me to dance take no for an answer pretty easily.

I guess I'm good at saying no.

Lauren and Mason are one exception. They make me go out on sales calls. But I've also never actually pushed back hard. I've never actually said no.

I wonder how they would react to that.

Torin is another exception.

I did say no to him. But he kept pursuing me anyway.

And now I have a feeling that if I keep saying yes to him, I'm definitely going to be asked to do some hard things.

"And you're going to be a great princess and would be an amazing queen," Ami says.

I look at the phone quickly. "What makes you say *that*?" Then I laugh, though it sounds just a touch hysterical. "I wear green rubber boots all day every day. I have dirt under my fingernails *all the time*. I drive a truck that has rust along both doors and hasn't seen a car wash in about five years. I throw up when I have to talk to crowds of people!"

"So what? People like you should be in positions of power, Abi. You should be making big decisions that impact lots of people," Ami says. "You already have the heart and the knowledge and the passion. Now you'll have the power and resources to make amazing things happen."

I don't know what to say to that. I've already witnessed what can happen when Torin and I join forces. Or when Torin joins *his* forces with my ideas.

But strangest of all, my sisters are not treating this idea like it's crazy.

I'm staring straight ahead, trying to absorb all of that. I'm not seeing the gold swirls on the wardrobe in front of me. Instead, I'm replaying memories. I've always known that my sisters think I'm smart. They were proud of me in a 'oh Abi's great' way. But I always thought they wrote off so much about me as 'something else'. Something...weird. They *never* called me weird. I've always felt loved. But I've always felt different from them.

This conversation makes me think that maybe my perfect, beautiful, bold, can-do-anything sisters, think I'm some of those things too.

"Thank you," I finally say quietly. "I do want to do amazing things."

"Abi," Charlie says, pulling my attention to her face. "I know that your brain is huge, and you rely on it a lot, and it gives you good information and helps you make great decisions..." She smiles. "...but it's okay to rely on your heart, sometimes too. Sure, it makes mistakes sometimes, but the times when it gets it right, are really, really worth it."

Ami smiles and nods. "Really, *really* worth it."

My stomach flips. My *heart* flips.

Damn. This might be a huge mistake. But if I don't go and at least try to help Torin be everything he wants to be, I'll regret it. I know I will.

I look at my sisters again. "I love you both. So much."

"We love you too." Charlie gives me a wink. "Princess."

I give a little choked laugh as I blink away tears.

They want me to be happy. My sisters might not always get me, or understand the things that I do, and maybe we don't have a *ton* in common, but they are there for me.

"Thanks, girls," I tell my sisters, hoping they can hear how much I mean that.

"Our pleasure," Charlie says. "This is so fun for us."

"What's so fun?"

"Watching you get swept off your feet."

Ami laughs. "It really is. And *of course*, you would do it bigger and better than everyone else."

"Bigger and better?" I ask.

"Yes." She laughs again. "I mean, I have a hot, single dad firefighter, but *you*—always the overachiever—got a *prince*."

I laugh, feeling light and again realizing that maybe my sisters look at me differently than I thought they do. "Yeah, well... my *prince*—" I love the little shiver calling him 'my' anything gives me. "—has a ranch in Cara. Horses, cows... cowboy boots. The whole thing."

Charlie gives a mock gasp. "What? You mean you might be into cowboys after all?"

I laugh. I'm so *happy* all of a sudden. "No. Just *one* part-time cowboy."

"Well then," Charlie says, a devious smile on her lips. "You know what you need to do?"

"What?"

"Tell him that *you* want to be a cowgirl. In bed," Charlie says.

"Oh, yes," Ami agrees. "And in reverse."

"I want to be a reverse cowgirl?" I ask.

"Oh, yes, you do." They both giggle.

I'm smiling too, even though I'm not sure why. "I don't know what that means."

"Torin will," Charlie promises.

"Should I look it up ahead of time?" I ask.

"No," Ami says quickly. "Let Prince Torin show you. He'll *love* that."

"And we'll easily be his favorite sisters-in-law," Charlie adds with a huge grin.

CHAPTER 23
WAIT 'TIL I TELL YE

EPISODE 759 TRANSCRIPT

Lindsey: What the hell just happened? Oh my God!

Jen: Um hey, everyone! We're here at a special time with an extra episode because...we have some news!

Lindsey: That's an understatement! We have THE news! Probably the biggest news of the year!

Jen: I would agree. And we got it from Lady Linnea Olsen herself! So, whatever you're doing, wherever you are, stop for a second, take a breath, and turn the volume up.

Lindsey: Yes, especially if you're driving or something like that.

Jen: Oh my gosh yes! Or doing...surgery or something!

Lindsey: Do you think people listen to us while they perform surgery?

Jen: Maybe? They probably listen to *something*. Why not us?

Lindsey: We might be a little distracting.

Jen: True. Well, just in case...if you *are* doing surgery or, I don't know, anything that could be dangerous to you or others if you get distracted for a minute, stop.

Lindsey: Unless you can't! Don't stop a surgery for this! Just turn us down and listen or read the transcript later!

Jen: Yes! Geez!

Lindsey: Okay, everyone ready? Here we go...<takes a deep audible breath> We were right! Prince Torin *was* in the US to get engaged!

Jen: <laughing> But that's about the only thing we got right! He not only *got* engaged, he's also getting *married!* And it's *not* to Linnea!

Lindsey: No, it's not.

Jen: Oh come on, don't look so upset! Clearly Linnea is fine! She's the one who sent us this story and these *photos*. And they're so great! Our producer is posting them right now so you can all go take a look!

Lindsey: Upset? I'm devastated! Heartbroken! I'm *outraged!*

Jen: Okay, okay. Calm down. We have a new princess! Our prince is *married*. Lindsey, this is *great!* Okay, everyone, our new princess is Abigail Landry. She's from Louisiana and is a super brainiac scientist. How amazing is that? They met at her sister's wedding. Not the one he was just at, but one a couple of years ago. So this has been going on for *two years*! That's so sweet! No wonder he hasn't dated anyone else! And no wonder he and Linnea haven't been anything but friends! And...now they're back! They're coming home today!

Lindsey: Yeah. But tell them the *rest* of the news.

Jen: But we should be happy for Torin!

Lindsey: Sure, sure. But what about *our* happiness?

Jen: It's not about us!

Lindsey: It should be a little about us! Everyone, we don't get to have a wedding. They're getting married *today*. In Louisiana! Before they come home!

Jen: Yeah, but...we have a new princess! And just look at these photos! She's beautiful and just look at the way he's looking at her. He's clearly in love!

Lindsey: Well, I can admit they *are* really cute together. Okay, so...<heavy sigh> Welcome to Cara, Princess Abigail. We can't wait to meet you, I guess.

CHAPTER 24

ABIGAIL

"Abigail, do you take Torin to be your husband?" the judge asks twenty-six hours after I told Torin we should get married.

I look up at Torin and my heart does a weird flipping, fast-thumping thing as our gazes meet. I nod, and Torin gives my hands a squeeze and the corner of his mouth curls up. I almost laugh.

"I do."

Of course I had to *say* those two words, but the look of pleasure and heat on Torin's face makes me want to say them again. And to say more.

I might be in trouble here.

Lord knows what this man might get me to say.

"Torin, do you take this woman to be your wife?"

"I do."

His voice has so much conviction in it, my heart thumps hard again.

Jonah hands me a ring that's a heavy gold band with purple stones and diamonds much like the one Torin gave me last night. The one that's...mine. I swallow hard as I slip it on Torin's finger and for some reason feel tears sting the backs of my eyes. He's been avoiding these purple stones and diamonds. He's reluctant to wear even the prince's crown. But he's now going to wear what I assume is referred to as the Prince's Ring as a wedding ring.

Torin simply lifts my hand and presses a kiss to the ring he gave me last night when it's his turn.

A minute later, the judge says, "By the power given me by the State of Louisiana, I now pronounce you husband and wife." He smiles. "You may now kiss your bride."

Torin doesn't hesitate. He cups my face in both hands and says quietly, "*Mine.*"

Then he kisses me deeply. Possessively. I feel the way he claims me all the way to my toes. And in several key spots in between my lips and toes.

Finally, Jonah clears his throat and Torin lifts his head. He gives me a wink, squeezes my ass, and says, "Let's go home, princess."

And fifteen minutes after walking into the judge's chambers...I'm officially Cara's new Crown Princess.

Holy shit.

I'm still in a bit of a daze as we head to the airport to get on Torin's private jet.

Until Jonah pulls me aside while Torin is talking to the pilot and our luggage is getting loaded.

"May I have a word, Princess Abigail?"

"Oh my God, you have to keep calling me Abi," I tell him. "No...P word in front of it either."

He laughs softly. "Okay, Abi."

"And of course you can have a word. Have several."

Jonah doesn't waste any time with small talk. "You make Torin happy," he tells me.

"I'm...glad." I'm not sure how exactly to respond. Jonah knows this is all temporary and very outcome oriented. "That will make this next year easier, right?" I smile.

Jonah doesn't return it. He's not frowning, but he looks very serious. "Torin is conflicted about his role as prince. He's not sure he believes in the monarchy, but he feels the pressure to step up to *be* the monarch. His family needs him to. The country needs him to. If something happens to his grandfather without Torin there and ready to take over, his family and the whole country will be in turmoil. His primary desire is to provide stability to them all. To accomplish that, he could simply continue doing things exactly the way his grandfather does them. But Torin is...Torin. He's not really the bare minimum type." Jonah tips his head. "Why just dance when you can waltz?"

I take a breath and nod. I know all about Torin being...*more*. Seemingly in every way.

I realize Jonah isn't telling me all of this as Torin's bodyguard. This is my new husband's best friend talking to me.

"He wants what he does for the rest of his life to *matter*," Jonah goes on. "And he believes the country needs more than what they have now. There needs to be innovation and growth. But he really wants his grandfather, the only person who really knows what it's like to be king, to tell him he'll do a good job and that his ideas are right."

I understand that to some extent. It's nice to hear that you're doing something right. But I learned a long time ago that people's words don't mean much without actions behind them. "It's even better to *see* you've done something right. To prove it. To yourself and to others," I say.

Jonah gives me a small smile. "I agree."

My heart starts thumping.

I know how much words mean to Torin, though. "The king doesn't tell Torin that he'll be a good king?"

Jonah shakes his head. "The king focuses on the things Torin isn't doing right and tries to correct those. They butt heads a lot. Torin has a lot of ideas, things he'd like to try, but the king hasn't let him put any of it out there yet."

"Torin *abdicated*. Surely, it's clear to his grandfather that he doesn't agree with how Diarmuid does things."

Jonah nods. "Exactly the problem. Torin's not really able to hide his feelings or bite his tongue when he has something to say. As you might have noticed."

I nod and can't help but smile. "Now that you mention it."

"You need to know that since Torin met you and learned about your farms, he's been committed to the throne in a way I haven't seen before. He's excited about your farms because they're tangible. They make sense, and he knows he can depend on *you* to make them happen. Torin believes in *you*. The farms give him a specific purpose. Something he can really *do* with the power of the crown."

I take a deep breath. That's a lot. But it also makes me feel warm and excited.

"That's what he needed," Jonah says. "*Torin* needed to see that he can do good—specific, visible good—with his power. He's uncomfortable with the idea of power with no purpose. He left the throne and the chance to rule behind. He came back to Cara reluctantly. He's only there because of his family. But to really step up enthusiastically, he needs a plan that will for certain make things better for the people."

I feel my heart start thumping hard.

The idea that someone understands and believes in my

farms in the first place is exciting but imagining that what I want to do could also give someone like Torin a real purpose, a *reason* to embrace his position, is thrilling.

"I'll be there for him," I promise. "I know he'll be a great king. I'll do whatever I can to help him."

"Temporarily," Jonah says.

I frown. I can't tell if Jonah thinks that's a good thing. Or not.

"Yes," I say. I have to be honest.

Jonah sighs. "Well, that's better than nothing I guess."

I just smile and shrug.

He studies me for a long moment. Then he says, "Let's talk again in about a month."

I don't know what that means exactly. I assume that I'll be talking to Jonah a lot. "About Torin?" I ask.

"About his happiness," Jonah says.

That almost sounds ominous. But I nod. "Sure. We can talk any time."

"Good." He pauses, then says, "Welcome to the family, Princess Abigail."

Right. Torin is Jonah's family. Jonah is also in charge of protecting Torin. Torin's best interest will always come before anyone else's for Jonah.

My thoughts still swirling, we board Torin's private jet and head for Cara.

I sit next to Torin. He gives me the window seat. And he immediately takes my hand, entwining our fingers and resting our hands on his thigh.

I'm *married*. I'm going to be living in not just a new house, or town, but a new *country*. One that my husband is in charge of. Kind of.

Everything happened so fast, I almost don't believe it.

Until I look out the window nine hours later and get the first look at my new home.

It's just after six p.m. here, but Cara gets nearly twenty hours of sunlight this time of year. So I can see the palace clearly.

From this viewpoint, the structure is smaller than I'd expected. Still, it is definitely a castle.

It's square, with an opening in the middle. I assume that's considered a courtyard. As someone who's spent a lot of time in New Orleans, I know and love a good courtyard. Though this one could have fit ten typical NOLA courtyards in it.

The four corners have spires on top of huge columns—I suppose technically those are turrets—but the rest of the structure is all solid, thick squares.

There's also a moat, an actual *moat*, around three-fourths of the castle. There's no draw bridge. Instead, a wide paved drive leads up to the front gate.

"Is that a hedge maze?" I ask pointing.

Torin leans in to look out the window with me.

It obviously is. It's gorgeous.

"Yes," Torin says with a grin. "And throughout the hedge are fountains, benches, little flower beds, and a butterfly garden."

"That looks like a greenhouse," I say, pointing to a structure beyond the maze.

"It is. There are also vegetable gardens, and those—" He points to the cluster of trees. "—are fruit trees. We have a good-sized orchard. There are apples, and pears, and... others." He laughs. "I'm not sure."

I look at him. "So the royal family has whatever they want year-round?"

He nods. "Castle staff are also free to take home whatever they want from the gardens, greenhouses, and the castle's small farm. We provide meat, eggs, milk and cheese, as well as wine, whiskey and beer from the distillery, and bread and pastries from the kitchen. We've modernized the production of everything over the years, but the recipes are original, and it's considered a huge perk of working for us."

I stare at him. "So, everything I want to do with the indoor farms is already happening at the palace?"

He shrugs. "On a *much* smaller, less technical scale, but yes."

No wonder all of my work makes so much sense to him. "Then why doesn't your grandfather understand the program and support it?"

His jaw tightens. "I wish I knew. We haven't discussed it at length."

Torin instructs the pilot to take another pass over the island.

"Only about a third of Cara is settled," he says.

The villages are nestled into the hills, mostly along the coast as they depend so much on fishing. The houses sit close together, but the rolling hills up behind them show that the island has lots of space.

"The largest village is the one just down the hill from the castle. It's walking distance from the front of the castle to the middle of town," he says, pointing. "The town has six thousand people, give or take. The others vary from a few hundred to a couple thousand."

The island really is remote, and he tells me that all of the land animals on the island have been introduced by humans. The only animal life that's native are sea mammals like seals. There are several types of birds, but they're all sea birds.

"But Fiona has an endangered animal sanctuary here that takes up about another third of the island," Torin says, pointing out the window again as we fly over the other side of the island.

I gasp and lean in. I can't see any animals from here, but the third of the island that isn't mountainous and doesn't have any clusters of houses and buildings, is clear.

"Really?"

"You know she rescues wild animals?" he asks.

I nod. She's the reason the petting zoo in Autre has turned into an animal sanctuary with everything from lemurs and tigers to camels and giraffes. She rescues exotic animals from "zoos", circuses, and collectors who have them illegally or who are abusing or neglecting them. She doesn't keep them all, but she rehomes them.

"She talked my grandfather into making Cara a sanctuary for endangered animals of all kinds. The island is truly, fully protected geographically and also by the fact that our family makes the rules." He shrugs looking a little sheepish. "I guess maybe there are a few perks to a monarchy. We have wildlife protections here that the US has spent decades debating and negotiating. All because my grandfather said that's how it will be."

"That's amazing." I squeeze his hand. I want him to understand that he really is in a position to do so many good things. "Are the animals just free range?"

"More or less. We have buildings for all of them since the weather varies. We also have some barriers between predators and the animals they consider prey. But they all have plenty of food and the sanctuary is nearly four hundred thousand acres, so they have enough space that I don't think they even notice that they can't get from one side to the other."

My eyes are huge, I'm sure. A four hundred-thousand-acre sanctuary for endangered animals and now everything I need to make indoor farming a reality for every person on the island.

I'm going to really like it here.

Then we fly over a homestead that's a distance from the castle, up in the hills, away from the coast. It's also very well lit, though, from the house to the long drive leading from the road, up the hill.

"And that's my ranch. The *Rogue*."

I look at him. "The *Rogue?*" I lift a brow.

Jonah had told me Torin was a reluctant royal, that he was home only because of his family, and that he struggled with the idea of power without purpose. It seemed that Torin was very aware of his reluctance. That he's made it obvious to those around him, as well.

He shrugs. "We name ranches here like they do in the US. The full name is the *Rogue Royal Ranch*. It's appropriate. It's where I go to get away. It's the only place I can go here in Cara and not be the prince."

I study his face. I realize that I don't want him to hate being the prince. I've always loved what I do in general, but Torin has made me excited about it in a new way that I didn't realize I wanted and needed. I want him to feel the same way about what he does.

"Do you go there often?" I ask.

He meets my eyes. "I do." He pauses, then admits, "Probably more than I should."

I don't say anything.

"But," he goes on, watching his thumb stroke over the back of my hand. "Maybe that will change now. I'll feel more useful at the palace."

Right. That would be good. I want him to feel useful

and to find his purpose. To embrace his position and understand how important it can be. But, that also means I'll be at the palace.

The *palace*.

How did my life suddenly swerve so hard that I'm going to end up living in a palace?

"Can I hang out at the ranch when I need to get away?" I ask, hoping he doesn't realize that I already want to get away.

"We're building the first farm on the ranch," he says, slipping an arm around me and kissing the top of my head. "So, that's where you'll be most of the time. And I'll be back and forth. I assume that's okay?"

Oh. My. God.

I just fell a little in love with him. "*So* okay," I say, trying not to let too much enthusiasm seep into my tone.

But on the ranch, I can go barefoot. I don't have to worry about using five forks at dinner—that many forks for one meal is ridiculous.

I might not even have to see the king that much.

This is awesome.

But first it has to be not-as-awesome. We're going to the palace tonight.

An hour later, our car is making its way up the winding drive toward the palace that, from the ground, is *much* bigger than I'd thought from the air.

The *palace*. Where I'm going to meet the king and queen.

I press my hand to my stomach.

How is this real?

"Are you okay?" Torin asks, lifting my hand to his lips and kissing my knuckles.

"I'm just not looking forward to this part. The whole being judged thing." I give him a wobbly smile.

He turns in his seat. "I know." He squeezes my hand. "Remember, you're already the princess. The people already know our story and love it."

Linnea has filled the podcasters in on the story of how we met, fell in love, and our elopement. And that we're returning to Cara. They've already started talking about it. The whole country knows.

Including King Diarmuid.

"We'll break ground on the farm tomorrow," Torin reminds me. "It will only be *good* judgments."

He's genuinely happy about this. I swallow. I blow out a breath.

This is the right decision.

It has to be.

Cara, and Torin, need these farms. So making them happen has to be the right thing to do.

Of course, this might be a case where a monarchy is also a bad thing for us because *one* guy can just shut it down if he doesn't like the idea.

I don't know the king. I don't know the rules. So I just did what I thought was right...

I frown.

"What?" Torin notices the way I tense and leans in. "What are you thinking about?"

"I just...realized something." I swallow. And then I even laugh lightly.

"What?" He strokes his thumb over the back of my hand.

"Just that, I think I've been a bit of a...um..." I look at him with a smile. "A princess for awhile already."

He stares at me for a few seconds, then slowly smiles. "Is that right?"

I nod as the thought fully forms. "People have tiptoed around me and treated me like I'm different for a long time."

"You're *special*."

I laugh, appreciating that. "Okay, well, I think those are synonyms. But anyway, when I was growing up, I eventually realized that everyone was going to just think I was strange. No matter what. I *am* different. I'm smart and I can't change that or hide it. And I don't really fit in a lot of the time.

"So I just started doing things my way. Collecting flowers and frogs instead of swimming and boating. Enjoying hide and seek because of the hiding part and being able to get wrapped up in reading while they looked for me. Going home from parties early or not going at all. Growing my own food instead of worrying about what to buy.

"I realized that I wasn't breaking rules. I was just bucking norms. And norms are only considered 'normal' because a lot of people do them, not necessarily because they're better.

"So anyway…" I pull in a breath and my gaze roams over his face, then I look out the window at the enormous structure—the palace—that we're pulling up to. "People think royals are different, right? They're going to talk about me no matter what I do. But…I'm used to that." I press my free hand to my stomach. The butterflies have calmed. I meet Torin's gaze again. "I'm not what the king expected for you. But I'm good at being different."

Torin cups my face and kisses me. Then sits back,

looking at me adoringly. "You certainly are, Princess Abigail."

And hey, even if I'm a little weird, at least I landed myself a prince.

The car is met by several staff members. One man directs the others on where to take the bags, greets Linnea and Jonah, and then turns to Torin.

"Welcome home, Your Highness."

"Hi, Samuel," Torin greets.

He turns to me. "Abigail, this is Samuel. He's my butler. Takes care of everything I need and is kind of a personal assistant. Samuel," he says, looking at the older man. "May I introduce you to my wife. Princess Abigail."

Samuel actually gives me a tiny bow, bending at the waist. "Princess Abigail, pleasure."

He's the first person, other than Jonah or Torin, to call me that. It feels weird.

"We'll have all your things taken up to your rooms," Samuel says. "You can freshen up and then the king will see you in his office."

I assumed that we would see the king fairly soon, but it had occurred to me that possibly we would wait until tomorrow. I guess not.

"After you meet with the king, everyone will retire, but your mother and grandmother would love to see you for breakfast."

"Of course." Torin looks at me. "We'll be happy to speak with the king. And breakfast is fine, obviously."

I let out a little breath. Waiting until breakfast to meet Torin's mother and grandmother does sound nice.

The staff all precedes us into the castle with our bags and boxes. Linnea and Jonah have already disappeared. Now it's just Torin and me standing at the base of the steps looking up at the huge front door.

"Are you ready?" he asks.

"No. But does that matter?"

He laughs and puts a hand on my lower back. "I'm right here with you. Are you nervous about meeting the king?"

I check my feelings. "Not nervous. I just don't want to."

Torin laughs and nudges me forward. "I completely understand."

The doors open for us as we approach, and I step into the O'Grady family castle.

And whoa...

I'd looked the castle up online, so I knew what I was going to find, but coming through the doors in person completely takes my breath away.

While it is an old stone castle, they have made the inside much more modern, and warm. There are rugs all over the stone floors, the woodwork is warm browns and highly polished, and artwork adorns the walls. There are thickly upholstered chairs and tables holding colorful bouquets of flowers, and warm golden lighting everywhere.

The ceiling rises several feet above me and there are windows everywhere. A staircase wide enough that four adults could stand side by side and take the steps at the same time is about twenty yards in front of us, yet the space we're in still feels welcoming.

I had expected something colder. Something definitely more museum-ish.

This actually feels like a home.

"Our room is on the third floor," Torin says, escorting me to the stairs.

"I get a tour later, right?" I ask.

"Anything you want." He hesitates. "I was going to say this is your home and you're free to go wherever you want, which is true, but I think we'll both feel more truly at home on the ranch."

I nod. "It really is okay that we spend most of our time there?" I have a niggle of doubt about that. Torin is the prince. He'll be the king someday. He needs to be here. He can't hide out on the ranch.

"Of course."

"How far is it from here?"

We get to the first landing, and we turn to mount the second flight of stairs.

"It's about sixty minutes by car," he says.

"Oh, that's farther than I imagined."

He chuckles. "It's where I get away."

Yeah. Like to the United States as often as possible.

I'll feel much less overwhelmed and more comfortable on a ranch where I can't even see the palace. But the niggle tells me that's not the right choice for Torin. Not only because he needs to be more involved in leading, but because he *likes* being involved, and talking to people.

And it might not be ideal for the farm. Yes, it probably needs to be set back a bit, but we want people to see what we're doing. I want people to be able to come and tour. I don't want to lead the tours, of course, but I want the farm to be accessible.

And I want the king to see it. If the point is to convince Diarmuid of what a great idea this is, then he needs to see it all happening.

We finally get to the third floor. It looks like there's at least one more floor above us. Torin guides me down a wide hallway with another high ceiling. The rug under our feet is thick and soft. The artwork on the walls is a mix of land-scapes and portraits. We stop at the fourth door on the right and he opens it, ushering me through.

"Wow, this is beautiful," I say as I step into Torin's private rooms.

Yes, rooms. Plural.

It's much more than just a bedroom. We step into a sitting room first. There is a sofa, a chair with an ottoman, a stone fireplace that looks like it's been upgraded from wood-burning to gas. There is also a television, a coffee table, and a huge bookcase. It looks like a very typical living room. Through a wide, arched doorway I can see a huge king-sized bed. Of course it's king-sized. It's a four poster and up on a two-inch platform.

"Your bed's on a stage?" I tease.

He chuckles. "I definitely like stepping off onto that wooden platform first thing in the morning in the winter then onto the cold stone floor."

I look down. There are plush rugs all over the floor in here as well, but sure enough, there are stone floors under-neath our feet here too.

I assume the bathroom is through the bedroom. To my right is a small kitchen area, with a refrigerator, very fancy coffee machine that I'm excited to use, and microwave.

"I almost don't ever need to leave *this* area," I tell him. "

"Believe me, if I could keep you in here to myself, I would. We'll try to make the meeting with my grandfather brief."

He kisses me but it's just a brush of his lips. I want so much more. I start to arch closer, but he lifts his head.

"I'm going to take a quick shower," he tells me.

Oh.

It's going to be difficult to ignore the fact that he's just on the other side of the door. Naked.

And we're officially married now.

"Okay."

He grins. "Feel free to snoop around the room."

CHAPTER 25

TORIN

Ten minutes later, there's a light knock on the bathroom door that I barely hear over the shower. But I know who it is.

I grin. Maybe we can settle her nerves another way. "That better be you, Abigail," I call out from inside the all-glass shower stall.

"Yeah, it better," she says, nudging the door open and peeking inside. "Nobody else better be sneaking up here to be with you."

I rinse the shampoo out of my hair. "You don't have to *sneak* up here to be with me, *wife*."

I like that nickname too much.

I like that one as much, if not more, than princess.

She doesn't comment on the W word though. She just says, "Good."

She's stepped fully into the room and is watching me.

My body reacts, heating and hardening right in front of her eyes.

"You sound a little possessive," I tell her, wiping my face so I can see her better.

"Maybe I am."

Fuck, I like that a lot. "Come here."

She walks toward the shower stall. Slowly. Teasing me.

She stops outside the glass and just watches as the water continues to fall on me, running down my body. Her gaze slides over me from head to toe. Then she sighs. She sounds very contented.

"You good, princess?" I ask.

"Really good."

"This is all you need?"

Her gaze quickly bounces from my cock to my eyes. "No."

"Then come here."

"Now? In there?"

"Yep."

"Can I just watch?"

"Watch what?" I know what she means, but I'm reminding her to use her damned words. All of them.

"Watch you wash."

She pauses and I wait her out.

She takes a breath, then says, "Then wrap your hand around your cock and make yourself come."

Well, damn. She turned these tables, didn't she?

I smile and shake my head. "Nicely done."

She grins, obviously proud of herself. "Yeah?"

"Yeah. Now come the fuck here."

"I'll get wet." But she's already shrugging out of the zippered hoodie she's wearing. We both changed into more comfortable clothing before getting on the plane. She must have taken her shoes and socks off out in the bedroom because she's barefoot.

"Yes, you will definitely be very wet very soon."

She's now just in her jeans and a tee. "I'm already wet," she tells me.

My cock hardens even more and I grip it. "Get. Your. Sweet. Ass. In. Here."

Her eyes are on my hand as her fingers go to the button and zipper on the jeans and she pushes them off too. "I hate wet denim," she tells me.

Her in nothing but tiny white panties and a fitted pink T-shirt that's going to be plastered against her breasts as soon as the water hits her is definitely fine with me.

I squeeze my cock, then take a long stroke as she opens the door and steps inside.

Her gaze is locked on my hand. She wets her lips.

"The light in here is really good." Her voice is already a little breathless.

"Yeah, it is." I reach out and trace a finger around one hard nipple pressing against the front of her shirt.

I grasp her wrist and tug her forward under the water, wetting her shirt, and all that gorgeous bare skin. Much better. The cotton clings to her and her breasts rise and fall as she breathes fast.

I cup her breast, running my thumb over the tip, but I keep stroking my cock. If that's what she wants, that's what she'll get.

"Can I touch you?" she asks, reaching out and putting a hand flat on my stomach before I answer.

"Always."

She strokes her hand up and down over my abs, to my chest, then down again, not quite touching my cock. She does it again. And again. Her gaze locked on my hand moving on my shaft.

"Abigail?" I finally ask.

She looks up. "Yeah?" Her cheeks are pink, her throat flushed by more than the warm water, and the hand that's not moving on me is on her stomach moving back and forth as if she wants to touch herself too but is holding back.

"Tell me what you want."

"I'm waiting for you to tell me to kneel like you said you would."

I stop breathing for a moment. Then I squeeze my cock hard and groan. "Christ," I rasp.

She catches her bottom lip between her teeth.

I take her chin in my hand and lean in. "Do you want to be on your knees for me, princess?" I ask.

She nods. Or tries to. I'm holding her too tight for her to move much. "Yes."

"Do you know what to do once you're down there?"

She tries to shake her head, but I hold her head still and lift a brow.

"No," she says. "Not really. I understand the basics, but you have to tell me how to make it good."

Oh, hell yes. "You sure you want my cock in your pretty little mouth? This mouth that says amazing things and is trying to save the world? You sure you want to dirty it up like that?"

"Well, see, I have high standards." She pauses and her lips curl into a sexy, almost sly grin. "I only suck royal cock."

I stare at her. I'm teasing *her*. *I'm* being dirty with *her*. And then she turns it around like that.

I give her a slow grin. "I fucking love that you've found your words, Abigail."

She grins back. "Does that mean yes, you're going to put your cock in my mouth?"

"That's absolutely what it means." I kiss her, hot and deep and thoroughly. Then I pull back, let go of her chin, meet her gaze directly, and say, "Kneel."

She goes to her knees, slowly, trailing her hand down my body as she does it.

This isn't going to last long, so I tell myself I'm not overly worried about her knees. But this is hard marble, and it only takes me two seconds to reach outside of the door, grab one of the bath towels, fold it, and push it under her knees.

She gives me a knowing smile and I know exactly what she knows—I talk dirty and tough, but I'm gone for her. I might be the one ready to give up my crown, my fucking soul to have a blow job from this woman, but she will, by God, be comfortable while she's taking everything I have to give.

I put my hand on top of her head, the other wrapped around the hardest erection I've *ever* had. "Open up, Abigail."

She puts her palms on my thighs, leans in, and opens.

Fuck. Did I say it won't last long? It's going to be about five seconds.

I slide my head over her lips, then onto her tongue. She closes around the top and licks, then sucks lightly. My fingers curl into her hair and I suck air in through my nose.

She's barely doing anything and I'm ready to blow.

But the fact that this woman even said yes to a dance, returned a single text, even knows my name is amazing to me. That she understands what she and I can do together in Cara makes me feel something I don't even have a word for. And that she's here like this with me is fucking incredible.

"More," I urge, pressing forward.

She opens again, wider, and I slide in further. I keep my hand at the base. No way can she take all of me yet. But we can work on that.

And oh, fuck, I want to work on that. And everything else with her.

"God, you feel so fucking good," I praise. I press in a little further. She tightens her lips around me. "You're doing so well. Such a good girl."

Her eyes find mine and my knees feel a little weak.

"Oh, you like that?" I ask. "You like hearing that you're a good girl? When you're on your knees with your mouth full of my cock?"

She nods. And I give her a pass on not using words this time, because, well, she can't.

But *fuck*, she likes the praise. I've gotten that impression before, but I *know* it now.

A lot of people have praised Abigail Landry. She's been a straight-A, award-winning, top-performer in every academic endeavor she's ever undertaken.

She knows she's extraordinary when it comes to books and labs. But this is very personal. She needs to know she's just as amazing when it comes to reaching into a man's chest and taking his damned heart in her hands.

She doesn't have as many one-on-one *people* connections. Other humans telling her she's important and she matters and that the things she does for them are mind-blowing.

I, however, can absolutely say that.

"You're so good with that tongue, honey," I tell her, stroking her cheek. "God, you feel good. I love seeing you try so hard to take me. You're pleasing me so much."

She sucks me harder, then slides up and off. She runs

her tongue up and down my length, then sucks at my head again.

"Fuck, Abigail. Yes." I grip her hair a little harder, pressing her down further on my length and she lets me.

But I need more. We can spend time on this another night. I need inside her.

"Need your pussy," I say, pulling back. "I *need* to fuck you."

She gazes up at me, just blinking. Waiting for my next command? I grin. Well, I could get used to this.

"Bed." I pull her to her feet, and she steps toward the door.

She also strips off her shirt, bra, and panties as she steps out of the shower.

My mouth goes dry as she looks back at me over her shoulder.

Fucking hell. I love every part of this woman, but that mischievous smile she gives me is maybe my favorite part.

She reaches for a towel as she steps out, but instead of wrapping it around her body, she *bends over* and wraps it around her hair, then straightens, twisting the towel somehow up on top of her head, holding her wet hair.

And I'm still standing like a dumbass under the shower.

But she *bent over while naked*. Every man on this planet would forgive me.

"You okay, Your Highness?" she asks.

"I'm completely unable to do basic tasks like walk, since all of my blood is now in my cock," I tell her.

She laughs as she reaches for another towel. Presumably to cover her body.

I quickly shut off the water and get out as well.

I crowd close to her on the bathmat, reaching past her for a towel.

And that's when I see it. The honeybee tattoo. Previously I was too preoccupied, and I'd forgotten to look. But there it is. At the base of the back of her neck, where her hair usually hangs. That's why I've missed it so far.

I lift my hand and trace the pad of my finger over the ink.

She shivers and turns.

"Found it," I say softly.

She smiles. "I was thinking about giving my bee a flower. Maybe a *trifolium dubium*. It's a clover."

I nod. I actually know this one. "It's planted all over Cara. It's the one that is most often called a shamrock."

She turns, her smile growing. "Yes. Its yellow flowers attract bees."

I'm in the bathroom, naked, having just had a partial blow job from her, but my throat feels tight with emotion and I can only nod.

"No words?" she teases, softly, her eyes soft.

I shake my head and lean in to kiss her.

She wraps her arms around my neck, and I lift her, carrying her to bed. I don't care that we're both still wet.

I toss her on the bed and lean over, tugging the towel from her hair. "You are so fucking gorgeous." I start kissing her neck, then down to one breast, where I suck a nipple into my mouth. "I'm so goddamned grateful I have you, Abigail."

She arches closer, her hands going to my head. "*Torin.*"

"Need you, princess," I tell her gruffly, switching to her other breast, as my hand slides down her belly and between her legs. I slip one finger inside, just to the first knuckle. "So wet," I praise. "You need something too?"

She nods. "You."

"What do you need from me?"

"Your cock. Filling me up. Fucking me. Making me come."

I growl and lower my lips to hers. Damn, she's going to kill me. And I'm going to love every torturous second of it.

"Say you want me to fill up your *pussy*. P word number one."

She sucks in a breath. Then she says softly, "I want you to fill up my pussy."

Yes. I kiss her again, deeply, hungrily, moving my finger in and out, loving the way said pussy grips me.

Then I say, "Now say, I want you to fill up my *princess* pussy."

She gives a soft laugh and shakes her head.

I press my forehead against hers, stopping her head, and looking directly into her eyes. I'm smiling slightly, but I know she sees how serious I am. "Yes, Abigail. I want to hear you call yourself my princess."

Fuck, I want to hear that more than I want to hear dirty words from her, I realize.

She wets her lips. She swallows. She stares up at me. And finally says, "I'm your...princess, Torin."

The words punch me in the gut, and I groan, taking her mouth again in the most carnal kiss of my life. I kiss her, finger fucking her, pressing my body into her, wanting to somehow meld our bodies together. I want to *own* her.

Finally, long moments later, I let up. "You have no idea what you do to me," I tell her, moving my finger slower, sliding up to circle her clit.

She moans, then murmurs against my mouth, "I have something else to tell you."

I lift my head and press my finger all the way inside her again. She gasps. "Tell me anything. But make it quick."

She meets my gaze directly and says, "Turns out I do like cowboys."

My heart thuds even as I grin. "Is that right?"

"Well, *one* cowboy."

"Damn, you've got good dirty talk, girl." I give her ass a squeeze and give her another finger as a reward.

She moans and wiggles against my hand. But then says, "*And—*"

"There's more?"

"I think I might like being a cowgirl in bed." She pauses. "Maybe even a reverse cowgirl."

I freeze and stare down at her. She's watching me with her lips pressed together.

I grin slowly. "Do you know what that means, Abigail?"

Her eyes widen slightly, and she shakes her head. "No. But you do, right?"

I move my fingers out, then back in. "Oh, I certainly do."

"I think I have to dress up," she says, her voice a little breathless. "Right?"

I chuckle. "Well...not technically."

She frowns. "Not even the boots?"

My cock pulses against her leg. "Who told you about cowgirl and reverse cowgirl?"

Her cheeks pinken a little. "My sisters."

Ah. "Remind me to send them a couple of *very* nice gifts."

She laughs, but says, "Why?"

"You'll see."

CHAPTER 26

ABIGAIL

"Are we going to be late for the meeting?" I ask as Torin stretches out alongside me, running his hand over my stomach.

"No one will bother us," he says. "I'm the prince. I do what I want." He gives me a wink. "Not that it doesn't annoy the fuck out of some people. But no one's going to knock on that door, I promise you."

This man was made to be naked. He looks so damned good. I can still feel him in my mouth and I want to do that again. I want more time to explore him with my lips and tongue. And to really relish all the reactions that gets from him.

But this is our *wedding night*. I shiver with that realization. I get to have him, like this, every night for the next *year*.

"You are going to be such a good cowgirl, Abigail."

A swirl of heat goes through me from head to toe.

I'm not sure why Torin's praise makes me feel hot, but it really does.

It's not that I haven't been praised in my life. One of my theories—because of course I've pondered this—is that it's because I started to tune praise out as a kid since I actually got a lot of it. But it was always about my intelligence or accomplishments. It's just kind of hot to be wanted for something else. Something more human. More raw and primal.

"I don't know anything about being a cowgirl."

He runs his hand up the inside of my thigh but stops short of my pussy.

"I'm very happy to coach you through this," he tells me. "*Very* happy."

"Well, you know that I've always been an A+ student," I tease.

I'm *teasing*. A hot guy. I didn't know I could do that.

And it's working. He looks turned on and very pleased with me.

"Oh, I have no doubt that you're going to pass with flying colors." He drags a hand up to cup a breast. He plays with my nipple and I'm already wriggling, wanting more.

I roll toward him. "Just tell me what to do."

"You just get on and ride," he tells me with a grin.

My gaze moves up and down his body. "*Oh.*"

I love how blunt and graphic he is in bed and about sex. I don't like that words can get misconstrued and misused, but with Torin that doesn't happen. He says what he thinks and feels and wants and there's no mistaking any of it.

He chuckles. "Yeah, *oh.*" Then he grabs both my hips and drags me over on top of him as he rolls onto his back.

He grasps one of my thighs and pulls it over his body, so

I'm straddling him. Then his hands settle on my hips, and he presses me against his cock.

His hard length moves between my pussy lips and rubs over my clit. I moan and rock my pelvis, increasing the pressure.

"That's my girl," he encourages, one hand splaying over my ass.

"Do you have a condom this time?" I ask.

"Multiple."

"Excellent."

"You ready for that? Already?" he asks, one brow up.

It's our first time, but this all feels perfect. I completely trust him and I'm *so* ready.

"Yes. Please." I circle my hips, loving the way it makes him groan and his hand on my ass tighten. "I've been thinking about you every single night since Ami's wedding." I lean in and kiss him, then say against his lips. "I've been using Charming *every* night."

"Charming?"

"My vibrator."

He grins. "As in Prince Charming?"

"Yep."

"You think getting your pussy filled is *charming*?"

God, I love when he says those graphic things. "Well, there's no Prince Hot As Fuck in the literature."

He pulls me down for another deep kiss. "I want to put you on your back, spread these legs, and drive deep," he says huskily. "But you riding me the first time is probably a good idea. Then you can control how deep I get and how fast we go."

"I don't know what I'm doing," I confess. "Maybe you should be in charge." I love when he's in charge. "We can do cowgirl another time."

"First of all, I'm still in charge." He squeezes my ass again. "And second, I don't know if you're actually ready for how much I want you. It could get rough."

I'm sure he feels the shudder of lust that goes through me.

He chuckles, but it sounds naughty. "Yeah, we'll get to *all* of that. You'll be ready for everything eventually."

I don't even know what that means *exactly*, but my response is *yes, yes, I will*. I wiggle against his cock. Then I reach between us and stroke him. "Where's the condom?"

He reaches toward the bedside table. "You stashed condoms in there already?"

"Of course." He pulls one out, opens it, and reaches between us to roll it on. Then his hands go to my hips again. "You ready?"

I nod.

He squeezes my hip. "*Say* it."

"Yes, I'm ready," I say, enunciating clearly.

He grins. "Prove it."

I shake my head with a little frown. "Um..."

"Put your fingers in your sweet little pussy and show me how wet you are."

Heat hits me. I push myself up to a more upright position and, blushing from head to toe, I reach between my legs.

"It's okay with me if you spend a little time on your clit. I completely understand how tempting that delicious spot is. I swear I can still feel it in my mouth and taste you on my tongue when I close my eyes."

Oh my God. I circle my middle finger over my clit and feel the pleasure ripple through me. My thighs tighten around him.

"That's it. Just like that."

I do it again, pressing a little harder and faster.

"Damn, that's a pretty sight," he says. He squeezes my thighs and moves them a little wider. "Do you want to come like that? All spread out on top of me, playing with yourself?"

I keep circling but I shake my head. "I want you inside me."

"Nothing's going to keep me out," he says in a firm promise.

I circle a few more times, but then I slide my fingers lower, dipping inside, feeling how wet I am. I moan, then withdraw my fingers to show him.

He grabs my wrist and pulls my fingers to his mouth, sucking on them as his eyes lock on mine.

The sucking pressure around even my fingers makes my pussy clench.

"Perfect," he says, letting my hand go. "Ride me, Abigail."

I take a deep breath and then move against him. He's long and thick and I know it's going to be a tight fit. I know it will work and all of that, but I'm going to feel every inch.

I can't wait.

"That's it," he encourages. "Line me up."

I reach down and take hold of his cock, then position him at my entrance.

"Take me," he coaches. "Slide me into my favorite place on this planet."

I laugh softly at that, feeling high...on him. "You haven't been to this place yet."

He grins up at me. "Doesn't matter."

Geez, how can he be so hot and dirty, then sweet and cute all at the same time?

I let myself sink down a little around him. We both

groan. Then a little more. Then more. It's definitely a stretch. I'm hot and so full. But *damn*, this is so, so good.

Him filling me up is so much of it, but the way he's watching me, looking at me like I'm the most amazing thing he's ever seen, definitely helps.

As do his freaking words.

It's just a constant litany of things like, "Abigail, Jesus, yes. Grip me. Yes. You're so perfect. So tight. Fuck, princess. So fucking tight and perfect. This pussy is mine. You are mine."

I'm moving. My hips are rotating, I'm lifting and lowering, just following my body's cues, searching for *that spot*.

Then Torin grips my hips. "Want to try the reverse cowgirl?"

I nod quickly. If it's even half as good as this...

He swats my ass.

I gasp. "Yes, yes, I want to try it."

He lifts me, turns me so I'm facing the foot of the bed, then lowers me back on his cock.

God, taking him again is as good as the first time. And this new position gives us a new angle. He's hitting a spot that makes me cry out and clench around him.

"Yes, fuck," he grits out. His hands are on my breasts, teasing my nipples, pinching and tugging with the perfect pressure to make my clit throb.

"I need..." I'm breathless. "Oh, God."

"*What*, princess? Anything. But you have to say it."

"My...clit," I manage.

Then his hand is on mine and he brings both to my clit. "Like this? You need some attention here?"

I nod. Then say, "Yes," between panting breaths. Then I say more, because I want more. I want to give him more. "I love your hands on me. Please, Torin. Make me come."

"Oh yes, coat my cock, Abigail. Give me all your sweetness."

He pinches one nipple, we rub my clit together, and within seconds, my orgasm crashes into me.

It takes my breath and I feel a little light-headed.

"Fuck." Torin swears low, and harsh. Then he's grasping my hips and hammering up into me. "Yes. Fuck yes, Abigail."

Then he's coming too, gripping me hard, filling me up, calling out my name. He lies still underneath me for a moment, then he sits up and presses his lips against my shoulder. He moves my hair to the side and kisses my tattoo. He takes a deep, shuddering breath, wraps his arms around me, tucks his face against my neck and then lies back, taking me with him. He rolls us both to the side, cuddling me, my back to his front.

And he just holds me like that.

For several long minutes.

Finally, when our bodies are cooled and our breathing is normal again, he gets up. "Be right back." He kisses the top of my head and pads into the bathroom.

When he comes back into the room, he climbs up onto the bed behind me, and pulls me back into spoon with him.

"So...I'm a cowgirl after all."

He kisses my shoulder. "I knew you would be. You're a very good rider."

I wiggle my ass against him. "And you like how I look in the boots."

"And out of the boots."

I grin. "I'm glad. But maybe being a cowgirl isn't all about the boots." I pause, then say softly, running my hand over the forearm he has wrapped around me. "Just like being a prince isn't really about the crown."

He pulls me in even tighter, like he's hugging me. He doesn't say anything for a long moment, and I just enjoy the feel of his hot breath on my shoulder.

Then he says, "You should bring your green rubber boots inside, and we'll try them out. See if being a farmer is about the boots."

I smile. I do love teasing with him. "Oh, is there a reverse farmer position?"

He puts his hot mouth against my neck and says gruffly, "Well, now there's going to be."

We cuddle for a few minutes, but then shower *again*, quickly, only able to play a little. We soap each other up and kiss a lot, but we really do have to get to our meeting with the king.

Torin, however, makes big promises for later. For the rest of our wedding night.

I'm *married*.

To a prince.

And I'm going to meet the *king*—my grandfather-in-law, I remind myself.

It's all still a little crazy when I think about it too hard.

So instead, I concentrate on picking something to wear.

"Can I wear my boots now?" I ask Torin. "To the meeting."

He looks up from where he's tying one of his dress shoes. "You can do whatever you want, Princess. No one tells you what to do here. Or anywhere, as far as I'm concerned."

"But I'm only a princess in Cara."

He stands and crosses to me. He cups my cheek. "No. You're always a princess. Everywhere. And you're my *wife*, everywhere. That means, you answer to no one."

I grin up at him. "Hmmm...so later when you tell me to kneel..."

"Except me," he says on a growl, lowering his head. "In this bedroom. Or any bedroom," he amends.

I kiss him back, very comfortable with that rule.

Finally, we're making our way back down the hallway. Torin is wearing a button-down shirt, the top two buttons undone, no tie. He also has the sleeves rolled up on his forearms, a look I very much enjoy. He's wearing casual blue slacks and his dress shoes.

He looks polished, sophisticated, CEO-at-the-end-of-the-day, without looking too uptight or formal.

We go back down to the second level.

"Our offices are here on the second floor," Torin tells me. "The first floor is for entertaining, tours, public meetings, that kind of thing. The second floor is all of our offices, staff offices, conference rooms, etcetera. Third and fourth floor are personal quarters for the family and guestrooms."

I nod. "Are there staff that lives in the castle?"

"Only a few. My grandmother's personal assistant, who has been with her for forty years, lives here. Samuel and Emil, our butlers too. Jonah has rooms here. Other security staff members do too, though Jonah's are on the family's floor."

I love the way he smiles when he talks about Jonah. It's clear he loves the other man like a brother.

"Staff quarters are on the east side of the castle other than Jonah's. But most of the staff live in town and commute back and forth just like anyone would to their workplace."

We stop in front of two huge wooden doors with gold handles. An older man with completely white hair, wearing a perfectly pressed dark blue suit is standing outside waiting for us.

"Emil, this is Princess Abigail. Abigail, this is my grandfather's personal assistant and butler, Emil."

Emil also gives me one of those bows. "Princess, welcome to Cara."

"Thank you. It's nice to meet you."

"Is he ready?" Torin asks.

"Quite," Emil says.

I feel Torin tense next to me. "Then let's get this over with."

The doors open, Torin's hand goes to my lower back, and I step into the office of King Diarmuid of Cara.

CHAPTER 27

TORIN

Abigail actually doesn't seem nervous. She didn't puke before coming down here to meet my grandfather at least.

I want that to be a good sign. I don't want her to be nervous.

On the other hand, I'm afraid maybe she has a bit of a false sense of security.

Yes, she's now a princess.

Damn. Every time I think that or say it, a rush of possessiveness and desire goes through me. She's the Princess. She's *my* princess. Because she's my *wife*.

I fucking love that.

And yes, of course, with that comes some power, influence.

But King Diarmuid could still make her fairly miserable.

He can't undo our marriage. He won't tear down the farm. But...he could be a real asshole to her.

We step into the room, and I look around trying to imagine how it looks to Abigail.

It looks like a typical office to me, but I know that isn't true.

There's nothing corporate about it. It's actually warm and comfortable. Despite the various *uncomfortable* conversations I've had in here.

The ceilings are high, the room is enormous, and the artwork on the walls is worth millions of dollars. But the colors are warm, the golden light from the lamps is soft, the furniture is welcoming, and the man behind the desk does actually look like a grandfather.

He has white hair peppered with a little gray. He has a short beard. He's wearing a button-down shirt and trousers like mine. His tie has been discarded, his suit jacket is hung over the back of his chair, and his shirtsleeves are rolled up.

He doesn't look his age. He could easily pass for ten years younger, but when he looks up, he looks tired.

"Grandfather," I say simply.

He sits back in his chair and motions us forward. I escort Abigail to one of the chairs and wait for her to take a seat. I pull the other chair closer to hers, then I sit, taking her hand.

"Grandfather, this is Abigail. Abigail, this is my grandfather, Diarmuid O'Grady."

"It's nice to meet you, Your Majesty." Abigail looks between him and me with a questioning look.

"You only have to address him by his title when we're in public. Behind closed doors, we're family. You can call him Diarmuid." I look at my grandfather for backup. That's always how it's been for all of us.

When we were young children, we called him grandfather. Even in public. It was actually endearing to the people. As we got older, we called him King Diarmuid or Your Majesty when we were in front of other dignitaries. But even with family, friends, and even more professional acquaintances in casual settings, we would call him Grandfather.

He gives a short nod. "That's fine, of course, Abigail."

"Most people call me Abi," she says easily.

"And are you pregnant?"

I whip my head to look at him. "*Excuse me?*"

Abigail squeezes my hand. "That's actually a fair question. I mean we got married, rather suddenly as far as he's concerned. The first time he meets me, we've already had a wedding."

My grandfather has clasped his hands together and is resting them on his flat stomach. He's just watching her.

She faces him. "I'm not."

I actually squeeze her hand harder without meaning to. Children. That's not something we've discussed. Of course not. Abigail only intends to stay for a year.

"Well," Diarmuid says. "I want to assure you that I'm very fond of Saoirse, Fiona's daughter. So no pressure on you."

My brows slam together. "What the hell?"

Abigail puts a hand on my thigh and squeezes. "Actually, that's very nice to know," she tells my grandfather. "I've met Saoirse several times. She's delightful. I can see why you're fond of her."

I study Abigail's face. She seems perfectly calm and composed. The subject of who will sit on the throne *after me* doesn't seem to ruffle her.

Of course not. That's well past the terms of your agreement.

I ignore that voice and work on looking as relaxed as she does.

"But I guess it's good to know we have what...six years?" Abigail asks. "We can wait until Saoirse is eighteen and makes the decision for herself? Then if she's in, we can decide if we're really into the parenthood thing or not?"

I look at her quickly. And I can immediately tell that Abigail is being completely sarcastic. But I wonder if my grandfather can tell. And if so, what he thinks of that.

Diarmuid is studying her closely. "Good thing you're only twenty-three."

I blink at him. Did my grandfather just make a joke?

Abigail laughs softly. "Of course, I'm very fond of your grandson, so if the pregnancy happens before six years are up, you'll have to forgive us. Odds, and hormones, and biology and all that."

I'm unable to hold in my surprised laugh.

Diarmuid also actually smiles now.

"But seriously, I can understand that this is a huge surprise to you," Abigail says to him.

"Not such a surprise. Even if Jonah wasn't required to forward all of your security information to us ahead of time, I would have heard about it from the podcast."

Now Abigail looks at me with surprise. "Jonah forwarded security information?"

But it's my grandfather who answers. "Of course, we can't have just anyone sleeping within the palace walls. Not to mention joining the family. We need to know everything about you. But you passed everything with flying colors."

She's still frowning but says, "Of course I did. I get excellent grades in everything."

Diarmuid *laughs* at that, and I'm shocked. He nods. "Yes, that's what I understand." Then he sobers a bit and asks, "So what was the reason for the sudden wedding? A courthouse in New Orleans rather than a wedding ceremony? Even in the US?"

"We didn't want to wait," I tell him. "Once Abigail agreed to marry me, I didn't want to wait another moment."

She gives me a sweet smile, then turns to my grandfather. "Truthfully, he did it for me. I'm not very good in front of crowds. Even crowds of my own family. I'm much more comfortable in smaller, intimate settings. Torin respects that and protects me. The courthouse got us just as married as a bigger, more elaborate ceremony would have. It seemed there was no real reason to wait."

"There has already been grumbling here about the lack of ceremony," Diarmuid informs us.

I had expected as much. But now that I'm back on Cara soil, I can make some appearances, and charm the people. "They'll soon see that Abigail and I have even better things planned for them than a one-day party."

Abigail nods. "I'm anxious to get started on my work. There's no reason to take a bunch of time off to plan a wedding. We're married. The most important part of that is that we are together." She gives me a beatific smile.

"So you won't even honor us with the tradition of the ceremony?" my grandfather says to me.

I frown and Abigail turns in her seat, giving him a puzzled look.

"Is that actually insulting somehow?"

"There hasn't been a royal wedding in years. It gives the people a sense of security. Seeing the new leader settle down, celebrate age-old traditions, and include the people in a major life event will make the people happy."

"Hasn't Torin proven his commitment, and how much he loves the tradition of this country in other ways?"

My grandfather sighs and I brace myself.

"My grandson left the country, Abigail. Abdicated his throne. After telling me everything I was doing wrong. He took his siblings with him. Then stayed away for a decade. Now he's only been here for two years, and we've argued nearly every day. Now he says he wants to settle down, but he's doing it with an American and all of her work, all of *her* traditions and customs, all of her *roots*, are still across an ocean."

I feel the frustration twisting through my chest. I don't know how to convince him of what I feel for this country. I don't know how to convince him that I'm here to stay.

But Abigail is watching him with interest, rather than any hint of anger or exasperation. Her hand is still resting on my thigh.

I cover it with mine. "Let's go. We're here to stay for a few days before we go to the ranch. We can talk again later."

But Abigail shakes her head. "I completely understand what you're saying," she says to the king.

Shock tightens my gut. "What?"

She looks at me. "I'm just saying that how he's feeling is fair. Not only did you leave the country for a very long time, now that you're back, you've come and gone a lot. And then you suddenly bring home a wife who, as far as the king knows, could want to hop on a plane and leave tomorrow."

The king is watching her, as if contemplating something.

"I want you to know that I understand how you feel," Abigail says to him. "But Torin and I are here now, and we're going to show you what we want to do as Prince and Princess. We understand that's going to take some time." She stands up from her chair, not realizing that she needs the king to excuse her. "So we're going to get out of your way right now. But I do hope you'll come out and visit our farm soon. And regularly. You'll get to see it as it comes together and grows. Literally."

Then she reaches into her bag and withdraws a box with a big bow around it. I have no idea where that came from or what it is.

She leans over and sets it on the king's desk.

He frowned. "What is this?"

"Open it," she encourages.

He leans forward and pulls at one of the ends of the bow. He opens the package and separates the tissue paper. Then he removes three chocolate bars. "Chocolate?"

She nods. "I made that. I know that you love chocolate, and I wanted you to know that because of the farms we're building, Cara can have cacao trees right here on the island. I can make you that chocolate anytime you want."

He looks at her, astonished. Then he lifts the bar in his hand to his nose and sniffs. "It smells like lavender."

She smiles. "That's one of my specialty bars. I think you'll really like it." Then she turns and starts for the door. She looks over her shoulder. "Are you coming?" she asks me.

I push out of my chair immediately. I'm absolutely following this woman anywhere.

"We'll see you tomorrow, sir."

But my grandfather is watching Abigail, with a look of surprise still on his face. "Yes. I'll see you tomorrow."

We step out into the hallway and Abigail laces her fingers with mine. She starts for the staircase, clearly heading back to our room.

"Hang on." I pull her to stop. "You brought my grandfather chocolate."

She nods. "Did you know I make chocolate?"

I'd read about it in her bio from IAS. "Yes, but..." Then I decide to just admit it. "I didn't know my grandfather likes chocolate."

Her eyes go wide. "Torin O'Grady, have you never Googled your grandfather?"

I laugh. "I guess not."

"Well, it's one of the best-known facts about him. He's a chocoholic. When I read that, I knew he and I were going to get along just fine. My chocolate is the best."

I pull her in and press my lips to hers. She immediately melts into me, wrapping her arms around my neck. I feel calm just like that.

"Did you really tell my grandfather that you think it's fair that he's doubting me?" I ask when I lift my head.

She nods. "It is. You did leave. For a long time. You still leave a lot. Almost any chance you get it seems."

"Because he won't let me *do* anything," I say with a frown.

"You talk to him a lot, but he doesn't listen, right? You can't win him over. But, he doesn't know what you're capable of, Torin. You've just been trying to convince him by arguing with him, trying to get him to *hear* you. You haven't *shown* him anything."

For a second, I have a hard time taking a deep breath.

She might have a point.

"And he didn't just want you to marry Linnea because she would be a good advisor to you or a great leader for Cara. I mean, maybe that's what he said, maybe that's what he even believes, but I think it was more than that." Abigail puts her hand on my chest. "You are a reluctant royal,

Torin. You've made no secret of that. You *abdicated*. Then when you came home, you built yourself a ranch where you could spend time *away* from the palace. And you named it *The Rogue*."

I swallow, but don't say anything.

She goes on. "I think he believed that Linnea would keep you here. That she would've made you stay even if you got frustrated. She's from here, and loves the country dearly, feels like she's part of the family, so you wouldn't have just taken off again, and potentially abdicated, if *she* was your wife."

I frown. My heart is squeezing tightly in my chest. "You think my grandfather's worried about me abdicating again?"

"Maybe. It occurred to me when he mentioned that you married an American. Maybe he's worried I'll want to go home, and you'll go with me. It makes sense that you'd go with your wife."

Fuck, why is it so hot when she refers to herself as my wife?

"And maybe that's why he pushes you," she says, unaware that my frustration is now mixed with lust. "If he pushes hard enough, will you just up and leave? Or can he actually trust you to stay even when it gets tough?"

Well...fuck.

All of that makes sense.

Dammit.

"His best friend, his top advisor for years, left to move to America. For a woman," I tell her.

Her eyes widen. "Oh my God! Oisin! That's right!"

Of course, she knows Oisin. He's now in Autre, living with her grandmother's best friend. Who he met on my grandfather's first visit to Louisiana when my sister moved there. They fell in love and did the long-distance thing for quite a while but eventually Oisin retired and decided to move to the US to be with Cora.

My grandfather has been a little lost without him. And I know exactly how that feels. My year without Jonah sucked.

"That's one more reason for him to fear you leaving," she says.

"You know, princess, for someone who doesn't like words very much, you really are pretty good at them." I've told her this before, but she keeps amazing me. I need to encourage her words because I fucking love them.

She takes my hand in hers again and starts for the steps. "Well, I've got some more words for you, but they are definitely not appropriate to be said in a hallway where just anyone could walk by."

"Give me just one," I urge.

She gives me a sexy little grin. "How about two?"

"Yes."

"Reverse Princess."

I growl and lean in, putting my mouth against hers. "We. Are. Doing. That."

Then I do the only thing I really can—I hoist her over my shoulder and head upstairs.

She's laughing as I toss her on the bed.

"What's this?" she asks.

I'm pulling my shirt off over my head as I tell her, "This is a reward."

"I like it so far," she says. "Please tell me what I did so I can do it again and again."

"Well, I promise to use this reward more than once. You charming my grandfather was a huge fucking turn on, princess."

"I'm starting to not hate the word princess." Her voice is husky and soft as her gaze roams over my bare skin.

I can't describe the emotion that courses through me at those words. "I am very partial to *wife*, too, though."

She smiles. "Me too." She pulls her shirt off. "But I hope being a princess doesn't mean I can't still get on my knees for you."

The heat hits me hard and low. I shove my pants to the floor and move in. "Oh, no, not at all. There's the Reverse Princess, after all."

"Ohhhh, the princess kneels in this one?"

"Something like that."

She laughs as I slide my hands up her legs until I can hook my fingers in the top of her panties and pull them off. When she's naked, I flip her over to her stomach. She kneels without being told. I press a hand between her shoulder blades, lowering her chest to the bed, keeping her gorgeous ass up in the air.

"The other part of the Reverse Princess," I tell her as I run my palm up and down her spine, "is that *I* kneel as well." I go to my knees on the floor beside the bed. Then I pull her ass back towards me and lick her pussy.

She moans into the duvet. "I love this position."

"Oh, we're just getting started."

I eat her like this until she's screaming my name into the mattress. Then I stand, kissing up her spine. "I have to inform you, love, you do not have a princess pussy."

She wiggles her ass against my stomach. "No?"

"Oh no, this is Queen pussy."

She sucks in a breath, but then laughs softly. I roll on a condom, grip her hips, and sink deep.

I fuck her like that, pouring everything I'm feeling into it.

This woman is not only going to make the agricultural program happen, but she's going to be my Queen. And she's going to make me a better King than I ever could have been without her.

I know there are many things about being princess or queen that may not work for Abigail Landry.

On the other hand, I'll be the fucking king. And if I can't change everything to accommodate whatever she needs, then what's the point of that damned crown anyway?

CHAPTER 28
WAIT 'TIL I TELL YE

EPISODE 780 TRANSCRIPT

Lindsey: The trick is to leave it on for ten minutes after massaging before washing it off.

Jen: I didn't realize that you needed to keep the lip scrub on for any time. I thought you just used it to exfoliate and then washed it off.

Lindsey: Right? But leaving it on for a bit before washing it off will really help.

Jen: Great! You can find the recipe for that homemade lip scrub in the show notes.

Lindsey: Okay, so now it's time to talk about our favorite topic.

Jen: Finally! You know everyone's been dying to get to this.

Lindsey: I know, but holy shit, it's been three weeks and Prince Torin and Princess Abigail have just been hanging out on his ranch...okay, *their* ranch, I guess. But they haven't been seen out and about *at all*.

Jen: Yep. All we've got are the adorable photos they've been posting on their social media accounts with their little captions. <gives a happy sigh>

Lindsey: And we know for a fact, that the ones that aren't selfies are taken by Linnea, right?

Jen: That's what she said. I think it's so funny, and cute, that the only reason that Princess Abigail even had Instagram was because her sisters made her start one back in high school. But she only used it to post plant and flower photos. <laughter> I guess moving up to photos with her in them is a big deal. She's apparently pretty introverted. But then Linnea made her start posting on it after she and Torin got married.

Lindsey: It's weird that she's so quiet and shy, right? Don't forget, one of her sisters was a Miss Louisiana and is a cover model for Bella Bobbi Cosmetics! Amelia Landry-LeClaire has *amazing* social media pages. She does a ton of very cool cosplay makeup. Definitely check Amelia out, everyone! Her stepson gets on there with her for the cosplay stuff a lot and it's adorable. And her sister Charlotte is in charge of PR for an animal park in Louisiana and she, and a bunch of other family members, are all over social media with their animals and events going on at the park.

Jen: Their animals are adorable! And they've got some pseudo-celebs there! First, Donovan Foster had his own animal rescue show on the Go Wild channel and is now doing a second self-produced show. And then, of course, Princess Fiona and Princess Saoirse both live in that same town as we've recently discovered. Along with Prince Cian. Princess Fiona is rescuing and rehabilitating animals at a sanctuary connected to the animal park!

Lindsey: Much like the endangered animal sanctuary she founded here in Cara. So it makes sense that Prince Torin would meet Princess Abigail there, but it's... interesting that she's so introverted compared to all the others, isn't it?

Jen: She seems much more bookish than her sisters. She has three degrees and she's very young. It seems she made her way through school way ahead of schedule.

Lindsey: Well, Torin was always a great student in school. That's common knowledge. It seems they'd be well-matched that way. I know the photos we've seen over the years of him in his glasses are quite...

Jen: Hot.

<they both laugh>

Lindsey: Yes, he gives great hot professor vibes. And I certainly understand them wanting to take some time to honeymoon, but it's been nearly a month! They have to emerge at some point! We need to *see* them with our own eyes.

Jen: Well, I don't know that they've spent these past two weeks studying the periodic table, but I'm guessing there's some major chemistry.

<laughing again>

Lindsey: Still, I want them out and about. Come on, Prince Torin, Princess Abigail! Come see us!

· · ·

PODCAST EPISODE 794 TRANSCRIPT

Jen: Okay, the Prince and Princess are still hiding out and I'm *dying*. Their photos and captions are so cute!! I love them so much. But I NEED MORE!

Lindsey: Seriously! I'm starting to get frustrated, and I know I'm not alone. We've had so many comments from listeners. I get that they're all wrapped up in one another, but *five weeks* with no appearances?!

Jen: I know. And we hear you, listeners! Them not having a wedding isn't helping things. If they'd gotten married here, it might make this feel better. But we haven't really seen them together at all!

Lindsey: I know. I've heard people saying things like it feels like Prince T wasn't doing much if he can just take a month plus off.

<laughter>

Jen: Okay, but we don't know that he's not working from the ranch, right?

Lindsey: Palace sources say he's not. Linnea has basically confirmed that the newlyweds are just enjoying time together. Hey, I thought you were Team Linnea when they were in the US and we thought they were on vacation together.

Jen: I was. But she's clearly fine. It's obvious they really are just friends. I mean she's the one who's handling all the press requests for them and she's the one taking the photos that aren't selfies. Like that one of them where he's carrying her through some kind of field. Oh, and the one where they're dancing in the kitchen and then he dips her back. <sighs>

Lindsey: Okay, I do love that one. And then that really sexy one where he's wiping what looks like chocolate from her lip with his thumb. The way she's smiling up at him... ugh, so cute and hot.

Jen: I know! The way he looks at her in *every* photo... I just want that. I want to go on a first date and just show the guy a photo of Torin and Abigail and say, "Can you just do this with me?"

<laughing>

Lindsey: The selfies they take are just as great. The one Torin took of her reading on the couch...her hair was falling out of her ponytail, she had glasses on, and she looked totally absorbed in her book, had that half-eaten chocolate bar beside her...it was so relatable.

Jen: And the one he took of him braiding her hair? The caption was *twisting my heart around her little finger just as easily*. I had no idea Prince Torin would be such a cinnamon roll!

Lindsey: Do you consider him a cinnamon roll? I always thought he had a little golden retriever energy.

Jen: Yeah, maybe, but not if you compare him to Prince Cian.

<laughter>

Lindsey: Oh, God, for sure. It would be so nice if Prince Cian started coming home more often, wouldn't it?

Jen: So let us know in comments what you're thinking about the Prince and Princess!

. . .

PODCAST EPISODE 808 TRANSCRIPT

Lindsey: It's cloudy, windy, and...typical. Ugh. But the temps are nice so get out and take a walk already!

Jen: And while you're walking, think about how great it would be to walk with a dog! And how you can do that either by adopting *or* by volunteering at the shelter to walk with those waiting for their forever homes! Call Maeve at the shelter for more information.

Lindsey: Okay, so we talk about them every week.

Jen: Every *day*.

Lindsey: Almost every day. <sigh> But people, we're going on *seven weeks* now. Where are our Prince and Princess?

Jen: You're all asking similar questions. And making lots of comments. And we love that you all come here to talk it all out! So, let's dive into some comments and questions that have been posted lately.

Lindsey: Yes, we always get lots of comments and we love that, but you all have really ramped it up on this topic in the past few weeks and we *get it.*

Jen: This is a common one. Lots of people saying that the Prince and Princess deserve to have a private life and their alone time and we should just leave them alone and quit speculating.

Lindsey: I disagree. I don't think we need cameras in their house or bedroom or anything, but these people aren't just average citizens. They're not even normal celebrities. Like if Alex Olsen shows up with a woman on his arm, we'll talk and speculate and *want* more info, but no, we're not entitled to that. But with Prince Torin? He's one of our leaders. He's our future king. And Princess Abigail is his *wife*. They're already *married*. She'll be our queen. I think we do deserve to know more about her.

Jen: Yeah, I get that. And the total blackout, just hiding out, seems weird, doesn't it? Even if there's nothing weird going on, appearances matter.

Lindsey: Someone in the comments said the same thing. She says it makes it seem like Abigail is maybe not happy here, or isn't adjusting to living in a foreign country well.

Jen: Well, she's not really *living* here. She hardly knows if she likes it or not. If she's not happy on the ranch, maybe she should try coming into town.

Lindsey: Right? Someone else said maybe she's sick or something.

Jen: Maybe. But this is a long time. If she is, it's something serious. And again, as a leader of our country, we should *know*.

Lindsey: <gasps> What if she's *pregnant?*

Jen: <gasps> Oh my God! Well...damn, we definitely should get to know *that!* Okay, someone here says what if she wants to go back to the US but Torin's trying to talk her into staying?

Lindsey: Well...screw her. I mean, we don't want a queen that doesn't want us.

Jen: But they already got *married*.

Lindsey: They shouldn't have done that without her living here for some time.

Jen: Okay, that's a good point. I mean, I *guess* they could get divorced. But...how does that work? We've never had a king and queen divorce.

Lindsey: Wow, anyone out there an expert on the rules around that?

Jen: There is a comment here that says since they didn't get married here in Cara, does it even count here? Or are they only really married under US law? Damn. Who knows for sure? Anyone?

Lindsey: Someone replied that King Diarmuid did bless the marriage so that's really all it takes here in Cara. But... did he? I mean I suppose he hasn't said they aren't married, but there wasn't even a ceremony for the blessing. Shouldn't that be public? Why aren't they doing *anything* for us to see? I don't like how everything is happening behind closed doors.

Jen: I know. It seems odd at this point. Everything feels secretive.

Lindsey: It does. I mean, do we even know for sure they're *here*? What if she freaked out and they went back to the US? We know from past experience that Torin is capable of sneaking on and off this island when he wants to.

Jen: Wow, true.

Lindsey: Or...what if she's blackmailing them or something? Like Torin *had to* marry her, but it's not a love match or anything. She's extorting them for money or power or...something.

Jen: <laughs> You're reading too many spy novels.

Lindsey: Romantic suspense, thank you very much. And I'm just joking around. That was in the comments. We should not be spreading stuff around like that. We're just chatting, people! No one quote us!

Jen: People literally print off what we say into transcripts and screenshot our posts.

Lindsey: Oh yeah. Oops.

CHAPTER 29
ABIGAIL

Oh, I am definitely into cowboys.

At least the way my husband does cowboy.

I feel a little shiver of pleasure go through me at the thought of *my husband*. The way it has every time I've thought it, or said it, in the past few weeks.

I prop my shoulder against the doorframe of the barn and watch as Torin brushes his horse, murmuring softly to her. I take in the way the soft blue flannel moves over his broad shoulders and muscled arms. Along with the way the worn denim hugs his ass, hips, and thighs. I even like the beat-up brown cowboy boots on his feet. These are the same ones he sent in the photo when we were texting.

This isn't the first time I've seen him dressed for ranch work, of course. But it never fails to make a hot swirl of want go through me. He doesn't look like a prince right now. He looks like a hot guy who works with his hands for a living. Not a guy who can use those hands to simply sign a piece of paper and make policies that affect thousands of people's lives.

Every time I think too hard about who he really is, it makes my heart pound. But I'm not sure if it's anticipation of the amazing things he can and will do. Or if it's nerves.

Being here on the ranch together makes it easy to forget where we *really* are.

What we really are.

We've been here for almost two months, getting the farm up and going, and enjoying our honeymoon.

We've been *very much* enjoying our honeymoon.

We haven't left the ranch since we came here after arriving on Cara. We'd spent two days at the palace, getting to know Torin's family, getting a tour of the palace and grounds, and getting a crash course in How to Be a Princess. But those lessons were cut short when Torin got frustrated, packed up our bags, and Jonah drove us to *The Rogue* himself.

We're not entirely alone. There are plenty of staff. The ranch runs at full capacity even when Torin isn't here. There's a ranch manager named Finn. There are also several ranch hands as well as a young woman named Marnie who is the housekeeper and cook for the guys. She also takes care of the main house when Torin is here.

Jonah and Linnea are here too, staying in Jonah's house on the property. Jonah is here for security and Linnea has appointed herself our public relations director.

But we spend plenty of time alone.

Wonderful, sexy, sweet, often-naked time alone.

The first two indoor farm buildings were completed within three weeks, a feat that is still amazing to me, but which Torin noted proves what money, influence, and determination can accomplish.

The plants all arrived the very next day. Because we planted mostly mature plants and trees, most of the crops are already flourishing. But we want everything functioning well and producing abundantly, along with having the entire newly hired farm staff fully trained before we start inviting people to visit.

The final farm building has only been complete for about two weeks now. We have two additional buildings ready to go but they're empty, waiting for later expansion. We've started with small crops that will be the most impressive. Things that Cara has never grown fresh, and things that will really emphasize how amazing having indoor farms will be. Coffee, avocados, citrus fruits, vanilla bean plants, even a few tropical flowers simply because they are gorgeous and will make an impression.

All of this has been a great excuse for us to hide out.

We've been supplying Linnea with plenty of candid shots of us around the ranch, at the farm, and just around the house. Shots of us cooking together, cuddling on the couch, shots of Torin's arms wrapped around me from behind, kissing my neck, a shot of him dipping me back after dancing in the kitchen. Lots of shots and captions that are meant to show the people of Cara that their prince is happily married to their new princess.

It seems to be working. Our posts get an incredible amount of interaction. Sure, there are plenty of people who want to see us out in public, but for now they're content with knowing we're enjoying one another on our honeymoon.

"You're such a good girl," Torin murmurs to the horse. He pats her a final time.

"I'll bet you say that to all the girls you play cowboy with," I say.

He pivots to look at me. "Hey, princess." A slow, sexy smile curls his mouth. "I do actually," he says, pulling off his work gloves. "But I promise you're my best good girl."

I push off the doorjamb and walk toward him, carrying the basket full of the surprise I've brought to show him.

"Damn, green rubber boots never looked so good," he says, letting his gaze rake over me from head to toe slowly.

We've had so much sex. *So much sex.* In all different rooms, on all different surfaces, in all different positions. And yet, his eyes on me can fire my blood in an instant.

"Hang on." He pulls out his phone, holding up a hand to stop me.

I stop, balancing the basket on my hip, and give him a quizzical look. "What?"

He snaps a photo of me. "This is definitely going on socials."

I look down at myself and laugh. I'm wearing shorts with the boots. Even though it's August, it only gets into the upper fifties here during the day—cold for a born and bred Louisiana girl—but the farm buildings are hot and humid. Just the way I like it. I have dirt streaked on my legs and my arms. I'm wearing only a green tank top and my hair is pulled back in a ponytail. I look like I've been working in a garden all day.

"You can't post that."

He strides toward me. He turns the phone for me to look. "First, this is sexy as hell. Second, this is a great shot of you at work. People will eat it up. They love that their princess works in the garden, cooks, doesn't do her make-up everyday, wears her hair in ponytails. You're *real* and they love it. Third, this will only improve the rubber boots sales."

I look up at him. "Rubber boots sales?"

"Didn't Linnea tell you?"

"About what?"

He snakes an arm around my waist and pulls me close. "Ever since we started posting pictures of you working on the farm, sales of rubber boots, in all colors, have gone up."

"Come on," I say, disbelieving. "No way."

He leans in, nearly touching his nose to mine. "You are the Princess. Whatever you do gets attention. You're a trendsetter."

Butterflies kick up in my stomach. I hate attention. He notices my frown and leans back.

"This is *good* attention, Abigail. We want people to think about the farm. Hell, we want them out gardening themselves, right? If they've got gardening boots, maybe they'll actually get out into the dirt. Maybe little girls will get interested in gardening. And if a little girl sees you as a farmer, a princess who will get dirty, who doesn't have perfect nails and hair all the time, that's a *good* thing, isn't it?"

I let that all sink in and nod. I take a deep breath. "You're right. It's a good thing. Thank you."

He leans in to kiss me but a thought occurs to me and I say, "Maybe we could start a program where the little girls come out with their boots and we have gardening days together. Or we could have a photo contest where they show me their boots in their gardens. We can have them post online somewhere. Start a page for that. Or even if they can't get the boots—I don't want anyone to *have* to buy anything—we can do boots or bare feet." My thoughts are spinning. "Or if they can't garden—because not everyone has the means for that—we could have them make paper flowers or cut out fruit and vegetable shapes. We could have them "plant" the flowers in cups at home.

We could do an arts and crafts video for them. Maybe it could be a group project. They could all tune in at a certain time and do it together. It could be an online gardening club." I sigh. "I would have loved to have other kids my age into gardening when I was little."

I feel Torin's hand on my face and realize I was staring off, the words just tumbling out. He's looking at me with wonder and obvious affection.

"Sorry. I was rambling."

"Never, *ever,* apologize to me for words, Abigail. You know how much I love them." He leans in to kiss me. "You're amazing," he says softly. "We should do all of those things."

I smile. "Okay. Linnea would be a great person to help."

"She really would. She'll be so proud of you wanting to reach out." He winks. Then he kisses my cheek and pushes the button on his phone, clearly sending the photo to Linnea.

"What's all this?" he asks, looking into the basket.

He pulls me back to the reason for my visit. "Oh, I wanted to share the first harvest of your favorite fruit." I give him a grin as I pull back the cloth covering the basket.

He reaches to pluck out a strawberry. "How did you know strawberries are my favorite fruit?"

I laugh. "Haven't you ever Googled yourself, Your Highness?"

He grins down at me. "*You've* Googled me?"

I nod. "Absolutely."

"And what else did you learn?"

It's actually ridiculous how much information is available about Torin and his entire family. "I know that you put your grandfather's motorcycle in the river when you were twelve. I guess I know that your grandfather *had* a motorcycle. That surprised me more than you putting it in the river. Though it didn't say if you did it intentionally or not."

He laughs. "Not intentionally."

"I know that you got fourteen stitches from that escapade."

He nods.

"I know that you got *fifteen* stitches from another motorcycle incident. This one in Morocco and that was when you were twenty-four and Jonah was along that time." I'm watching him and trying not to grin. "I also know there was a stolen chicken, that you were accused of stealing two hundred American dollars from an Egyptian tourist, and a diamond bracelet from a Swedish tourist. But they could never find the two hundred dollars, and the diamond bracelet turned out to be a fake."

He's clearly fighting a smile, but he nods. "Which is why we stole the chicken. He owed us."

"The chicken belonged to the Swede? That wasn't in the article."

"Well, we *thought so*. But no."

"And you thought the chicken was worth the same amount as a *diamond bracelet* that I assume you thought was real at the time?" Now I'm losing my battle with my attempt to not grin.

"I did not. We thought the chicken was his beloved pet. Which would have made the chicken infinitely more valuable, no?"

I snort. "Maybe. If it had been *his* chicken."

He nods. "Exactly. But since it wasn't, he had no qualms swinging a plastic baseball bat at me while driving along beside me on a motorcycle, knocking me and the chicken off, and inflicting a wound that required sixteen stitches."

My eyes are wide. "You could have died."

"Yes. Which is why I punched him hard enough to require him to see a dentist the next day."

I shake my head. "The article says fifteen stitches."

He shrugs. "They were misinformed."

And now I just laugh out loud. "*That's* the part they got wrong?"

He's grinning widely. "They might have missed a couple other things."

"But you *were* in Morocco in a strange, exciting, and dangerous situation with stolen goods and a motorcycle crash?"

"Yes."

"What the hell are you doing with me?" I ask him, honestly.

Immediately, he steps closer, and his voice drops to a husky, lower tone. "Being a much, much better man." He lifts his hand and cups my face. "Anyone can get drunk, mouth off to the wrong people, get involved in a motorcycle chase, and steal a chicken."

I lift a brow.

He gives a self-deprecating eyeroll, but then says, "You're related to the Autre, Louisiana Landrys. Don't tell me this story is *that* crazy to you."

I laugh. "Fair."

He sobers. "The excitement and *rush* I feel with you is unlike any I've ever experienced. And...I feel it every fucking time I see you. It's absolutely amazing to me that I get to have this, you, every day, Abigail."

I feel that same rush as he says those words. Damn. This is all so surreal, but yet, it's so *real*. I have my hands in dirt and on various plants every day. My muscles are sore every night from working on the farm. I see a rainbow of colors, and smell the scent of plants, dirt, fertilizer, flowers, and fruit all day. I *taste* fresh produce I harvest and carry only a few yards into the kitchen. Every single one of my senses tells me this is as real as my work, my passion has ever been.

And this man...he can simply smile at me, and I feel every single cell in my body respond.

Torin watches me as he lifts a berry to his mouth and takes a bite. Then his eyebrows rise. "Damn, that's delicious."

I give him a smug look. "I know. I'm very good."

He lifts the strawberry to my lips, and I take a small bite. Then he rubs the berry over my lips before leaning in and kissing me, licking the juice off before sliding his tongue into my mouth. We kiss deeply and are interrupted only by the sound of clearing throats.

We pull apart, turning to grin at three of the stable hands who have come into the barn.

"Sorry to interrupt Your Highnesses," one of them says, giving us a short bow.

I laugh. I know very well that when they're out here working with him, they call him Torin.

"No worries, gentlemen," Torin turns to me, then leans over and hoists me over his shoulder. "The Princess and I were just leaving."

The guys are laughing as they say, "Hey, can we keep some of the strawberries?"

Torin keeps walking. "Nope. The next batch is all yours, but we're going to need these."

CHAPTER 30

WAIT 'TIL I TELL YE

EPISODE 815 TRANSCRIPT

Jen: Okay, that photo of the princess being carried over the prince's shoulder, his hand on her ass, with that basket of strawberries? That was cute and hot.

Lindsey: Yeah, that was apparently taken by one of the stable hands. He said they're always flirting and laughing and even making out around the ranch. <sighs> WHY CAN'T THEY DO THAT OUT IN PUBLIC?? I want to see it!

Jen: Same!! And that photo was posted right after the prince's own photo taken of the princess in her boots, all dirty from working. Have you seen that people are having a hard time finding rubber boots on the island? They're ordering online.

Lindsey: I saw that Linnea posted that they're going to be coming out with a special boot for little girls with a Princess Abigail design. You'll only be able to get them from one of the businesses here in Cara. And they're getting a local artist to design it!

Jen: Oh, I hadn't heard that! That's amazing.

Lindsey: It is. They're bringing business to the islanders and the princess is interacting indirectly with people in a really interesting new way. But I still WANT TO MEET HER IN PERSON!

CHAPTER 31
ABIGAIL

"You're so fucking sweet. Even without the chocolate sauce," Torin says, dragging his lips up my neck to my ear.

"I'm never going to get this done." I still lean my head back against his shoulder, giving him more access to my neck.

"I can make you not care," he says. He dips his finger into the melted chocolate again and drags it over the upper curve of my breast that's showing just above the tank top and apron I'm wearing. He leans in and drags his tongue over the swipe of chocolate.

I'm supposed to be making chocolate dipped strawberries. But yeah, I really don't care at the moment. I give a little moan. "You're right. But then all this goes to waste."

"How about I just pour this all over you and spend the rest of the night with my tongue on every inch of your body?"

I laugh lightly. "That's not really that different from how we spend most nights."

He lifts his head and grins down at me wickedly. "Have I mentioned how much I like being married to you?"

God, there is something so ridiculously hot about him saying stuff like that.

I really like being married to him too. I can't believe that two of our twelve months is already over.

Our lips have just met and I'm just tasting my chocolate on my husband's tongue, when I hear, "We need to talk."

We pull apart with little groans. We turn to look at Linnea as she comes into the kitchen, Jonah right behind her.

"What are you doing here?" Torin asks, glancing up at the clock. It's eight p.m. Jonah and Linnea are here often, but almost never this late unless we've set up a meeting.

"Well, if you would answer your phone, I wouldn't have to stop by in person. But I don't need you to tell me what you've been doing instead of looking at your phone," she says.

I laugh. I'm sure it's clear in spite of the chocolate I'm stirring and the previously dipped strawberries cooling on the parchment paper on the counter, that we haven't *just* been working.

"Is everything all right?" Torin asks. He straightens slightly but doesn't give me much space.

"Yes and no," she says. She and Jonah take seats on the stools across the island from us.

I can feel some tension in Torin's body now. I frown. "What's going on?"

"As you know, you are social media stars. Everyone loves everything they're seeing about you."

I roll my eyes. "*Most* of what they see from us."

Linnea tips her head. "*Everything* they see *about* you. The likes and comments on your posts are incredible."

"Yes, as long as we're holding hands or hugging or kissing. If we talk about the farms or anything more serious, everything plummets," I say with a frown.

We've posted a few shots of our produce, even posted photos of things like the chocolate dipped strawberries, salads, even more complex recipes.

There is definitely less interest in those posts.

At least the rubber boots are popular.

Linnea nods. "Well, it's true that those posts don't get quite as much attention. But you're here, newlyweds, hiding out on the ranch for your honeymoon. This is the only glimpse they're getting of you. Plus, you guys look amazing together. Your chemistry is incredible even in photographs. Of course, they want to see you being all sexy and mushy and kissing."

I understand that. And yes, our photos are great. Torin looks properly adoring in every photo. I have felt more free and relaxed and sexy in the past seven weeks than I have in my entire life.

"But we're also doing *work* here. We're planting these farms for the people. We want them to be at least slightly interested."

"But we're not really focusing on the farms on your social media right now," Linnea says. "We're just cultivating passive interest."

I put my spoon down and brace my hands onto the countertop. I pin her with a look. "No, we're not focusing on it, but we should start doing more of that. Maybe it's time to *work* more."

She smiles. "Exactly." Her gaze shifts to Torin. "Honeymoon's over."

I look up at him.

He's frowning. "What do you mean?"

"I mean the country has been very understanding, and actually enamored, with the idea that you're here, holed up on this ranch with your new bride. They've loved the whole honeymoon thing. Giving them bits and pieces that show you together has been fabulous. But now you need to come to the palace. You have to be seen. You have to go to meetings."

He sighs. "Meetings about what? The farm isn't quite ready to go. I'm definitely not at the point where I can go have any economic talks or talks with our trade partners."

"Of course not," Linnea says. "But the first step is selling this to the people, right? When *they* love it, it will be harder for your grandfather to hate it."

I look up at Torin. "Right. Definitely. And this is just the starter site. To give everyone a general idea of what's possible. We need to build a *real* farm. More than one. I thought there was a new farm being built by one of the schools."

"There is," Linnea says. "And it's finished. You need to come and make an appearance. You need to talk to the administrators, the teachers, and the parents. We need to get everybody on board and really explain what's going on now. We've been putting them off with, 'The Prince will come and make a statement when it's all ready to go', and now...it's ready to go."

Torin's hand grips my hip. "I think maybe we need to get a secretary of education. Someone who can handle all of this."

I turn to him. "What? No."

He focuses on me. "Why not? We can put someone in charge of all of this. To make sure all of it is being handled well. Make sure that the teachers and administrators and parents are given the information they need and want. Someone who can be available to them."

I push him back slightly and plant my hands on my hips. "We already have that. *You*. No one is going to explain this better than you. You understand these farms in and out. You've already sold this idea to people. Lauren and Mason. Everyone in Shreveport. You know how to do this. You're the prince. People want to hear from you anyway. You need to get out there and sell them on this idea. Explain the farms to them. Tell them why they're amazing."

He steps in close to me again. "I just want to stay here with you."

I lift a brow. "That's very sweet. And I love being here with you too. But, we came here to do a job. These farms are important. And *no one* is going to sell them better than you."

An interesting mix of emotions goes through his eyes. He looked pleased, then a little frustrated if I'm not mistaken. But that doesn't make any sense.

We've been holed up here together for nearly two months. We've talked and laughed and had so much sex I can't even believe it. Surely, he feels all right about leaving once in a while.

Finally, he nods. "You're right. I need to get out there and talk about this."

I smile up at him. "You're definitely the best one. And soon, this farm will be ready for visitors as well."

"And as soon as the farm at the school is up and running, and everybody is on board, then we can build more, and you can start having those talks with other countries, getting the scientists on board who you want to study the effects long-term, talking about job-training," Linnea reminds him. "There are a lot of parts to this. The first farm at the first school is just the beginning."

He pulls in a deep breath and finally looks away from me to Linnea. He nods. "When do you want me?"

She smiles. "Tomorrow."

He sighs. "I should've seen that coming, shouldn't I?"

CHAPTER 32

WAIT 'TIL I TELL YE

EPISODE 818 TRANSCRIPT

Lindsey: OUR PRINCE IS BACK! Welcome back, Prince Torin! So nice to see you! *Finally*.

Jen: And seriously he looked *good*.

Lindsey: Well, he's been chilling on the ranch and...well, I think we all know what he's been doing for two months. He *should* look good, right?

Jen: <laughing> I guess we can assume that part is going well.

Lindsey: Yes. But... WHERE IS OUR PRINCESS??

Dammit, I just want to see this woman in person. I want to confirm she's real. She's not a robot or a figment of our imagination or photoshopped into all those posts.

Jen: Well, we just said that we think Torin's been having a very good time for the past two months, so I think it's safe to say she's not imaginary or photoshopped. And if she's a robot...well, that's disturbing. Stop it. Don't say that.

Lindsey: Okay. You're right. So she's real. But where is she? We don't have cooties, Princess! We aren't weird! Well, maybe some of us are weird.

Jen: We're getting weirder by the day. The longer you wait to come meet us, the weirder it's going to be!

Lindsey: Yes! Can you just drive by and wave? Or stand on the King's balcony and throw stuff at us? I'd even take that!

Jen: <laughing even harder> Throw stuff at us? Like what? Soft things, please! Pillows? Socks? Flowers! Flowers would be classy!

Lindsey: But in all seriousness, Prince Torin was at the palace for *two days* without her. Why? I mean, why doesn't she want to be here with him? It's not just about being holed up with him in their little love nest anymore. Now she legit doesn't want to be amongst the people, and that's not cool.

Jen: It's really not. So, Princess, if you're listening...uh, we want to like you, but you have to come meet us.

CHAPTER 33

ABIGAIL

It's only been three days. I can't possibly miss Torin this much.

I can't be *lonely*. I love being alone. I have an entire ranch to myself. Well, there are still staff here, but I can go wherever I want, do whatever I want.

I have *three* indoor farm buildings to play in. I have *acres* of land to walk, ride horses—yes, I've learned to ride horses—and explore.

I have an amazing kitchen to cook in. Two living rooms and five bedrooms to read in, not to mention the porch and the patio with a firepit.

I have *so* much space and quiet and alone time.

I should be in heaven.

But I miss my husband.

I miss knowing he's nearby while I work. I miss meals with him. I miss flirting and teasing with him. I miss just talking to him.

I definitely miss him in bed.

Sure, the video call sex with the vibrator he bought me has been fun and different. But I miss him in bed with me just holding me, or just resting my hand on his chest while I sleep.

I've never been much of a cuddler, but I apparently seek him out while I sleep. I always have a hand on him when I wake up even if we're not curled up tightly together.

The sunrises here take my breath away. They come early, around 5:30 a.m., but I've been up to see the sun peek over the hills several times. I'm walking the paths between the farm buildings this morning, breathing in the fresh, cool morning air and thinking about the video call I'm doing after lunch.

The idea for the gardening club came to me completely spontaneously while talking with Torin and then we'd shared it with Linnea before I'd really thought it through. I'm going to be on a video meeting with Linnea, and a local artist named Bridget. Any kid—truly any *person*—can use the link that Linnea's posted everywhere to join. They'll be able to see and hear me, Linnea, and Bridget while we talk about gardening and make paper tomato plants that we're going to "plant" in coffee mugs. The craft project is supposed to be simple and use materials that everyone should have pretty readily available.

It's going to be our first online "gardening club".

And I'm going to be on camera live.

I press my hand to my stomach and walk toward the fifth farm building. It's one of our empty ones, but I've been thinking more about the idea of having an in-person gardening day with me once a month. Kids could come with their parents. We could run buses to and from the farm. We could provide all the supplies. Everyone could take fresh produce home after we complete the activities. But it could be a fun way to get people out here to the farm and a great way to get kids excited about farming.

It seems surreal to me, but I'm starting to actually understand that, simply by having the title 'princess' in front of my name, people want to meet me and will show up to events where I'll be. We have nearly two hundred people signed up for today's online garden club. So, if it will get kids interested in gardening then yeah, I could host a little in-person club too, I suppose.

I push against the glass door to building five and step inside. It's the smallest of our buildings, but surely it's big enough to...

I freeze as I take in the sight before me.

The building is not empty.

In fact, there are *lots* of plants here.

They're all planted on one level, filling the space from ten feet beyond the doorway to the back wall. And they all look like they're the same type of plant.

I move closer and it takes me a second to register what I'm seeing. Not because I don't recognize the five-inch seedlings filling this entire building...but because I do.

But why is there an entire building full of lavender?

Of course, I know the answer instantly.

Torin planted these for me.

My husband planted an entire lavender field, indoors, for me.

My hand covers my mouth and my eyes fill with tears. I don't know how to feel exactly.

I'm stunned. And touched. And I admit something that's been niggling at the corners of my conscious mind but that I haven't let in.

I do now.

I could fall in love with him. Easily.

That's such a huge problem.

I'm leaving in a year. That was the agreement.

I would be a terrible queen. I haven't even left this ranch since I arrived as the princess. Haven't wanted to. I'm so happy just concentrating on the things I do well and not having to worry about the things I don't.

How would I ever handle being *queen*?

Besides Torin deserves to know that he can be the king on his own. He doesn't need a queen. He can love and lead Cara on his own.

But he's making it very hard to remember that we're just...

Friends?

We're at least that. I like him. So much. I admire him. I enjoy his company. I believe in him.

And I love the way he makes me feel about myself.

He gets me.

He pays attention. He listens and absorbs the things that matter.

Yes, he made me a princess and I have a gorgeous ring ladened with gemstones and diamonds. But I don't wear it every day. I simply can't wear that thing while I *garden*.

And he hasn't given me any other jewels. Or gowns. Or expensive art.

He's given me a farm.

Two, if I count Shreveport, which I definitely do.

And now, instead of buying me lavender oil or even lavender flowers, he planted me an entire field of it.

I feel a tear slip down my cheek.

I walk down the center aisle of the building. Everywhere I look are tiny lavender seedlings. They're all still green. Short. Not the tall bushes with gorgeous aromatic purple flowers they will eventually be. But they're so beau-tiful to me even like this because I know what they will be. This is just a start. Just the beginning of what they can be.

They're like Torin and me.

My breath catches. But the comparison is fair.

No one has ever invested in my needs and wants and dreams like this. Not since my parents helped me build my first greenhouse. And even then, they didn't plant things for me or study the science or ask me a million questions or read any of my papers about it the way Torin has.

I stop and turn a full circle, taking in what he did here.

And then my heart squeezes.

Lavender plants are beautiful, and healing, and they come back year after year—a delightful constant.

Once they bloom. But it can take one to two years for them to get to their first bloom cycle.

It's very possible I won't be here to see this lavender bloom.

I press my hand to my chest as that gives me an actual pain.

A couple of months ago, a year seemed like a long time. Plenty of time to get everything done that I wanted to.

Now it doesn't feel like nearly enough.

CHAPTER 34
TORIN

I feel my phone vibrate in my pocket. I pull it out surreptitiously and swipe my thumb over the screen to unlock it. *God, please let Jonah read my body language and get me out of this meeting.*

For three days I've been in meetings that my grandfather has insisted are important. I'd optimistically told myself I could use the meetings or at least the down time during breaks to talk to some of the palace's most important advisors and contacts about the new farming initiative.

I'd been wrong about that. So I've been gritting my teeth for three days.

The text isn't from Jonah with some made-up excuse to get me out of here.

It's even better. This text is from my wife.

My heart gives an extra kick just seeing her name.

We've been texting. We've spoken every night I've been away. Hell, I'd insisted she get Charming, her favorite vibrator, out last night and I'd talked her through a sweet, hot orgasm.

But I've missed her like crazy and being away from her for even three days and nights has been hell on my mood.

Her text simply reads *Look what I found when I went on a walk today.*

Attached is a photo of her standing barefoot amongst some green plants about five inches tall.

I know exactly where she is.

Dammit.

I look up and glance around the table. I wait until the man speaking finishes, then I say, "Excuse me, everyone, I need to make a call."

My grandfather frowns, but I push up from my chair.

"Torin, we'll need your input—"

"This can't wait," I tell him. As if he'll listen to my input on anything anyway.

I move toward the door and give Jonah a quick head shake to tell him I don't need his assistance. I step into the hallway and start dialing Abigail's number as I stride toward my office. But I don't complete the call until I shut the door behind me.

"Hello?" she answers after only one ring.

"You weren't supposed to go into building five, princess," I tell her.

"You didn't say that." Her voice sounds thick. As if she's choked up. "You said buildings four and five were extras. I thought they were empty."

"I didn't think you'd go back in there," I say. Then I sigh. "I also didn't realize how long it can take for those plants to bloom."

She doesn't laugh. She sniffs.

"Abigail," I say huskily. "Are you crying?"

"Of course, I am. You planted me a lavender field."

I'm not surprised she recognized the plants even when they're far from blooming.

I smile. "Yes. Well, it won't be much of a lavender field for another year or so. I got mature plants but didn't realize they can take two years until their first bloom cycle." I'm seriously annoyed by that. I wanted to give her that building full of lavender. "I'm sorry."

She gives a shaky laugh. "Are you kidding? Don't be sorry! My God, Torin. Most men give women bouquets of cut flowers. You planted me an entire *field* of the flower I love and use the most."

I smile in spite of how disappointed I am. I knew I couldn't keep building five a secret from her for an entire year, but I'd been looking into having blooming plants shipped in and added to the building. It was going to cost a fortune, but no one had told me no yet.

"You're my princess, Abigail," I say, my voice gruff. "I'll always make sure you have what you need and what makes you happy."

"God, I wish you were here," she says, her voice wobbly. "I so want to..."

"Reverse farmer me?" I tease, trying to get her to smile.

She laughs and takes a breath.

"Yes," she says. "And...just hug you."

I feel my heart squeeze. The sex with her blows my mind. She's so eager and open and passionate. But I want that sweeter stuff too. The stuff that says this is more than farms and fucking. "I'd love that. Both of those. All of that."

We're both quiet for a moment. I'm wondering how the

hell I can get out of here tonight. There's almost nothing I wouldn't miss to go to Abigail.

There is a late dinner tonight and then again Friday night, and my grandmother will be in attendance at both, so I'll have to stay tonight and then come back Friday. But that's fine. I'll make it work. Not only would it be incredibly rude to miss them, but it would hurt my grandmother if I didn't show up. Especially because she specifically asked me to be there.

She said it was important to her that the family be together. Her emphasis on these being important family dinners was strange. My mother, grandmother, grandfather, and I have dined together often. It's hardly a major, formal event for us to eat together. But I know that if I go back to the ranch, to Abigail, it will be incredibly hard to leave again.

Still, it's not far. I can go back and forth. I promised Abigail that she won't have to do all the gatherings and appearances. She's so fucking happy on the ranch and having her there, on *my* territory, knowing my home makes her that happy, that comfortable, that I'm providing her the things she wants and needs, is satisfying in a way I've never experienced before.

I will not make her live at the palace.

But I can leave tonight as soon as the dishes are cleared. I *will* be with Abigail tonight.

"Abigail—" God, it's on the tip of my tongue to tell her I love her. But she's so comfortable. She knows I care about her. I'm *showing* her how I feel. She feels it. She has to. So I don't have to say it. I can do this her way. "I'll be home tonight."

"You will?"

I fucking love how excited she sounds about that. "Yes."

"But...you have more to do there, right?"

"Nothing that's more important than seeing you."

"Oh." She sounds...surprised by that.

That's not okay. She shouldn't be surprised that I'm putting her first.

"You know I want to be with you, right? More than all of this stuff here?" I ask.

"That 'stuff' is incredibly important, Torin. You need to be there. Not only because as prince you have a lot of priorities that are often going to come in front of my need...for hugs, but because you need to prove to your grandfather that you're here to stay. You've been reluctant to step up. But now you can show him your heart is truly in this."

Dammit. I know she's sincere and I appreciate her support, but...*no.* Of course, my position is important. It will be even more so as time goes on. And no, it's not a regular job. I get all of that. But I need this woman to know *she* is important. The most important thing.

And...

Fuck.

I want to know I'm the most important thing to her.

So much of my frustration is about where we stand with one another. When we were together twenty-four-seven, alone for the most part, on the ranch, with a singular focus, it was easy. I knew she was happy. I knew she wanted me.

But we were there, just us, for *two months.*

Jonah had said it would only take her *one* month —*maybe* two—to fall in love with me.

Well, it's been all of that and she hasn't said those words to me yet.

Then she let me go, to come back to the palace, easily.

She's been fine with texting and calling. She has been

the least clingy woman I've ever met from the very beginning, and it seems none of that has changed.

So, yes, Jonah's voice is back in my head reminding me that she married me for *practical* reasons. Not because she's in love with me.

As I've been falling deeper and deeper in love with her.

The farms are her prerogative. That's what gets her attention, her time, and her passion.

I know that. I've known it all along.

How I'm feeling is my own fault.

But that doesn't mean I can't hate it.

"I *will* see you tonight, Princess," I tell her. I keep it simple. But firm.

There's a long pause on her end. Then she says, "Okay."

Also simple.

Well, there will be time for more words.

Eventually.

F ive hours later, I'm finishing up my notes for the meeting I've set up with two members of the board for the University of Faroe Islands. I want to start talking about how to partner with them on education and training in the various fields we'll need here in Cara for our expanded agricultural programs and green energy initiatives.

"Hey, you need to look at something."

I look up to find Jonah crossing to my desk. He looks intent.

"What's going on?"

"Did Abigail tell you she was conducting a video call today with a bunch of kids?"

I frown. "What? No." That doesn't sound like Abigail at all.

He nods and pulls my laptop across the desk, types in a few things, then turns it back to me.

"What kids? What's it about?"

"Just watch."

Abigail is on the screen. So are Linnea and another woman I vaguely recognize as a local artist and early childhood educator. She's been on a couple of arts in education committees.

There is also a collection of young faces. The kids are of varying ages and they're all listening as the woman speaks.

"What's going on?" I ask.

"It's a—"

But then I know. "Gardening club," I fill in quietly, watching her on screen. She's not talking, but she's smiling and has a happy glow about her. My heart squeezes just watching her.

"So she did tell you about it," Jonah says.

"It was just a passing thought. It was only a few days ago."

"Well, she told Linnea and you know how *she* is." Jonah grins with pride and affection. "She gets stuff done."

I nod. She really does.

"This is the first one?" I ask.

"Yep. They'll learn about how plants grow by making the plants out of paper and sticks or straws or pencils. They're starting with a tomato plant. They talked about seeds and how they sprout. They're constructing seedlings today. They'll talk about what the plants need to grow bigger and then next week they'll make the plants a little taller and add more leaves." Jonah grins. "But this way all the kids can participate whether they can actually grow real plants or not. If they don't have art supplies, Linnea arranged with a local shop to stock free kits. And this way, no kids are disappointed if their plants die. Eventually they'll make tiny tomatoes, then bigger and bigger ones. When it comes time to 'harvest' their tomatoes, Abi is going to bring actual tomatoes into town and the kids can all show up and they'll make some fun, easy recipes together."

My heart starts pounding harder. "She's going to make a public appearance?"

"She's going to be on all the video calls and then yeah, I guess." He shrugs. "It was all her idea."

"Did she talk? Today, I mean?" I ask. The artist is still talking, taking the kids through the art project. Abigail and Linnea are both making tomato plants of their own along with the children.

"She did. She introduced herself and said how excited she is to talk to everyone about gardening and how much she loves plants and that she's been growing things and then eating them since she was a kid." Jonah meets my gaze. "She did great. She was very warm and genuine. And she said she'd answer any questions anyone has. *But...*"

I brace myself. "But?"

Jonah grins. "She thought it would be easiest if they type their questions and comments into the comment section or if they send them to her via email later so they don't interrupt the speaker and their art project and so she has time to answer them fully."

My eyes widen. "She gave out her personal *email address?*"

Jonah chuckles. "She started to, but Linnea jumped in and gave them an official one for Princess Abigail."

"Does Princess Abigail have an official email address?" I ask.

"I'm guessing she does now," Jonah says with a grin.

I turn back to watch my wife concentrating intently on gluing green leaves onto what looks like a stick she might have picked up in our backyard. My heart squeezes hard again.

Her social media presence used to be photos of vegetables and flowers. Then she let us start putting photos of her up. Now she's interacting. She's reaching out. She's letting some of our people get to know her. But she's still doing it in a way that works for her. She can sit in our kitchen—I can tell she's at our center island—and answer questions from her keyboard and not have to get up in front of anyone.

This is...so good.

It's not traditional. It's nothing my grandmother or mother has ever done. I'm certain my grandmother does *not* have email. But this is great. People can see how sweet and intelligent and passionate Abigail is and she won't have to deal with public speaking.

I take a deep breath. "This is fantastic."

Jonah claps me on the shoulder. "I thought you'd like that."

I look up at him. "Thank you."

"You could have watched it on replay. They're recording it for anyone who misses it. But I thought you'd like to see it right away."

I nod. "Yes, thank you for showing me this. But also...for helping protect her. And us. And please thank Linnea. She's been a wonderful friend to us both. And she's been so good with our public relations. And not forcing Abigail out into the public eye."

He nods. "I'll admit it was self-serving of me to get you a girl in the beginning," he says with a smirk. "But Linnea is happy too. This is what makes her such a great agent for her siblings. She knows how to make people shine. It's a gift. She's wonderful at bringing out people's gifts and talents. And there's no question that Abigail has several. It's just a matter of finding the best way to highlight them. Linnea will be a great agent for the new princess." He gives me a wink.

I laugh, suddenly feeling lighter. My eyes are back on the screen and I see Abigail smile brightly. I quickly unmute the meeting as she begins talking.

"I'm so excited to see how all of your projects grow and see what we can learn together," she says to the kids. "Thanks for doing this with me. I love to talk about gardening and growing things, and I never had a group of friends to do that with until I went to college. Then I moved here and besides Prince Torin, I don't have people to talk to about all of this. I'm so glad I found a new group of friends who are into all of this. Our gardening club is going to be the best."

And just like that she wins all of the kids, and their parents, over.

They get to call themselves friends with the Princess? They get to tell people they're in a *club* with the Princess? Yeah, she's got a club. But it's not just a gardening club. It's a fan club.

And I'm the president.

CHAPTER 35
WAIT 'TIL I TELL YE

On INSTAGRAM

[PHOTO IMAGE is of a brown ceramic coffee mug with a popsicle stick stuck in it and green construction paper leaves glued to the stick]

CAPTION: Lindsey: Okay, I'll admit it. I tuned in and I made a tomato plant seedling out of paper, glue, and popsicle sticks. Check it out. I'm in the Princess's gardening club! Sure, I tuned in to see and listen to her and not because of the arts and crafts. It was our first look! But she's charming and sweet and yes, of course, I'm coming back next week. See you all there!

CHAPTER 36

ABIGAIL

I'm nearly vibrating.

I know it's adrenaline and endorphins and all of that but...that was *fun*.

Linnea answers on the second ring. "Hey, Abi! You were so great!"

"That was amazing! Right? It went well? It felt like it went well."

"It went *really* well. It was perfect," she assures me. "We had a lot more kids on the call than expected! I'm sure some of it was because of their parents' curiosity about *you*, but I really think they're going to come back! I'm really proud of you! Well done."

I feel warmth bloom in my chest and spread. That feels good. I can't wait to tell Torin about it. I'm so glad we recorded it. I want to show him.

And I try to ignore the niggle in the back of my mind

that reminds me of why I chose tomato plants for the kids to pretend to plant today.

If a few of them really get into gardening, you definitely need to start them with tomatoes because they'll grow fast enough from seed that you'll still be here to see their finished crops.

I didn't want to miss that. I'd realized it subconsciously I suppose when we first set up the idea for the activity, but after seeing the lavender Torin planted for me, I realized that I would have been heartbroken to get a bunch of children excited about gardening and then not have been able to see the literal fruits of their labors.

I clear my throat and push thoughts like *a year is just not going to be enough* to the back of my mind. "So I was thinking...you know what would be more effective, and more fun for Torin, than meeting with all these business people and politicians and trying to explain why the farms are exciting?" I ask.

"What?"

"A farmer's market."

She pauses for a moment. "What?"

"We need to get people interested in the farms. We need the *people* to understand why these are important. Even before the king and all the big business people and advisors understand it. If the *citizens* want them, then the higher ups will have a harder time saying no," I say. I'm talking fast, but I can't help it. My blood is pumping, and my thoughts are whirring. "But the farms aren't ready for tours and visitors yet. We have these visions of people coming out here to pick fruits and vegetables and sample food made with the produce, but we're too far away for a lot of people to come and we're not ready. *But* we can take samples to them. We could set up little markets in the villages. Or at the schools. We can have fresh fruit and vegetables. We can make pies and tarts, salads, chocolate, jams, coffee, all kinds of things in smaller batches for them to taste. And we can have games and projects like today's for the kids. We can invite local artists and bakers and other farmers too. We can bring the farm to them."

Linnea again doesn't say anything for a second.

"We need to get out there and tell as many people as possible about Torin's ideas," I say. "But it's a lot easier to get people to listen to the bigger ideas while they're having fun and tasting delicious food."

She finally gives a soft laugh. "*Torin's* ideas? Abi, this is you."

"Well, the ideas about how to present it are mine, but the farms as a whole, on a large scale, are his. While we're there handing out chocolate covered strawberries, he can talk about how the programs at the schools will work, how this will create new jobs, how it will impact the economy. All the big picture stuff."

"I love it," Linnea says. "Instead of having him sitting in meetings, trying to convince the University to offer new programs, we get the people *asking* for programs. And if the Faroe Islands don't want to do it, we'll do it here in Cara."

My heart rate speeds up. "Exactly. So...markets. Who do we talk to about getting those set up?"

She laughs louder now. "Abi."

"Yeah?"

"You're the princess."

I frown. "I...um...okay."

"*You* just say the word, and I make some calls, and say 'Princess Abigail wants this'."

I open my mouth. Then shut it. I think about that. My heart flips. Wow. I feel myself smiling. "Really? That's it?"

"Yep."

"Really?"

"I thought you'd studied how the Cara royal family works."

"I…looked up their history and things like that."

"Well, there are only two people who have more power than you do on this island," Linnea says. "The king and queen."

"Not Torin?"

"Nope. The princess shares equal power with the prince. Just like the queen shares equal power with the king."

"Wait, *what*?" I don't know why this hasn't occurred to me to wonder about this before. I suppose because I've been so wrapped up in one particular member of the royal family, I haven't really thought about the rest of them much.

And, well, I didn't intend to be a member of the royal family for long.

Every time a thought like that crosses my mind now, I feel a sharp pang near my heart.

"Torin's mother is the king and queen's daughter-in-law," Linnea says. "She's respected by the people and is given financial support and protection as a member of the royal family, but she doesn't have any actual authority. However, the queen—Torin's grandmother—does have power. Equal power with the king."

I think about that. "Do they ever disagree?"

"If so, it's behind closed doors. They always support one another in public. But they're also in charge of different things."

"I need to know more about this."

Linnea laughs. "You do. In our constitution, the king and queen share equal power. An O'Grady has to sit on the throne, but his or her spouse also rules. When the O'Grady steps down or passes, the spouse also steps aside. But while King Diarmuid wears the crown, Queen Roisin has equal power."

My eyes widen as a realization hits me. "So Diarmuid wanting *you* to be queen really mattered. You would have had real power."

Linnea is quiet for a moment. Then she says simply, "Yes."

"And he thought you could correct anything Torin did wrong." I'm frowning again. "Or would just do things the right way yourself."

She sighs. "I suppose that's what he thought, yes."

"That's a big deal."

"It's not," Linnea says. "Not anymore."

"But it is," I say firmly. "It's why it's important that Diarmuid understands that Torin doesn't need a queen. He needs to truly trust Torin."

Linnea doesn't respond immediately, but then she says, "You really care about this. About Torin and the throne and his relationship with the king."

"I do," I say without having to think about it for even a second.

"I'm glad."

I can hear the sincerity in her voice.

"Okay. Then, let's make it happen," I say. "Let's show *everyone* what a great leader Torin will be. Let's get these markets set up so the people can understand the farms."

"Sounds good. I'll get started right now."

I can hear her smiling. I know I'm grinning like an idiot. I *love* a great plan in motion. "I appreciate this. Can you just be my assistant? Forever? Can I hire you for that?"

"You can." She laughs softly and I hear a warmth in her voice. "But...I'm also doing this because I'm your friend."

For a second that makes my throat tight. I haven't had a really good, close girlfriend in...forever. "Thank you."

"Thank *you*. You're doing amazing things for my country, Abi."

I have to blink fast at that. I swallow. "Oh, and hey?"

"Yeah?"

"I need to get to the palace."

"Oh." I hear her surprise. "Okay. When?"

"Tonight. Well, now. Right away. Torin has a dinner tonight with his family. I want to be there."

"Then pack a bag and get in the truck, Princess," Linnea says, her amusement clear in her voice.

"I can just take the truck?"

"You're not a guest, Abi. This is home and it's *your* truck," she says with a laugh.

I feel that pang near my heart again. *This is home.* I love those words. But I can't stop my brain from adding *for now* on to the end.

"Not that anyone would pull over and ticket the princess anyway," Linnea says.

"I can *steal* vehicles now? Wow, why didn't anyone tell me?" I joke, trying to lighten my thoughts.

She laughs. "Well, you'll have to explain it to the king and trust me, that dungeon is *not* a fun place."

"There's a *dungeon*?"

"Well, yes." She's still laughing. "But I don't think it's been used in a century or so."

I shake my head. Royalty is weird. "I don't know how to get to the palace."

"There's only one road, my friend. Just head away from the ranch. After a little while, you'll see the palace in the distance. It's the big building up on the hill with the spires and stuff."

I laugh. "Right. Okay."

"You're doing great, Princess Abigail," Linnea says, her tone softer and sincere.

"Thank you."

We disconnect and I go to pack an overnight bag. Then I pack for two nights.

And then I get in the truck and head *toward* the palace. On purpose.

With my nerves jumping, my heart beating with excitement. And my pink cowboy boots on.

The drive is easy and it's impossible to get lost.

The road from the ranch to the main village is a straight shot and once in the village everything opens up and basically directs me right to the castle's gates.

I pull up next to the guard's station and roll the window down. Okay, this might be interesting. I don't have an ID card or anything.

"Hi. I'm—"

"Good afternoon, Princess Abigail." The guard bows and opens the gate.

Or this might be super easy. "You know who I am?"

He looks surprised. "Of course."

"How? I've only been here once. And you weren't on duty."

"You remember who was on duty?" he asks.

I shrug. "Yes."

He seems strangely pleased by that. "Well, of course we

know who you are. We've seen photos and have a full description. We also know the truck."

"Oh." That makes sense. But it's strange, too. "So I can just go in?"

"Of course. Though I'm sure staff will meet you at the door." He leans in slightly with a concerned look. "We weren't expecting you, though. And you should have someone with you. Is everything all right?"

I'm supposed to have someone with me? "Do I need to call ahead when I want to visit?" I ask. "I don't know what number to call. I wanted to surprise the prince."

He smiles. "You don't have to call ahead, Princess Abigail. You are free to come and go however you like. But you should have security with you."

"Oh." I nod. "Okay. I'll remember that." I'm not sure who that would be if Jonah isn't around. "Don't tell the prince I came alone," I say. Torin might be upset about that if there's really a reason we need constant security.

"All right," he agrees without hesitation.

Then I lift a brow. "Are you able to keep information from the prince?"

He stands straighter. "Only if instructed to do so by the king, queen, or princess. Or you. The other princess."

Right. The people in power. But I have equal power. Got it. I smile. "That wasn't a test," I tell him. "I'm truly just curious. I'm learning as I go here."

"They didn't instruct you?"

Right. Well, they would have if Torin hadn't gotten frustrated and swept me off to the ranch after less than forty-eight hours. "I probably just missed that part." That almost hurts to say. I've never 'missed that part' in any instruction of any kind, ever.

"You're fine. You can do whatever you want," he says, and I swear he's fighting a smile.

"I do like the sound of that," I tell him honestly.

"Have a great day, Princess Abigail," he says, gesturing for me to drive through the gate.

"You too. What's your name?"

"Brian, Your Highness."

"Have a great day, Brian."

He gives me a bow and when I glance up into the rearview mirror, I definitely catch him grinning.

Well, at least I'm entertaining.

Callum, the main butler for the house when the other butlers aren't expecting people to show up, meets my truck.

"Princess Abigail." He's clearly shocked as he grabs the truck door I just pushed open. "I had no idea you were arriving today."

"No one did, Callum. Surprise!"

He doesn't look like he appreciates surprises. I get the impression everyone here likes to be very prepared.

"What can I do for you?" he asks, immediately looking for and locating my bag in the backseat. "Are you hungry? In need of...medical attention?"

I laugh. "I just need to know where Torin is."

"Oh. Well, the prince is in his offices as far as I know, but likely...busy." He says that last word weakly.

I don't think he's supposed to even insinuate that I'm not supposed to interrupt Torin if I want to.

"I'll find him. And I promise not to be a bother," I tell him, heading for the steps.

"You haven't hired an assistant yet, I understand," Callum calls after me. Clearly if I had an assistant, she or he would have been expected to call ahead and warn everyone I was coming.

But no, I don't have an assistant. I've got a freaking *agent*. And a friend. "No. I'm good," I call back, not even slowing.

I head straight to Torin's office. Samuel is at his desk outside and I prepare myself for his surprise and then his attempt to keep me from interrupting Torin. Instead, he gives me a smile and blows out a huge sigh of relief.

"Princess Abigail, it is *so* nice to see you." He rises and comes around his desk.

"It is? Really?"

"Yes." He strides to Torin's door. "Please go in."

"Really?"

"He's been even more impossible than usual here without you." He pushes Torin's door open. "I look forward to his vastly improved mood." He gives me a little bow as I pass.

I fight a smile but say, "I'll see what I can do."

CHAPTER 37
ABIGAIL

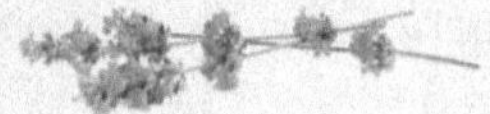

The door shuts behind me and Torin is already crossing the room. "Abigail. What are you doing here?"

"Surprise." I smile at him, but immediately notice his intense frown. "Uh, I should have called."

"Are you all right?"

Yes, surprising the prince is difficult. Everyone assumes it means something bad happened. I feel bad about that.

"Yes, of course! I was just eager to see you and didn't want to wait for you to get home. And I knew you had a dinner tonight and thought maybe I'd crash it." I wince. "Maybe that was a bad idea."

Then his arms are around me and his face is buried in my neck and he's taking a huge deep breath as he lifts me off the ground. I wrap my arms around his neck as he turns and carries me toward his desk. He sweeps a bunch of papers out of the way and deposits me in the center,

"

then braces his hands on either side of my hips, leaning in.

"I'm so fucking glad to see you."

"Oh good." I smile. "I wasn't sure suddenly if this was okay."

He shifts, putting both hands on my face. "It is *always* okay for you to come to me."

There's something about how he says that, or the look in his eyes, or something that makes me go all melty. "I've missed you," I tell him softly.

"I'm glad." He leans down and kisses me.

Immediately I wrap my arms around his neck, needing to be closer to him. He came back here because he needed to. I understand that. But *God*, being without him has been harder than I expected. I've been busy. I've been doing everything I would normally be doing if I was still living in Nebraska or Louisiana—working, reading, cooking—but I've felt more alone than ever and things have felt empty.

I scoot closer to the edge of the desk, and he leans into me, deepening the kiss. His hands are in my hair, his tongue is in my mouth, and he gives that low groan that always makes my pussy clench.

"God, princess, I need you."

"Yes."

He kisses me again, then lifts his head. "I have a meeting."

I blow out a breath. "That's okay. I can wait. I'm staying tonight. And tomorrow. I know there's a family dinner tonight, right? And I had this idea that Linnea and I—"

He's kissing me again. Thoroughly. His fingers are tight in my hair and he's devouring my mouth. When he lets me up for air long moments later, he says, "I saw your video call with the kids."

I feel my instantaneous smile. "You did? Oh, I'm glad. It was so fun."

He traces a finger over my cheek. "You light up. You did it on camera. And just now. Do you know that?"

"Really?"

"You were so fucking beautiful—*are* so fucking beautiful—when you're into your work and your passion."

My heart melts at that too. "Thank you. It was...good. It felt good."

"I'm glad. And I—" He shakes his head. "Just fucking need you."

"We have tonight. I'll be here."

But he leans past me and pushes a button on the phone sitting on his desk. "Samuel, push them back twenty minutes."

"Yes, Your Highness."

He disconnects.

I lift a brow. "Wow, no argument from Samuel."

"He's very glad you're here."

I smirk. "So he told me. You've been grumpy?"

"I've been an asshole."

I run my hand over his chest. "Aw. How can I help?"

"Take your pants off."

I laugh. "We only have twenty minutes."

"Princess Abigail," he says, his tone firm and low.

Just the way I love it.

"Yes?"

"Take your pants off and let me have *my* pussy."

A shiver of lust goes through me. And I don't argue, or even tease. I push him back, slide to the floor, and undo the button and zipper on my jeans. I push them as far as my boots will let them go.

"Do you want the boots off?" I ask, already knowing the answer.

"No. Turn around." He's drinking in the sight of me.

I know I look a little messy. I got on the video call with the kids in the same T-shirt I'd worn out in the farm buildings. Linnea had said I should look like a gardener. So I hadn't even redone my ponytail. I'd even worn my green rubber boots, though they couldn't be seen on camera.

To come to the palace, I'd showered, but I hadn't dressed up. New jeans, a new shirt, and my pink boots instead of the green. But otherwise, I'm just...me.

I turn so I'm facing the desk. He moves in behind me, running a hand over my ass. "I was so proud of you today," he says in my ear.

Goosebumps trip down my arms. "Thank you."

He's in a suit and tie. Of course. I feel him shift, shrugging out of the jacket. Then he rolls the sleeves of his white dress shirt up on his forearms. I bite my lower lip. I love him in everything he wears. He makes an exceptionally hot cowboy. But *this*—the suit, tie, and dark-wood-and-leather office—definitely makes me hot and needy.

He pulls his tie loose and tosses it on the desk beside me.

"I'll need a few minutes to put myself back together," he tells me, running a hand around my hip and over my belly, pulling me back against him. "So this is going to be fast and rough. I just need to bury myself inside you and make us both come hard. Later we'll take our time."

I nod. "Okay," I tell him breathlessly. "Yes. Good."

He runs his hand down to cup me, slipping a finger inside. "Already wet for me, princess?"

"Yes. Always."

"Spread your feet as far as you can."

I do. It's not far with my jeans around my ankles but it doesn't seem to matter. While one finger pumps in and out of my pussy, he presses his other hand to my back between my shoulder blades, urging me down onto his desk. I bend over, propping myself on my forearms.

Then he starts to pull his hand away. "I need to get a condom."

I grasp his wrist. "No."

I went on the pill almost immediately after getting to Cara. We both wanted to have sex bare, and we both got tested and I've been on the pill long enough now that we haven't used a condom in a while.

He pauses, that thick finger deep inside me, the other hand squeezing my hip. "It'll be messy."

"I like being messy from you."

"Christ," he breathes out. He adds a second finger, teasing my clit, then sliding in deep. He leans in to say against my ear, "If I fill you up right now, you can't change your panties the rest of the day, you hear me, Abigail? You will walk around this castle, playing your part, looking like a princess on the outside, but all sticky and messy between your pretty thighs because of me."

Desire licks through me, hot and strong and I nod. "*Yes.* Please, Torin."

"Fuck," he mutters. I hear the zipper on his pants. "You're so fucking perfect." Then he shifts again, moves his hand, and then drives his cock into me from behind.

I moan. "Yes."

"You also have to be quiet, honey," he says, lifting the hand that was just between my thighs and covering my mouth. "No one hears your sweet cries but me."

Then he pulls back and thrusts forward, sliding deep. Over and over. I'm up on my tiptoes, thankful the desk is holding me up. I can't do much more than just take it from this position and that, too, is hot. My body is on fire, everything in me melting and melding with him.

"You feel so fucking good," he tells me, his voice tight. "God, I can't get enough of you."

I could try to speak, but with his hand over my mouth, he wouldn't hear me anyway, so I just let myself get lost in his hard, rhythmic thrusts, his dirty words, and the heat and weight of him.

My climax is starting to build as his pace picks up.

"Fuck, Abigail. Yes. Milk my cock. Take it all, princess."

He moves his hand from my hip to my clit, circling and pressing, and I know I'm not going to last. My inner muscles clench around him in response and he doesn't need any words from me at all to know what he does to me.

"Come for me, honey. Make me messy too, Abigail."

He fucks me faster and harder and suddenly I feel that tightening twist and then I come apart.

"Torin!" I cry out, but his hand muffles the sound.

"That's right. That's it. Fucking perfect," he mutters.

And then I feel him tense and come, thick and hot inside me.

We just stay like that for several long seconds, him holding me back against him, me slumped over his desk.

Then he gives my ass a little smack and pulls back. "I've got a meeting," he says, all prince-like.

I look over my shoulder with a grin. "Yes, sir."

He heads toward the powder room attached to his office. "That's Your Highness. Though we can discuss sir for certain occasions."

I pull my panties and jeans back into place. Yes, I'm definitely going to be thinking about him for the rest of the day.

As if I wouldn't have been anyway.

He comes back into the room a few minutes later, buttoning the cuffs on his sleeves. He's all put back together, though he's still without his tie and jacket. "I'm so glad you're here." He pulls me into his arms.

I hug him. "Me too."

"You do not have to come to the dinner tonight."

I look up at him. "Really?"

"Really. You didn't plan to. I've told you that you don't have to do these things."

"But it's a family dinner, right?"

He hesitates. "Family will be there, yes."

I pull back and narrow my eyes. "What else?"

He sighs. "I just found out that Cian and Astrid will be here. Along with Miles and Henry. And Linnea's mom and dad. A few other friends who are really more business acquaintances. A couple of advisors. So we will be greeting them on the front steps. There will be photo opportunities for...anyone who wants to show up."

"Hang on." I frown and step back. "Cian? Your brother? And Linnea's sister Astrid? And who are Miles and Henry? Wait, do you mean Henry, Cian's best friend?"

"And bodyguard." Torin sighs. "Miles is Astrid's best friend. He's been her train—"

"Oh my God! Miles *Stafford*? The guy who was with her through her whole rehabilitation?" Anyone who's read about Astrid and her recovery knows who Miles is. He was the physical therapist who first worked with her in the hospital. They became fast friends and he stayed with her throughout her rehab, later quitting his job to become her personal trainer and assistant.

There are also rumors about them being romantically involved, though they both deny it when asked. They've never been caught in any photos or situations doing anything more than sitting close and laughing or occasionally with Miles's hand on her elbow or lower back when they're out and he's helping her up steps or through a crowd.

"Yes," Torin confirms. "And I'm not sure exactly why they're here except that my grandfather feels that having family and friends here for a dinner would be a nice way to show that everyone around us is supportive and happy about the marriage."

"Ohhhh," I say, catching on. "The whole we didn't have a wedding but no one's mad thing?"

Torin moves to lean against his desk. He pulls me between his knees, linking our fingers loosely. "Yes. Essentially. You and I haven't done public appearances together. We haven't attended any social engagements at all. I haven't even attended any alone. He wants to show the people that even if we're not having huge gatherings, we're at least seeing family."

"And Linnea's sister and parents are family," I say.

"They are." He says it matter-of-factly.

"So this *is* about us. I kind of have to be there, don't I?"

He leans closer. "I promised you wouldn't have to do this."

He told me I wouldn't have to do big public appearances. "I appreciate that," I tell him sincerely. "But I didn't presume that included family events."

"This is a 'family event' concocted by my grandfather,"

Torin says with a touch of irritation. "So, of course, it's not just a casual, intimate meal."

"What is it?"

"I'm not even sure. He knows you're not going to be there—at least the last I knew. And he was annoyed by that, but he didn't call it off." Torin seems suspicious of that for some reason.

And he clearly told his grandfather I would not be attending.

"You made a point of telling him I wouldn't be here. And he made a point of telling you the dinner was going to happen anyway," I say.

He nods.

"This is another battle for the upper hand between the two of you."

He sighs. "Yes."

Well, at least he's willing to admit it.

"Why are you doing that?" I ask, sincerely curious.

"You are my *wife*. He doesn't dictate what you do and don't do. I decide what's good for you and what's not, and how and when and *if* we will do public appearances."

I lift a brow. "Torin…"

He shrugs, unapologetic. "I promised to keep you from events that would make you uncomfortable."

I can't say I'll be perfectly *comfortable* at this dinner, and I love that he's being protective and upholding his promise, but I can do this. "It's a family dinner."

"It will be a public event at least in part, Abigail. There are guests. My brother and Astrid being here makes it even more of a spectacle."

"I know that he's not giving you control over anything else, yet. And the farms aren't up and running to the point that you can really show them off and control *that* program. So, our marriage and how it's presented and how we function as prince and princess is the only thing you feel that you *can* control."

He studies my eyes for a few seconds. Then he nods. "That's probably it."

"But you being the rebel, the uncontrollable one, the one bucking his rules, is not helping him feel secure about you taking over a position that takes a lot of self-control and putting others in front of what you want and feel. It also requires a lot of transparency."

I realize the truth of all of that even as I explain it out loud to Torin.

I'm the princess now. Torin's wife. At least for now. I need to make sure people see *him* as the king they want and need him to be. And that means that sometimes—okay, often—the feelings and needs of other people are going to be more important than *my* own.

I squeeze his fingers. "Do you really think Diarmuid is a bad king?"

Torin looks startled. "I've never thought he is a bad king."

"So why do you push so hard against him? You believe he cares about the people and wants what's best for them. You believe that the things he does are done with good intentions. You will do things differently when you're king, but you will do them with a heart for taking care of people. Just like he does."

Torin takes a moment to answer. "It's because he didn't lean this hard on anyone else."

"Do you mean Declan? When he was preparing to be king?"

Torin shakes his head. "My brother never seriously

prepared to be king. Not really. I mean…" He takes a breath and blows it out. "My father."

We haven't talked much about his father. I've seen photos. I know he was killed in a car accident. I know he was beloved and his death devastated the family and the entire country.

"Your father was ready to be king?"

"Very. And the pressure of following in his footsteps was enormous. For Declan and then for me after Declan left. The country wanted my father. My grandfather wanted him."

"So they saw eye to eye. Does it bother you that you would have disagreed with your father on a lot of things too?" I ask, wanting to understand Torin's frustrations and reluctance about his future role.

He gives me a smile. "My father and I agreed on almost everything. He and my grandfather argued all the time. Loudly and passionately."

My eyes widen. "What?"

He nods, running his thumb over my knuckles. "My father didn't propose a conversion to a true democracy, but he also wanted more input from the people. He had ideas about how to include the people. I remember hiding in the secret chamber behind my grandfather's office and listening to their 'discussions'." He shakes his head, but he's smiling. "They were passionate conversations, but they would talk for hours. I learned more history, and political science, and philosophy, and was introduced to more ethics ideas eavesdropping on them than I did in any university class."

I smile, delighted by this insight. "And that's how your ideas got planted?"

"My father never advocated for a move to a true democracy, but I'd like to think my father would have loved my presentation," he says with a small smile.

"So you poke your grandfather in memory of your father?"

He laughs. "Not consciously. But I do get very...frustrated... that my grandfather won't listen to me the way he did my father. It's like after my father was gone, the king felt like he had to try even harder to control things."

I nod. "That's probably exactly how he felt, Torin." I squeeze his hand again. "I can't imagine how losing his child, not to mention that man who was assumed, by everyone, all his life, to be his successor—who wanted the job and who he believed would do a wonderful job—would make him feel." I step closer. "In fact, that explains a lot. Diarmuid is comparing you to your father, and maybe that's not fair, but I'm sure he can't help it. You probably remind him so much of your dad...except you've got this rebellious streak that makes him nervous. And that's what he's trying to..."

"Squelch?" Torin asks dryly.

"Understand?" I offer.

He laughs softly. "That's generous. But all of that makes sense." He shakes his head. "Doesn't this make the perfect argument for elected leaders, though? So when someone dies, they're easier to replace? It doesn't throw everything into such turmoil?"

I shrug. "I don't know. I mean, should our leaders be easy to replace? Shouldn't they be the best of the best? People who really make a difference? People who are exceptional? I hate the idea that they might be a dime a dozen. And," I add, "an easy, obvious line of succession—of *good*, honorable, worthy people, of course—is easier and comforting. When someone dies, you know who is next and you know they've been preparing and come from a long line of great leaders."

He twists his lips.

I go ahead and say what we're both thinking. "Unless, of course, they go rogue and spend a decade in another country, disassociating from their leadership responsibilities. That could make people a little nervous I guess."

He growls and grasps my hips, pulling me close. "I can't believe you're not a thousand percent on my side."

"Why? Just because you're hot and dish out orgasms whether I'm good or bad, I should agree with everything you say and do?" I tease.

He slides his hands to my ass and squeezes. "Those orgasms really should help my case."

"Oh, they do. Imagine how hard on you I'd be if you didn't do that?" I say, grinning up at him.

He laughs.

"And admit it, you like that I'm honest with you and don't think you're perfect but like you anyway," I say.

Something flickers in his eyes, but he nods. "I do like that. I never have to wonder how you feel or what you're thinking."

"Never," I promise.

He pulls me close and wraps his arms around me as my arms go around his neck. He puts his face against my neck. "Some days in this office, thinking about what's ahead, I miss my dad so fucking much."

I hug him tightly. "I'm so sorry you've had to be without him."

"You've made it better, Abigail."

My heart gives an extra thump at that. "I have?" That's...not good. I'm not going to be here long term.

But I can't deny that hearing I'm helping him makes me feel amazing.

"You're someone I can talk to. You don't fit the mold here. You can see outside of these boxes that are generations old. And when it comes to new ideas, instead of asking, 'should we?' or saying, 'it's never been done that way', you simply ask, 'why not?'. I was looking for that, for you, before I even realized it." He pulls back and looks at me. "You're the best decision I ever made."

An emotion I can't even put a name to rocks through me. I've never had anyone say anything like that to me before. I've never had anyone look at me the way Torin is looking at me right now.

I swallow hard. "Same," I tell him honestly. "I've never had the support and freedom that you've given me. Thank you."

"Every minute has been my pleasure."

I kiss him. Just sweetly. Just because I can't put what I'm feeling into words. I'm not sure I could even if I was good at saying things.

Then I pull back. "And as for this family dinner...I can do this. I already know Cian and Henry. I've met your grandfather, grandmother, and mother. And I won't need to give a speech, right?"

"Definitely not. One on one conversations. And I won't leave your side."

I can see that he's pleased that I'm willing to do this. I think deep down, he wants me to do this, but he won't ask.

"I'm in."

"Really?"

"Sure. And meeting Astrid Olsen will be exciting."

He grins. "Are you going to fangirl and embarrass me?"

"You never know. I've held it together around a few

royals, but we're talking about someone who's *really* impressive now."

He laughs and then swats my ass as I step out of his embrace and start for the door.

I shoot him a little smirk over my shoulder.

"I'll see you later, Princess," he tells me, watching me leave. "And don't forget...no new panties. I'll be checking."

I step out of his office with a little shiver of heat, and a whole wave of happiness, sweeping through me.

CHAPTER 38
TORIN

I'm so fucking happy she's here.

I had thought to protect Abigail from this and keep her away from this dinner. Even before I knew that it was turning into somewhat of a circus, I hadn't thought of asking Abigail to be here. I told her she could stay on the ranch, away from the palace and all the ceremonial duties.

But I'm so fucking glad she's here.

And she came to me.

She missed me. Enough to come to me on her own. After I found out that she'd driven herself here in the truck, without telling anyone where she was going, I was even more pleased. And yes, feeling cocky.

I think my wife kind of likes me.

And I probably shouldn't have fucked her in my office. We could've waited. That wasn't the most professional thing or the most romantic thing I've ever done.

But the second I saw her I had to touch her, the second I touched her I had to kiss her, and the second I kissed her I had to do more.

Being away from her is not something I'm good at it seems.

I step through my bedroom door three hours later. "Abigail—" My words are cut off as my wife, my princess, walks into the sitting room.

My hand drops away from where I was loosening my tie, my mouth falls open, and I can't think of anything to say except, "Holy shit." Also not very professional or romantic.

She laughs softly and runs her hands down the front of the long, royal purple sheath dress she's wearing.

It's strapless, with a train off the back. The bodice has sparkly threads woven throughout, becoming more dispersed as the skirt falls to her feet.

It's simple, not overstated, not anything like what my mother and grandmother will be wearing.

But she's fucking breathtaking.

"Do you like it? It was already here for me," she says.

I nod. "Yes. They would've come up with something for you."

She walks toward me, brows furrowed. "Is it okay?"

"You're gorgeous. You look very...regal."

She gives me a bright smile. "Really? I'm certain that word has never been applied to me before."

"People haven't been looking close enough."

Her mouth forms a little "o", then she says, "Well, I haven't been in a dress like this before."

"It doesn't have anything to do with the dress."

I reach out, knowing that touching her is dangerous,

but absolutely unable to resist. I drag my fingertips down her arm from her bare shoulder to her wrist, then lace our fingers together. "You know the dress matches the stones in your tiara perfectly."

She nods. "They brought it up earlier. I'm not sure if there's a certain way I'm supposed to wear it."

"Do you want me to help you with it?"

"I was hoping you would."

I notice that her opposite hand is resting against her stomach, the way she often holds it when her nerves have kicked up. The ring on her left hand sparkles in the light. That stone also matches her dress perfectly.

I'm slammed with the surge of possessiveness and lust that always hits me when I look at my ring on her finger.

"Where is it?" Suddenly I cannot wait to see her with the princess tiara on her head.

I didn't want any of this. I walked away from this. I didn't want to be prince, royalty. But right now, in this moment, I cannot wait to put that crown on my wife's head.

She leads me into the bedroom and points to the cushion on the bed where the tiara is resting.

Her hair is down, and before picking up the crown I move behind her, gathering her hair in my hands. "I think we should put your hair up."

Her hand goes to cover her tattoo at the base of her neck. "Everyone will see my honeybee. I don't know if *that's* very regal."

"It is. Because it's you. And I love this fucking bee." I lean over and kiss it.

I feel a little tremor go through her body. "Whatever you want," she tells me.

Words like that seem so innocent, and yet I'm semi-hard from them. "I do love when you're submissive to me, Princess." I kiss her again, dragging my lips from the back of her neck to the tip of her shoulder. "How are the panties?"

She leans back against me. "Wet," she said softly.

I drag my lips back across her soft skin and up the side of her neck to her ear. "Good. They're only going to get wetter."

"We're going to dinner with your family."

"Are you saying that you don't think I can turn you on no matter where we are? Challenge accepted."

She turns in my arms and smiles up at me. "I might actually end up enjoying this dinner after all."

I run my hands down her back to her ass and give her a little squeeze. "Don't distract me. We need to get your hair up. Then I need to get dressed. And we need to get downstairs. We have guests to greet." I lean in and give her a kiss. "But if you're a good girl, I will reward you appropriately later."

She wiggles her hips against me. "What if I'm a bad girl?"

I give her a wicked grin. "Fuck around and find out."

She laughs and pulls out of my arms. We go into the bathroom, and I help her put her hair up. She's always amazed by my ability to help with her hair and I silently thank both Fiona and Saoirse for all of the times they demanded help with theirs. At the time I wasn't as grateful as I should've been. I should probably mention that to them sometime.

I change into my tux, and then help Abigail place the tiara on her head, arranging a few curls around the base.

I suck in a breath as I stand behind her, looking at her in

the mirror. "Abigail—" I have to clear my throat. "You look more gorgeous in that than I even expected."

She touches the cool metal reverently. "Do you think so? It doesn't look strange on me?"

"It absolutely does not. You were born to wear that."

The statement, and the truth of it, hits me directly in the chest.

This woman was meant to be mine.

We're an unlikely pair. She seems like an improbable princess. Hell, I'm a reluctant royal myself. But here we are. I've never felt this way about anyone before. And we're going to make a fucking difference. Together.

I'm keeping her.

So, I'm going to need to tell her how I feel soon. I'm the guy who loves words and mine are bubbling up higher and stronger every time we're together. I'm not going to be able to keep them inside much longer.

I don't want to freak her out. I don't want to make things awkward. But I'm going to have to tell my wife that I'm madly in love with her.

I know we agreed we weren't going to make this about feelings. I know she said she didn't want that. She wanted this to be straightforward and goal oriented.

But Jonah said she'd fall in love with me in two months and while she hasn't said it, I can't expect her to. Abigail doesn't use words. She uses actions.

And she's here. With me. Going to a family dinner, wearing a fucking princess crown.

That has to mean something.

I'm the word guy. I have to say it first.

"Okay, let's see yours," she's says. "I've only seen it in pictures. And I have to admit it was pretty hot. I'll bet in person it's even better."

I grin down at her. "You like the pictures of me in my crown?"

"I like pictures of you in anything."

"That is a very good answer."

I puff out a breath and then lift my crown to my head. It always feels weird. Heavy. Strange. There's so much more that goes with wearing this crown than just having a piece of heavy metal with jewels on my head.

But tonight, as I settle it on my head in the mirror and watch my wife's eyes light up, and a smile curve her lips—a smile that's proud, a touch possessive, and more than a little turned on—suddenly the weight of the crown is a little lighter.

We gather at the front of the palace on the steps with the rest of the family. My grandfather and grandmother are here, along with my mother, and my younger brother, with his best friend, Henry, standing in the background.

Linnea, her sister, and her parents are also here with us. The other assistants and bodyguards, including Jonah and Miles, stand behind all of them. It's a strange assortment of people. But the cameras are flashing as if we are truly a bunch of celebrities.

Technically we're here waiting for guests to arrive so that we can greet them. But we're out here a little early so that people—media, and the public, whoever wanted to gather—can get any shots they want.

Unlike the paparazzi in the States, no one here calls out questions or asks us to turn to give them a different view of what we're wearing. But there are a lot of people gathered, and we all know, even though we're not saying it, that it's because Abigail is here.

Though, in fairness, the country loves Cian. He's not wearing a crown because he has not rescinded his abdication. He's technically just a guy here at the palace for dinner. But Cara still considers him a prince, and his charm, good looks, and philanthropic contributions around the island have made the country forgiving toward the youngest royal, who would have likely never taken the throne anyway.

Astrid is also popular and beloved by the people. Everyone in Cara has followed her since she first started competing in international gymnastics competitions. Every household in Cara owns her book, and the gymnastics academy here—founded by her grandfather and named for her—is full of little girls who worship her.

When news got out that both Cian and Astrid would be here, it brought an even bigger crowd than just having Abigail finally out in public view. In fact, there's a giddy electricity in the air tonight.

Abigail's hand is in mine, and she's clutching my fingers tightly. She has not thrown up, and I assume that's only because she is not out here alone and does not have to actually address the crowd. That said, I'm ready to sweep her up and I know exactly the potted plant we're going for if she does suddenly say the magic words "I'm going to be sick".

Finally, our guests start to arrive.

The first three men and their wives are men who could be labeled as my grandfather's closest friends now that Alfred is gone. But they don't play poker with him, have probably never seen him drunk, and, as far as I know, do not have any granddaughters promised to marry either of my brothers. They are also, of course, important men who conduct business both in Denmark and here in Cara. They also serve as Royal Advisors. They are supposed to advise my grandfather on trade agreements and business policy. However, they tend to share opinions on just about everything.

The next two cars deliver my grandmother's best friends and their husbands.

Again, they are mostly friends, but the women absolutely give my grandmother counsel when it comes to various issues and, of course, gossip around the island.

The last to arrive is my mother's best friend. Her husband was also close to my father. I've known Ella and Anton my entire life and it is nice to see them.

They greet me warmly and seem genuinely happy to meet my new wife.

Finally, greetings are complete, photos are done, and we are inside and seated around the table. I made sure that Abigail was seated between me and Linnea with Astrid and Jonah straight across from us and Cian just next to him. She is surrounded by friends and people that she's comfortable talking to.

"Wow. This salad is amazing," Astrid says to no one in particular.

Abigail immediately straightens. "You think so? We grew everything that's in that salad on our farm."

Astrid looks over, clearly not sure what to say. "Oh. That's...cool."

"I mean, our new indoor farm. At Torin's ranch. Linnea's probably told you all about it."

Astrid looks at her sister, then back to Abigail. "No. We haven't talked about farms."

"We're building indoor farms," Abigail tells her, before Linnea can say a word. "We can grow *anything*. Year-round. The farms were Torin's idea." She gives me a bright smile, but immediately turns back to Astrid. "Besides the salad, the Brussels sprouts also came from the farm. And later there will be chocolate dipped strawberries and apple tarts. Of course, just the apples were grown on the farm. Not the crust. They made that here. Obviously."

She's rambling. I can't help but smile. Some might think it's because of nerves, but I know it's because *this* is what gets Abigail going. I put my hand on her thigh under the table and squeeze.

She puts her hand on top of mine and keeps going. "The strawberries are especially great though. They're Torin's favorite. And I make the chocolate. From bean to bar. I have cacao trees and I harvest the beans and do everything from scratch. Oh! And I brought cacao pulp and juice. A lot of people don't even know about the pulp and juice that come from cacao pods. It's delicious *and* it's got vitamins B, D, E, and magnesium. You all really need to try it."

I squeeze her thigh. "Take a breath, princess," I say quietly. And it's maybe the funniest thing I've ever said to her. My quiet, never-uses-her-words girl hasn't paused once, and Cian and Henry are staring at her as if they've never seen her before. I'm sure they've never seen this talkative side of Abigail.

I lean over and kiss her temple. "God, you're hot when you're worked up," I whisper. Then I tell Astrid, "I love cacao juice. It's sweet, and tangy, and tropical."

"Um, wow," Astrid says, clearly not sure what to think of this new information about cacao pods she never expected to get. "I would...yeah, I'd try that."

I put my arm around her. "This is Abigail's passion." I

kiss her temple. "We're really proud of this work." I look down at my wife. "It's amazing you brought all this food tonight. I didn't know you were going to do that."

"Well, I thought it was a perfect opportunity to introduce everyone to what we're doing. And it turns out as Princess, I can get a lot of stuff done." She smiles at Linnea. "With a little help."

Part of me finds that adorable. I love that she's getting more comfortable being the princess and that she's realizing having a little bit of influence can be a good thing. On the other hand, here we are talking about the farm again.

I'm proud of it. I really am. But this isn't the crowd we need to sell it to.

"My grandfather loves chocolate," Cian says as he scoops up a forkful of Brussels sprouts.

Abigail turns her attention away from Astrid and onto Cian. I think I see Astrid sigh with relief.

"Oh, I know. I've been sending him bars on a regular basis."

"No kidding." Cian grins. "How's a guy get in on something like that? I mean I'm your favorite brother-in-law."

"You are?" Abigail asks, with a grin. "Griffin and Michael are pretty great. Plus, I haven't even met Declan."

Astrid snorts. "Lucky you."

Abigail glances at her. "You don't like Declan?"

Astrid shrugs. "Declan's hot and rich, but he's not really a guy you *like*. You respect him, hate him, are intimidated by him, admire him, or lust after him. But I don't think anybody really likes him."

Abigail gives me a look.

I can't really argue with most of that except maybe the lust part, but yeah, my brother is not exactly a warm, fuzzy guy. "Declan definitely does things his own way," I say.

"You know Declan from growing up here with the O'Gradys right?" Abigail asks Astrid.

"Well, yeah. But he also owns the team that my brother plays for. So we run into each other once in a while."

"So do you respect him, hate him, or are you intimidated by him?" Cian asks with a smirk.

"None of those. Just some lust," Astrid says without blinking.

Linnea chokes on a drink of water.

I have my arm resting on the back of Abigail's chair. I take the opportunity to brush my fingers along the back of her neck. Right over her honeybee tattoo.

She leans back into my touch. I love having her here. With my family and friends. Yes, sitting around this dining table is much different than sitting around the table at Ellie's with her boisterous and fun-loving cousins. But, at the same time, this is family. These are people I grew up with. People I've known my whole life. Cian and Henry and Jonah were with me when I went to the US. They believed in what I had to say and got on the plane with me. They were by my side when I left Cara and stayed there for ten years in the States.

And none of them ever said a negative word about me changing my mind and coming home.

I stroke my fingers over Abigail's neck. This is my past, present, and future all melding together.

"Are you all going to the pub tonight?" Linnea asks, probably trying to change the subject from her little sister having dirty thoughts about my big brother.

Astrid leans in, smiling at Cian. "We should. Like old times, but we won't have to sneak out now."

"Hell yeah," he says. He looks at Henry. "You up for a trip to the pub?"

Henry shrugs. "If I can handle you in the Quarter in New Orleans, I think I'll be okay in a pub in Cara."

Henry and Jonah didn't become our bodyguards until we went to the US so they've never been our protection while here on the island. But Henry has a point.

"Are your same policies in place here as in the US?" Jonah asks Henry.

"Policies?" Miles asks.

Cian claps him on the shoulder. "My best protector and dear friend takes it upon himself to eat half of all my food and drink half of all my drinks before I do to be sure they aren't poisoned, and spends time with all the pretty girls I find interesting to make sure they aren't psychos."

Henry just smiles and lifts his glass of water.

But everyone else laughs.

"Wow, such dedication," Miles says.

"I live to serve," Henry says.

"Well, while you're out, mingling with the people," Linnea says, "be sure to mention how great Abigail and Torin are together and how much you loved meeting her."

"No problem." Cian gives Abigail a wink. "Abi's the best. Gorgeous, smart as hell, sweet, looks hot as fuck in purple. I've got it."

I look down and see my wife blushing. I give Cian a frown. No one makes my wife blush but me.

"Just be sure to mention the market tomorrow," Abigail says.

They all look at her.

"What market?" Cian asks.

"We're having a market outside the school." She glances at Linnea. "You didn't tell them?"

"What are you talking about?" I ask. I look from Abigail to Linnea.

Abigail pivots toward me. "I forgot to tell you." She's lit up again. "We're bringing fresh produce, and fresh goods—though we used up the strawberries tonight, but we'll still have tarts and fruit salad and scones and salsas for everyone to try—to the town square and setting up booths for samples and games and crafts for the kids. We'll be there when everyone is getting out of school, so the kids and their parents can participate and the teachers and administration too. But of course, the whole village is invited. It's the perfect way to start showing them what the farms can do, directly. The things that will be available to them." She looks at Astrid. "So you can mention that when you're out tonight."

"We're going to be at the *pub*," Astrid says. She looks at Linnea. "I thought we were supposed to talk up the love story."

"You are," Linnea assures her. "Abi," she says, looking at Abigail, "Cian and Astrid are going to be asked about you and Torin. People are going to want to know what it was like to meet you."

"Great," Abigail tells her. "That's the perfect time to talk about the farms and Torin's ideas."

"I don't know if scones and craft projects are really pub talk," Cian says.

"They're just going to want to know what *you're* like," Astrid adds.

"So tell them I'm really into farming. And that I'm kind of weird and that I wouldn't shut up about cacao pods." She frowns. "And the *market*."

"Abi," Cian breaks in with a laugh. "No one in that pub is gonna give a fuck about cacao pods or whatever."

Abigail is scowling now.

I rest my hand fully on the back of her neck. "Abigail—" I start.

Linnea leans in. "Abi, Cian and Astrid are very popular here. They often show up at the pub when they're home to visit. People love hanging out with them. And I thought it would be a good idea for them to give an A+ report card on the new couple. They'll say that you're shy and quiet, which is why you haven't been doing appearances, but that you're lovely and the family is thrilled with the marriage."

I pin my brother with a direct look. "Be careful what you say."

He nods. "I've got this. I would never say anything but gushing, hugely complimentary things about Abigail. Even before she became my sister-in-law."

"And what are you going to say about the farms?" Abigail asks.

Cian's brows arch. "Um...probably nothing."

"But *that's* the big news."

He laughs. "No, darlin'. *You're* the big news."

"Only because they don't know about the farms. Torin is working so hard for them. You need to tell them what a great prince your *brother* is," she says. "If you and Astrid are such great ambassadors, you should be out there gushing about *Torin* and how lucky Cara is to have him back."

I feel a mix of emotions. I love that she's defending me so ardently and that *she's* acting as an ambassador for me. But I'd love for her to want to be a part of this, linked with me, and that she'd enjoy having people talking about us as a happily-in-love couple who is going to take the world by storm.

"And *he'll* tell them all about that soon enough," Cian tells her. "Right now they want to know about the gorgeous blonde that's wrapped our handsome prince around her little finger and who's going to be making little princes and princesses with him."

Exactly. And I want her to want that.

Why is our relationship being the center of attention such a terrible thing? We're the fucking prince and princess. Of course people want to know more about us.

I'm proud of her, not just the scientist who is making the farms a reality, but the woman I'm in love with. I want to have photos of us splashed up everywhere. I want to give interviews about how I felt when I met her and how we fell in love. I would love to marry her in front of the entire country.

I can't wait to announce things like the international awards she's sure to win for the farm initiative, and the expanded programs we'll be introducing. I'm eager to introduce her to all of my friends and every dignitary who will be important to Cara's future.

And yes, I'm looking forward to throwing her birthday parties, and celebrating our anniversary, and announcing when she's pregnant and when our children are born.

I suck in a deep breath.

I'm getting *way* ahead of things here.

The woman likes me. I'm sure of that much.

I think she might even be falling for me.

She's willing to come to family dinners at least, and that's actually pretty huge.

But she still thinks we have an expiration date. She's not going to be here long enough to even see the lavender bloom. On our first anniversary she'll be getting on a plane.

My gut clenches and I have to consciously relax my neck and shoulders.

Abigail's frown has deepened. "Tell them Torin will be at the market. That will make them want to come out.

Maybe *you* and Astrid could go too. Help turn people out for your brother."

"Abi, baby," Cian says with a laugh. "They don't care about the market! They want to know how you danced the night away, staring into each other's eyes at Charlie's wedding."

"But that's not how it happened," she protests.

He chuckles. "I know. But I'm going to make you both look good. As amusing as I, and everyone, found your general disinterest in my big brother at first—"

"Cian," I interrupt.

"Wait, *disinterest?*" Astrid asks, eyes sparkling. "What's this? Torin, did you have to actually *work for it?*"

"Stop it," I tell them both. This is not the story that needs to get repeated. These two are both mischievous and if they get a little beer in them at the local pub, God knows what they might say. "Abigail is amazing. She's not easily won over, but when she finally..."

I trail off. I was about to say 'when she finally fell in love with me' but...I don't know if she's in love with me even now.

I clear my throat. "It took more than charm and waltzing, but I finally won her over."

Astrid grins. "Obviously."

Yeah, I wish it was obvious.

Abigail knows me. She knows a side of me no one else really does. She knows my dreams and hopes and my vulnerabilities. Jonah has guessed at many of those, I'm sure, but we've never *talked* about them. I've never admitted them to him. Abigail knows what I'm like in my most intimate moments.

But she hasn't said she loves me.

I think she loves my ideas. I think she loves that I want

to do good things. I think she loves the idea of me as King of Cara.

But I don't know if she loves *me*. The man. The regular guy behind closed doors, who gets tired and frustrated and who often wants to hide from the responsibilities and pressure.

My reluctance bothers her. I do know that.

She's here to help me get the farming programs going so I have something concrete to focus on, to point to as a plan.

But she didn't promise to be there for me beyond that. She didn't vow to stand with me as king. She only agreed to help me get there.

"Just tell them that they met at the wedding in Autre. Just repeat the story," Linnea says to Cian. "And then tell them that you like her. That she's fitting in perfectly. That she's got amazing ideas for Cara and she's sweet and intelligent and we're lucky to have her."

"Tell them they're *Torin's* ideas. And you can mention the market as an example," Abigail interjects.

My frustration is building. Can't she let the farms and this market go? Just for tonight? The plan to have Cian and Astrid be our ambassadors in the village is inspired. Everyone loves them. They're also personable and fun. And they are definitely royal insiders. People will believe whatever they say.

But Cian is right. The people want to know about Abigail. And me. Us. Our relationship. Our courtship. The whirlwind romance that was so big, we couldn't even wait until we returned to Cara to get married.

"You have to sell our love story," I say. "We need to be sure everyone is so enamored with us and our relationship that they forget to be mad that there was no wedding."

Astrid nods. "Lindsey and Jen are still talking about that. You should just have a wedding here. Even though you've already officially done it, it wouldn't hurt to have a ceremony here."

Abigail shakes her head. "Oh, no. That's not necessary."

Right. Because she doesn't want to stand up and lie to anyone about us being in love and wanting to be together for more than a year.

"It's not *necessary*," Astrid agrees with a smile. "But it would be fun. And the people would *love* it. There hasn't been a royal wedding here in my lifetime, of course. That would be amazing!"

But Abigail is still shaking her head. Of course. "I'm not really a big wedding kind of girl."

She's not a big display of emotion girl at all.

I feel my frustration building.

Unless, of course, she's on a video call with kids talking about fucking plants.

Then she lights up and practically glows with happiness.

"We could make it small-ish and simple," Astrid says. She looks at Linnea. "It's a good idea. You've seen how everyone is whining online about not really knowing Abi."

"Well, yes, but—"

"They don't *need* to *know* me," Abigail protests. "I'm just—"

My patience snaps. "Okay, so everyone is heading out then." I shove my chair back and stand. I gently squeeze the back of Abigail's neck with one hand and hold the other out to her. "*We* have some things to take care of tonight."

I will not sit here and listen to her talk about how she doesn't want to lie to people about how she feels about me, how she won't even *pretend* in public to have feelings for me, how she won't even consider that things between us could be good for more than twelve months.

And I swear if I hear the word *market* again tonight, I'm going to...

"Yes, we have a lot to talk about before the market tomorrow," Abigail says, taking my hand.

I pull her out of her chair with a growl.

CHAPTER 39
TORIN

I start out of the room with Abigail in tow. The room is quiet behind us.

And I don't care what they say once we're out of earshot.

Abigail also doesn't say anything until we are in our bedroom with the door closed.

Then with my eyes on her the entire time, I take off my crown, and pull my tie loose, sliding it out from my collar and tossing it to the floor.

I unbutton both of my cuffs and start rolling up my sleeves.

"Torin?" Her tone is curious, and her voice soft.

"You had a lot to say at dinner, Princess."

She nods. "You know how I get when I'm excited. When I talk about the farms."

"And you have big plans for tomorrow."

She wets her lips. "Yes. I should've told you about that before. Are you upset?"

"I'm frustrated."

Both of my sleeves rolled up, I unbuckle my belt and slide it out of the belt loops. She watches intently. She's not worried, that's clear.

"Frustrated. Why?"

"Because I love our farms. I love how involved you're getting. I love that you get excited. But I would very much like to be able to excite you and completely overtake your thoughts. Like that fucking farm does. Like you do mine."

She takes a step toward me. "I think about you all the time."

"But you'd rather talk about the farms and have everyone at the pub talking about the market than about us."

She shakes her head. "That's not it."

"That's how it sounded."

"The farms are about you. Your plan for the country. I want everyone to know that. It's why I'm here. And the market—"

"Abigail," I say, low and firm, cutting her off.

I know it's not entirely rational. I know she's not trying to anger me. And it's not truly anger that I'm feeling. It's intense exasperation. But the combination of *that's why I'm here*, as if that's the only reason, and that fucking word —*market*—again, makes my remaining thin thread of patience snap.

"Yes?" she asks.

"Stop. Talking."

I can't believe I'm saying those words to this woman. But I am so caught up in her. I'm obsessed with her. I would really like her to at least be *distracted* when I'm around, if not thoroughly consumed by me.

"Take your clothes off."

She presses her lips together. And makes no move to take anything off. "The farms are not more important than you are, Torin."

"Show me," I say shortly. "I want to be the only thing you are thinking about. Give me your *full* attention, Abigail."

I see her catch her breath.

Then she nods.

"Take everything off except your crown, your wedding ring, and the panties that better be the same ones you've had on all day."

She doesn't say anything more. She simply watches me as she reaches back and unzips her dress. The purple fabric pools at her feet. She leans over to unbuckle the thin straps on her shoes, then kicks off her heels. She straightens and reaches behind her to unclasp her strapless bra.

Then she's bare except for the tiny triangle of her panties. She even reaches up and pulls the clips from her hair, letting her long blond tresses tumble around her shoulders.

I stand, still in my pants and shirt, staring at her blatantly.

She's so fucking gorgeous. And she's mine. She may not obsess over me the way I do her, but she belongs here. Her body is mine, her words are mine, her huge heart is mine... even if I have to share it with a number of other things.

"Come here," I order simply.

She steps out of the circle of fabric and walks toward me. When she's standing right in front of me, I reach out and run my hand from her shoulder to her fingertips. Then

I grasp her hip and bring her closer. "I want this tiara to stay on your head. No matter what we do. Keep your chin up, princess, or your crown will slip."

She nods. "Yes, Your Highness."

That doesn't even sound sarcastic.

I run my hand from her hip over her stomach, then down to cup her through the damp silk fabric. I run my middle finger over her clit, and she sighs softly.

"So wet."

She swallows. "Your fault."

"Damn right." I move both hands and strip the bikini panties down her legs. "Step out."

She does, and I bring them up to my face. I take a long breath in, inhaling her scent.

"Good girl."

"So do I get rewarded?"

God, I love when she teases me. "Well, you were bad at dinner. I wanted everyone to gush over what a wonderful couple we are. All you wanted to do was talk about your vegetables."

She shakes her head. "That's not true."

"You're obsessed with the farm."

"I'm obsessed with making it successful. For you."

I toss the panties to the side and reach up to cup her face. "You light up about your work. The farms, the video call with the kids, even the idea of the market makes you so fucking happy."

I don't like that they make her happier than I seem to. It's not her fault. I can't blame her for not feeling for me the way I do for her. I knew that going in. Jonah pointed it out and I waved it off. If anything, it's my own fault.

I do think over time she'll come to love me.

But I can't tell her yet or she'll run. We made a deal. She

specifically told me what she wanted...and what she didn't want.

I can't mess this up or I could lose her for good. I have to be patient.

Not my strong suit.

But I can keep *showing* her how much I love her.

And for the rest of tonight, I want her thoughts completely absorbed by me.

I move to lock the door, though I doubt anyone in the palace would dare interrupt us. I will tolerate no distractions. Not in actuality, and not in my wife's head.

Then I turn to face her.

"Undress me," I tell her.

Her eyes light up with eagerness and I fight my smile. She loves this. She loves the graphic words, the straightforward actions, my bossiness in the bedroom. I understand that it makes the intensity between us easier for her. She can just follow my commands, give in to the pleasure, take what I say about how she makes me feel physically and not overthink anything, or guess, or wonder.

She comes forward and starts unbuttoning my shirt.

"Who do you belong to, Princess?"

I see her hesitate just a moment. She wants to say herself. She wants to push back. Or to tease. Or test me.

I reach up and cup her breast, flicking my thumb over the tip, then squeezing gently. "In this bedroom, when your body is on display, who do you belong to?"

She answers this time without hesitation. "You."

I slip my hand behind her neck and squeeze gently, bringing her close, so our lips are nearly touching. "That's right. You're mine. And I don't want anything else in this beautiful head right now except me. How I touch you, how I make you feel, how I can consume your body with pleasure."

It might not be love, it might not be the same level of obsession, but I know how I make her feel physically. I know that how she feels with me can fill her mind with pleasure just as it does her body.

She nods. "Yes. Always you."

That's enough. For now.

I turn her so her back is against the door. This isn't going to be soft and sweet. This isn't going to be making love. This is marking her, reminding her, claiming her.

"Open my pants. Take my cock out."

She reaches between us, and I feel the button then zipper on my pants give. She reaches past my boxers and strokes her small hand along my length. I grit my teeth.

I feel a clawing need. It's unlike the way I've felt with her before. In the past I've felt a nearly overwhelming desire, a lust that clamors for me to be *with* her. This is different. This isn't about my pleasure, so much as it is making *her* crazy. Reminding her that I am the only one who touches her like this. I'm the only one who can do this to her.

"I'm going to fill you up again. And you're going to sleep like that. Your thighs sticky and your pussy dripping with me."

She takes a shuddering breath. "Oh my god."

I lean in and kiss her neck then suck gently, then bite down not as gently. She gasps, then groans.

"I'm going to mark you, Abigail. You're mine, and no matter what else fills your head or your heart, no matter what else stirs your passions, or excites your mind, at night in this bed it's me. On my desk, over the back of the couch, in the shower, wherever I want you, I will take you over and over and over. I will fill up your body and your thoughts, at least during these hours we have together."

"Torin—"

I sense that she wants to ask me what I'm talking about because there is obviously more meaning behind my words, but I cover her mouth with my hand. "No. You've said enough tonight. All I want to hear from you is *yes, Torin*, or *my Prince*. Or, *sir*, if you'd like. I'll even allow *Your Highness*. But *yeses* and my name or title. That's it."

Her eyes are wide and she's looking at me with surprise and a touch of confusion. But she's not afraid. She knows I will never hurt her.

I run my hand to the front of her throat and lower my mouth to the side of her neck again sucking hard enough to make a mark. I press her back against the door and keep one hand on her throat as I scoop up under her ass with my other hand. She's light enough, but she also helps by lifting her legs so getting her weight shifted against the wood behind her and her thighs wrapped around my waist takes very little effort.

"The only word you need to stop me is no. If you don't stop me, I'm going to try to make that crown fall off your beautiful head," I tell her gruffly.

I see the heat flash in her eyes.

"Yes, Your Highness." Then there's a spark of mischief when she adds, "Please."

A word I did not give her permission to use.

But she knows I fucking love it.

She's slick and hot and ready for me. I slide home immediately, filling her completely.

She moans, her head falling back against the door. Her crown slips a little but stays on her head.

And it's such a goddamned turn on to fuck her with that thing on her head.

I'm so conflicted by that. I love her in that crown and yet my title, my role, the fact that I brought her here to this palace, is most of our problem.

If we were still in the States, if I could have dated her in Louisiana or Nebraska, this would all feel a lot easier.

Instead, I *married* the only woman who has ever consumed me like this.

And who just kind of likes me.

And I do think she likes me. I think she even cares about me. We definitely have shared passions.

But fuck, I want her to be over the moon for me.

I shift my hips back and thrust into her again. I feel like punishing her for making me feel this way. And yet, her gasp of pleasure fires my blood.

I thrust into her hard again and again. "I feel like you're under my skin, inside me, part of me," I tell her, almost accusingly. "How do you do that? How did that happen?"

I keep pounding into her, pushing her against the door.

But she doesn't seem to mind. She's gripping my shoulders, as if she needs to be closer. Her thighs are tight around my hips and she's gasping in pleasure.

"Yes! Torin, yes!"

I tighten my fingers around her throat just slightly, and she moans. I squeeze her ass and pick up my pace. I know if anyone is on the other side of the door, they know exactly what the pounding sounds are.

"Dammit, Abigail, you're everything to me."

She gasps and suddenly, just like that, she shoots over the edge. Her pussy clamps around my cock and I feel her coming. She shudders in my arms, legs locked around me, her pussy milking me.

Her eyes are squeezed shut, but she's crying out my name. "Torin! Oh my God, Torin!"

The ecstasy on her face shoves me over the edge of my climax and I roar her name. "*Abigail!*"

Everything in me empties into her. Physically, and emotionally.

She has my heart. My soul. My everything.

I put my face against her neck and stay pressed into her for nearly a minute before I realize that I have my wife, the princess, smashed against a hard wood door.

Still buried inside her, I pull her against my chest and stride to the bed. I lay her down and she murmurs in protest as I pull out of her.

I realize it's a little depraved, but I do enjoy seeing what a mess I've made of her. And no, I don't intend to clean her up.

I lean over and kiss her forehead. "Be right back."

I pad into the bathroom and shrug out of my clothes. I don't need to stay in my tux anymore. Not that I needed to be in it to fuck her, but there was something primal about stripping her and taking her like that. Lust tightens my gut again. Dammit. I have very strong feelings for this woman. Maybe I should just concentrate on the ones that I know are returned—admiration and respect, friendship, desire.

Yes, we can be very happy with just those things, right?

I return to the bedroom and see that she's still lying exactly where I laid her down with her eyes shut.

I scoop her up and pull the covers back, then lay her down again, climbing into bed with her and pulling the covers up over us. She snuggles into my arms as she always does. And it's only a few minutes before she's asleep.

Okay, so I guess we don't need to talk about the fucking

against the door. I don't need to ask if she's all right or if she has bruises.

I scrub a hand over my face. She better not have bruises. I'm sure she will on her neck where I sucked and bit. That's different. But if she has bruises on her back from that door, I'm going to be pissed at myself.

I lie there for far too long. I'm tired. But I can't fall asleep. I want to wake her up to talk. To declare my undying devotion. To tell her I'm madly in love with her and to beg her to feel the same way. And that is fucking pathetic.

It's also ridiculous. I can't wake her up. And her feelings are her feelings. I can't *force* her to love me.

Finally, I get up and get dressed, in casual clothes this time, and head out. I know the perfect place to go. I can forget about how Abigail is twisting me up and can just relax and have a good time.

CHAPTER 40
ABIGAIL

I wake up alone around midnight. I stretch, reaching for Torin. He's not there and his side of the bed is completely cold. I sit up and stretch. I wince a little too. That sex against the door has me a little sore. But I smile. It was hot. I don't know exactly what came over him, and I'm going to have to ask him about it later. It was like he couldn't wait and he wasn't about to make it soft and sweet, because he just had to have me right then and there.

I smile and stretch and then feel how badly I need a shower. Yes it was definitely hot and messy.

I don't know where my husband is, but I want to find him. I want more of whatever that was before I fell asleep.

I reach for my phone and text him.

Where are you? I'm two minutes away from reaching for Charming.

That should do it. If he's downstairs getting a snack or

something, he'll be back up in less than two minutes for sure.

Not that he won't maybe let Charming be involved...

I grin and wait for either a dirty text in response or for Torin to come storming through the door.

But three minutes later, neither has happened. And there's no *way* I can go downstairs like this.

I try calling him instead, wondering if maybe he didn't hear the ping of the text.

But he doesn't answer. I frown. That's strange.

I slide out of bed, grab my robe, and quickly pull it on. I go to the door and pull it open just enough to look up and down the hallway. It's empty and quiet and I contemplate going down to the kitchen as is. We don't have guards stationed right outside the doors, of course. But I won't get far without someone seeing me. The palace is never completely asleep.

Typically I could probably pull on loungewear and go down to the kitchen but I'm a mess and while I'm sure it's no shock that Torin and I are having sex, I'll be far too self-conscious if I run into anyone in this state.

I shut the door and chew my bottom lip. I could just go back to bed and wait for him to come back. But I'm now wide awake and sneaking around the dark castle together sounds kind of fun.

I head into the bathroom for a shower. If he gets back before I'm done, I don't mind the idea of him joining me in there either.

But he's not back by the time I'm done.

Or by the time I'm dressed in black leggings, a large sweatshirt, and slip-on tennis shoes.

Or by the time I'm opening the door again and sneaking out into the hallway.

I'm not stopped until I hit the second-floor landing.

"Princess Abigail?"

I suck in a sharp breath, my hand flying to my chest as I turn. The security officer approaching is named Sean and I give him a smile. "Hi, Sean."

"Is everything all right?" he asks.

"Yes. I'm looking for the prince."

"Oh." He frowns slightly.

"Have you seen him?"

"I don't believe he's back yet."

"Back?" I repeat. "He left?"

"Yes. Around eleven."

It's almost twelve-thirty. I blink. "He *left* the palace?"

"Yes." He frowns again. "You didn't know?"

"I didn't. Do you know where he went?" Is it my business? Yes, I think it is. I guess we'll see if Sean agrees.

Then I remind myself that as princess, I have as much authority as Torin does. Unless he told Sean specifically *not* to tell me, then he'll have to let me know where Torin is.

"I assume he's still at the pub. I can't imagine there's much else to do in town tonight," Sean says with a smile. "But he's got people with him, don't worry."

I'm not worried. I'm confused. "He's at the pub? You mean the one where Cian and Astrid were going?"

"There's only one pub," Sean says.

Right.

So Torin couldn't sleep and decided to go down to the pub with his brother and friends. That makes sense.

And the most out-of-character thought crosses my mind.

I want to go to the pub.

I enjoyed the few outings I had in Sapphire Falls at the

bar with my friends there. I'm sure the pub with Cian, Astrid, Torin, and God knows who else, will be fun.

And...I take a deep breath...for some reason that seems like an easier way to be out "among the people" than up in front of them in some formal manner. Even earlier, standing on the front steps of the palace and receiving guests while people looked on and took photos, felt strange.

But having a drink at the local pub like I did in Sapphire Falls? Sure. I can do that.

Especially if Torin is there. He won't let anything happen to me. He won't let me be uncomfortable. He won't let people ask me probing questions or expect me to say anything. He'll do the talking. As always. I can just be *with* him.

"Can you tell me how to get to the pub, Sean?" I ask, starting down the steps.

"Um...what? The pub?"

I look back. "Yes. The center of town is walking distance from here, right? Can I walk to the pub?"

"Well, yes."

"Great. Just take the main road? I assume, since it's the only one and probably one of the few places open this late, I'll find it?"

"Princess Abigail, you can't go alone," he protests, starting down the stairs.

"Okay," I say agreeably. I'd rather walk with someone anyway. "Do you want to come?"

"I...can't. I'm on duty."

"Isn't part of your duty to take care of me?"

That clearly trips him up for a moment. "Yes, but—"

"It's fine. Can you find someone else?" Now we're on the landing just above the first floor.

Sean obviously realizes I'm serious about this and he nods quickly. "Yes. Yes, I can. Will you wait? Please?"

He looks almost worried now. I stop and smile. "Yes. I'll wait for someone to escort me to the pub."

"Thank you," he says, relieved. "Just…" He looks around. "Wait here."

"I'll wait by the front doors," I tell him. I hold up a hand when he starts to protest. "But I promise I won't leave."

He nods, then hurries off.

I continue down the steps. I pass one of the large mirrors in the main hall and check over my appearance. This is *very* casual. Even if it is a pub, should I dress up more than this?

I run my hand over my sweatshirt. It's a deep maroon with the crest of my college on it.

Hmm…maybe not very princess-y.

Then again, I've been in lots of photos in my green rubber boots.

I do reach up and pull my ponytail loose, though. I shake my hair out and run my fingers through it. I never wear a lot of make-up, so people haven't seen me too made up. And I've only worn my tiara once.

Still…I wonder if Sean will have an opinion about what I'm wearing.

"Abigail?"

I turn quickly at the familiar voice. "Jonah," I say with surprise.

"You want to go to the pub?"

"Oh no, they woke *you* up?"

He frowns. "Of course they did. I'm to be informed of all of your and Torin's movements."

"I didn't know that. I'm sorry."

"Don't be." He holds out a black cap. "You should probably wear this."

"What's this?"

"A hat," he says with a brow up. Then he smiles. "It's Linnea's. I think you going to the pub is fine. Really great actually. But it might not be what you're expecting. We can keep you a little incognito until you decide you really want to stay."

"You think I might not?"

"I think you're a serious introvert who just recently even started appearing on camera in videos with little kids. I think it's huge that you even think you want to go to the pub and I'm very happy to take you, but I think having an out might not be a terrible thing."

I think about that. That's really sweet. I take the cap. "Thank you. I really appreciate that."

"I really appreciate how good you are for my best friend," he says. "And the woman I love. And...just in general. You're good, Abigail. I'm here to help."

Then I do the second most out-of-character thing. I step forward and hug Jonah.

He's not just surprised. He's shocked. But it only takes a second for him to hug me back. When I step away, smiling, he's also smiling.

"Am I dressed all right?" I ask, looking down.

"Yep. Perfect."

I turn to the mirror and put the cap on, adjusting it on my head and arranging my hair. Then I turn back to him. "Ready."

"I'm glad you think so," he says with a light chuckle. He pulls the door open, gives Sean a little wave, and ushers me through.

As we walk, I ask, "Why aren't you at the pub with Torin if you need to keep track of every movement?"

"When we're in Cara, it's okay to just know where he is and that someone is with him. I don't need to be with him physically all the time."

I shoot him a smirk. "But you always were anyway, before Linnea right?"

He smiles. "Yes."

"Who's with him tonight that makes it okay for you to stay behind?"

"There are a couple of security officers from the palace there because of the whole entourage, but Henry is there with Cian and Miles is with Astrid, so Torin is covered by proxy."

"Is Miles a bodyguard? I thought he was Astrid's trainer."

Jonah nods. "He is. But he's very protective. I don't expect anyone in Cara will be violent or anything. No one wants to cause them harm. They might just get...exuberant. Miles won't let anyone get too close or handsy or anything."

"That makes sense."

We walk about three hundred yards and as we crest a small rise, I can see light glowing and already hear the sounds of a party. My eyebrows rise. "Is that the pub?"

"It is."

"Wow."

He chuckles. "It's not always quite that loud, but I'm sure Cian, Henry, and Torin are helping make it raucous."

I study him. "You're not *upset* about getting a chance to go in there, are you?" I ask. "You like this."

He looks over at me. "My years with Torin have been amazing, Abi. He's..."

He trails off for a second and I nod. "I know."

Jonah smiles. "Torin is a force of nature. There's really no resisting smiling and having fun when he's in your life. There's no avoiding being fucking frustrated as hell by his stubbornness and exasperated by his impatience, either. But there's also no avoiding thinking big, taking the world in differently, asking a shit-ton of questions, starting to wonder *why* about everything—why people do the things they do, why things run the way they do, why *can't* we do something else—because of him."

I feel a warmth in my chest that makes me lift my hand and rub at it. "I'm so glad he has you."

"He always will."

We walk for several feet, drawing closer to the light. And noise.

"You'll always have me too, Abi," he says.

I look over. "Thank you."

"Even after the year is over. You can always call me. Any time."

I nod. But the words make me look back down at the ground as I walk. *After the year is over.*

It's so nice to know that Jonah would still be a friend after I leave Cara. I think Linnea will too.

Torin might even be.

But that feels so weird to even think.

He *is* my friend. I'm closer to Torin than I am to anyone. Even my sisters, I realize. I feel closer to them than I ever have, but they still don't know me the way Torin does. They don't make me feel safe and understood and supported the way he does.

I don't know if anyone else ever will.

"You sure you want to do this?" Jonah asks.

I really don't.

But then I look up and realize that he's not talking about me leaving Cara. He's looking at the squat stone building we're approaching.

Light is spilling out of a multitude of windows and at least three doors. There's music, but also voices—laughing, shouting, cheering, and just talking.

And there are so many people. So, so many.

They can't all fit inside. They're spilling out of the doors, gathered around all sides of the building, partying all the way out to the road.

I stop. "Oh my God."

"Yeah," Jonah agrees. "That's because of your husband."

I turn wide eyes on him. "Not Cian and Astrid?"

"Them too. There were about a hundred too many people here when they were here, but when Torin showed up, the number doubled."

"How do you know that?"

He just gives me a smile. "It's my job."

I turn back to the scene just down a short hill from us. "Wow. So Torin is more popular than Cian and Astrid?"

"He's their prince, Abi."

Jonah's tone indicates that it should be obvious to me that would bring crowds.

And, I guess, it is.

He's their leader. He's their someday-king.

I take a breath. "Okay."

"You want to go in?"

"I'm not sure. Can we just get closer?"

"Sure. Here, around back." He guides me down the hill, closer to the trees along the edge of the road that throw shadows on us. He takes me to the back side of the pub that butts up against more trees. There are far fewer people back here because there simply isn't room for a crowd. Or for dancing and passing trays of drinks.

Jonah manages to get us up near one of the windows. It's open and we can hear everything.

Including the man currently speaking to the crowd.

From the top of a table.

A very familiar man.

My husband. The prince.

"Marlin, I know your son went to London for school and didn't come back," Torin says, pointing his finger on the hand that's also holding a bottle of beer at a man standing near the door across the room from us. "Let's train our kids *here* and give them jobs *here*. Let's keep them home."

The crowd cheers.

My eyes are wide, but I feel my smile.

"And I know last year the produce prices went way up," he says pointing at someone, or maybe a group, at the back wall. "I know that *sucked* because there was nothing we could do. We don't have anything to negotiate with. We have to just be nice and hope Denmark is good to us."

There are a few boos now.

He nods. "Right? We need our *own* crops. We need to produce our own food, you guys!"

There's some clapping to that.

"What about the fishing?" someone calls.

"He's having a town hall meeting?" I ask Jonah softly.

He's grinning. "Looks like it. I guess, why not? The town is here."

"Is he drunk?"

Jonah's smile turns more affectionate. "No, Abi. He's... Torin. He's in his element. He's just being very much himself."

I turn back to watch.

"Yes, the fishing!" Torin exclaims with a grin.

"It sucked this last season!" someone calls.

He nods. "I know. I need you to come talk to me about that, Jack. Come up to the palace." He looks around the room. "Any of you. All of you! And any other businesses that are struggling, I want to hear it. We need solutions."

"Like what?" someone yells. "How are you going to solve it?"

Torin points at the man. "That's just it. I'm not!"

There's grumbling and a few more boos.

But he waves his arms. "*We* are!" he says. "I need your help. I can get stuff done, but I need to know the stuff to do. That's where you all come in. I'm not a fisherman."

"No kidding," someone shouts.

But Torin just grins. "Seriously. I need you all to help me figure out what we need to do."

There's murmuring in the crowd, but no one says no.

"That's perfect," I say quietly.

"He's going to be really good at this," Jonah says.

"I know." I'm so proud of him.

He might be on a table in a pub, but it's so clear this man was meant to lead. His enthusiasm and sincerity and earnestness are so obvious.

He needs that throne right now.

"Maybe I should go in," I say.

"You think so? Everyone will notice you immediately," Jonah says. "*Torin* will notice you immediately. There will be no hiding out."

My breath catches in my chest. I will be the center of attention. A lot of attention.

My stomach starts to cramp at the thought.

Then someone calls out, "So are we ever going to meet your *wife*?"

I look at Jonah. He looks at me with a 'well?' look.

And I'm suddenly frozen.

"Oh *fuck*," Torin says. "I want that so much."

I swing back to look at him.

Did he just say 'fuck' in front of all of these people? And then I notice something I hadn't at first. There are dozens of phones out and held up.

People are recording this. Recording Torin.

Which is great when it comes to him talking about meeting with them about business concerns and how Cara needs to start producing its own crops but now...

"I want you all to meet Abigail. You are going to *love* her."

"So where is she?"

"We want to meet her!"

"Tell her to come out with us!"

People all start shouting and cheering.

My stomach cramps even harder and I'm aware that I'm breathing fast and shallow. Oh, God. Oh, God. Oh, God.

"She's *amazing*," Torin goes on. "But she's not big on crowds and stuff."

"She's the princess!"

"We want to see her!"

I feel Jonah put a hand on my back and I know he's saying something to me, but I can't hear him over the blood rushing through my head.

Torin puts a hand over his heart, grinning broadly. "I know you do. I know. And you don't even know how incredible she is. My gorgeous genius," he says, with feeling. "She's so fucking amazing, and she's *here*, doing all of this for us."

People applaud, but there are still people calling out.

"We need to see her in person!"

"We want to hear *her* talk!"

"I want her to, too!" Torin calls back, laughing.

Hey, isn't he supposed to be covering for me? Telling them it's fine and I don't need to come talk to them?

Torin puts his other hand to his chest now. "I am so madly in love with her."

My heart gives a very hard thump and I feel my mouth drop open.

There are *whoops* and some cat calls and more applause, but I'm just staring at Torin.

He just said...

"Seriously, over-the-moon, 'til-death-do-us part love!" he proclaims. "I fall more in love with her every day!"

Oh.

My.

God.

Torin just said he's in love with me.

In love with me.

While standing on a table in a bar.

We said we weren't going to do that. We weren't going to talk about feelings. We weren't going to make any vows about emotions. We weren't going to make any public proclamations.

And then he goes on. "I didn't know that was going to happen," he tells the crowd. "I met her at a wedding and asked her to dance because she's so damned beautiful, and there was just...something about her. But then...I had to talk her into it. That's never happened to me before."

That gets a bunch of laughs.

He grins and nods. "I know. But from that moment, I couldn't stop thinking about her. We danced, and then...she walked away. And I was done for. I saw her again at the next wedding, and I just *had* to have another chance. And then I found out how *fucking amazing* she is." He looks around the room. "You don't even know. She's so incredible. And she's willing to be here with me. With us. I just…" He shakes his head. "I can't believe it. I love her so much."

The crowd goes crazy cheering, applauding, and pounding on tables.

I swallow hard and look at Jonah. "Why…why is he doing this?"

Jonah doesn't look anywhere near as shocked as I feel. "He needed to say this. He told me yesterday during our run that it's been trapped inside for so long, he's been afraid he's just going to blurt it out to you. I guess if he can't say it to you, he had to at least say it to someone."

I blink. Then frown again. "He couldn't say it to me? But he could say it to an entire pub full of people he barely knows?"

"These are his people, Abi. They're the ones who most need to know where his heart is."

My frown deepens. "More than *I do*?" I ask.

Jonah nods. "They need to feel close to him long term. After you leave."

My rib cage tightens. So these people get to see a side of Torin, hear genuine thoughts and feelings from him—even ones that are about me—because he knows they're going to be here and support him and love him…even after I'm gone.

My stomach is in a knot. It feels so…*wrong* for him to be sharing something that's clearly something he feels deeply with anyone else before me.

I want to be the one to know all his thoughts and feelings.

I want to be the one he shares everything with.

I want to be the one he knows will be there for him.

I want to be the one he tells how much he loves me.

"Yes!" Torin shouts. "I am madly in love with my wife!"

The crowd cheers, hoisting their drinks in the air.

"And we're going to have a wedding!" Torin suddenly announces.

I gasp.

"We're already married, but I want to pledge my love to her forever in front of all of you."

Okay that is *definitely* something we specifically said we were *not* going to do.

The pub burst into cheers, the sound of feet stomping and hands pounding on the tables again filling the air.

"And our marriage deserves a huge party!" Torin declares.

And I stand just staring with my mouth hanging open.

My husband, the man who promised to protect me from public spectacle and judgment and being the center of attention, has just announced his feelings for me to a bunch of people I don't know, including who knows how many people on the internet.

And promised them a wedding. A royal wedding that *everyone* will be excited to see.

I turn to Jonah. "I need to get out of here."

"Okay," is Jonah's simple answer. He doesn't look a bit surprised.

Well, at least I was willing to walk down to the pub even if I didn't go inside.

Even if I didn't get up on a table and tell the whole world how I feel about my husband.

CHAPTER 41

ABIGAIL

I need to call my sisters. I'm thankful for the time difference, this time. It's only seven p.m. back home.

Charlie picks up on the first ring. "Hey, how are—"

"You need to get Ami and call me back," I blurt, cutting off whatever she was about to say.

"Okay." She disconnects just like that.

I pace across our bedroom, nibbling on my thumbnail, waiting for the call back.

It comes surprisingly quickly.

"We've figured out how to both be on video without being in the same room," Charlie says.

Ami's face is in a second square. "Are you okay?"

Just seeing them, I almost start crying. My nerves are strung tight. "Have you seen the video?"

I know they have. If they're following Cara's royal family, especially Torin and me, they've seen this video.

"Yes," Charlie admits. "We were actually going to call you, but weren't sure where you were. Were you *there*?"

I shake my head.

"I didn't think so," she says. "Surely someone would have gotten you on video if you were."

My stomach cramps. But I'm also considering it a sign of progress that I haven't thrown up because of all of this.

"I was there," I say. "But no one knew. Not even Torin. So I...saw it. But..." Tears start rolling.

"Oh fuck," Ami mutters when she sees them.

"So, I take it you're upset?" Charlie asks.

Charlie would love a declaration like what Torin did tonight. Hell, Charlie would *do* what Torin did tonight. The funny thing is, her husband, Griffin, would never do something like that. Griffin is more like me. Quiet, happy behind the scenes, very content to let his significant other shine in the spotlight.

I stop pacing and stare into the phone.

Charlie and Griffin are a lot like Torin and me in a few key ways. The roles are just flipped. "It took a while for Griffin to tell you how he felt about you, right?" I ask.

Charlie seems surprised. "Yes. And he didn't *want* to have the feelings."

"Right." I'm studying the edge of my phone as I think about that.

"Do you *want* your feelings?" she asks.

My gaze bounces back to her. "What?"

"You're in love with Torin," she says with a gentle smile. "But you haven't told him. I'm just asking if you *want* those feelings."

I nod. I don't even have to think about it. "I do. And...I really loved hearing his feelings tonight."

I realize that's true. I've never had anyone proclaim

their feelings for me like that. Claim me like that. Be so proud of me and so in love with me and so *happy* with me that he just couldn't hold it inside.

I...liked that.

Words matter. I've always believed that. But up-front, in-public words have always been scary.

Until...tonight.

As I think back over it, I was shocked that Torin was doing that. But I wasn't shocked by the words themselves.

Torin is in love with me.

That doesn't feel shocking. That feels...obvious.

Yelling it to a roomful of strangers from a tabletop isn't how I expected to hear about it, but it was...very Torin.

And I feel a little healed from it.

I suddenly have to sit down.

My butt hits the mattress as my heart pounds and I stare off into the distance, my thoughts swirling.

For a girl who was made fun of and judged and bullied when she was in the spotlight in the past, *this* felt so damned good.

A *prince* climbed up on a table and shouted his feelings for hundreds of people to hear.

"Abi?" I hear Charlie ask. "You okay."

I focus on her. "Yeah. I'm great. I guess I just wish he'd said them to me first."

Ami leans in. "He's never told you he's in love with you?"

I shake my head. "Tonight is the first time I've heard it. Along with a bunch of other people. Without him even knowing I was there."

Charlie gives a little wince. "But he knows you hate the spotlight," Charlie says.

"Yeah." I pause, then look at my sisters. "Jonah told me

Torin said he couldn't keep the words inside any longer and since he couldn't say them to me, he had to say them to *someone*."

Ami frowns. "Why would he feel he couldn't say them to you?"

"I don't know."

Charlie gives me a 'come on' look. "Abigail, you do know."

I frown. "What?"

"The man knows you," she says. "He knows you and he *listens* to you. You talk about how you don't trust words and talk. You need to see what people *do* before you trust them. You said getting married was practical. You talked about the farming program and how great it would be for Cara. You were very interested in how being the princess would mean you could get things done faster and easier. You didn't marry him or move to Cara with him because you were in love with him, and he knows that."

I feel a pang in my chest.

I know I said all of those things. I know that's what Torin thinks.

But I'm not sure it's true.

Moving to Cara for the farms and taking on the title of princess did seem practical. But I think it was an excuse. A way to make myself feel like falling in love with Torin made sense.

Ami nods. "He didn't want to freak you out by telling you that he'd fallen in love with you and there are now a bunch of emotions complicating something that he thinks, for you, is supposed to be simple and straightforward."

My throat tightens. "I care about him," I say. "A lot. I love being here with him. I think he's amazing. He's going to be an amazing king. I want him to believe in himself. I love what he has planned for this country. And I love his heart. I love his insecurities. I love being with him. I love the things he believes in. I love how he makes me feel about myself."

My sisters are quiet. They both just sit smiling at me, letting me think about what I just said.

Yeah, okay, I heard it.

I take a breath. "Fine. Yes. I love him. I've loved him since..." I sigh. "A long time. But we haven't said it. We agreed *not* to. And *he's* the big talker. If he had something to say, why did he do it this way instead of saying it to me? Now I've got a huge spotlight on me."

"You definitely do," Ami says. "Have you heard the podcast?"

"The podcast from here?" I ask.

She nods. "They did a special edition tonight once Torin showed up. This was his first public appearance with the people, Abi. Lindsey and Jen were *there*. And they've been talking *all* about this big love declaration."

My heart turns over in my chest and my stomach roils. "What are they saying?"

"That it's your turn." My sister has the audacity to grin. "They want you to publicly declare your feelings for him the same way. They mentioned there's some farmer's market thing happening tomorrow where Torin is introducing your farm to the village. They have challenged you."

"Oh...no..."

My finger is shaking as I click on the link Ami just sent me.

• • •

PODCAST EPISODE 821 TRANSCRIPT

Lindsey: Well, wow. I feel like I just got injected with a B12 shot. Or Cupid's arrow hit me. And that is very unlike me.

Jen: No kidding. That was amazing. I mean, Prince Torin has never really shied away from the spotlight. But that was next level even for him. The public declaration, the just putting it all out there like that. I can see why Abigail fell for him. If he has been feeling like this for her for like two years, she didn't stand a chance.

Lindsey: Okay, Princess, your turn! We want to see your big public declaration!

Jen: I don't know. Maybe she's not that type. He's the big, sunshiny, energetic, golden retriever type. She's the quiet, nerdy bookworm. I have to admit, that's pretty cute.

Lindsey: Yeah, it is. At the same time, now the guy has declared his feelings, for all of us to see, and she knows we all love him. She has to give us *something*. Can't leave a guy hanging like that, can you?

Jen: Oh my God, you know what it reminds me of? Have you ever seen the Drew Barrymore movie *Never Been Kissed?*

Lindsey: Sure. My mom loves that movie.

Jen: This reminds me of how she does the public declaration of her feelings for the guy and says meet me on the pitcher's mound at the baseball game and give me my first kiss. And then the huge crowd shows up and she's standing there, waiting for him, and the clock's running down, and he's not showing up and he's not showing up... <dramatic sigh>

Lindsey: So you're saying Prince Torin has said, "Hey, Abigail, come kiss me in front of everyone" and now we're just waiting to see if she'll do it?

Jen: I'm just saying that would be pretty great.

Lindsey: That *has to* happen! You hear us, Princess? Get your bejeweled behind down here and kiss your prince! I hear there's a pretty cool farmer's market happening tomorrow. That would be the perfect place.

I stare at the transcript.

Oh, this is bad. This is really bad.

"You're going to do it, right?" Ami asks.

I look at my sisters and instantly start shaking my head. "Of course not!"

"You have to!" Ami insists. "If you don't, that will look so bad! It will be embarrassing for Torin!"

"Well, he should have thought of that when he got up on that table!" I say. But I don't mean it. Even as the words leave my mouth, I want to take them back. I take a deep breath. "Okay, what he did tonight was kind of great."

"It was," Charlie agrees. "Ideal? For you? No. But pretty romantic. And very..."

"Torin," I fill in. "It was very Torin. He's the get-up-on-a-table type. And I knew that when I agreed to this. I mean he *built me a farm*. He's...over the top and larger than life."

"And he's a prince," Charlie says. "He will always be in the public eye, in the spotlight."

"And he loves that. It's where he belongs," I say quietly, thinking about how he looked up on that table tonight.

He didn't look ridiculous. He didn't come off as obnoxious. He was genuine, passionate, approachable, and as *him* as I've maybe ever seen him.

"Can you deal with that?" Charlie asks.

"I don't know," I tell her honestly.

"And if I get up in front of everyone and kiss him and say that I love him—" I take a deep breath, imagining it. "—if I tell *him* I love him, I have to mean it."

"Do you?" Charlie asks.

"I do love him. But I won't promise anything up in front of everyone that I don't mean."

"So what can you say that you'll mean?" Ami asks.

"That's what I need to figure out," I tell them.

We say goodbye soon after. They make me promise to call again tomorrow. After we disconnect, I strip out of my sweatshirt and leggings and climb into bed. I curl into a ball and squeeze my eyes shut.

What can you say that you'll mean?

That's a really, really good question.

CHAPTER 42

TORIN

"You should probably sleep in another bedroom."

I stop several feet down the hall from my bedroom door. Jonah's sitting in a chair outside my bedroom.

"Is Abigail all right?" I ask, starting forward.

"She was at the pub tonight."

I stop. I stare at him. "What?"

"Not the whole time. But she was there to hear you tell the whole place that you're madly in love with her. And that you're going to have a wedding."

Oh.

Fuck.

I scrub a hand over my face. "How did that happen?"

"She woke up without you, went looking for you, Sean told her where you were, and she wanted to go. So I took her, of course."

"She wanted to go to the pub?" I ask, more surprised by that at the moment.

He nods. "Yep. Pretty good progress I'd say. She was in very casual clothes, I gave her a cap, and we went around back to check things out before going in." He lifts a brow at me. "You were already on the table by then."

Oh, man. I'm so fucked.

I have done the worst thing I could possibly do to the woman that I love.

I dragged her into the spotlight. I told the whole world I'm in love with her. I've put my heart at her feet and very fucking publicly asked her to pick it up and take care of it.

"How angry is she?" I ask, my gut is tight.

"She didn't seem angry, actually." Jonah shrugs. "She seemed thoughtful, if anything. She was quiet the whole way back."

"She didn't cry, did she?" I ask. That would kill me.

"No. No tears. Just quiet. Like she was thinking things over."

Oh, I'm sure she was. Abigail thinks *everything* over. She's probably already figured out a way to leave the island and get back to Louisiana without seeing me.

And honestly, that would be easy enough. She's the princess. She can ask any palace staff member to take her to the airport and they will without question. She can then simply ask for our pilot to be contacted. Then he'll fly her wherever she wants to go. They won't need to say a word to me.

Which means, I need to camp outside this door so she can't leave without me knowing.

"I'm going to grab a pillow and blanket," I say. "Stay 'til I get back?"

"You're going to sleep in front of the door?" he asks.

"Of course."

"I don't think she's leaving."

I sigh. "She can't win here. If she doesn't reciprocate, everyone will wonder why. They'll think she's cold. If she doesn't love me with equal fervor, they won't like her." I shake my head. "Hell, if she tries to reciprocate, she'll probably throw up.

And I don't think Abigail Landry O'Grady can pull off a lie that big. She's too genuine. She's too matter-of-fact. If she doesn't love me and tries to publicly proclaim that she does, people will know she's lying. And they'll hate her for that too.

They've seen her genuinely happy and excited. I'm sure people who didn't initially see her adorable video doing the craft project with the kids have seen it by now. People will no doubt be searching for photos and videos of her first thing tomorrow.

They'll be able to tell the difference between her confidence and genuine happiness there and whatever she might try to pull off in public with me.

"She's going to leave. This is the exact thing she told me she didn't want."

Jonah nods. "Yeah. It sure is."

I frown. "Team Abigail already?"

"What makes you think I wasn't Team Abigail from the start?"

"The whole 'you deserve to be loved' thing you laid on me."

"Well, you do."

"Thanks. So you *are* Team Torin."

He grins. "I'm Team Abi and Torin."

"Jonah..."

"She loves you, dumbass. Just give her a minute to

figure it out. And to figure out how to tell you without puking."

His words make my heart thump hard and I almost hate how much I *need* that to be true. "I have to sleep here tonight. I have to see her first thing."

"I'll stay here," he says. "You go actually sleep. You have the market in the morning with Linnea. You need to be good for that."

"But if she tries to leave, go to the airport and whatever, you'll stop her?" I ask.

Jonah shakes his head. "Of course not. She's the princess. I can't stop her."

"Jonah," I almost growl.

"But," he continues. "I *will* tell you. In time to catch her."

I believe him. He wants me to be happy and he knows Abigail is key to that. So he'll tell me if she tries to leave the island. "Thank you."

"Get some sleep," he says, slouching in the chair, seemingly getting more comfortable. "I have a feeling tomorrow is going to be a big day."

CHAPTER 43
ABIGAIL

I still have no idea what I'm going to do.

Or more specifically, what I'm going to *say*.

I slept fitfully all night and woke up early. I've redone my hair three times. I've changed my clothes four times.

And I don't know what to do.

Except go to the market today and find Torin.

He didn't come to bed last night.

I assume he came back to the palace.

He has a lot of people looking out for him, so I know he's safe.

But I don't know how I feel about waking up without him. It feels wrong. And empty. And lonely. And I don't want to do it anymore, ever again.

So I guess that means I need to figure out a way to tell my husband that I'm in love with him.

And accept the fact that once I do that, I'm officially on a world stage. Forever.

Sure, it might be a small world stage. But, knowing Torin, it *will* get bigger.

I press my hand against my stomach.

I really want to see him on that stage. He'll be so, so good up there.

So that means, I need to figure out a way to stand beside him up there.

Because I'm not letting him go.

Just then my phone beeps with an incoming call. I frown when I see the number.

The king is calling me.

This day just got even weirder.

"Hello? Good morning, Your Majesty."

"Abigail, will you please come to my office?"

"You're...calling me for that," I say stupidly.

"Yes. I figured that was faster. I could have texted, I suppose."

The idea that the eighty-something-year-old king of Cara would *text* me about anything makes me smile. "This is fine. I'll be right there."

A few minutes later, I walk up to Emil's desk. He rises and opens the king's office door for me with nothing more than a quick bow.

I step across the threshold with a deep breath.

"Your Majesty," I greet.

He stands and comes around to the front of his desk. "Diarmuid when we're in private, Abigail," he says with a smile.

He leans against the desk, and I relax. He doesn't seem upset.

"Okay," I say. "Then you have to call me Abi."

He tips his head. "Torin calls you Abigail."

I nod. "He's the only one."

"Ah. Then Abi it is." He gestures to the chairs in front of him.

I take the closest one, crossing one leg over the other. "Are you upset about the scene at the pub last night?" I ask. I'm sure he's seen the videos by now.

"That's exactly what I was going to ask you," he says.

I'm surprised, but I say honestly, "I'm not. Anymore. Actually, it's kind of my fault he got to that point."

Diarmuid nods. "I know how that feels. There are a few things he's done where it's been *my* fault he got to *that* point."

I relax further and give him a smile. "I think you are one of the reasons he was drawn to me when we met."

The king looks interested. "Is that right?"

"He's used to being challenged by people who love him, and he knows, deep down, it's a form of support and love—making sure he's really up to the things we will demand from him. But he loves winning us over and proving himself."

Diarmuid nods. "I think you're exactly right." He pauses, then says, "Linnea would have been an excellent queen."

I lift a brow. "I agree." What can I say? Linnea Olsen is awesome.

"But she would not have made Torin as great a king as you will."

I'm astonished. I sit a little straighter. "Oh."

"She would have done any number of great things. She would have led the country. She would have made good decisions. But *you* will make Torin do great things. You will *help* him lead the country. You will support him in his decisions. And he'll do the same for you. With Linnea we would have had a great queen. With you, we will have a great queen *and* king."

My heart is pounding. I swallow. "You don't think Linnea would have helped Torin be great?"

"She would have advised him. Encouraged him. He might have even listened. But you will make him *want* to do it. You've helped him find purpose. Standing *beside* someone, as he would have with Linnea, is different from standing *with* someone, as he will with you."

I suddenly feel stinging at the back of my eyes. I blink. "So you're not worried about him leaving Cara?"

"No. His heart is here." He smiles at me. "Because *you* are here."

I sniff. "But I could leave. I'm an American."

"You're not going to leave Cara, Abi," Diarmuid says confidently.

I'm not going to leave, but I don't know how he knows that. "You're sure?"

"Of course, I'm sure. You know he's going to be a great king. You want that for him. Because you love him. And he needs to be *here* to do that. So you'll stay."

I swallow hard. Then simply nod. Because he's right.

"You believe he's going to be a great king, too," I say.

"I do."

"So you need to talk to him." I sigh. "You and I are both going to have to suck it up and get better at *saying* the things Torin needs to hear. Just because it's not what we like to do, doesn't mean we don't have to do it."

He studies me for a moment. "People think that being king means that you never have to do things that you don't want to do."

I nod.

"But if you're doing it well, it's actually doing a lot of things you don't want to do," he continues. "Choosing the greater good over individuals. Weighing every single option. Twice. Sleepless nights. Sometimes cutting off relationships because they are selfish and political. Sometimes maintaining relationships even though they are selfish and political. Putting a country full of people, who are more strangers than friends, ahead of family, actual friends, and yourself. Making mistakes very publicly. Being given respect without ever really knowing if it's been earned or if it's just expected." He gives me a smile that seems genuine but also, tired. "Questioning if this is something you should even want to pass down to your children and grandchildren whom you love very, very much."

I watch him, thinking all of that over. Finally, I ask, "Were you a little relieved when your grandchildren left Cara? Just a little part of you? For even a day?"

"For much longer than a day," he says with a nod.

"But you did want him to come back." I can tell, somehow.

Diarmuid nods again. "Over the ten years he was gone, I saw who he was. I suppose being away from all of this helped me see it even more clearly. I could see who he could be. Who he really wanted to be. He's a leader. He wants to do great things. He was restless because he didn't have a purpose. Now he does. He'll be the best king we've had in a while."

I smile. "You need to tell him all of that."

"I do," Diarmuid agrees. He straightens. "Would you like to walk down to the market together?"

I shake my head. "You go ahead. You should talk alone."

"All right. I'll see you there."

I laugh softly. "I'm guessing *everyone* will see me."

He reaches out, takes my hand, and squeezes. "Lucky them."

CHAPTER 44

TORIN

Linnea turns back from straightening things on top of the final table that's been set up for the market. We're just double-checking things, but of course, everything's perfect.

Abigail arranged to have everything brought from the farm. Our staff at the ranch and palace worked to produce the food and baked goods. We have additional people on hand to staff the booths that Linnea has trained to answer questions along with handing out samples and helping kids with the games and craft projects.

It's all under control. I honestly believe that between Abigail and Linnea, they could solve every world problem.

"Did you see the video?" I ask Linnea. "Of me, at the pub last night?"

It's all over the internet and the podcast girls talked about it last night and this morning.

Apparently a lot of the crowd that's starting to gather isn't here for the fresh produce and baked goods. They're here to see if Princess Abigail shows up and publicly declares her feelings for me.

The podcast girls challenged her to do so.

This morning they even put a time on it.

Ten a.m. At the amphitheater in the center of town. Only a few yards from where our stand is set up.

It's ridiculous. It's childish.

No one *really* expects it to happen. Right?

I'm nervous as hell.

"Are you kidding?" Linnea asks. "I've watched it six times."

I sigh. "Jonah filled you in."

"Of course."

"I haven't spoken to Abigail yet."

Linnea turns fully, her brows up. "Why not?"

"I don't know what to say. I said it all last night. I suppose I feel like the ball is in her court."

"The woman who took a huge step even getting on a *video call* with a bunch of children? You're leaving this big question of does she love you and want to stay with you in Cara forever in *her* court?" Linnea shakes her head. "Sure. The Prince of Patience. I bet this lasts till noon. At the latest."

"You don't think she'll show up at ten?"

"Are you seriously going to *make her* show up at ten? In public? To do the most terrifying thing she could do?" Linnea asks. She looks legitimately shocked.

"I should head her off." She's right. I should find her right now and put a stop to this. "Should I make another public announcement? Something about how Abigail..." I frown. "What the hell would I say? That she *doesn't* love me? How does that go over? People will hate that. But I can't say she *does* love me. She hasn't told me that and I can't tell other people she's feeling something like that without her saying it."

"You should absolutely *not* make any more public statements," Linnea says, holding up a hand. "At least not until you talk to Abigail. Maybe just go find her and tell her you're sorry. Start with that."

I take a breath. "But I'm not sure I am. I'm sorry if she's feeling anxious or uncomfortable. Very fucking sorry about that. I'll do whatever I can to make that better. But I'm not sorry for what I said."

Linnea considers that. "I think that's good. You should probably just tell her that." She steps closer. "Torin, you and Abi need to just start *saying* what you feel and think to one another."

I take a deep breath. I can't believe that's the advice I'm getting. I'm all about the words. But I nod. "If she is leaving, I'll just go with her."

"What do you mean? She's leaving?"

"I don't know. She might want to. I messed our whole agreement up. I won't force her to stay here. But I'll go with her. I'll follow her wherever she goes. And I'll try like hell to convince her to come back." I scrub a hand over my face. "Fuck, my grandfather will never forgive me if I get on a plane to the US though."

"I don't know about that."

I swing around at the sound of my grandfather's voice.

I stare at him.

He's...here.

He's dressed in blue jeans and a casual button-down shirt. I glance behind him and find his security detail, along with Emil. It appears he walked down here from the palace.

"What...are you doing here?"

"I decided to come to the market," he says, looking around. "I saw a very persuasive video telling me that this event will give me a chance to sample the produce, check out the new farm building, and hear all about the Prince and Princess's plans."

I feel a niggle of embarrassment. Not for what I said, but the whole on-a-pub-table thing. For the first time in my life, actually. "You saw the video."

"I did. A couple. The one Linnea did." He gives her a smile. "And yours," he says, looking at me again.

Linnea has done a few promotional videos for the event, but I didn't even think of those.

I sigh. "Should I apologize to you as well?"

"For what?"

"For behavior unbecoming of a prince?" I offer.

"Speaking passionately to our people, in the *midst* of our people, about things that are important to you, is actually *quite* becoming of a prince. Or a king. Or a leader of any kind."

I study him. He seems sincere. "So the public sharing of intimate, personal feelings didn't bother you?" I ask.

"Sharing personal, intimate feelings makes you more human. Though I would think Abi might have some thoughts and feelings about *what* you shared." He moves in closer. "You got your message across clearly. You are passionate about three things that are important to both you and this country—the farms, the people, and your princess. I think it's very good for everyone to see that."

I'm shocked. "You're really okay with what happened last night?"

"I am. There might be better ways to do it in the future, for your liver's sake if nothing else. But perhaps you'll start doing pub talks with the people regularly. Hearing their concerns and questions in person over a glass of soda seems like a great idea. Perhaps you'll address people in the town square. Perhaps you'll continue hosting markets. The message is the important thing. And letting people see your sincerity and enthusiasm."

I have so many things I want to say. But most importantly I need to ask a follow-up question. "You really won't be upset if I get on a plane today and *leave* Cara again?"

"If you are going after your wife, then of course not. You have to do that."

"Cara doesn't come first?"

He nods. "But Cara needs Abi. So you going after her would be a good thing for the country too."

I feel shock and...relief—yes, I'm pretty sure that's relief—wash over me. "You're calling her Abi," I say, not missing that detail despite the emotions coursing through me.

He smiles. "She said I should."

I feel the corner of my mouth curl. "You like her."

"I do. So much that if you *didn't* get on the plane to go after her, I would probably do it myself."

My eyes widen. "*Is* she getting on a plane?"

He laughs and shakes his head. "She is not. At least, not today. And not without you, I would imagine. I believe she's planning to come to the market, as a matter of fact."

Again a mix of emotions hits me. Surprise, relief, worry, protectiveness, love. "She shouldn't," I say. "Everyone will notice. The crowd will overwhelm her."

"She'll be okay."

"She throws up when she's up in front of crowds."

"So, she'll maybe throw up. I'm sure she knows how to handle that by now. She'll be here for the right reason, Torin. She'll be okay."

I take a breath. He seems so sure of her.

He regards me for a moment, then says, "You got what you wanted, you realize."

"What do you mean?"

"I realize this isn't a true democracy, but Cara can be a type of representative government. If you let the people have input, if you listen to their needs and wants, if you answer their questions, if you consider what they need not only on a large scale like feeding everyone and improving the overall economy with indoor farms, but on smaller levels like what hours the farm needs to be open, what the people actually want inside the farm, and who would be best to staff it, and then you make that happen, that is still giving people a say in how their country runs."

I nod. "I love getting out, talking to people, discussing their needs and what we can do. Even talking through what we can't do and asking for patience, or for new ideas on things that I don't know how to solve."

My grandfather gives me a warm, genuine smile and for a moment I can't remember the last time I saw that. And then I remember that it was in his office when he first met Abigail.

"I'm proud of you," he says.

My heart bangs against my rib cage. "Oh," is all I'm able to manage.

"This is what I've been waiting for, Torin," he tells me. "Not for some big idea or amazing plan written out or on a projection screen. I wanted you to get out amongst people and see what leading is really about. Being in charge isn't about coming up with all of the ideas. It's about understanding the problems, finding the right people with the right ideas, and pulling together the resources to get things done."

I take that all in and it hits me—when I was most truly, fully myself, up on a table in a simple pub in the heart of my country, just letting the words spill out, was when my grandfather finally saw what he needed to. When I was just *me*, I finally showed him the king I would be. And that's the king he wants to give his throne to.

I take a deep breath and nod. "You're right," I say. Those are words that he didn't expect to hear from me either. "But Abigail and Linnea have done a lot of this."

"You have wonderful people around you. People who will always be there for you. You're learning you don't have to do this alone. The job is to ask questions, listen to the answers, and give the right people the resources, time, and space to make things happen."

I nod. Then take a breath and admit something I almost can't believe I'm saying. "But I'm not quite ready for the throne."

My grandfather nods. "I know. But you will be. And you have a lot of people to help you. A monarch, at least a good one, is the least lonely person in the country."

I think about that. But I smile. "Are you the least lonely person in this country?"

He chuckles. "Sometimes I wish I were a little lonelier."

I laugh. Then I think about the gorgeous genius who became my wife and helped me get to this place. "Things are going to be good," I promise.

My grandfather shocks me yet again and pulls me in for a quick hug. "Things already are."

I hug him back, feeling, for the first time, that he truly trusts me with the next steps.

Over his shoulder I spot something that makes my heart stutter.

Abigail is here.

"I...have something I need to do," I tell him, pulling back.

He glances over his shoulder. "Yes. We have lots of time for talking."

I nod and immediately move toward her.

She's wearing a white dress with small pink flowers, tied loosely at her waist. The skirt falls to her calves, stopping just at the top of the hot pink cowboy boots she's wearing.

This is not a princess dress she got when she came to Cara. This dress came with her. And it's absolutely perfect.

She looks gorgeous.

And, thankfully, she doesn't look angry.

She also doesn't seem to notice that the crowd has already spotted her, and they are whispering and moving closer. Jonah is with her along with a couple of other members of the security team, so no one will get too close, but I still need to get her out of the public eye as soon as possible.

We need to talk.

Without anyone recording it.

"Hi, princess," I say, arriving at her side in seconds. I loop my arm around her waist and steer her toward the building to our left. "We need to talk."

"We really do."

I usher her inside the tiny room at the back of the amphitheater.

I jump right in. "I understand that you saw...everything last night."

"I did."

"I'm very sorry I did that."

"So you didn't mean it? You were drunker than you looked? Or you were just caught up in the moment?"

I watch her closely. I realize that *this* is the moment. This is not at all how I planned it. It is not how I would have done it if I'd had the chance to plan it. But I can no longer keep my feelings inside.

I step closer to her. "I meant every fucking word, princess."

The little wrinkle between her brows forms. "You did?"

"Of course. I regret telling...everyone...before I told you, though."

"So you love me?" she asks.

"More than anything. More than I ever imagined I could love someone."

The wrinkle smooths, but she presses her lips together, not saying anything.

"I know I agreed this was all practical," I tell her. "I know I promised to keep you out of the public eye. I know I told you it was about the farms and the throne, but I think I fell in love with you the first time you walked off the dance floor away from me. And it's just grown stronger every day I've known you. I thought you were beautiful and wanted you more than anyone I've ever met the moment I saw you. But then I got to know you and, dammit, Abi, I don't know how I could live knowing that you're out there somewhere in the world and I don't get to see your smile, or watch you work, or sit near you while you read, or make love to you every night."

She's staring at me.

"What?" I ask. "Say something."

"You just called me Abi."

I think back and...she's right. I nod. "Your friends call you Abi. The people who love you call you Abi. The people who are closest to you. And fuck, princess, you're my best friend. You see me as someone I *want* to be. You see my heart. You see the things I dream of and you want to help me make those come true. And no one loves you more than I do. You are...everything."

She steps closer. "No one has ever looked at me, or listened to me, or *valued* me the way you do. All of this stuff with the farms...it started out as work, as my dream job, but now...it's about you. It's for you. For *us*. For our country. It was what I could do to show you how much you matter to me."

"You don't have to build farms for me, Abi," I say, my voice husky with emotion. "What you do for me is make me happy. You make me want to be better, every day. You make me passionate for my work, for my position, for my *life* again." I step closer and cup her face. "What you can do for me is just love me."

I see the tears well up in her eyes and brace myself for her to say that she just isn't there yet.

"God, Torin, I *do*," she says. "So much. I love you, so so much."

I stare down at her. Blood is rushing in my ears. "Say it again." My voice is gruff.

She lifts her hands, holding my face between her hands. "I love you."

CHAPTER 45

ABIGAIL

His eyes scan over my face. I can see amazement, surprise, and hunger in his gaze.

"Say that again," he says, low and firm.

"I love you. My husband. My prince."

He puts his hands on either side of my face. "I love you so fucking much. You've taken my *soul*. You've taken everything—my future, my dreams, every hope. I don't know what I would do without you, princess."

My hands cover his. "You never have to find out. I'm here to stay. We're going to build this first farm together. Then another. Then another. Then other projects. Bigger dreams." I pause, tears stinging my eyes. "We're going to build a *life*."

His mouth crashes into mine and he kisses me deeply. I arch closer. Going up on tiptoe, I push my hands into his hair.

We separate only when we hear someone clear his throat.

I peek around Torin to see the king standing in the doorway.

"Okay, we'll talk more later," I tell Torin. "There's something we have to do right now."

He frowns, looks at his grandfather, looks at the doors that will lead out to the stage, then looks back to me. "What's going on?"

"It's almost ten. I'm addressing our people. With you. And I'm probably going to say something very romantic. And maybe even kiss you. In front of them all."

He starts shaking his head quickly. "No, Abigail. No. You don't have to do this. I won't *let you* do this."

I widen my eyes. "Excuse me, but I'm doing this. I'm not asking your permission."

"Seriously, Abigail. You don't have to do this. We'll make a statement together. A *written* statement. Or you can do a one-on-one interview with someone. We can go on the podcast. But you don't have to go up in front of all those people." He leans in. "I know what this does to you. I promised to protect you from this. I know I thrust you into the spotlight, but we can get around it. You don't have anything to prove."

But I squeeze his wrists. "The thing is, I do. It doesn't matter what it does to me. I want all of *them* to hear this. And I want *you* to hear this. Actions are wonderful. They completely count. They're so important. And that is why we are also going to have a wedding here, just like you promised. But words are important too, and *I* will always give you whatever *you* need."

His fingers tighten against my face and he's shaking his head again.

"You're not asking me to do anything hard, Torin," I tell him, my voice gentler. "You're just asking me to love you out loud. And I can absolutely do that. I'm more passionate about you than I am about the farm, and you *know* how I feel about that."

Jonah moves in behind Torin. I hadn't even realized he and Linnea were in the room.

He puts a hand on Torin's shoulder. "Let her," is all he says.

I pull Torin's hands away from my face. "It'll be fine."

"Okay," he finally says. Clearly, he's still reluctant. "But if you don't want to talk, you don't have to. Just be there beside me."

We step to the doors, I'm smiling brightly, and then...I see the crowd.

The amphitheater is just off the main square. There's a wide stage between us and the crowd, but the crowd is *huge*. They're all going to be looking at me. Listening to me.

And the nausea hits me hard.

I turn to Torin. "I'm going to be sick."

And he reacts as quickly as he did that first time at Ellie's. He drops to his knees, yanks one of my boots off, and shoves it in front of my mouth, just as I throw up.

When I'm finished, I stare in horror at the boot.

He shrugs. "It was the only thing close enough and big enough."

"These are my *lucky* boots."

"Yep, really lucky they were here or *that* would have been quite a spectacle."

I glance at the crowd. That's *horrifying*. I blow out a breath. "You are so buying me new boots," I tell him.

He truly grins for the first time since I met him on the path outside. "As many as you want, Princess."

Linnea shoves a water bottle at me, which I gratefully accept. After I drink, she hands me a breath mint. Wow, she is *really* a handy person to have around. Then I grab Torin's arm and balance on one foot as I take off my other boot.

I take a deep breath.

Then say, "I need a minute."

Torin doesn't look a bit surprised. He steps to the side and I rush back into the room behind the stage.

I press my hand to my stomach. Oh my *God*. I just threw up in front of all those people. I cover my face. Great. Just *great*. I was prepared to show Torin, and *myself*, that I could do this and now...ugh!

I can hear the noise of the crowd and it's rising as they all realize we're not coming right out, so I head for the back door of the amphitheater. I just need another minute to gather myself.

As soon as my hand hits the door, my eyes slide shut. I push the door open and slip outside, pressing myself against the side of the building. I take a deep breath. I don't need to puke again. This will pass. I need to get over this. I don't have to talk. I just need to stand there next to Torin.

You're fine, you're fine, you're fine. I just keep repeating the words over and over.

Until I hear a little voice say, "It's the Princess, Mommy!"

My eyes fly open, and I see that not only is there a little girl staring up at me, but there's a whole group of people staring at me.

Apparently, some of the crowd has gathered along the side of the building and wrapped around the back. And I'm standing right in front of them, pressed against the side of the building like an idiot. A quick glance tells me there are about thirty women and children.

I'm not great at judging ages in children, but the girl is probably about five. I give her a smile. "Um...hi."

Her eyes go wide as if she's shocked that I can speak.

"Mommy, it's the Princess," she repeats in a stage whisper. She grasps for her mother's hand without looking.

The pretty young woman next to her, takes her hand and offers me an apologetic smile. The woman is obviously very pregnant with this little girl's future sibling.

I give her a smile too. "Hi, I'm Abigail."

Suddenly everyone drops into a curtsy as one.

I'm appalled.

I push myself away from the wall. "No, no, don't do that," I tell them, waving my hands. "I just slipped out here to take a quick break. This is not a formal occasion. Please don't curtsy."

In fact, I'm putting it on my to do list to do away with curtsy-ing for the princess altogether if possible.

Everyone looks back up at me. The little girl's mother says, "Hello, my name is Sorcha. And this is Aisling." She puts her hand on the little girl's head.

I force a smile. "It's nice to meet you."

"Why are you out here with us?" the little girl asks.

"Aisling, don't ask questions like that. The princess can go wherever she wants to," her mother admonishes.

I run a hand on the front of my dress and take another deep breath. *Do not throw up again, do not throw up again, especially in front of this little girl. You might scar her for life.*

"Honestly," I say. "I got nervous. This is the first time I've done something like this as princess. I'm not good at speaking in front of big crowds. I was standing up in front with Prince Torin and I realized all of these people were here to see me and suddenly I just couldn't talk." I lean in. "In fact, I threw up."

The little girl's eyes go wide. "You did?"

"It happens a lot. I have bad anxiety. Do you know what that is?"

The little girl shakes her head and looks up at her mom.

"Well," I say. "It's when you get really nervous or scared about things. For me it's being up in front of a lot of people. Especially if I have to talk. It's really hard for me to control. And even though it's super embarrassing, one of the things that happens is I throw up."

"I hate throwing up," Aisling says.

"Me too. And it really makes being a princess hard sometimes. I want to get up and talk to people, and I want to stand beside Prince Torin, but it's really hard to be up in front."

I notice the crowd is staring at me and everyone is completely silent. There is some surprise, of course, but I notice that they seem to be relaxing.

"Well, I throw up about eight times a day, and I hate it too," Sorcha says. "I'm sorry that happens to you."

I give her a smile. "You have a little better reason."

"Being nervous is a fine reason." This comes from a woman to her left. "Being nervous is a very normal thing. We all feel it sometimes."

I look at her and give her a grateful smile. "Thank you. I'm just a really bad public speaker and it makes this new position hard."

"Well, you're obviously good at other things," another woman says. "This farm idea sounds pretty great."

I look at her quickly. "Really?"

"Yes, we've been reading about it, and we're excited to have oranges and fresh lettuce and things like that right here. My son is hoping to get a job helping with the building."

I feel some of my nerves give way to excitement. "That's wonderful."

"And you're doing okay talking now," another woman says.

This woman is leaning on a walker. I quickly take in the details about the rest of the women. There are varying ages, some are dressed casually in blue jeans and T-shirts, while others are dressed up in professional wear. There are even a couple in heels.

"Are you all out here because there's no room upfront?"

Several of them nod.

"Got here too late," one of the women in a pantsuit says. "My meeting ran long."

I look at her in surprise. "You left work to come?"

She shrugs. "Of course."

I focus on the woman with a walker. "Where are you coming from?"

"Home. I started out early enough, I thought, but it's tough to get around with this thing." She shakes her walker.

"Are you all here because of the video of Prince Torin last night?"

Some of them actually seem confused by the question.

"What video?" Aisling asks.

"Were you coming here to see if I would kiss the prince in front of everyone?" I ask with a teasing grin.

The little girl wrinkles her nose. "Ew. No. I made a tomato plant with you the other night," Aisling tells me. "And Mommy said today I could see real ones that you grew on your very own farm."

"Oh..." I don't know why I'm surprised by this. "That's so nice. I'm so glad."

"And we're here to listen to whatever else you want to

talk about," Sorcha adds. "We always come whenever the queen or princess addresses the public."

I didn't know my mother-in-law or grandmother-in-law did that. "How often does that happen?"

The woman with a walker shakes her head. "Not very often. That's why we have to show up when it does."

"And what do they talk about?" I ask.

"The queen leads all of the women's initiatives. Maternity leave, healthcare, fair wages, childcare, things like that," the woman in the pantsuit tells me. "So we come and listen to her ideas and plans, and then we're able to offer input and suggestions."

I like hearing that. I need to sit down with the queen and hear more about the initiatives and her plans. But I frown. "You have to show up in person to do that?"

They all look at one another and nod.

"That seems unnecessarily complicated and burdensome," I say. I can't believe women with walkers and who are very pregnant with young children in tow have to come all the way over here to see the queen in person. Not to mention women leaving work for it.

"You could just email me anything you want the queen to know, and I can take it to her," I say.

"You have email?" someone asks.

"Of course. Oh! And they recently got me an email as princess! After we did the video call with the kids."

"That was so fun!" Aisling tells me. "You should do more of those."

My eyes widen. "I should. I don't get nervous doing those. I don't need to throw up." And now I'm staying so I can make plans like that. I can do *lots* more video chats and kids' programs and... I feel butterflies start flitting through my stomach. *Good* butterflies. I'm staying. That feels so, so good.

A thought occurs to me. "Maybe I could use some video chats like that to talk with everyone." I look around the group. "We could have them at varying times, but then you could join and listen to me talk about new plans and ideas, and you could give me input without having to come all the way over here in person."

Sorcha rubs her belly. "That would be a lot easier."

The woman in the pantsuit nods. "We could probably even join from work. But certainly afterwards. If you have them after hours or record them."

I nod. "We'll do a variety of times so everyone can join."

Aisling smiles up at me. "You don't look nervous anymore."

I laugh. "I feel a lot better, actually. I suppose sometimes I'll also have to do these public speeches. And sometimes I might even throw up. But as long as I get to talk to people like you, I think it's going to be okay."

Maybe it will help if I just imagine Aisling and her mom and these other women in the crowd.

Suddenly, the door behind me opens.

"Abigail?" Torin steps out.

He has the same reaction I did when he realizes there's a little crowd gathered out here.

He pulls up short, straightening. "Well, hello, ladies."

"It's the prince!" Aisling says.

I actually giggle. His eyes snap to me when he hears the sound. Then an eyebrow rises. He can tell that I'm happy. That I'm good. That I'm surrounded by people, but that I'm very, very good.

"Everything okay out here?" he asks.

"Everything is great out here," the woman in the

pantsuit says. "I think you have yourself an excellent princess here."

He gives them a grin. A real, genuine Torin grin. And I know at least a few of the women swoon a little.

"I'm very glad to hear that you are finding my princess as charming and delightful as I do."

"She's smart," the woman with the walker tells him.

He nods. "Extremely."

"So that means whatever she tells you about later, you're going to agree with, right?" Sorcha asks him.

Torin looks from her to me, takes in my grin, then back to her and nods. "I've already learned that's a very good thing to do."

She winks at me. "He already knows how to treat a princess."

I step close to him and slide my hand into his. "Oh, he definitely does." I look up at him then I look at Sorcha. "I don't suppose you have a cell phone?"

She laughs. "Of course, I do."

"Would you mind taking a photo for me? Or better yet, a video?"

She pulls her phone out from her pocket and holds it up. "Sure."

Then I turn to my husband, slide my hand up behind his neck and pull him down for a kiss. Torin only takes two seconds to respond. He dips me back and kisses me deeply as the crowd awws and claps.

When he rights me, we're both grinning. I look at Sorcha.

"Got it," she says.

"Would you be willing to send that to a certain podcast?"

She laughs. "Consider it done."

I grin up at Torin. "Okay, I'm ready to go on stage."

"You sure?"

"Of *everything*," I tell him confidently.

He puts his hand on my lower back and ushers me through the door.

"Is it okay if I go out there barefoot?" I ask, realizing I was outside without shoes this whole time.

He puts his mouth against my ear. "It's one of my favorite ways to have you."

I laugh, and then we're stepping out onto the stage in front of all of our people. Together.

I let their applause wash over me and take a few deep breaths. Then I look up at Torin. "How quickly can we put a royal wedding together?"

His eyes actually twinkle as he smiles down at me. "You're the princess. All you have to do is say the word and it'll be done."

I give a happy sigh. "I think I might be okay at this royal thing after all."

He slips his arm around me, resting his hand on my hip. "I never had any doubt of it, Abi."

EPILOGUE
WAIT 'TIL I TELL YE

EPISODE 850 TRANSCRIPT

Lindsey: Well, the big day has come and gone. And um...wow. Just...wow. Jen, do you have any better words for it?

Jen: <laughing> I do not. And I know that's not super helpful for people who listen to a podcast! But just, okay, imagine everything you love about weddings... the gorgeous dresses, the flowers, the beautiful location right? But then...make it <happy sigh> *meaningful*.

Lindsey: Right. So most of you might have read about

this because a lot of this got written up ahead of time, but let's do a rundown.

Jen: I'm ready!

Lindsey: Okay, so first, they got married at the palace. Out in the flower gardens, of course, because this is Abigail, our own personal farmer-princess. Which means they just used the flowers and trees that are already there. Nothing was cut, so nothing is going to dry up and die.

Jen: Exactly, though Torin insisted she and her brides-maids—who we'll talk about in a minute—carry bouquets that were a combination of clover and lavender. Those have a special meaning for the couple, we're told. Now, the lavender from her bouquet is going to be dried and used for handmade sachets that will be sold and the money is going to be the first deposit into a new fund that Abigail has tagged as a scholarship for any Cara citizen who is inter-ested in studying botany or agri-business in the US or Europe.

Lindsey: Not just *any* Cara citizen. Specifically women.

Jen: Yes, that's right. Women who want to go into those fields will have access to this scholarship fund.

Lindsey: So then next, we'll talk dresses.

Jen: Yes, *all* of the dresses—the princess' wedding gown as well as her bridesmaids' dresses—were all sown by women here on the island. Each was different and this not only gave business to local seamstresses but also gave them a world stage to show off their designs.

Lindsey: I know the ladies were *so* nervous, but so delighted! In addition, their hair and makeup were done in town. So again, local business was supported and high-lighted. The entire thing was wonderful, involving all of us. Everyone was invited to the palace grounds to witness the ceremony and enjoy the reception afterwards. Those who couldn't make it could watch the whole thing live online. And I understand cakes and chocolates and champagne were delivered to all the villages so that people could partake in local parties and feel included in the entire celebration no matter where they were.

Jen: <sniffling> It was lovely. Everything was specially thought out and had Prince Torin and Princess Abigail's touch. It felt very much like they were friends getting married and we were all a part of it.

Lindsey: I agree. You know I'm the more cynical one, and I thought maybe Princess Abigail would talk everyone into keeping it small and intimate and maybe even keep cameras away. But our new princess really embraced her wedding day.

Jen: She did. I understand from palace insiders that the procession through the middle of town up to the castle was her idea.

Lindsey: I was *stunned* by that. It was so lovely to see them and their wedding party and even the esteemed guests up close like that. Her sisters and Lady Linnea were her attendants. Prince Cian and Prince Torin's long-time bodyguard and friend, Jonah Greene, along with Cian's bodyguard, Henry Dean, were Torin's groomsmen. Interestingly, *disappointingly*, Prince Declan was not even in attendance. *But* Iris Kim, his long-time friend, assistant, and often-rumored girlfriend, *was* here.

Lindsey: *Yes.* I did make a note of her as well. That *is* interesting. I would have died if Declan had showed, and yet I was also disappointed that he didn't.

Jen: Same.

Lindsey: So, when I asked about the bodyguards, I was told that their time in the US really made all the men very close and they're much more friends than anything else.

Then the rest of the procession was made up of Abigail's parents, grandparents, brothers-in-law, and seemingly dozens of cousins who all made the trip. They were grinning and waving and seemed to be having a great time. It was quite charming.

Jen: And can I just say that speech she gave from the king's balcony was...just perfection? I nearly swooned.

Lindsey: I did too... from shock. I knew that Prince Torin would say something amazing. And, of course, he did. The man is head over heels, to the moon and back. I'm not sure I've ever seen anyone as in love as he is. And the best part is he wants the entire world to know. So, of course, he gave an amazing, romantic, heartfelt speech. But then... much to everyone's surprise... so did Princess Abigail.

Jen: She sure did. And it was short and sweet. Honestly. She didn't go on and on or anything. She said—hang on, I have it here. I wrote it down—"Torin, you took everything I believed about love, life, home, and myself, and turned it upside down, made it bigger and brighter and just...more. More than I ever knew it all could be. Thank you for not giving up on me when I turned you down the first time. And the second time." And then he grinned at her and leaned over and said something in her ear that made her blush and laugh. And I almost *died*.

Lindsey: *Gah!* Me too!

Jen: And then she said, "I love you and I love this country and I can't wait for...everything that's ahead of us." And then...that *kiss*!

Lindsey: <big sigh> I *know*. It was like Torin just couldn't *not* kiss her anymore! He dipped her back and I mean, that kiss went on and on! I was fanning my face, I'll tell you! There were lots of whoops and cheers. It was better than any movie kiss I've ever seen. Period.

Jen: And let's just acknowledge *why* the speech and kiss were amazing. Yes, they were romantic, and no, we haven't heard much from the princess. But let's just point out that ever since that farmer's market when we first saw Abigail and Torin together in public, people have been talking about how incredible it is to have a princess who is so open and honest about dealing with social anxiety. She's been very transparent about how difficult it is for her to do public speaking, how she dealt with some bullying as a kid, and how it's always been a struggle having people looking at her and judging her.

Lindsey: Yes, we should acknowledge that. But she has really garnered a lot of support. Rightfully so. First of all, for any public figure to talk about anything that makes them vulnerable is huge. Especially when it's something that is so relatable. I think she's really made a lot of people feel more comfortable talking about their own vulnerabilities. Then to think about a woman like that falling in love with a prince and becoming a princess? Talk about having to overcome your issues and step into the spotlight.

Jen: But that's the thing, right? She hasn't completely overcome it. She's been very honest about how nervous she still gets and how she still throws up a lot before she has to speak to us. But she's still there doing it. I just think that's really cool.

Lindsey. I agree. A thousand percent. Which is really why none of us expected her to say anything at the wedding. That made it all the more meaningful.

Jen: <another happy sigh> For sure.

Lindsey: I even heard that she was supposed to give a speech at one of her sisters' weddings as a maid of honor and she struggled with that.

Jen: Was it one of her cousins who told you that?

Lindsey: Yes! At the pub the night before the wedding!

Jen: Yes! Another one told me that Torin was at that wedding reception and totally stepped in and rescued her from that speech.

Lindsey: Oh my God! Was that the wedding where they met?

Jen: No, the second one. The first one was her sister Charlie's wedding.

Lindsey: Right. The second was Ami's. I'm telling all of you, her family is delightful. They filled up the pub the night before the wedding and I know a bunch of you got to meet them. Wow, are they a lot of fun.

Jen: And wow, they can drink Irish whiskey like they were born here! <laughing> And they grow them just as handsome and charming in Louisiana as we do here. I'm not so sure that there weren't some Irishmen sneaking down the bayou at one time long ago and mixing some Irish into those bloodstreams.

Lindsey: <laughing> Would not surprise me a bit.

Jen: Oh, and what about when Abigail told Torin in her speech that she's so glad he didn't give up when she first turned him down?

Lindsey: <sound of a hand smacking the table> Right? She *turned him down* the first time he asked her out. And the first time he asked her to *marry* him. He even said he couldn't get a second *dance* with her.

Jen: I know! The woman turned down a prince. *Our* prince. One of the most handsome, charming, intelligent, amazing men in the *world*. What if she'd *never* said yes?

Lindsey: <laughing>. It really just makes their whole story better.

Jen: It really does. Okay, we need to run down the rest of the guest list quick for everyone.

Alex and Astrid Olsen were both there, of course. They're friends of the family. Their parents were there too. I will say, it was very sad to not see Duke Alfred. He's been such a fixture here with the royal family. I missed him.

Lindsey: Me too. I'm sure the king missed him too.

Jen: I'm sure. Of course, the royal family from Denmark was here. There were also several friends from Ireland and the US—besides the entire Landry clan.

Lindsey: Oh, and I see a couple of comments...well, questions really... yes, all of the Landry boys are married. Yes, even Wyatt and Mitch. Their girls, Trudy and Paige, were in attendance and those guys are very spoken for. Sorry, ladies.

Jen: Yeah, I had a chance to talk to some of the Landry girls and they have great senses of humor, but I don't think any of us want to mess with them.

Lindsey: Agreed! <laughs> It was *really* awesome to see Princess Fiona back. And, of course, little Saoirse. Who has grown up *so* much. They are always welcome here. And I think this is the second time we've had a chance to kind of see Fiona's husband. This time he was actually out socializing a little as well.

Jen: Even Colin, Fiona's longtime bodyguard and friend, is married now.

Lindsey: Honestly, there was this just huge group of people that landed and kind of took over, and I think everybody had a hell of a good time. I think it's safe to say that anytime the Landrys and their friends want to come back, they would be very welcome here.

Jen: I agree. Especially after Abigail's grandmother, Ellie, taught our bartender how to make a couple of drinks. Everyone's a pretty big fan at this point.

Lindsey: <laughing> I had one of those and yes, she

needs to come back! So anyway, huge congratulations to our prince and princess. We love you. Welcome home, Princess Abigail, we're so happy you're here. And to Prince Torin, if all of your decisions for us are as wonderful as who you chose to be our next queen, then we are *all* going to live happily ever after for sure.

*Thank you so much for reading **Reluctantly Royal**!*
I hope you loved Torin and Abigail's story!

Want more from the prince and new princess?
You can get it right here > https://bit.ly/RRoyal-Bonus

And don't miss Jonah and Linnea's story, **Reluctantly Rogue!**

The gorgeous, brilliant woman I have dirty dreams about every damned night?
She's supposed to marry my best friend.
She's supposed to be queen someday.
She's off-limits.
But I can't walk away.

Find ALL of my books at **ErinNicholas. com**

And the best place to find out all the news about that
(including upcoming books and more!) is right here!
bit.ly/Keep-In-Touch-Erin
Be sure you get those dashes and upper case letters in there!

And this is your personal invitation to my Facebook group,
Erin Nicholas's Super Fans where you can get first looks,
behind the scenes peeks, and daily fun with fellow romance
lovers (including me!)!

CONNECTED BOOKS FROM ERIN NICHOLAS

All of these can be read as stand-alones, even though they are part of interconnected series! Jump in anywhere and enjoy!

Want to know more about Torin's sister Fiona, his brother Cian, and their bodyguards, including Jonah?

Check out **Kiss My Giraffe** (a grumpy-sunshine, princess-in-hiding, small town rom com!) and **Better Safe Than Safari** (a bodyguard-rockstar, curvy-girl, steamy rom com)**!**

Want Abi's sisters' stories?

Charlie's story is **Otterly Irresistible**, Boys of the Bayou Gone Wild book one—a grumpy-sunshine, hot boss, steamy small town rom com!

Ami's story is **Bayou With Benefits,** Badges of the Bayou, book two—a single dad, friends to lovers, steamy small town romance!

You can also get to know everyone in **Sapphire Falls**! The first book is Mason's and is called **Getting Out of Hand**! A hot nerd, opposites attract, grumpy-sunshine small town rom com!

Find all of these and so much more at www. ErinNicholas.com!

About Erin

Erin Nicholas is the New York Times and USA Today bestselling author of over sixty sexy contemporary romances. She's known for her blue-collar book boyfriends and big, boisterous found families in small towns. Her stories have been described as toe-curling, enchanting, steamy and fun. She loves to write about reluctant heroes, imperfect heroines and happily ever afters.

She lives in the Midwest with her husband who only wants to read the sex scenes in her books, her kids who will never read the sex scenes in her books, and family and friends who say they're shocked by the sex scenes in her books (yeah, right!).

Find her and all her books at
www.ErinNicholas.com

And find her on Facebook, BookBub, and Instagram!

Editor: Lindsey Faber

Cover design: Qamber Designs

Digital ISBN: 978-1-952280-81-8

Paperback ISBN: 978-1-952280-82-5

Special Edition ISBN: 978-0-9983506-9-1